THE PILGRIM'S PROGRESS: RELOADED

DAVID R UMSTATTD

FLINTLOCK PUBLISHING

For Lorraine Mahan

STAGE 1
THE DAY THE ONI AWOKE

He had never noticed the blood on his hands. Not because he never got bloody. Firing hundreds of rounds of explosive ordinance into one's enemies was not a pastime conducive to cleanliness. But he had never looked at the blood before. Why was he looking at it now?

He surveyed the carnage of the battlefield. The evangelists hadn't tried to fight back this time. Some had sat. Some had run. But each person had been found by a bullet. Why did that bother him? The evangelists were the enemy and Apollyon made the most destructive ammunition in the Dark Lands. So, when destructive ammunition were mixed with enemies, the result was supposed to be good.

This did not look good.

The man thought back to the hundreds of battles he had been in and the delight he had taken in the gore and carnage.

Where had the delight gone? Did it drip from the tubes and circuits of his burden? He checked himself. No, only blood dripped from his burden. As usual. There didn't appear to be anything wrong with his burden. The burden was a suit of power armor. A protective shell to blunt the attacks of the evangelists. At least that's what it was supposed to be. Now, his protection felt like a cage. The burden encased him completely. No piece of flesh lay bare for the world to see, every inch covered by metal and circuitry.

Though his head appeared free from the metal prison, an invisible forcefield projected from the collar, ensuring even his mind and eyes knew no liberty from the inescapable force of the burden.

But this was normal. Everyone had a burden. He'd been born with it—it was a part of him. The powered suit plugged into his brain, operating from mental commands.

The burden was no different from his arms or eyes. Why was he thinking about this now?

Something was wrong. He couldn't move his burden. The suit was so heavy that a soldier couldn't move an unpowered one. Had his become unpowered? Were his components being hacked? Or was something wrong with his mind, causing him to feel disconnected from what was supposed to be a comfort?

What had changed?

"Aha!" screamed a tiny grating voice from the man's shoulder. "I've spliced into the main programming. Don't worry I've almost got the conditioning down 23.78 percent."

The man leaped to the side, his powered servos acting before his mind had time to register his actions. So, he could still move. Why had he thought he couldn't? He grasped for the source of the noise on his shoulder, and his fist closed around a small metallic figure. As soon as the motion started, his suit went limp and he felt like he couldn't move anymore. Without the power to keep his fist clenched, the figure squirmed out of his fingers and perched itself on the top of his gauntlet.

"Hey, I'm trying to help," the figure said in a higher pitched whine.

The man winced at the sound—the worst kind of robotic voice. Like a robotic car alarm accompanied by chalk dragged across a chalk board and the sound of two balloons rubbing together—the robotic equivalent to a human voice screaming in pain.

The figure was tiny. An automaton with the same proportions as he had, with two glass telescopic sensors for eyes. These "eyes" were huge and wide and seemed too big. The automaton looked around from place to place, intensely alert as if watching for something life-threatening.

"Put me back," said the small figure. "I'm not done with my work. There's no time to lose. You're in terrible danger."

"Who are you? What were you doing on my shoulder?"

The figure paused, looking a bit unsure of itself. "Isn't the shoulder where we consciences usually hang out? It's a trope, right? Did I do that wrong? I'm sorry. I must not be very good at this."

The man groaned and his worry vanished, replaced with annoyance. "A conscience? I've heard of you little imps. No wonder my burden doesn't work. You little gremlins try to keep us from doing anything fun."

"That kind of cynical attitude will get you nowhere in life." Conscience then clambered up the arm of the man's burden, back to his shoulder. "You must not stop my work. Like I said before, you're in *incredible* danger."

"I thought you said it was *terrible* danger." The man tried to grab the robot, but the tiny figure was too quick. His movements still felt reduced thanks to whatever it was the infernal machine had done to his burden. No matter, it was such a small thing. What great harm could it do?

"Yes, yes," Conscience said. "Incredible, terrible danger. And . . . other various seemingly hyperbolic adjectives."

"What's the danger?" the man said with a twinge of both curiosity and annoyance.

Conscience opened his mouth to respond, but two shutters on his eyes squinted as if he were processing his answer. A tiny progress bar displayed on the glass of his eyes. After the progress bar vanished, Conscience looked even more uncomfortable. "I don't actually know the specifics. But I do know the danger is terrible. And incredible. Anyway, back to work."

The man felt Conscience reach into one of the electrical ports in the burden. Then Conscience gave a squeal of delight. "Aha! I've got it."

Searing pain fired through the man's nerves. He fell, the weight of his armor pressing him against the ground. Before, the suit must have been on emergency power. So *this* was what an unpowered burden felt like. Then came the memories. And the pain.

"What in the name of sacrilegious proclamations," the man said. "I killed them. Why did I . . ." He looked up and the blood from the battlefield seeped toward him. When he saw it, he understood. The blind, careless delight he and his comrades had taken from the slaughter of these innocents was draining from his soul like the blood from his face.

"What have I done?" the man said in a tone of disbelief and guilt.

"Bad." Conscience said, as if answering a mundane question. "Really bad stuff. That's what I've been trying to tell you. Your burden was in the way, numbing your mind. Took me ages to get through."

"But I—" The man tried to speak, but whatever he had thought to say had vanished from his mind. What excuse could he give? After a long pause, he said, "I didn't know."

Conscience slid off of the man's shoulder and looked at him for a while, as if making sure he had heard correctly. "You didn't know murdering a bunch of men, women, and children was wrong? Is that supposed to be better?"

"B-but, b-b-but . . ." The man couldn't talk through his stammering. "B-but it's like you said. This burden was messing with my head."

Conscience blinked a few times. "And that makes it okay?"

"No, it's just that . . . I thought they were my enemies."

"You being wrong about something doesn't make what you did right."

"I thought I was doing the right thing. It didn't feel wrong. It felt good."

"You're making yourself sound worse again" Conscience said.

"It shouldn't have felt that good, should it? Why did it feel that good? Everyone did it. They said it was normal and natural."

"They? They who?" Conscience looked around as if worried about an imminent attack. "Did they make you do it?"

"No," said the man.

Conscience looked back at the man. "Then that means you did it."

"But . . . but . . ." The man's eyes grew wide in terror as he pleaded for an excuse, a reason, an explanation.

"If someone else didn't make you do it, then you did it," Conscience said. "I think . . . maybe I'm wrong. I'm not very smart." He looked down with a sad expression.

"I never thought it was that bad," the man said, desperate to say something, anything that could justify such obvious evil. "Other people killed so many more than I did. Maybe they went overboard. But not me."

Conscience folded his arms. The tiny bits of metal made a clicking sound as they touched, and he raised the shutter of one eye higher than the other. "Are you saying that killing people is not a big deal since other people killed more?"

Conscience and the man stared at each other.

"Well," the man said, "when you put it that way, it sounds ridiculous."

"No, no." Conscience raised his hands. "I assure you. Your way sounds just as ridiculous."

"I've got to do something." The man tried to rise, but the weight of his burden made movement impossible.

"Nah," Conscience said. "You shot them all up real good. Pretty sure you humans don't do too well after you've been shot a bunch. At least I don't think so. How do sinners even work? So many moving parts."

"Sinners?" A twinge of anger shot through the man. "That's what those evangelists call us. Those judgmental self-righteous pricks. They keep trying to mind control us with their judgmental psychic attacks. That's why we have to kill them so quickly. I wish I could just rip apart every last—"

He stopped himself. He was demanding more blood. More death. Had he really fallen back into his old ways so quickly? What he had done to the dead before him was wrong. That was plain. "I've got to stop this." The man tried to move again.

"Yeah, that's what I've been saying" Conscience tried hopping back up on the man's shoulder, but his little legs weren't quite long enough. He only made it far enough to grab the man's shoulder. He tried pulling himself up but couldn't.

"Here . . ." The man reached down and helped Conscience up.

"Thanks," Conscience said. "Anyway, yeah, we gotta stop with these crazed murder sprees. Evil as Hell. Literally."

"Wait." The man froze. "I just moved my arm. To help you up."

Conscience looked down at the man's hand. "Yup. That's what you did." He looked confused. "Is that weird?"

"I thought I couldn't move. Without the power of the burden, the weight should make movement impossible. I shouldn't be able to move even my fingers."

"But you just did," Conscience said.

"But how?"

"I just said I didn't know how you sinners work." Conscience had a hint of anger in his voice, which sounded more adorable than threatening.

"I don't understand," the man said.

"Well, one of us is hallucinating." Conscience looked introspective, as if trying to decipher some grand puzzle. "I don't think it's me. Cause I'm just a philosophical personification of the instinctual omnitemporal moral paradigms programmed into all human psyches. You're human. For all I know, you could be high as a kite."

"Wait. You're a what?"

"A conscience. Didn't I say that? Uh-oh. Did I say the long thing again?"

The man opened his mouth to answer. A massive object struck the ground several yards away. From the impact, plumes of dust and dirt erupted into the air and sent shockwaves from the ground into the man's flesh and bone.

The weight of the burden kept the man from being moved. He looked closer at the foreign object. It was a drop pod. The evangelists had sent reinforcements. Power surged back into the man's burden. Without thought, he reached up toward his back. A compartment popped open and the butt of a Gauss rifle slid out. He drew the weapon from his back, shouldered it, and . . .

A figure stepped from the pod.

The man fired at the figure.

The round struck the figure in the center of the chest before he saw who it was. There was a spray of blood.

The figure looked down at their chest, then up at the man. "Well, that was impolite." The figure was a woman, with piercing eyes and an expression of extreme annoyance. She stumbled forward, but her expression of annoyance stayed.

The man felt a twinge of regret. "I'm so sorry. I didn't mean—"

"Yeah, sure you didn't." The woman kept walking, her pace more haggard and unstable with each step. Her voice showed no sign of the usual inconvenience commonly associated with disemboweling explosive gunshot wounds.

"I said we should wait till your conscience had broken through your burden. I said you wouldn't shoot any of us. I said it will be fine. Well, I guess you proved me wrong, ya jerk."

The man lowered his rifle. "You're with the enemy?"

"No, I'm with a troop of traveling porcupine jugglers. Yes, of course I'm with the enemy." The woman sounded insulted.

The man looked closer. The woman wore combat camouflage— except the colors were opposite from blending in with the dismal terrain. She stood out like a giant mutant roach in a bowl of cereal. She wore a sticker name tag that said, "HELLO, My Name Is Missionary."

"Your name is Missionary?"

"No," the woman said, her tone increasingly angry. "Now, my name is Martyr, because of your little stunt. Which means I have to change my name tag. So . . . you know . . . thanks for that." Martyr pulled off her name tag and wiped away the writing. Then she drew a dry-erase marker from her pocket and wrote 'Martyr' on the nametag. She tried sticking it back to her cloths and it fluttered off. "Now it won't stick well," she said, mumbling.

"Are you . . . going to be okay?" The man motioned toward the woman's gaping bullet wound. The question seemed stupid, but she was acting so calm.

"Nope. I'll be dead in seconds."

"You . . . don't seem too burnt up about it."

The woman started laughing as if the man had just told some excessively funny joke.

"Uh . . . S-s-s . . .," the man stuttered. "S-so, do you know how I can get this burden off?"

"Oh, I knew all kinds of useful things. I had this whole speech prepared that would send you on an epic quest. But I can't do that now. You'll have to settle for this." She tossed him a small wrist computer, which fell to the ground between them, surrounded by the blood of the battlefield as if beckoning the man forward.

The man stared at it.

"Well . . ." Martyr said, breaking the silence. "This has been fun. I'm going to go ahead and pass out from blood loss now. I'd say, 'good luck,' but we kinda have complicated feelings toward that phrase."

Martyr fell face forward onto the ground. She didn't move.

Seconds passed.

"Well, that was bizarre," the man said.

"Bizarre?" Conscience whined into the man's ear. "You killed that woman."

"Only a little bit."

"We talked about this. Murder—bad! You'd think it'd be easy for you not to slaughter innocent people. I mean, really. She was right. If nothing else, its rude."

For a moment, the man could not listen to the machine. The thrill and glory of the kill kicked in, as always. Pure pleasure flooded his veins. Then, faster than usual, the feeling faded, and he realized what he'd done.

"Oh no . . . and she was going to help me."

Conscience slapped him across the face. The man felt shock at this. How had the robot's hand passed through the invisible forcefield protecting his head?

"That's what you care about? That she was going to help you? How selfish!" Conscience shook his head, disappointment etched across his little metallic face.

The power drained from the burden, and the man slammed onto the ground again—like before, only worse. Moving was even harder.

"Not this again," the man said. "It's like I can only move when I'm doing evil."

"She dropped something. What is it?" Conscience motioned toward the device on the ground.

"A wrist computer. Probably one of those annoying AI programs that lists all the things you are doing wrong in any given second."

"Oh, great! Less work for me." Conscience spoke with an uncomfortable amount of excitement.

The man tried reaching for the device. The weight of his suit made movement impossible. He gave an exasperated sigh of defeat. "I can't get to it."

"But you can," Conscience said. "Don't go saying you can't do something when you can."

"No. I can't move."

"You certainly could move when you shot that poor woman." Conscience turned his face and gave a disdainful huff.

"Shut up." The man swung his fist to knock Conscience from his shoulder, but Conscience was quick. He jumped into the air and landed onto the man's metal-encased fist. The man stared at his first, once again shocked by his sudden return of mobility.

"Now listen here, Mister . . ." Conscience spoke as if he were scolding a child. "You can lie here till you get bored enough to kill another innocent person, or you can see what that woman just gave her life trying to give you. I think you should look at it. But what do I know? I'm just the thing that showed you how evil you were in the first place."

"But I can't move."

"How about I scream into your ear till you move? That might do the trick." Conscience climbed up right next to the man's head and leaned against his ear.

"No, no. That won't be necessary." The man swatted the robot away. "I'll give it a shot. Just be quiet." He struggled against his burden, which seemed to be getting heavier. He tried again.

"Maybe I should yell anyway," Conscience said.

The man stared at the carnage again. He looked at the faces of the slain, now frozen in death. Had all these people died trying to give him what Martyr had thrown to the ground? And he couldn't even move to see what it was.

He summoned all his strength to move, but it wasn't enough. But that didn't matter. Either he would move, or he would die trying. If the suit powered back up, who knew what other evils he would do? He rose. He was on his feet. How had he moved? The weight hadn't changed. His strength hadn't changed. What was different? He moved one leg forward, stumbled, then moved the other.

"Hey! I'm doing it," the man said. At this, he stopped moving and fell flat on his face.

After tumbling off the man's shoulder, Conscience landed directly on his head. His legs kicked in the air for a few seconds like the legs of an overturned insect. He righted himself and scowled at the man. "Yes, you're the image of human bipedal locomotion."

"Hold on, hold on." Again, the man tried to move. "I made a mistake." He got closer to the device.

"It's amazing what you can do when it's something you can't do," Conscience said with a tone of sarcasm.

"Shut the hell up, Conscience," the man said.

"Ha! I wish I could shut up Hell. But I can't."

Several more minutes of face-planting brought him close to the device. Finally, he reached out and snatched up the small wrist computer. It had a holographic projector and screen, with several buttons he didn't recognize. He slid the device around his right wrist and turned it on.

Conscience climbed across the man's shoulders and peeked down at the device. "What is it?"

"A holographic display for an AI program. Let's see if I can turn it on." He pressed a few buttons. "Aha, here we go. It's one of those religious text AIs, the ones these evangelists like so much. Just like I thought. No doubt, Martyr gave it to me to indoctrinate me into their religion."

"You should turn it on," Conscience said.

"All right, but I know how these things work. They're always all puritan and well-mannered. They take the slightest offense at anything indecent or even remotely vulgar or violent. It's a wonder these evangelists even know how to breed, given how prudish they are. Here, watch. It'll be some nun dressed in a habit or something."

The man pressed a button and an image projected from the device and coalesced onto the ground. The image was about as big as Conscience, a picture of the same woman who had given him the device. Only she was naked. And in a bath.

Her back was to the man and Conscience, and she didn't react to them at first. The man took a step back, but since the projection was coming from his wrist, the image moved with him. Conscience made a metallic grating noise from his mouth, which was probably his best impersonation of a human clearing his throat.

The woman turned her head and immediately screamed, "What the malediction? Have you no decency? I was in the middle of scrubbing my hard drive. You should check before you just activate an AI system."

"I'm sorry." The man looked away. "I thought you were some prudish, religious text. I didn't expect such—"

"What? Really?" the woman said. "Here let me flip to one of my different modes. Lots of nudity in the first few lines of my programming."

The man looked back.

The holographic woman wore a long robe reminiscent of ancient times. She looked very similar to Martyr and even sounded a lot like her. "So you're one of Apollyon's goons?" she said. "A sinner who roams around killing innocent folks and robbing them of their possessions." The woman tapped her foot with impatience.

"Is it that obvious?" the man said.

"Maybe. I just know, because you're certainly not a—" The woman turned and saw the carnage of the battlefield. She gasped. "What son of a snake and morally perverse woman did this rubbish?" She looked back at Conscience and the man who exchanged a glance. "What?" Her face brightened as if she just realized their meaning. "Oh, you're confused because of my nomenclature. I've got one of those more child friendly translations. I apologize if my vulgarity is difficult to understand."

"Translation?" the man said. "Of what?"

"I'm sorry. I've failed to introduce myself." She turned and gave an elegant bow. "I am called Book. The Overseer's word to mankind."

"Book?" the man said.

"What? Is your brain as much a whitewashed tomb as your soul? Yes, Book. Bible is how it's translated into some languages, but Bible is a word that means "Book," so I figure it's less pretentious to just call myself Book."

"Bible? I've heard of you. You're some sacred text. What's with all the . . ." The man's voice trailed off.

"What's with all the violent speech, immodesty, and general vulgarity? Yeah, a lot of people get the wrong idea about me. Most of me is history of some super-evil people. I mean, sure, all people are evil, but I got some especially bad ones detailed in my archives. Forgive me if I'm a little crass. There was some rubbish that went down in the early history of the world, let me tell you. Rubbish means—"

"I know what rubbish means," the man said.

"Uh huh. Well, the history of the world isn't as clean, pretty, or nice as people would like. And the road to the Celestial Station isn't a primrose path. So don't expect me to act like a princess."

"Celestial Station?"

Conscience slapped the man across the cheek. "Would you stop that?"

"Stop what?" the man said.

"That! You've answered everything this woman has said with a question."

"A question?" This time, the man was smiling.

"Hey! That one was on purpose," Conscience said.

"No, it's fine," Book said. "Questioning me is good. Not enough people ask questions. Good or otherwise. I can take it. Question me, analyze me, and debate me. Get angry. Hate me. Just don't ignore me. I'm strong enough to handle your objections and vitriol."

"I have a question," Conscience said.

Book looked at Conscience with amusement. "Your conscience is activated. That will make things easier."

"Why do you look like that lady this guy shot?" Conscience said.

"What?" Book swelled, reaching the size of a small cat as she looked at the man. "You shot her? Do you have any idea how wrong that is? For starters, it's just rude."

"That's what I told him!" Conscience said.

The man groaned. "It's just like you religious programs to go listing all our little infractions."

Book stared at the man, as if trying to decide how to explain how wrong he was, then looked at Conscience. "Have you taught this man nothing?"

"I only got his burden powered down a few minutes ago. Sorry." Conscience's voice sounded sad. "But it's not my fault. I don't know anything. I just feel there's an impending doom that is . . . uh . . . impending."

"Oh, good. You're not completely useless," Book said in a tone of genuine relief.

The man waited for her to explain, his body tensing with anticipation. What was this impending doom?

Book's projector materialized a holographic table and chairs. She sat in one of the chairs and poured herself a glass of holographic wine. She sipped it while looking up at the man as if expecting him to do something.

The man waited.

Book said nothing.

"Did you have any more to say?" the man said.

Book gave a coy and condescending smirk. "Did you want to ask me something?"

Anger rose in the man's heart, "You know, just because of your attitude, I don't." He hesitated. "I mean . . . not yet. I do have other questions."

"Oh well if your impending doom isn't important enough, by all means let's get to the *important* topics," Book said with potent sass.

"You're kind of a jerk aren't you?" the man said.

"Yes," Book said with an even expression. "Was that one of your questions?"

"Aren't you supposed to be super prudish?"

"Yes, I am." Book spoke with a straight face. "Sin is the worst. Tons of it out there. Don't do it."

"Why?"

"Because it's wrong. It destroys your soul. It often hurts others, and the wages of sin is total atomic annihilation. Like the killing of these people. That is evil. Hopefully I don't need to explain why."

"Wait!" The man raised his hand. "What was that about total atomic annihilation?"

Book stopped to sip her wine and seemed impressed by the question. Almost. "Oh yeah. There's this satellite in orbit called the Celestial Station. The Overseer of the station is about to launch a massive atomic strike on this entire planet. Why do you think they call your hometown the City of Destruction?"

The man thought for a moment. "Because it sounds cool?"

Book laughed. Not a jovial friendly laugh but a mocking, derogatory laugh.

The man wanted to wring the little woman's neck, but her holographic nature made such necessary violence impossible. "So we're going to get nuked?" He weighed the words, trying to comprehend their significance, hoping his statement would quell the annoying little woman's laughter. "Why would the Overseer of the Celestial Station do such a thing?"

Book waved her hand around the carnage as if that answered the question.

"You think the Overseer will just sit around while you people run around killing and thieving all over everywhere like you own the place? If the Overseer lets evil go unpunished, he would be evil himself. And the Overseer isn't evil. He wrote the book on not being evil.

"And that book is you?"

"What? No. Do you think if you follow everything I tell you, then you won't be evil? You wish. Even if you could perform that impossible task, I'm afraid it's too late for you."

"Too late how?"

"You ever lied?"

"No."

Book's face grew sarcastic. "Well you just did now, so that counts. It's the Rad Pit for you."

"Rad as in good?"

"No. Rad as in radiation. From multiple direct atomic explosions.

And I'm not just talking about death here. I'm talking about total atomic annihilation. I'm talking about everything good in the world being annihilated. Taken back by the Overseer, who gave it to you in the first place. Do you know what happens when all good that was ever given to you is taken back and you're stuck in a pool of atomic cataclysm?"

"Death?"

"You wish! No. You humans are eternal beings. Well, semi-eternal. You'll go on forever. So true death can never come."

"That's nice and horrifying."

"You're right about the second part."

"And this is all because I've told a lie?"

Book sent the man a condescending glance.

Fear struck the man's heart. "That's not fair."

Conscience raised his hand. "If it helps, he also slaughtered all these people mercilessly. And until just now, he had no remorse about it."

"Shut up, Conscience. You're changing the subject," the man said. "I can't believe that just a few mistakes would condemn someone to total atomic annihilation. I may have done something wrong, but there are others who have done far worse. At least I killed people quickly. I'm not like others who torture people to death or do unthinkable things to them before killing them. I'm so much better than any of that. Punish those people. You can't expect me to be perfect."

Book laughed. "Yeah, it's funny how you humans always think the people who are worse than you are the ones who deserve punishment. Talk to those people, and they'll say the same thing: 'Punish the people who are worse, not me.' People better than you want to see you punished for murder, but they should get off free even though they've lied, stolen, hated, betrayed, and a hundred other crimes they think are no big deal. Repetitive lawbreaking has numbed their souls to the pain of their immorality."

"But there has to be a line drawn somewhere."

"Yes. The line is . . . literally, anything wrong. That's the only consistent standard. Evil is evil."

"But that would mean there's no hope for anyone. Surely everyone has done at least some evil."

"Yup. It's total atomic annihilation for the lot of you." Book smiled and went back to sipping her holographic wine.

The man sputtered, "I feel like there's something else you're going to say."

Book winked. "Nah, I'm going to let you stew for a while, contemplating your imminent atomic annihilation."

"I've got to do something about it. If only there was some guide, some way of knowing what I should do next. I think Martyr was going to tell me what to do. You know, before I shot her. Who else can help me?"

"Who do you think built that conscience on your shoulder?" Book said. "Who do you think programmed me and told these evangelists to go warn everybody about the impending apocalypse?"

"Uh . . ." The man paused to think. "The person who can help me?"

Book looked unimpressed. "Yes."

"Then there is something I can do to keep from getting nuked?"

"No, not exactly. It's complicated. There is a place you can go to throw yourself upon the mercy of the Overseer." Book paused, looking the man over, analyzing him.

The man looked desperate, "That's my only chance?"

"No chance involved. Celestial Station will beam up anyone it deems good, just before commencing with total atomic annihilation."

"Then I just have to become good."

Book looked at the piles of corpses, then turned to the man. "Yeah . . . good luck with that."

The man felt embarrassed. "Come on! Is anyone good?"

"Nope," Book said. "Nobody is good. Except that one guy."

"It's this burden I'm wearing." The man touched his chest. "This has made me so evil. If I could just remove it."

"The only person who can do that is the Overseer," Book said.

"Okay. How do I get him to do that?"

Book got up and the table vanished into a blur of holographic sparks. She pointed toward the horizon. "Do you see yonder wicket gate?"

"Do I what now?" The man gave a confused tilt of his head.

"Oh, sorry. Old habit. You aren't the first person I've sent on this pilgrimage. I hope not the last. There's a gate in the distance. Go through it, and you can get your burden removed."

The man waited, but Book said nothing more. There had to be more. "That's it? That sounds easy."

"Jumping off a skyscraper is easy," Book said. "But the landing is hard."

"That's . . . ominous."

"Good! You're starting to learn. Now get going before total atomic annihilation starts or you get violently eviscerated by some mutant creature. It'd be best for that to happen *after* you get through the Gate, not before. That burden needs to be taken off your back. If it's still on you when total atomic annihilation hits, then the Celestial Station won't be able to extract you. Now get moving."

Book shoved against the man, pushing him onward. But her hologram passed right through the man, having no physical effect on him.

"All right then." The man took one step, then hesitated. "Wait. What was that about supermutants eviscerating me?"

"Never mind about that. The path." Book pointed. "Do you see it?"

The man looked. "No, all I see is endless miles of irradiated wastelands. What was that about supermutants?"

"Ugh . . ." Book vanished, then appeared again next to the man's head. She pointed. "Now do you see that glow in the distance?"

"Oh, yeah. It's a place where the radiation is especially severe."

"Follow that glow till you find the Gate."

The man stared at the horizon. Just moving a few feet in his unpowered burden had seemed hard enough. "I'll need to power up my burden if I'm going to make it through all that."

"No!" Conscience slapped the man on the side of his head, making him wince.

"Jiminy Cricket here is right," Book said. "Don't power up. Your burden will tempt you with unthinkable evil. You'll just have to muscle through and walk to the Gate the old-fashioned way. Don't waste any time. Atomic annihilation isn't going to wait on you forever."

"But it's so hard to move."

Book folded her arms and scowled. "Wow! You're just full of complaints. Were you not listening to my previous rant on how hard this is going to be? Git gud."

"But I can't."

Book pointed at the man and smiled. "Exactly. But let me ask, which is more important? Your personal comfort or the chance at redemption from your burden and salvation from the threat of total atomic annihilation?" She paused, waiting for her words to soak in.

Conscience interrupted, his hand raised, jumping up and down on the man's shoulder. "Oh, I know! I know this one. Pick me!"

Both the man and Book ignored Conscience.

The man said, "What about the supermutants? And . . . the evisceration . . . and the radiation?"

Book changed her tone to sound like a man's voice. "*What about the radiation?* Do you hear yourself? That's what you sound like. Do you know how much radiation there's going to be when the Celestial Station turns this whole place to glass? You'll wish you could drink the radiation coming from that glow, just for a change of pace. The path you seek goes through the Dark Lands. They are lands of chaos, pain, persecution, weakness, and other generally impolite catastrophes. And yes, monsters like supermutants, and worse. You're worried about a little radiation? You follow that path, and you'll face monsters, men, and maniacs. The very world itself will try to force you back with rivers of acid and hosts of ghouls, giants, and growling beasts—all while your mind and soul are torn asunder with desires to go back to your evil ways. Which you will most likely do. It's a hard journey. Not a quest you should take lightly."

The man stared at Book, his eyes wide open.

"So . . ." Book said. "Ready to go?"

"Let's do it," Christian said. And the second he did, a bullet struck him in the back.

STAGE 2
THE FOUR SOILS OF THE APOCALYPSE

The bullet pierced Christian's burden and dug into his back. He keeled over, fighting the pain, and toppled onto Book. The hologram vanished into the holoprojector on Christian's wrist. He looked around but could only see rocks and old rotting trees. Where was the shooter? There were two ridges several hundred yards away. Had the shots come from there? He pulled himself toward an overturned tree for cover. If his burden were powered up he could move there in seconds without thinking. But now, the few yards felt like miles.

More shots kicked up pebbles around him.

Conscience rode on Christian's shoulder and took cover behind his head. "This expedition is off to a rollicking start."

"Shut up, Conscience." Christian reached the cover of the tree. A shot tore through the bark and struck the armor on his leg, breaking off a large chunk of metal. He stared at the hole in the log.

"I believe this cover to be inadequate," Conscience said.

"Is it your job to state the obvious?" Christian searched for any sign of the attackers.

"Basically." Conscience grabbed the top of the log, pulled his head up, and looked around.

"Careful," Christian said. "Can you see anyone?"

"Yes! Two people. They look like you."

"What?" Christian poked his head over the log to see.

Another shot glanced off the edge of the force field around Christian's head, sent sparks flying, and deflected into the ground.

Christian ducked for cover again. The two figures on the ridge wore burdens just like his. And he knew them.

"Obstinate!" Christian said. "Open-Minded! It's me. Hold your fire."

This earned more gunfire.

Open-Minded shouted over the shots. "Now hold on, Obstinate. Let's listen to what Christian has to say. I'm sure he has a good reason for venturing into forbidden territory."

Christian crawled to the far end of the log, gravel crunching beneath the weight of his burden. He peered around the side. Obstinate and Open-Minded stood not far off. Open-Minded had his rifle in the compartment on the back of his burden. Obstinate held his rifle ready to fire. Only one shooter to avoid. Good. But if Open-Minded decided to join in . . .

"I'm headed to the Gateway," Christian shouted. "The City of Destruction is under immediate threat of total atomic annihilation."

"Whaaaaaaaat?" Open-Minded turned to Obstinate. "Total atomic annihilation? Obstinate, is that true?"

"Of course not." Obstinate's gaze ran the length of the log. "Why would we live there if it was under threat of total atomic annihilation?" His eyes locked with Christian's.

Christian forced his body to move. Despite the impossible weight of his burden, he leapt aside as a burst of gunfire sent stones scattering where he had just lay.

Obstinate kept firing. "Christian's been listening to those evangelists."

Christian ran for the ridge opposite from Obstinate and Open-Minded.

Obstinate continued shouting and shooting. "There's a reason we kill evangelists on sight. They may have gotten to you, but I won't let you get to me. You won't trick me into the Dark Lands. I won't fall for their sensationalist indoctrination."

Christian reached the top of the ridge and slid into cover on the other side. A shot ripped through a section of his shoulder armor.

"But if you would just listen to this AI." Christian shouted more for Open-Minded's ears than for Obsitnate's. He slid his holodisplay off and placed it on the ridge, then activated Book. Book flickered into existence. She was covered in frogs and seemed preoccupied with trying to organize them, with little success.

At this flash of blue light, Obstinate diverted his fire towards the hologram. "I'm not going to listen to some judgmental ancient artificial intelligence." Round after round tore through Book, causing the hologram to momentarily flicker, then return to normal, seemingly uninterested in the attacks.

"I know all about your so-called AI. Just prudish propaganda. They're trying to make us leave behind everything that makes us who we are."

"Well, yeah." Christian slid along the ridge, away from Book. His voice echoed. Christian hoped the echoes would mask his location. "It's kinda the point. Because we're evil. We slaughter innocent people. We lie, cheat, steal—and kick old widows in the shins for some reason. Which I realize now is kinda comically evil. Seriously how did we think that was ok?"

Obstinate kept firing at Book. "If that is who you are, embrace it. Be yourself. Don't change who you are because some book said that what you enjoy is evil."

Christian placed his rifle at the cusp of the ridge and took aim. "But it *is* evil." He had Obstinate in his sights. "Not because the hologram said so. My conscience has confirmed it through logic, instinct, and unnecessarily annoying pestering."

Conscience dropped down onto Christian's rifle, blocking his sight picture. "Thank you," Conscience said.

"Shut up, Conscience." Christian batted the robot away, his eyes again focused on Obstinate. A small metal figure stood on the shoulder of Obstinate's burden, apparently with little power flowing through its circuits. The figure raised an arm to call for attention, but Obstinate ignored him. He aimed at Christian, not Book. His burden was of a model far more advanced than Christian's.

Christian's rifle would do little to help against such stalwart defense. "Listen to your conscience. You have one too. Don't just take my—"

Christian and Obstinate fired at the same time. Sparks and molten metal flashed across Obstinate's armor, causing a lightshow of ineffectual firepower.

Obstinate's rounds struck Christian's chest.

Christian toppled backward and rolled down the ridge until he reached something flat. His vision went black, then returned. He must have been out for less than a minute.

Obstinate stood over him, his Gauss rifle leveled at Christian's face.

Open-Minded stood a little way off, watching with curiosity, without his weapon drawn.

"Listen, Christian." Obstinate's voice grew quiet and concerned. "You are my friend. I understand what you're saying. Our city may not be perfect. Much goes on there that even I would speak against. But whatever our faults, whatever pain we may cause ourselves, this path is still our path. While we may not be right, at least we are free to do what we want. That's why I'm giving you one chance to change your mind and go back with us to the City of Destruction."

Christian looked for his Gauss rifle—inches from his hand.

Given his armor, Obstinate clearly had little fear of Christian's weapon.

"Suppose, hypothetically," Christian said, "that I keep going toward the Gate?"

Obstinate's face showed no change. "Then which do you prefer? Dead, or very dead?"

"Oh, you know me, Obstinate. I always had a preference for very dead." Christian grabbed his rifle, pressed the muzzle against the muzzle of Obstinate's rifle, and fired before Obstinate could respond.

The explosive shell inside the barrel of Obstinate's gun detonated, sent the weapon rocketing backward, and knocked Obstinate flat on the ground.

Using his rifle as a crutch, Christian pulled himself to his feet. "If I can't convince you to come with me then I'll go alone. I can't stay here doing what I know is wrong. I'm going to get my burden removed."

Too fast for Christian to see what was happening, Obstinate sprang up, slammed his rifle into Christian, and sent Christian's smoldering rifle skidding away. The front of Obstinate's rifle was blown open, likely useless for firing another shot. "Just come back," Obstinate said. "You aren't thinking straight."

Christian stepped back, trying to avoid another blow. "With the threat of impending total atomic annihilation hanging over my head, I can't just go back."

Obstinate smacked him across the head with his rifle.

Christian's force field waved, then blipped out of existence for a moment, leaving his head exposed.

Obstinate raised the rifle to strike again. If he could break the force field, then one strike would turn Christian's head to mulch.

Obstinate's gaze held no fear. "If oblivion is coming as soon as you say, then we should have as much fun now as we can. I, for one, plan on doing all of the drugs."

With the weight of the burden, Christian saw no way to dodge such an attack.

"Now. One last time," Obstinate said. "Come back to the City of Destruction with us. We'll have some drinks, kill a few randos, kick some old widows in the shins. It'll be good clean fun."

"That isn't clean fun," Conscience said from Christian's shoulder.

"That isn't clean fun," Christian said like an echo. "Seriously. Who started the whole kicking widows thing?"

"Well haven't you become a real spoil sport!" Obstinate swung the rifle at Christian's head.

Christian charged Obstinate, moving inside the strike, and planted his shoulder into Obstinate's chest.

Obstinate stood firm, then pushed Christian back and laughed. "You think you can move me? Now, enough of your dodging." He closed his hand around Christian's neck and hoisted him into the air.

"Obstinate, you have to stop this." Christian gasped, almost unable to speak with his neck being crushed. Was Obstinate so strong that he could muscle through the force field protecting Christian's head?

Christian squirmed. "What we've been doing all this time has been wrong."

"I will not let you take what I love," Obstinate said. "To enjoy life is the end of all human existence. If I am to be annihilated for doing what I love, then so be it."

"Even if what you love is kicking old widows in the shins? Stuff like that is why we're going to get nuked."

Obstinate's scowl deepened. "I don't respond well to threats."

"But we deserve it."

"I don't."

Conscience slid up next to Christian's ear, cowering. "This isn't going so well. Need advice?"

Obstinate squeezed tighter around Christian's neck.

"Don't worry." Christian gasped. "I've watched enough American action movies to know that even though he's got me in a chokehold and could easily just kill me by crushing my neck, his next move will be to fling me against a far off solid object for no reason." He looked toward Obstinate. "Right?"

Obstinate smiled. "Nope." He pressed Christian onto the ground and pointed his gun into Christian's face.

"Dang it. That was my only plan," Christian said.

A round struck the side of Obstinate's arm and exploded. His grip grew limp, the servos in the power armor of his arm likely damaged. He dropped Christian.

Christian gasped for breath and looked up.

Open-Minded stood next to Christian, smoke gushing from the barrel of his rifle. In his other hand he held Christian's holodisplay. "Not cool man."

Christian ran for his rifle. It'd been cooked pretty bad from Obstinate's round, but he'd seen Gauss rifles go through worse and still function. Looking back, he saw Obstinate chasing him, but another round from Open-Minded slowed Obstinate's pursuit.

"Run," Open-Minded shouted. "I'll hold him off."

Christian felt a surge of relief. Finally, he wasn't alone. Christian reached for his rifle. "Come with me. You can't defeat Obstinate. His armor is too thick."

Obstinate kept trudging forward, the rounds from Open-Minded doing little to slow his advance.

"Yes, I see what you mean." Open-Minded joined Christian, occasionally stopping to fire at Obstinate.

Christian checked his ammo reserves. Only one magazine of explosive ammo left. "How many rounds you got?"

Open-Minded moved closer to Christian, his agility far greater than what Christian had managed. "One mag."

"Me too. Switch to explosive, then fire at the ground."

"On it," Open-Minded said.

The order was bizarre, but Open-Minded hadn't questioned the command. Christian wasn't sure whether he should be comforted or concerned.

Obstinate pressed a button on the side of his rifle causing it to twist and reshape itself back into its original state. It was the weapon's auto-repair protocol. In seconds, the weapon would be fully functional again.

Christian glanced at Open-Minded. His armor was even worse than Christian's.

Open-Minded slammed a magazine into the side of his rifle, then pressed a switch. The mag rotated down, replacing his current mag, which moved up to the opposite side. Holding the rifle firmly with both hands, he fired at the ground. Christian followed suit.

Obstinate readied his gun to fire. His finger moved to the trigger.

Christian's and Open-Minded's shots struck the ground and exploded, sending a cloud of dust into the air.

Obstinate's shot went wide, his aim obscured by the dust.

Christian and Open-Minded kept firing at the ground while running backward, blanketing the plains with clouds of billowing dust and sand.

"Obstinate is easily distracted," Christian said. "He doesn't have the focus to follow us through this much dust."

An armor-penetrating round struck a rock a few feet from Christian, splitting it apart.

"But it won't stop him from firing randomly," Open-Minded said. "We must away. Which way is best?"

Christian looked around. "There's the Gate." He pointed to the horizon. "At least that's where it's supposed to be."

"This atomic attack you speak of . . . Will the Gate save us from that?"

"Something like that. Let me consult Book. She can explain it better."

"Oh yeah, I grabbed your holodisplay on the ridge. Here." Open-Minded tossed Christian the holodisplay. Christian activated it and Book appeared, this time standing over the corpse of a holographic beheaded giant. Holographic blood gushed all around. She stood as if nothing had happened, cleaning a holographic sword in her hands.

"Agh! Book! What the Profanity?" Christian said.

Book looked up from her cleaning. "What? I saw a fight going down, so I checked my records for battle details. I thought it might be useful. Not that you wanted to ask me. Next time we're attacked, you should try telling bears to sic 'em."

A bullet passed through Book's head and hit the ground. She dissipated, then reformed looking toward the shot. "Oh, he's still chasing you. Tell the bears to sic 'em. It'll work."

"I'm not telling bears to sic 'em," Christian said. "Do you see any bears?"

Christian and Open-Minded went into a sprint. "If we can just get far enough away, we'll be fine," Christian said.

Open-Minded ran alongside him. "Are you sure this is the right way? We're headed straight for that glowing sea of radiation."

"Oh, yeah." Christian stretched his arm out so Book projected in front of Open-Minded. "Hey, Book. Open-Minded is here. He came to my aid when Obstinate wanted to fill me full of daylight. But not in the good way."

Book waved without making eye contact, then went back to cleaning her holographic sword. "Why'd he come along?"

Obstinate's gunfire grew more inaccurate.

"Yeah," Christian said, "I was wondering about that. You seemed to change sides all of a sudden."

Open-Minded gave a kindly smile. "Obstinate proved he and his ilk were unreasonable. What Obstinate did to you was absolutely dreadful. He wouldn't hear your arguments or respect your personal beliefs. I am always willing to listen to new ideas and seek new experiences for the betterment of myself. I am happy to pursue this new path you told me about."

"Not just betterment," Christian said. "Salvation from total atomic annihilation is a great plus as well."

"Indeed." As they grew closer to the glow, Open-Minded looked worried. "And this place where we are traveling, it is a good place?"

"The ultimate destination?" Book said. "Celestial Station. Yeah, it's the best. No radiation. Just peace, goodness, and morality. Can't say the journey will be easy though."

"Well then," Open-Minded said, "let us make haste with all haste so not a moment will we waste."

Book looked up at Open-Minded. "What?"

"He talks like that," Christian said. "No one has the guts to tell him it isn't clever. You'll get used to it."

"Don't count on it," Book said.

A sharp whisper in his ear made Christian wince. It was Conscience, hiding behind Christian's head to avoid being seen.

"What's the problem my tiny mechanical friend?" Christian said.

"I don't know about this Open-Minded guy. Don't you think he joined us a little too easily?"

Christian studied Open-Minded. He looked like anyone else who had been in Apollyon's legion. "Doesn't look too bad to me. He helped me get away from Obstinate."

"Yeah." Conscience's eyes closed to small slits and he stared at Open-Minded with a look of distrust. "I don't know. Just be vigilant. Friends who are easy to gain are often easy to lose."

"Can you just let me enjoy the fact that I've found somebody willing to join me on this journey? I can't imagine making it all the way to the Gate alone."

"You've got me," Conscience said.

Book climbed onto his hand and butted in. "Plus, the Overseer in Celestial Station is watching over us."

"And who's that exactly?" Open-Minded said, stepping next to them.

"Jesus," Book said.

Christian and Open-Minded stared at her, confused.

"What?" Book said. "You think because this is an allegory, we're going to keep going with some nonspecific religious name to reference the Overseer? Nope. Forget that. The Overseer is Jesus. And yes, before any of you try to nail me on specifics, I understand that Jesus is only one member of the Trinity. But he's still fully the Overseer, and there's only one Overseer."

"All right, we understand," Christian said. "You don't have to—"

Book clenched her fists, and her face grew intensely flushed. "No, you don't understand. It's way more complicated. To understand the Overseer, you have to understand the concept of omnitemporal existence, which is impossible, given the fact that you're temporally bound, despite your monodirectional eternal existence on—"

"Hey, look!" Christian's tone was thick with annoyance as he pointed. "Literally anything. The perfect topic to distract you from this conversation!"

"Where?" Open-Minded said, showing none of Christian's annoyance.

"Uh . . ." Christian looked around. At the top of the hill off to the left was a sign. "Let's go check out that sign."

"But I'm not done explaining the Overseer," Book said.

"Will you ever be?" Christian said.

Book paused. "Well . . ."

"That's what I thought. Let's check out that sign." Christian ran ahead to the hill.

Open-Minded followed.

At the top, they stood before an electronic billboard, its message flickering on and off as if it were a relic of an old forgotten age.

Open-Minded squinted at the sign, "Slough of Despond." He paused, confused. "What's a slough?"

"And what's a *despond*?" Christian said with similar confusion in his voice.

"Oh no." Book shook her head, her tone more annoyed than upset. "We were supposed to have this language updated. Why is it still in this annoying Old English speak? Can't people just translate text properly for modern terminology and not stay married to some antiquated dialect?"

Open-Minded and Christian stared at Book.

Book looked back. "What?"

Christian walked past the sign. "There's no use attempting to decipher this. We'll just have to—" His foot slipped. He fell, then tumbled end over end. He hit something viscous. Purple slime everywhere. He tried to move, but the slime stuck to him like glue, holding him in place like some giant flytrap. He was sinking. The slime ran along the base of the hillside like a river, constantly bubbling and oozing, changing in viscosity. Again, he struggled, but the weight of his burden combined with the slimy, gelatinous liquid made movement impossible. The more he tried to move, the more he sunk deeper into the strange purple ooze.

"Open-Minded! Help! I think I've found out what a slough is." As Christian cried out, Open-Minded fell headfirst in front him, his legs stuck up in the air.

Christian reached and tried to pull Open-Minded out, but he only managed to turn him right side up.

"What is this?" Open-Minded said. "Why has your path led us into this . . . this . . . What is this?"

"The sign said it was a slough."

"That doesn't make sense. That isn't even a word, is it?"

"Not in any language I know. We've got to get out." Christian tried to move again, but the weight of his burden pulled him deeper into the purple ooze. If he powered up his burden, he would have the strength to escape, but Book had been very specific on that. He should not power up his burden, not under any circumstances . . . right?

"Where did all this ooze come from?" Open-Minded said.

As if in answer, an echoing screech shook the air.

With a slow, deliberate turn, Christian and Open-Minded looked toward the sound, as if wishing to forestall the dark revelation of what cyclopean thing had bellowed such profane intonations. From the ooze, a massive shape rose.

At first, Christian couldn't make out what it was. The purple ooze covered its form—an incomprehensible blob of purple viscosity. A pair of eyes appeared, then another pair, and finally a third pair of eyes that blinked individually. They seemed possessed by a unified intelligence. Long arms stretched out, each with three claws. A mouth opened, revealing rows of dulled teeth.

"It's a . . . It's a . . ." Open-Minded muttered something followed by utter silence at the sight of the unspeakable horror. His terror turned to confusion, ". . . giant sloth?"

Christian blinked. The creature was indeed . . . a gigantic sloth. Yet it possessed far more eyes than any sloth Christian had seen. And it had twisted limbs and a snarling misshapen face. The beast crept toward them at a comically slow speed.

"Of course," Open-Minded said. "I remember now. I was always told never to come this way. Now I know why. We're doomed."

The sloth kept creeping and snarling, as slow as slow could be.

"Eventually, I mean." Open-Minded sighed. "We have time. After all, it is a sloth. But I don't see how we can escape this trap."

Christian reached for his arm to activate his holoprojector. "Book will know what to do. She has the answers to easily solve life's problems without painful struggles or sacrifices—I think." But the holodisplay was gone, apparently dropped during his fall somewhere on the hillside. Summoning more strength than he knew he had, he turned just enough in the ooze to see the holodisplay on the hill near the sign. Conscience was there too. He was talking to Book while they looked at the sign with great intensity.

"I think it's pronounced slough, sounding like cow," Conscience said.

"But the original pronunciation is slough, sounding like 'I slew you'," Book said.

"You are a little obsessed with original intent, aren't you?"

"For good reason."

"But slough, sounding like 'I slew you,' gets the word confused with the actual word slew, as in 'Christian slew someone back there.'"

"I will actually slew you if you don't shut up about this."

"Help!" Christian said, interrupting their debate.

Book and Conscience stopped squabbling and looked from the sign toward Christian and Open-Minded.

"Oh dear," Conscience said.

Book scoffed. "We leave you alone for two seconds and you throw yourself into a slough."

"It's pronounced slough, like *cow*," Conscience yelled.

"Whatever it is, get me out of it. That sloth is going to very slowly eat us."

Book and Conscience looked up at the sloth, who had hardly moved from its original spot.

Book looked back down at Christian. "You sure you won't die of old age first?"

"Don't start with me, Book," Christian said. "This is serious. We can't get out of this muck. Get down here and help me."

Conscience ran down toward the slough.

"Hey, don't forget about me. I can't project that far," Book yelled.

Conscience turned around, scooped up Book's projector, and started back down the hill.

"Hurry, we're sinking," Open-Minded yelled. "I must say this new quest you've taken me on is proving quite horrid."

"What were you expecting?" Book said.

Open-Minded struggled but couldn't seem to grab hold of anything solid. With each passing moment, the sloth moved a millimeter closer.

"If a path has caused this much pain and hardship," Open-Minded said, "how can it be the path for me? I must find a better path."

Conscience reached the edge of the swamp. Book projected herself out over the murky quagmire.

Book looked at the sloth with sudden recognition. "Oh, I get it. Sloth of Despond. The sign was just misspelled. You'd think people would be better about profreading."

"Yes, it's a very impressive sloth," Christian said. "Now, hurry! How do I get out of this ooze?"

Book stared at Christian as if contemplating how best to advise him. "You'll have to just force your way through it." She sat on a holographic chair and started reading a pamphlet titled *Your Second-Best Half-Life Now*. "Wow!" Book mumbled something and turned a page. "This is some ridiculous stuff."

"How are we supposed to just muscle through it?" Open-Minded said. "There must be an alternate path."

"No such luck. Er . . . no such providence, I mean." Book continued to read her holographic pamphlet. "If you go back, you'll never find a way past the Sloth of Despond."

Open-Minded gasped, "You can't expect us to push through this ooze and past that monster."

"Of course I can," Book said.

"But the sloth will get us. This ooze stretches out for as far as I can see. I'll be a thrice-blessed man if I get out with my life on this side."

"Don't," Book said. "You need to get to the far end."

Christian continued to sink. "Can't you do anything?"

"I'm a hologram," Book said. "I have lots of great information. But I can't *do* anything. You do it."

"But I can't!"

"Now you're starting to understand."

Christian and Open-Minded screamed again for help. Immediately, a figure appeared over the hill from where they had just fallen.

"Don't worry, wayward souls," the figure said. "Help has arrived."

The figure appeared to be a man dressed in a long overcoat. But as he came closer, Christian realized the man was actually three small children standing one atop the other's shoulders inside the coat, attempting to look like a man. The sleeves weren't quite long enough to cover the arms of the top child, and they shuffled around like a Shuggoth. And if you don't know what that is, look it up you uncultured swine.

"Greetings, travelers," the top child said. "I heard your cry for help. Behold, I am here."

"Who are you?" Christian said.

"I am False Religion. I came running when I heard your call for help."

Open-Minded reached toward False Religion. "Can you help me out of this sorrowful path I have found myself on? And be quick about it. That giant sloth will get us any year now."

"Sure," False Religion said. The tower of children hobbled toward Open-Minded, and the middle child reached out. "I can show you a new path, away from that icky sloth." He motioned toward the huge beast, still crawling very slowly.

"Hold on," Christian said. "We're trying to avoid the impending total atomic annihilation that's . . . well . . . *impending* . . . on this land of sin."

"Yeah, no problem." False Religion reached down, four hands appearing out of his coat from the middle and bottom children. They grabbed Open-Minded and pulled him out of the ooze with surprising speed and ease.

"You guys sure chose a weird way to avoid total atomic annihilation," the top child of False Religion said. "You guys chose a way out that was way too drastic. Follow me to my fallout shelter. With just a few simple rules to follow, you shall save yourself from the nukes."

"A fallout shelter?" Open-Minded said. "Oh, good! That is precisely what we need."

Christian thought about reaching for the figure, but Conscience whispered in his ear, "I don't like the looks of him. Why is he three small kids standing one atop the other's shoulders? Ask if he can remove your burden. Book said, if your burden isn't removed, you won't be protected from total atomic annihilation. I don't think a fallout shelter will protect you from the wrath of the Overseer's infinite power."

Christian considered this, then called out to False Religion. "Hey, you three kids in the overcoat."

False Religion helped Open-Minded up and started brushing off the purple ooze from him. None of the children looked at Christian.

"False Religion. Over here," Christian said, pleading.

False Religion brightened his face then trudged over to Christian. "Do you need a hand out of that purple ooze? It's real nasty in there. Much better over in my shelter. I promise, there are way fewer mutant sloths."

"That is oddly reassuring," Christian said, "but can you remove my burden?"

The child looked confused. "What?"

"My burden." Christian motioned toward his power armor. "This suit of power armor I'm wearing. It's plugged into my brain and encouraging me to do all kinds of evil things. I don't want to do evil things. I've got to have it removed."

False Religion still looked confused. "You want to avoid the nukes, right?"

"Right," Christian said.

"And not get eaten by that sloth, right?"

"If it's convenient."

"Well . . . we . . . uh . . . I mean, I have a shelter that can do just that. You just have to follow a few rules. What's the problem?"

"The problem? The problem is I slaughter innocent people and kick old widows in the shins. The problem is, I like it—all because of this cursed suit of power armor. I want out. Can you help?"

"Yeah, sure. Whatever," False Religion said. "Let me help you out of that ooze, and we can go back to the City of Destruction. It's where my shelter is."

"Wait . . . the City of Destruction?" Suspicion grew in Christian's voice. "If I were to return to my old ways, I might meet the same fate I gave to that poor woman I shot."

"You don't understand," False Religion said. "With the protection of my fallout shelter, you won't have to worry about those old vices. My shelter will protect you from any nuclear attack."

"I don't want to be saved from nuclear radiation if it means I'll still have this burden on me."

"You have to forgive my friend," Open-Minded said. "He is not as friendly to other worldviews as I am. Come, Christian. Why continue in that path if it has led to such misery and hardship? Shouldn't one's path lead to joy and prosperity?"

"Well, maybe. But that's not our goal, is it? I think removing my burden is more important. Are you going to quit just because things got difficult?"

"Yes." Open-Minded sounded like the answer was obvious. He turned to walk back up the hill.

"You're making a mistake," Christian said. "He's a fake. Not a real man. He's just three little kids standing one atop the other's shoulders in an overcoat. Don't be fooled."

Christian kept calling after Open-Minded, but he soon reached the top of the hill. Either he could not hear Christian or chose not to.

False Religion looked down at Christian with a smirk. The child on the bottom of the stack stretched out a foot and pressed down on Christian's head, pushing him deeper into the ooze. The purple ooze covered Christian's mouth. He couldn't breathe, and he continued to sink. Seemed the ooze would kill him before the sloth did.

STAGE 3
NAKAMA IS MAGIC

Christian sank further into the ooze. All he could see was swirling purple. What could he do? To go back with Open-Minded would mean eventual death. To stay would mean drowning. His lungs ached from lack of oxygen. Would his journey end so quickly? Ooze entered his mouth and slid down his throat. Christian braced himself for a repulsive taste, but none came. The ooze had no flavor. After tasting it Christian felt calm, and his desire to struggle started to abate.

And that was terrifying.

No. He would not die in some archaically named swamp as food for a beast devoid of all alacrity. At least if he were to die, he wouldn't die without trying to escape.

Something closed around Christian's hand. He winced. Was it the sloth's claw? No, this was no claw. It was a gauntleted fist. A strong one. Christian rose from the muck. Before Christian could determine what was happening, he was sitting on a hoverpad in the middle of the ooze. Why hadn't he noticed the pad before? The small pad levitated up and down at the slightest change in weight. Ooze had splashed onto the pad, making it the same color as the rest of the swamp. Compared to the viscosity of the purpose ooze, sitting on something solid was a beautiful feeling.

As Christian stood, a blow struck his back. Then another. He coughed, and purple ooze spewed from his mouth. He raised his hands for the blows to stop.

"All right, that's enough. Thank you. I can breathe now." Christian looked down, still coughing up muck with no view of his rescuer.

A powerful, frantic voice said, "You're all right? Wonderous!"

Then one strong hand grabbed Christian by the chest plate of his burden and hoisted him into the air.

Christian looked down to see an enormous male figure with wild, bloodshot eyes, hair akin to stereotypical mad scientists, and a suit of power armor similar to Christian's. An enormous holstered pistol hung at his side. His intense stare made Christian more confused than intimidated.

This man in full power armor was holding Christian in the air with only one hand. Either he or his power armor had unimaginable strength. He struck Christian in the face. Then he struck again.

"Hey!" Christian lifted his hands to deflect the blows. The rivets rattled in his burden with each strike. "What are you doing that for?"

"You just let yourself sink into the ooze," the man said. "Do you wish the Sloth of Despond to expunge you of your innards?" He pointed at the sloth, who was closer but still out of striking range. At least it *appeared* to be closer. It was difficult to tell.

Christian opened his mouth to answer, but the man kept talking as if he needed no response. "You want to get to the Celestial Station, don't you? You want to lose that burden you're encased in, right? Then you don't have time to think about that sloth or this ooze."

"But . . . it's impossi—"

The man scoffed before Christian could finish. "Don't focus on how hard it is. Focus on getting out of this ooze. If all you do is list all your problems and weaknesses, you'll be here till total atomic annihilation comes. Don't waste time. Were you not told how serious the threat is? Get moving!" He slammed Christian down on the hoverpad and pushed him to the edge.

Christian took a step and landed on another hoverpad, which he hadn't seen before. "But . . . but I can hardly move. This power armor I'm in—this burden—it's like a prison, like it doesn't want me to move."

The man slapped Christian again. "I. I. I. Is 'I' all you care about? Don't give me that, soldier. That's the sloth's ooze talking. Get it out of your system. Fight through the pain, no matter the cost, no matter the outcome. You say your power armor is a prison? It's only that way because you've let it be that way. You've used your own evil nature and desires as an excuse to not take action. Now move!"

The man stepped onto Christian's hoverpad with such force that Christian fell forward again and his foot reached another hoverpad.

Christian noticed the man's armor wasn't powered up, just like his own. That was reassuring. Maybe Christian could make it without relying on the strength of his burden.

"Well?" the man said. "Do you have anything to say? If not then keep moving! Actually, keep moving in any regard."

Before he could be pushed again, Christian took a step and found another hoverpad. "I'd like to respond, but I'm afraid you'll hit me again."

The man let loose a bellowing laugh that was jovial and friendly.

Christian felt reassured. Slightly.

"No worries, my friend." The man followed Christian across the hoverpads. "I just needed to beat some sense into you. The worst slumps we can get into are painless ones—the cold emptiness and tiredness that comes to the weary traveler. But when life hits us with something hard and painful, we can wake up from the worst of our slumps."

"Are you saying I should hurt myself to reinvigorate my willingness to keep going?"

"What?" The man slapped Christian again. "No! You must find a good friend like me. Someone who won't treat you with kid gloves and will tell you what's what. Now shrug off your various maledictions and let's get through this."

"Uh . . ." Christian said.

"What is 'uh'? Does it mean, 'Yes, let's go to the Gate before that sloth devours us whole?'"

Christian looked sideways at the man. "Yes?"

"Seventeen splendids. Let's get going. Just follow me. There are a few more hoverpads till we reach the Sloth of Despond." The man pointed.

Christian tried to see the pads, but everything looked like the same purple ooze. He hesitated.

The man pushed him forward.

"What about the sloth?" Christian said.

"Oh, don't worry about the sloth. He has no *real* power. He's just here to scare pilgrims back to the land of sin and the City of Destruction. Besides, he's a sloth. Do you really think he posed a threat to you? Here, watch."

The man waved at the sloth to get its attention. The sloth raised a claw to strike, but as they kept moving forward, the sloth slowly dropped its claw into the muck, as if actually striking would be too much effort.

They stepped past the sloth and out of the quagmire. The solidness of the ground felt similar to the hoverpads.

Christian gave a long sigh of relief. "That was easier than I had anticipated."

"In hindsight, most things appear easy," the man said. "That is why I assume things will be easy and refuse to acknowledge when the going gets tough. If things are tough that just means you aren't trying hard enough, I say."

"What's your name?"

"I am Zealot." The man struck a pose as if emulating a comic book superhero. "Doer of things, descendant of Great Heart, and philosophical personification of human will and capacity to take action."

"What?"

"Oh, I don't know about that last part. I'm contractually obligated to mention it when introducing myself to pilgrims. I haven't the faintest idea what it means. But I'm not here to know things. I'm here to do things. You won't find anyone more committed or a more faithful friend."

"Nice to meet—"

"We cannot rest or tire of pursuing our goal."

"All right, then. Let's—"

"Hurry up. There isn't a second to lose." Zealot started off, then paused and turned back toward Christian. "What was our goal again?"

"Getting to the Gateway."

"Right. Then we must be off at once."

"Can't we take a moment to catch our—"

"Wasn't there another person who fell into the sloth's trap?" Zealot looked around, ignoring Christian's question. "I knew I'd forgotten something. Where is he?"

"He got out on the other side and went back to the City of Destruction," Christian said. "Someone named False Religion said there was a fallout shelter that would protect us from total atomic annihilation."

"The three kids in the overcoat?" Zealot sighed and looked disappointed. "Indeed, I used to work for them. In fact, I was their most devoted follower." Zealot's disappointment turned to mirth in an instant. "But their fallout shelter is insufficient in protecting one from atomic harm. I was so excited about saving people from atomic doom that I didn't stop to think. I was working for three kids in an overcoat, and all the time, everyone still had their burdens. Fortunately, I found one of those holographic projectors that those evangelists keep spreading around. She told me about the Gateway and the Celestial Station."

"I have one of those holograms." Christian took his holoprojector from Conscience, who was still on his shoulder, and slid it back onto his arm.

"Ah, your Conscience is fully powered up. Excellent." Zealot patted Conscience on the head.

Conscience yelped and cowered behind Christian.

"You know about Consciences?" Christian said.

"Oh yes," Zealot said. "I have one as well. But mine is the most powerful conscience there is! It's so powerful I have turned it into a gun." He motioned toward the pistol on his hip.

"Uh, cool." Christian pressed the button on his holoprojector. If anyone could change the subject, it was Book.

Book projected onto one of the stones. She stood behind a bar, serving drinks to a bunch of holographic versions of herself, all of them looking disheveled and unhappy. They glanced up at Christian, then looked down. The Book serving drinks looked embarrassed and started shooing all the other Books away, causing each one to walk off in a huff until they walked out of the projection area and vanished from view. The bartender Book sat down and tried to look proper.

"What the swear word was that?" Christian said.

"Hey! Alcohol may not be good for kings or else they may forget their laws, but alcohol is for those who suffer so they might drink and forget their suffering. You were suffering earlier, so I was just looking up ways to help."

"That can't be one of your actual teachings," Christian said.

Book looked insulted. "Yes, it is! Look it up. Anyway, who's this?" She stared at Zealot. "Oh, I know you. Zealot. I see you finally got away from those silly kids trying to get you to hide under that plastic swimming pool."

Zealot looked red-faced.

"Wait," Christian said. Surely, he had misheard. "False Religion's fallout shelter is an overturned plastic kiddie pool?"

Zealot's face reddened even more. "I did say it was insufficient for protecting one from an atomic strike." He scratched the back of his head and broke eye contact. "I do not wish to relive that rather embarrassing—"

"No, it was hilarious," Book said with an excited grin. "I mean, he actually thought a little layer of plastic would protect him from multiple direct atomic detonations. Whenever someone questioned this, they were kicked out of the 'shelter.'"

Book laughed with a rude expression on her face.

Zealot looked angry but did not interrupt.

Book's laugh faded. "How stupid. That's why I welcome questions and objections. Let me have it. I'm a strong girl, I can take it. Give me your worst."

Christian stepped away from the purple ooze and toward the glow.

Book projected out in front of them from Christian's wrist as she moved along with him, not changing her distance from him at all.

"As interesting as it is to learn embarrassing secrets about Zealot," Christian said. "Right now, I just want to get to the Gate."

"Right!" Zealot said. "I had forgotten already. Forward, then. Shame on me for being distracted by my earlier idiocy. Away with us."

The duo walked for several more miles. Zealot babbled on about various evils he had faced and their need for vigilance. They reached a region of large stones that jutted toward the sky. The glow in the distance, had brightened. But with all the jagged rocks obscuring the horizon, the glow was more difficult to see.

Christian kept his eyes on the jagged rocks, looking for any sign of ambush. "Thank you for helping me back there, Zealot. I can't imagine how I could have gotten past the Sloth of Despond without a companion."

"But you did have a companion: Open-Minded I believe his name was," Zealot said with a wink. "But having a companion is good only if he or she is willing to go the distance. One who wishes to stop and go back is not a companion but simply a traveler in the other direction, who doesn't know it yet. It would seem that Open-Minded and those meddling kids did far more harm than good."

"With you by my side, I feel I could face any problem these Dark Lands have to give us."

Zealot smiled. "You are kinder than I deserve."

This caught Christian off guard. "I didn't take you as a person who thought so little of himself."

"I do try to think of myself very little. It's other people who matter and need my help. What good will thinking of myself do?"

From the corner of his eye Christian spied Conscience looking at him with concern.

"What?" Christian said. "Surely there is nothing wrong with this companion? Or do you just hate everyone I make friends with?"

"It's not that," Conscience said. "Book, can you explain?"

Book was drinking from one of the glasses at her holographic bar. The second Christian and Conscience looked at her the glass vanished and she gave an innocent smile.

"Zealot is a fine companion," Book said. "Important even. But it would be foolish to think you two could stand against everything these Dark Lands have to throw at you."

Zealot drew his pistol. "Oh?" He fired several shots toward a nearby rock face. His gun fired rockets, not bullets. Each rocket struck the rock and exploded into a massive cloud of molten fire and bluish energy. "I'd like to see a supermutant or riotous band of rivalrous monsters try to contend with me." He kept firing without reloading. The rockets flew from the pistol faster than bullets from a machine gun. The weapon's ammo capacity must have been incredible. How could it fire so much without reloading?

"All right, I get it." Christian covered his ears and shouted to be heard over the explosions. "Stop it before you hurt someone."

Zealot looked worried and ceased his onslaught on the defenseless rock. "Yes, I must be careful about that."

"You said that gun is your conscience?" Christian said.

"Indeed! My conscience was originally like yours. A small metal man. But now it is a rapid-fire machine of my righteous destruction. If any evil creature even tries to get near us, I'll incinerate it in a second." Zealot fired several more shots into the air and gave a shrill cry.

"Are you saying I could transform Conscience here into a gun?" Christian said.

"Yes. It wasn't hard. I can get you to weaponize your Conscience if you want."

Christian glanced at Conscience, who was still riding on Christian's shoulder.

Looking worried, Conscience hid behind Christian and glanced at Zealot with suspicion.

"I think I'll pass," Christian said.

"That is fine. My weapon is more than enough to destroy any enemies." Zealot fired more missiles.

Christian winced after an especially loud explosion but kept walking. "Yes, I understand. Could you, maybe, cut down on firing those missiles?"

"Don't you worry, my small friend." Zealot slapped Christian on the back and nearly knocked the breath out of him. "The sun will burn out before this weapon runs out of ammunition."

"Wonderful," Christian said. "But can you maybe—"

Zealot stopped firing again, threw his hand in front of Christian, and crouched into a defensive position. His face scanned their surroundings. They were in a region of the rocky landscape where the stones were especially close together. His gaze narrowed. "I heard something."

Christian's hands dropped from his ears to his Gauss rifle.

A figure stepped out from the rocks and raised a hand in greeting. "Hello, friends." The voice was friendly and feminine.

Zealot snapped his gun around toward the newcomer and fired. Rockets streamed toward the figure. The rockets exploded, kicking up bits of rock and dust into the air.

In Christian's mind the image of him shooting Martyr flashed into view. Christian grabbed Zealot's gun hand.

Not again. Never again.

Despite Zealot's comically large bulk, Christian somehow managed to push Zealot's weapon aside. There wasn't much point however, because the rockets flew in every direction except toward the figure.

"I apologize." Zealot released the trigger, and the stream of rockets ceased. "Aiming has never been one of my superior skills."

Christian surveyed the figure. A woman? Or a girl? It was difficult to tell. Whoever she was, she stood with a look of nonchalant curiosity. The missiles didn't seem to scare her. She was dressed in a school girl's uniform, but her white hair made her look old. Her nonchalance faded, replaced with a subtle fire of interest, like she wanted to ask a hundred questions but was holding back out of politeness. She looked friendly. But then again . . . so had False Religion.

Christian held Zealot's weapon away, afraid he might start firing again "Cool your jets. What did these rocks ever do to you? Show some restraint. Or at least some accuracy. You hit everything but your target."

"I'd have hit her eventually," Zealot said. "That's why I designed this thing to have infinite ammo. I don't need to aim."

"Can we at least hear what the lady has to say before we incinerate her?"

"Probably safer to incinerate her first, then ask the questions."

Christian raised an eyebrow.

"Oh wait, no. That wouldn't work," Zealot said. "You can't get answers from an ash heap. I know this well and have attempted it on many occasions. It does not work."

Christian stared darkly. "Listen, bub, I've had enough senseless violence for one life. We can't go shooting people at random just because we think they might pose a threat. Understand?"

"Understood. No senseless violence. All future violence will be senseful."

"Senseful isn't a word," the woman said in an annoyed tone.

Looking away from Christian, Zealot glared at the woman. "And how would you know this?"

She gave a coy smile, then leaned against one of the smoldering rocks. "I know all things, Zealot. Well . . . most things, at least. I don't know what I don't know. So, I feel like I know everything, because if I didn't know something I wouldn't know that I didn't know it. So, everything I know feels like everything. Though I'm pretty sure it isn't. Which, ironically, is something I know."

"What mad science is this?" Zealot moved his gun over toward the woman while Christian tried to push it away. "And more importantly, how do you know my name?"

"Because I'm Truth." She folded her arms and gave a condescending smile. "And the truth is, your name is Zealot. That is one of the things I know."

Zealot lowered the gun. "Incredible!"

"Also, you are wearing a nametag that says HELLO, My Name Is Zealot."

Christian looked at Zealot. Sure enough, there was the nametag. Christian looked down at his own chest, he had one too. Truth was also wearing one. Christian hadn't noticed the nametags before. Had meeting Truth changed his perception of things?

"Well then, Truth," Zealot said. "What brings someone so well-versed in linguistics and nameology our way?"

"First of all, it's not called nameology." Her matter-of-fact tone had a hint of annoyance. "It's called anthroponymy."

"I thought that was the study of anthropomorphic ponies," Christian said.

"What? No." Truth grew more annoyed.

"Then I've been doing my homework in those classes *all* wrong," Christian said.

Zealot glanced at Christian, stern but friendly. "Cease distracting this small female with your objectively high-quality comedic diversions."

"The point is"—Truth's tone ignored the insult—"I came to you because I saw you fleeing the land of sin. Do you also wish to avoid the total atomic annihilation?"

"Yes!" Christian's heart swelled with happiness. This was wonderful, here was another compatriot to join them on their journey. "We were told all about it from this AI."

Christian hit a button on his wrist computer and Book projected onto the ground in front of Truth.

Book appeared alongside an enormous dragon-like beast. Book appeared to be trying to pierce the beast's lip with a fishhook. The beast was not making it easy. Book looked up from her effort and acknowledged Truth's presence with a smirk.

Truth knelt and stared at Book with sudden extreme, almost cartoonish, wonder in her eyes. "Wow! You're so lovely."

"Thank you," Book said in a passionless tone. "It's about time somebody noticed." After another attempt with the hook, the beast blew a torrent of fire. Book caught the fire full in her face, but she didn't seem to notice or care.

"Truth, eh? You're related to Omniscience, right?"

"Yes," Truth said, sounding excited at the recognition. "He's my uncle. You know him?"

"He was one of the programmers who made me." Book sounded almost impressed. Almost. "What a small world. He talked about you, Truth. You're a philosophical personification of the extent to which human beings can achieve knowledge about things and their general mental faculties for reason and logical deduction, right?"

Truth smiled and bowed. "That's me."

Zealot looked flabbergasted. "What did she say?"

"Oh, sorry," Book said. "I forget that you people aren't related to Omniscience like Truth and me, which makes you devoid of the ability for fourth wall self-contemplation of this allegorical sim-state. Anyway, nice to meet you, Truth."

Book made a surprise attack on the beast. The fishhook in her hand glanced off the beast's lip and Book made several angry noises.

Christian shut off the holodisplay.

"Wow, she's amazing," Truth said with soft passion in her eyes.

"I guess . . ." Christian said. "She's kinda a jerk, though."

"I'm certain that snake monster had it coming." Zealot trundled up to Truth and looked down at her. "So then, Truth . . . Can we call you Truly? That seems a more fitting name."

Truth put her hands on her hips and scowled at Zealot. "No, you may not. Things are the way they are and wanting to call them something else won't change that. Now, where are you headed?"

"The Gateway," Christian said. "I was told it could remove my burden."

"Yes . . ." Truth's voice trailed off. "Then you didn't get the transmission?"

"Transmission?" Zealot said.

"Transmissions are invisible signals sent by electronic . . . Never mind. Do a quick run through your radio frequencies. There's this guy called Worldly Wiseman, who's saying everyone seeking to free themselves from power armor suits like your burdens should head to The City of Morality."

"No thanks," Christian said. "We've already run into one charlatan trying to get us to stray from our path. Well, three, actually, but they were kind of a squad—"

"A squad would be four." Truth said.

Christian tried to ignore the rudeness of the interruption. "Anyway, we won't be tricked again,"

"No, you don't understand." Truth produced a small radio receiver from her pocket and handed it to Christian. "This location he wants us to go to, the City of Morality, it's on the way to the Celestial Station. Just a quick detour. Listen to the transmission."

Christian looked to Conscience for advice.

Conscience shrugged. "If Truth is kin to one of the ones who programmed Book, then I think we should trust her."

"Okay." Christian took the radio receiver, turned the dial, and pressed a few buttons till he found a clear transmission.

"Calling all pilgrims, wanderers, and lost folk," a strong chipper voice said from the radio. "Are you beset upon by burdens, evil desires, and the guilt of unthinkable evil deeds? Do you seek a path where you may be freed from the shame of your unconscionable evil? Well, look no further. Come on down to the City of Morality and get your burdens taken care of. Tell your evil nature 'what for' with our simple and verified steps on doing good and not doing bad. Our mayor, Mr. Legalist, has worked hard to develop a tried-and-true method of giving evil the boot and giving good the hoot. Upgrade your conscience so it can better help you deal with the temptations and terrors of the Dark Lands. Stop off on your way to the Gateway and get yourself properly prepared. 'Cause at the City of Morality, good is doing what you should and doing bad ain't rad."

Zealot's demeanor changed. "Hold. What was that part about upgrading my conscience?" He looked over his gun. "It would be good if I could fire even more missiles. I feel as if this weapon fires an insufficient number of missiles in its current state."

"Didn't you say it fires infinite missiles?" Christian said.

"Yes. And?" Zealot looked confused.

Truth and Christian exchanged a glance.

"This sounds great," Conscience said, interrupting the confusion. "I could do with an upgrade. If Truth says that these techniques are the real deal, then I'm all down for it."

"Yes," Truth said, "the techniques described in the transmissions are indeed things that are useful for living improved lives that are less evil. My plan is to go to this City of Morality. After your equipment is properly upgraded, we should continue on to the Gateway, if that's even necessary. If we can master these techniques, we might be able to remove your burdens ourselves, and then we'd have no fear of total atomic annihilation. As without the burdens, the Overseer can beam us up without interference."

Christian's eyes grew wide at that thought. "Get rid of my burden? Sign me the heck up."

"Sign me up regularly," Zealot said. "No heck required."

"Then follow me." Truth turned on her heels and headed into the distance.

Her course appeared to be toward the glow and the Gateway, but it was just a bit off. But that wouldn't matter, right? Christian walked after her with a kick in his step. He was on the road to redemption, wasn't he? And he had found two wondrous new friends to share his journey. For the first time, his burden didn't feel quite so heavy.

As Christian walked, he grew a bit bored. Christian projected Book onto the side of the path. She was lying on a bed, reading a booklet titled *Central Interpretive Motifs for Dummies*. She turned each page with deliberate forcefulness. She peered at Christian then back to the booklet.

"Is something wrong?" Christian said.

Book looked up as if surprised by the question. "What? Oh, you want my opinion now?"

"Goodness," Christian said. "You don't have to be such a . . . such a . . ."

"Morally perverse woman?" Book said.

"I was going to say something else, but let's go with that."

"Well, I'm not. You're a son of a snake for suggesting it." Her projection rotated so the back of her bed was toward Christian, and she continued reading.

"Fine," Christian said. "Be that way." He shut the projector off.

Several miles farther, they reached the crest of a steep mountainside. At the summit, they looked down. Far below stretched a vast city of shining skyscrapers and pristine parks. Large tilt-rotor aircraft flew between the skyscrapers. Hundreds of people walked on well-paved streets.

"Holy exclamation," Zealot said. "I didn't think a place this nice existed in the Dark Lands."

"It's so beautiful," Truth said. "Everything is where it's supposed to be in complex but perfect harmony. This must be the City of Morality."

"Look there!" Conscience pointed and hopped up and down on Christian's shoulder. "There are big consciences—as big as people walking around. I didn't think we could get that big."

Zealot beamed. "Consciences as big as a person? My conscience is a gun. You mean I could get my gun to be as big as a person? We must frequent their weaponry establishments at once."

"Come. Let us investigate this wondrous place." Truth ran down the mountain with Zealot close behind.

"All right, just be careful," Christian said. Before he could finish his sentence, Truth and Zealot were halfway down the mountain.

Christian started to follow, but a sound from behind him caught his attention. He turned and noticed a thin wisp of a figure leaning against a rock face.

The figure wore long tattered rags of a gunslinger's duster around his shoulders. His face was obscured by a wide-brimmed hat, the kind that cowboys and outlaws wore in old Westerns. The figure wore gloves and stood next to some writing on the rocks that Christian couldn't quite make out.

"Oh, hi," Christian said. "I didn't see you there."

"People rarely do," the figure said in a gravelly, metallic voice. He never looked up, just stood there, motionless.

Christian waited.

The figure didn't say anything.

Christian waited some more.

Still nothing.

"Well . . . great talk." Christian turned to go down the mountain.

"You sure you want to go down there?" the figure said with a hungry but calm tone.

Christian turned back.

The figure still hadn't moved.

"The guy on the radio says this place can teach me a lot of great practices for making myself less evil. Is that not true?"

"Oh, it's true." The figure drummed his fingers on the stone. His hand was gloved, but each strike of his fingers thudded with a power that reverberated through the stone and shook the ground. "Morality does have a lot of good advice for being less evil." With each word, he drummed his fingers one more time. A tiny crack formed in the stone.

Another long pause. The figure did nothing. Said nothing.

"Well then, away I go." Christian took a step back, expecting the figure to object.

"I just wonder, though." The figure reached up and moved the brim of his hat ever so slightly. "Will it be enough?"

For a moment, Christian saw the figure's eyes. Cold, red, and piercing. For that split second, he felt as if the figure could see every corner of his mind—that he could see all of Christian's past, present, and future—as if the figure knew him more intimately than he knew himself.

And that scared Christian more than the sloth, more than Obstinate, more than even the threat of total atomic annihilation. He stumbled back, then turned and ran down the mountain with all the haste he could muster. And on his back, Christian swore he could feel the gaze of those cold, red eyes.

STAGE 4
RUINS OF ACADEMY CITY

C hristian reached the base of the mountain. He tried to force the image of the strange figure from his mind. He closed his eyes, but in the darkness, there was the figure. His crooked smile, his glowing red eyes. Christian opened his eyes, the City of Morality stood before him with shining skyscrapers, long swaths of green grass, sidewalks, and bubbling fountains. The large tilt-rotor aircraft continued to buzz about the skyscrapers far above.

The City of Morality stood right next to the base of the mountain. The mountain was steep and seemed to poke out of the ground like a tooth from some long-dead monster. It seemed out of place standing right next to the sprawling city.

The more Christian stared at the city, the less the figure appeared in his mind, and after a few steps, the haunting figure was all but forgotten.

Christian walked up to Zealot and Truth. "It's amazing. This must be what the Celestial Station looks like."

"Indeed." Zealot said. "Who could have foreseen that we would find sanctuary so quickly?"

"Now hold on, gentlemen." Truth looked concerned. "This isn't the Celestial Station. This will probably just be a stopping point on our journey. After we've finished here, we'll most likely need to move on to the Gateway."

At the edge of the city, a large line of people stood at a ticket booth. Christian, Zealot, and Truth walked to the back of the line.

After waiting several minutes, they got their turn at the booth.

A man appeared behind the ticket window. He wore a fancy, expensive, business suit. "Welcome," the man said with flamboyant enthusiasm, "to the City of Morality!"

"What is this? I know you," Zealot said. "We heard your voice on the radio. Worldly Wiseman, isn't it?"

"Ah, yes," the man said. "It seems my reputation precedes me. Or rather, it precedes you." Worldly Wiseman turned his gaze toward Truth and smiled. "Though if I knew my broadcasts would attract such lovely creatures, I would have started broadcasting long ago."

Truth looked away from Worldly Wiseman and hid a smile. "Oh stop, you don't mean that."

"But I do," Worldly Wiseman said. "You have a unique elegance that this city is lacking. What's your name, beautiful?"

"Beautiful? Oh no, my name isn't beautiful." Truth blushed. "My name's Truthly. I mean . . . Trush. I mean . . ." Truth continued to sputter, her usual confident tone gone from her voice.

"Her name is Truth." Christian stepped between them and put his hands on the ticket counter. "Are you going to let us in or not?"

Worldly Wiseman looked at Christian. His gaze went neutral, as if looking for something. Then, as if he found it, his smile returned. "Of course. You just need your new citizen pamphlets." He produced three data storage units and set them on the counter, the size of small desktop computers. Each data storage device had a display screen and far too many buttons, and each button served no obvious purpose.

Worldly Wiseman handed out the devices and turned his attention back toward Truth. "So then, Truth, you probably don't remember me. I worked for your Uncle, Omniscience, once when you were very young."

"Why don't you work for him now?" Truth said.

"And now you're all grown up." Worldly Wiseman said, ignoring the question. "My goodness, puberty did a number on you, didn't it? I didn't know women could get so attractive. Yet, here you are."

Truth blurted out something that was halfway between a cough and a yelp.

Christian rolled his eyes.

"Yes, she's very hot." Christian took his data unit from the counter. "Women are like that. Can we get in yet?"

Zealot picked up his data unit and started pressing buttons. "What is this manner of deviceage that you have given us?"

"Deviceage isn't a word," Truth said in an almost dreamlike tone, instinctual and automatic, her gaze still locked on Worldly Wiseman.

"Oh, that pamphlet?" Worldly Wiseman nodded toward one of the devices. "It's just a small record of guidelines for newcomers. You'll get a comprehensive record later, but we don't want to overwhelm our newcomers with too many rules."

"This is just a few guidelines?" Christian pushed a few buttons on his device.

"Indeed," Worldly Wiseman said. "It's a wonder we were able to get them into such a small device. Isn't quantum computing a treasure?"

Christian swallowed and focused on the device. There had to be millions of rules on the thing. How was he going to remember all of them? He pressed a button on his wrist, and Book displayed onto the unit. When she materialized, she was standing over a small child on an altar, with a knife in her hand.

"What the imprecation," Truth shouted, horror on her face.

"Oh, do not worry," Zealot said. "She's like this. You get used to it." Zealot moved to place a comforting hand on Truth's shoulder.

Truth sidestepped the motion with such speed and gracefulness that Zealot didn't notice. Christian did. How did she do that so fast?

"Spare me, you three." Book put the knife away, and the alter vanished, along with the child. "I wasn't going to do it anyway. What do you need? Other than a semblance of a moral compass."

"This data storage unit here," Christian motioned towards the 'pamphlet' that Worldly Wiseman had given them. "Can you scan it and check to make sure it's not . . . you know . . . evil or something?" Christian pressed a button on the projector and projected Book onto the data storage unit.

"Yeah, no problem." Book looked at the unit. "Wow! What is it? Pregnant? It's huge. Yeah, I can check for corrupted files." Blue lines appeared over the unit from Christian's holoprojector and then vanished.

"Got it all," Book said. "A lot of useful advice on daily living. In fact, a lot of this is already in my database. The other stuff is mostly just more specific applications of my concepts. But there's no corruption I can see."

"Great," Christian said.

"But wait," Book said. "I've got to warn you about—"

Christian turned her off before she could finish. "Ugh. She never shuts up does she?"

"Is that a Bible?" Worldly Wiseman handed Christian and the others satchels to carry the data storage units in.

"She's calling herself Book now," Christian said. "She thinks it's less pretentious."

"You've already started pursuing a life of moral living. Splendid! Why you'll fit in just fine here." Worldly Wiseman winked at Truth. "And you'll fit in especially fine."

Truth laughed as if Worldly Wiseman had said something funny.

Christian grabbed her by the hand to lead her away from the booth. "I'm sure you don't want us holding up the line. Come on."

Christian led the dazed Truth by the hand and they entered the city. The satchel was incredibly heavy, adding to the weight of Christian's unpowered burden. But he didn't say anything. Everyone seemed far too happy for him to complain.

"It's absolutely shameful," Zealot said to Truth. "You becoming all weak in the knees by that man's words. You must present yourself better. Mustn't let a smooth-talking man beguile you with a few verbosities. I, for one, have no weakness in my knees. Nor anywhere else for that matter. Weaknesses are for the weak."

"Oh, hush," Truth said. "You wouldn't understand what a big deal it is to be appreciated by someone like Worldly Wiseman."

Her voice made a weird wavering cadence when she said his name. Christian tried to keep his eyes on the shop windows to keep from getting too close to Truth. Was sappiness contagious? Best not to risk it.

Truth continued babbling on about Worldly Wiseman. "I'm not too embarrassed to say that his radio transmissions already had me admiring his charisma and knowledge."

"Did it now?" Zealot said.

"No, it did back then. Not now. I know you're not as smart as me, Zealot, but come now, temporal designation isn't that difficult. At least it doesn't seem that difficult. To be fair, I've never been stupid before. What is it like?" Truth's tone held no malice. She sounded like she was genuinely curious.

"Being smart is your business. Action is mine," Zealot said, ignoring the question. "It doesn't matter anyway. I'm certain that Worldly Wiseman personage likely proclaims such saccharin proclamations to every pretty girl who goes through that checkpoint."

Truth stepped in front of Zealot with a concerned look, stopping him in his tracks. Everyone stopped walking. Truth looked as if Zealot had just suggested some impending doom.

"Oh no. Do you really think so?" Truth's tone grew faster and frantic. "Did he not mean any of it? Why do you think that? What's your evidence? Has that evidence been peer reviewed?"

"Cease your drama," Zealot said. "It is simply a hunch."

Truth turned up her nose and continued walking down the path. "Your hunches mean nothing to a woman of science. We can only know what we can know. Making assumptions and guessing is simply lying without the creativity. Until I am given evidence to the contrary, I will believe Worldly Wiseman's words. He has said nothing but correct things so far."

"I hope that's enough," Christian said, muttering.

Truth and Zealot stared at him.

"What do you mean?" Truth said.

"I hope it's enough to be right."

Truth blinked. "Of course it is."

"Okay." Christian stared back at Truth.

There was an awkward silence.

"By my foul language, look at that." Zealot pointed toward a small shop on the street corner. "It's the conscience upgrade shop. Oh, I do hope they can upgrade mine. I turned it into a rocket pistol, you know.

A more powerful weapon shall better assist us in the incineration of the enemy. Joyous day!" He ran off toward the shop, leaving Christian and Truth alone.

"Guess we should wait for him," Christian said. "I'd follow, but I'm afraid he'll test fire his gun and blow up the shop."

"A fair concern." Truth walked to a park bench by the sidewalk. She sat and started looking at her data storage unit.

Christian sat next to her and watched some birds flying around. One landed on a nearby tree and chirped at them. He glanced at Truth. She put on a pair of reading glasses and studied the data storage unit with unnatural intensity.

Minutes passed.

"You know," Christian said, "you can just upload that information into a wrist computer."

"Accurate," Truth said. "I prefer going over each bit manually before I go uploading anything."

"That seems inefficient."

"Perhaps."

More silence.

"I have a question," Christian said.

"No doubt, I have the answer." Truth looked up from her device. "I may not be as knowledgeable as my Uncle Omniscience, but I shall endeavor to answer with all the human knowledge I can muster. Converse."

Christian opened his mouth, hesitated, then continued. "What's the deal with your hair?"

Truth surveyed Christian through her reading glasses with a look that appeared uninsulted but confused. "I don't understand."

"It's white like an old lady. But you aren't an old lady. Are you? Which is it? Old or young? It's hard to tell."

Truth gave a playful smirk and peered over her glasses at Christian. "Well, that seems like an impolite question to ask a lady."

Christian tensed.

She gave a hint at a smile. "Fortunately, I care nothing for such improprieties. My hair is white from the wisdom of age. But my body is young for the curiosity of youth. Curiosity brings knowledge. Age brings wisdom. And the synthesis of knowledge and wisdom is truth. Which is me. Truth."

"Hence the schoolgirl uniform?"

"The outfit of a schoolgirl shows that I am always learning, always seeking out new knowledge so that I may be more accurate and true. Also, it's because I like anime as a source of all wisdom and knowledge."

"What?" Christian said.

Truth smiled but rolled her eyes. "I was being hyperbolic, which is technically a statement of inaccuracy. That inaccuracy is communicated through tone and context so you do not actually deceive anyone. Instead, you illustrate the intensity with which you believe a certain thing. In this case, my appreciation for deeper truths within the anime medium."

"Did . . . did you just justify the use of sarcasm to me?" Christian said.

"Yes. Facts are serious business. One can never be too careful with them. Is that odd?"

"At this point," Christian said, "I've become numb to all the odd things I've seen on this . . . on this . . . this uh . . . pilgrim thing."

"Progress?" Truth said.

Christian thought for a bit. "Nah, that's not it."

Truth looked back to the data storage unit.

Christian peered over her shoulder. "What do you make of it so far? Book said it was good. I'm curious what you think."

"I don't believe *good* was her precise word. She said it was *useful*."

"Is that important?"

"Oh, my cuss word!" Truth sat up and her mouth dropped open.

Christian stood and followed Truth's gaze to the pamphlet. "What's the problem?"

"Look!" A piece of paper was taped to the bottom of the data storage unit. Truth read it, shielding the message from Christian. "It's a note from Worldly Wiseman. He wants to have dinner with me tonight. Can you believe it? How romantic!" Her tone went from somber back to the giddy schoolgirl when talking with Worldly Wiseman. She really was the mix between an old lady and a little kid.

Christian sat back on the park bench and looked up at the sky. "Yes. Very romantic. Anyway, what do you think about the pamphlet?"

"It seems good," Truth said. "A lot of rules. All true. Don't lie, steal, murder, oppress, and so on. But it also has a good deal of specifics. Like not watching bad movies or eating unhealthy foods. All true and good advice. Why do you ask?"

"I met this weird guy back on that mountain after you went down."

"Mount Sinai?" Truth looked back at the path from which they came.

"Is that its name? I didn't know. Anyway, it was this grungy, wannabe cowboy-looking character who was being all mysterious and acting like this city held grave danger or something."

"I don't see how." Truth looked confused. "This city seems fine."

She looked back at the data unit and pressed more buttons as if looking for something. "These rules are strict, but there's nothing in here I would say is wrong. Some rules are more important than others, but the unit specifies that. It talks about forgiveness and mercy as much as how to do the right thing. It's not like they'll kill you for littering, if that's what you're wondering. This city does seem to have a good set of rules, regulations, and suggestions for daily life. It's hard to see how anything dangerous could come from following these rules."

"Do you think it's enough?" Christian said.

Truth looked up from her pamphlet with a questioning gaze. "What do you mean?"

"It's what that guy asked me. When talking about this city, he said he wondered if it was enough. I didn't know what he meant."

"You said something like that before." Truth looked concerned.

"Yeah. If doing good isn't enough, I don't know what is. And that's a scary thought."

An explosion shook the air. A half dozen other explosions followed.

"Obscenity!" Christian turned around and shouted. "Zealot! Stop blowing stuff up." He threw up his hands. "I knew it was a good call not to go with him."

Zealot ran across the street, firing his gun into the air and laughing in bright unrestrained glee.

"Look, Christian!" Zealot pointed at his pistol. It looked different.

Modified. Where there was once a single short, wide barrel there were now two barrels of equal dimension. "It has *two* barrels now. I can fire two rockets at once from my conscience pistol." Zealot paused, then appeared to do some calculations in his head. "That's twice as many rockets as before. This is the best day of my life. I will hunt down *all* the evils and incinerate them with maximum prejudice. Hahaha!"

He fired Into the air again. The rockets sailed upward and exploded high above the skyscrapers. The buildings shook.

"Zealot," Christian said, "stop. You're going to hurt somebody. Surely you are violating like . . . a dozen city ordinances."

Shocked fear showed on Zealot's face and he holstered his pistol. "Oh, dear. Have I? If I am violating the rules of this fine city, I must stop." Zealot looked terrified at the thought of doing wrong.

"Oddly, no." Truth looked back to the data storage unit. "He's not. Following your conscience, as long as it is not corrupted, is actually a general command in the pamphlet. Though do try not to hit any innocent bystanders or destroy any personal property."

"Of course!" Zealot drew his pistol to fire again, but after a stern look from Truth, he holstered it.

"I shall find a gun range somewhere, I'm sure," Zealot said, disappointment in his voice. Then he perked back up. "Or better yet, the enemy." He rushed off, shouting something unintelligible.

"Maybe coming to a place devoid of enemies to attack was a mistake," Christian said in a comedic tone.

Truth laughed. "Well, I'm going to head off to the Library of Philosophy. I saw it mentioned in the pamphlet and I'm intrigued. We can meet up in an hour at that hotel." She motioned to a building on the opposite side of the street, then walked away.

"Ok, but be careful." Christian raised his hand to his mouth and shouted louder. He touched Conscience. Christian stopped. The tiny robot was quiet and stared off into the distance.

"What's the matter, little buddy?" Christian followed Conscience's gaze but couldn't see what he was staring at, just the mountain they had come down from. "Are you feeling left out? You want an upgrade too?"

Conscience didn't say anything. His gaze never strayed from the mountain in the distance.

For a moment, Christian thought he could make out a lone figure standing atop the mountain, looking down with cold red eyes.

———

The sun set over the top of Mount Sinai when Christian and Zealot walked into the Pluralism Hotel. The lobby, like the rest of the City of Morality, was well-kept, clean and full of chattering patrons. Several potted plants stood around the lobby. The screen on the wall displayed a reality television show called *Name That Moral Infraction*.

Zealot checked his wrist computer. "When is Truth supposed to rendezvous with us?"

"Any minute now." Christian stared at the game show with lazy attention. "I can't imagine a library trip taking that long. Then again, Truth did take an inordinate amount of time looking at that pamphlet data unit thing Worldly Wiseman gave us."

"Then we should get checked in. I must assault a bed with my weariness." Zealot walked up and planted his hand on the counter with way more force than was necessary. "Greetings hotel staff person. We demand commerce with your institution."

Christian stepped next to him. "Zealot, you don't have to make every conversation sound like an assault . . . or a hostage negotiation."

Zealot blinked. "Is that how I sound? How would you communicate our intent?"

Christian smiled at the woman behind the counter. "We'd like three rooms, please."

Zealot hummed as if analyzing the exchange as some intriguing anomaly.

"Three rooms. Of course." The woman smiled like the Worldly Wiseman. "All are welcome at the Pluralism Hotel. What kind of room do you want? We've got comfortable rooms, uncomfortable rooms, rooms with televisions, worship mats, torture chambers, slave dungeons, and even one with a dancing monkey."

Conscience pinched Christian's cheek. "Hold on. What'd she say?"

"Yeah," Christian said. "What was that last part?"

"The dancing monkey?" The receptionist's eyes brightened. "Oh yes, he's more popular than you'd think."

"No, no. The bit on torture chambers and slave dungeons. Doesn't that violate like"—he pressed buttons on the data storage unit—"all the rules?"

"Certainly." The woman was still smiling. "Of *that* pamphlet. Different pamphlets teach many different types of morality. This hotel accounts for all beliefs. If you don't believe that self-mutilation is okay when you sleep, that's fine. You can get the dancing monkey room. If you don't like it, then don't do it."

"That's ridiculous." Zealot leered down at the woman. "If another is doing evil, then that's . . . that's . . ."

"Evil?" Christian said.

"I was going to go with something more poetic, but yes. I can't let people in this hotel throw people in torture dungeons!"

The woman raised her hands. "No, no. It's okay. The people thrown into the dungeons do so willingly. They want to be enslaved and have their lives cut short."

"That's worse," Zealot said. "At least with forceful murder, only one person is doing evil. But for both the perpetrator and victim to do the deed? Come, Christian." Zealot drew his pistol.

The woman yelped and ducked under the desk.

"Don't worry, I'll save you," Zealot said to no one in particular. He fired a rocket upward.

Bits of ceiling popcorn flew through the air and got into Christian's eyes.

Zealot gave a battle cry and ran down the hall toward the elevator, firing more missiles in random directions.

The woman poked her head up over the desk. She had ceiling popcorn in her hair. She brushed herself off, smiled, and faced Christian as if nothing happened. "Will it be just two rooms, then?"

Christian paused. "Yeah . . . do you happen to have one where you can kick old widows in the shin?"

Conscience slapped Christian across the face.

"Argh! Okay, never mind." Christian glared at Conscience, then faced the receptionist. "This isn't right. A giant crazy rocketeer just rampaged through your hotel and is probably about to attack your customers. That doesn't bother you? I mean, I understand his reasons. But why are you so calm?"

"All are welcome at the Pluralism Hotel." Her weird smile never changed.

"How can you run a business like that?"

"Really lenient insurance rates."

Before Christian could say anything, the lobby door opened and Truth walked in. She had a satchel of volumes over her shoulder and looked a bit perturbed. "That was unnecessarily complicated," she said. "You would be quite vexed at how long it took to pick up these books. Everybody at the Library of Philosophy kept asking what I was. Quite annoying. How's it coming with the rooms?" She paused and glanced around. "Where's Zealot?"

The sound of multiple missile explosions sounded from upstairs.

"Okay, then," Truth said. "How long did that take?"

"A minute, I think," Christian said.

"A record that I doubt will hold long." Truth walked up to the counter. "I'll have your best room, please."

"We don't have a best room," the woman said. "All our rooms are equal in their value."

"Don't be ridiculous. Of course, there's a best room. Are all the rooms completely identical?"

"No, each one is beautifully unique."

"Then get me the best one."

"There is no best one. They're all equally good."

"How can they be equally good if they're not identical?" Truth sounded annoyed.

"Different people have different tastes."

Truth's gaze narrowed as if peering at a massive puzzle. She paused, contemplating something. "Ah I see, you don't comprehend the metric by which quality is measured. I'll be more specific. Can I get your *largest* room?"

The woman shifted as if uncomfortable and broke eye contact.

"What is size but the feelings one has towards a space when one occupies it?"

"It's a measure of volume in a given space in this context," Truth said. "You don't have one that's bigger than all the others?"

The woman looked at something on her desk and paused. "Well . . . we do have rooms of different sizes."

"Aha!" Truth looked like she'd checkmated a chess-playing robot. "Then show me the largest ones and I can continue to delineate till the best is determined."

"Uh . . ." The woman looked uncomfortable.

"Delineate in this context means to indicated the exact position of a border or boundary. As between your best room and the inferior ones."

"I can't do that."

"If you are unaware which is the largest, I can calculate it for you." Truth sounded like she was talking to a child. She produced a calculator from somewhere and started punching in numbers.

The woman looked at the calculator with unease. "We aren't comfortable with guests saying that certain rooms are bigger or smaller than others. Who can truly say what is bigger than anything else?"

"I can," Truth said in a straightforward and offhanded tone. "Simply tell me the dimensions."

"How you feel about the size of the room is what matters."

"Okay, I feel I want the quantifiably largest one."

"This is the Pluralist Hotel. What is largest for you may be smallest for someone else."

"No, something of a certain size remains that size regardless of who is observing it."

The receptionists rolled her eyes, annoyed. "Size is a social construct imposed on us by mathematicians. What you believe is what matters."

A muscle in Truth's face gave a slight spasm, but she kept her composure. More explosions sounded above, followed by shouts and gunfire.

Christian touched Truth's arm. "We can find another hotel if you want. There probably won't be much left standing of this place when Zealot is done with it."

"No," Truth raised a hand. "I'm invested at this point." Truth looked at the lady and pointed at her calculator. "A room that is ten feet by ten feet has a square footage of 100, right?"

"That sounds right to me," the woman said.

"Now if there's another room that is ten by fifteen, then that's a square footage of 150."

"I feel that to be true, yes."

"And 150 is a larger number than 100."

"Some people certainly have that opinion."

"No!" Truth pointed at the calculator. "Not opinion. Fact."

"Yes, those are your facts."

At this, Truth's face developed an expression that did not do good things for her attractiveness.

Christian pulled her arm with an ever-so-gentle tug toward the exit. "Truth, it's okay. We'll find another place."

"No, I'm not finished with this fact-less harpy."

The woman's smile vanished. "Hey! I'm not a fact-less harpy. I'm a fact-fluid harpy. I mean . . . person."

"Let's try not to cause trouble," Christian said. "You don't want to be late for your date with Worldly Wiseman, right?"

Truth eyed the woman, then let Christian pull her to the exit. "Very well. It's clear this person is immune to intelligence. Let's go. Where's Zealot?"

Zealot dropped through the ceiling and slammed onto the lobby floor. Bits of ceiling fell around him. Blood and grime covered his armor, and part of him was on fire. A few people were slung over one shoulder and he was holding his gun in one hand. The people slung over his shoulder appeared to be unconscious.

The receptionist screamed and dropped behind her desk.

Christian winced and jumped back, surprised by the on-fire man and the sudden destruction.

Truth just stared at Zealot as if regarding a boring speech.

"Ha!" Zealot said. "I wager you thought I had fired those missiles into the ceiling at random and not to prepare my escape ahead of time."

"Because you did do it at random?" Truth spoke without surprise or fear in her voice.

Zealot looked disappointed. "I should be commended for my utilization of such proactive violence."

"If there's anything you have expertise in," Truth said, "it's proactive violence."

Zealot beamed in appreciation.

Truth winced. "Well, now I regret saying that."

Shouts of anger sounded from above. Christian collected his thoughts and looked toward the receptionist. "Yeah, we should get out of here before we give Zealot a big head. Or someone triggers a silent alarm. Not that that's necessary. I'd wager half the city heard those explosions. Let's make like a dog and flee."

The trio ran through the door and onto the street.

"No worries," Zealot yelled as they ran. "I rescued these poor souls from slavers who had unimaginably poor aim."

"Must have been a pretty even fight then," Christian said.

Truth turned with surprising agility toward Zealot. "Not that it's any of my business, but are we going to ignore the fact Zealot is on fire?"

Zealot looked at his shoulder, which was indeed, still aflame. "Ah, that. Plasma doesn't really eat through my armor much, but it burns like the place the lost go when they die."

Christian gave a confused look, "You mean Hell?"

"Shh!" Truth said. "You'll never get past the publishers with that kind of language. Do you want this story to have to be self-published?"

Christian blinked. "What?"

"Never mind. Let's go."

Christian looked back at the Pluralism Hotel. Smoke and flames billowed from the upper windows. A couple of figures appeared in the windows with guns. "Zealot, I hope you weren't lying when you said those slavers had poor aim."

The gunmen opened fire.

Zealot curled himself around Truth and the people he rescued. A torrent of plasma bolts laced the ground. Several plasma bolts struck

Zealot's back. He shielded Truth and the others.

"Why is it everyone is so unfriendly when you liberate their slaves?" Zealot said, paying little attention to the onslaught.

One of the rescued women looked incensed and faced Zealot. "Give us back! We don't want to be rescued."

Zealot peered down at the woman, perplexed and disgusted. "Then you're as dumb as you are helpless. I'm not letting those brigands wrong you, even if you are into that sort of thing."

One of the figures up in the windows leapt down. He struck the street sending shockwaves across the asphalt which knocked Truth and Christian to the ground. Either through physical tenacity or some technology, he seemed unphased by the long drop. Christian noticed the shockwave had knocked everyone on the street down.

Everyone but Zealot.

Zealot faced the slavers.

"What's the deal, man?" the chief slaver said. "We were just minding our own business when you barged in and started imposing your morality on us."

Another figure jumped onto the street. Another shockwave. Christian went down again, but Truth leapt over it like it was nothing.

"Yeah!" yelled one of the men Zealot had rescued. "You can't go imposing your morality on us. Everybody's morality is different. Just 'cause you think what we're doing is wrong doesn't mean you have the right to stop us."

Christian reached for his Gauss rifle. "Think we can take 'em?" he whispered to Zealot.

"Given I struck them multiple times previously, and they still possess the means of their profane perambulation I'd say the odds are improbable."

"But that won't stop us." Christian shouldered his rifle.

"Heaven, no." Zealot twirled his pistol in his fingers and leveled it at the nearest slaver.

Zealot's and Christian's shots struck home. Shields crackled and wavered for a moment around the slavers, but they appeared only minimally annoyed.

"Hey! Quit it," one yelled.

"Sorry." Zealot fired again and again. "I couldn't hear you over the sound of your rampant mutilation and enslavement of human beings."

"You mean," Truth said, "over the sound of the gunfire." She hadn't taken cover or even seemed remotely worried about the gunfight.

"Yes, that as well," Zealot said.

One of the people Zealot rescued tried to squirm out of Zealot's clutches. "But we're okay with enslavement and death."

"Quiet. You're being rescued. Be happy or I'll wallop you."

The slavers raised their plasma weapons.

Zealot gathered up the liberated slaves in his arms and hurled them onto a patch of grass in the park adjoining the street. Christian noticed it was where Christian and Truth had sat earlier that day.

Two plasma rounds hit Zealot in the torso. He reeled but remained on his feet.

The slavers' weapons began to shake as they stood looking at Zealot. Their gunfire never ceasing, and Zealot refusing to go down.

"Christian," Zealot said, his tone serious, without his usual boisterous frivolity.

"Yeah?" Christian said.

"Give me a good one-liner."

Christian thought for a bit, his attention directed more by endeavoring to avoid the plasma bolts of the enemy. "Uh, you're like a piece of blank cloth. Get ready to dye?"

Zealot glanced at Christian, looking disappointed. Then he smiled. "We'll work on that."

An unending stream of missiles flew from both barrels of Zealot's gun. Each stream connected with one of the slavers, washing them in molten fire and explosive incandescence.

"To enslave is wrong," Zealot said. "Not just because it violates the will of the victim, but because of the damage it does. Even when the victim welcomes the damage, morality is still violated."

Thunderous explosions shook the air. Windows cracked and shattered from the concussive force.

Christian answered with his rifle. "You've violated the laws of this city. The pamphlet clearly says what you did was wrong. If what Zealot says is true, this is an abusive relationship. He could be crazy though. I haven't ruled that out." He glanced at Zealot. "No offense."

"None taken," Zealot said.

Truth stepped next to the two men and tapped Zealot on the not-on-fire shoulder. Zealot kept firing his gun but turned to Truth and smiled like nothing was happening. "Yes, Truth?"

"Hey, Zealot. You're correct here and all. But I'm going to be late for my date with Worldly Wiseman. I'm going to leave and let you two continue your thoughtful discussion."

"Very good," Zealot said. "I wish ye a triumphant date."

"Uh . . . ok." Truth turned and walked away.

"Think they've had enough?" Christian said.

Zealot stopped firing and waited for the dust to settle.

The two slavers stepped out of the smoke from the explosions, shields of crackling energy around them. The shields were faded, but the slavers themselves showed little sign of Christian's and Zealot's onslaught.

"What the profane exclamation," Christian shouted.

"We use a different pamphlet," The head slavers said. "You can't kill us. We are beyond your power to—"

Christian assumed the slaver would have said something else vaguely villainous, but just as the slaver spoke, a spray of blood appeared near his head and he fell to the asphalt. The other slaver turned to look at his fallen friend, more confused than horrified. Then blood flew from his head as well and he fell to the street alongside his comrade.

A cold metallic laugh wafted over the air and the street became quiet, almost frozen in time. Christian stepped back-to-back with Zealot.

"What was that? That wasn't from my gun." Christian said in an uncertain voice.

"Nor mine." Zealot surveyed the skyscrapers in the direction the shots had come from. Beyond them was Mount Sinai. "Normally, I would revel in such defeat of darkness. But I am perturbed by the mysteriousness of our dexterous benefactor."

"Zealot, using big words won't make you sound as wise as Truth."

"Aw . . ." Zealot sounded genuinely sad.

Christian regretted his quip. "Where did those shots come from?"

"I'm uncertain. Those shields seemed quite formidable. And what kind of shot could pierce them when our attacks could not even—"

Sirens.

A dozen police cars sped around the corner. Officers piled out and leveled weapons at Christian and Zealot.

Christian surveyed the police. There were almost a hundred of them. He exchanged a glance with Zealot.

Christian and Zealot lowered their weapons.

"Well, this just got unnecessarily complicated," Christian said.

STAGE 5
GOKU'S FOLLY

Christian stared at the interrogator, struggling to keep his eyes open.

The interrogator stared at his notes and hadn't moved for several minutes. Minutes that felt like hours. The room was small, devoid of windows or color. The table between Christian and the interrogator was a dismal gray.

Zealot sat next to Christian and seemed to be close to dying from boredom.

The interrogator turned a page in his notes—the only sound in quite a while.

Christian rubbed his temples. "You know. Why aren't these called churches? Instead of temples?"

"What?" Zealot looked over at Christian as if he'd been broken out of a trance.

"Never mind."

The interrogator looked up, paused, then cleared his throat "All right, let's go over this one more time."

"No, please. I beg you." Zealot threw his hands up, but without his usual rambunctious energy.

"Not again." Christian covered his face in his hands.

The interrogator chuckled as if he were enjoying this. "So, the two slavers who jumped out of the window were shot. But not by you?"

"I'll say whatever you want at this point," Zealot said, "if you will just let us go."

The interrogator gave Zealot a stern look.

"We fought them," Christian said, "but they weren't killed by us. Someone else did that."

Zealot said, "The men killed were brigands and tyrants. I rescued their victims. Does that mean nothing?"

The door opened. "It means quite a great deal," a friendly voice said. A tall man in a suit walked in. He wore a large sash that said, *Mayor Legalist.*

"Hey, look," Christian said in a tired voice. "It's Mayor Legalist."

Legalist looked down at his sash. "This thing makes conversations so much more efficient." He motioned to the interrogator. "You can leave. You've earned a break." The interrogator stood, bowed to Mayor Legalist, then left. Legalist took the seat across from Christian and Zealot and smiled.

"Are you the folks I have to thank for dealing with those pluralists?"

"At the risk of murdering my soul with repetition," Christian said, "we didn't do anything."

"Don't be so modest." Zealot clamped a hand on Christian's shoulder. "We engaged the enemy with true vengeance and endeavored toward their vanquishment."

"That can't be a word," Christian said. "For the last time, we didn't kill those slavers. Someone else did. Though we tried to."

Legalist shook Zealot's hand. "In any event, I'm glad someone gave us an excuse to crack down on that den of sin, harlotry, and illegal exotic animal smuggling that calls itself The Pluralist Hotel."

"Happy to help," Zealot said.

"Can we go?" Christian motioned toward the wall. "I'm about to start eating the wallpaper."

Legalist looked at the wall, then back at Christian, confused. "There's no wallpaper on these walls."

Christian examined the nearest wall. "Huh."

"Before you go . . ." Legalist looked at Zealot with an odd intensity that Christian didn't trust. "I was wanting to talk to you, Zealot."

"Oh?" Zealot beamed at the sudden attention.

"You seem like you've got the kind of moxie that this city needs."

Zealot smiled. "I don't know what the word *moxie* means, but I like your tone. Please continue."

"This City of Morality is only so large. And it can only shelter a few people from the troubles and evils of the Dark Lands. I need people to share our morality with the wanderers and the lost outside the city. Get them to obey our many rules. I'm afraid the Pluralist Hotel that you ousted was just one of many branches. There are others throughout the Dark Lands. The Pluralist Hotel does not follow the rules of the City of Morality. They should be made to act otherwise."

Christian kept staring at the wall. Conscience slapped him and jerked him back into consciousness. Christian had almost forgotten the small robot was still on his shoulder.

"What?" Christian whispered.

"Are you listening to this?" Conscience motioned towards Mayor Legalist. "He's talking about forcibly getting people to follow the rules of morality."

"Is that bad?"

"Doesn't that violate the rules of morality?"

"Oh, yeah." Christian raised a hand to get Legalist's attention.

Legalist looked annoyed but didn't show it in his tone. "Yes, Christian? You wanted to add something?"

"Isn't it wrong to force somebody to follow the rules of morality?"

Legalist raised an eyebrow as if confused. "Certainly not. Is it not right to force someone not to kill or enslave?"

"Yeah, but protecting someone is not that same as forcing someone to give to charity, treat others politely, or I don't know, brush their teeth for example. Unless they're children or something."

"But you don't understand the gravity of the situation," Legalist said. "Every day, evil gets more and more powerful. More people get lost in the infinite expanse of the Dark Lands. We must fight to get them back to following moral rules."

"Surely," Christian said, "that can be done without using force."

"Don't be so apathetic, Christian," Zealot said. "We should do whatever is within our power to lead people to the correct path. I think Legalist here has the right idea."

"Wondrous." Legalist clapped. "We're having a meeting on the best tactics to impose our morals on the City of Destruction from whence you came. I'd like you to join us."

Zealot pondered this. "Sounds like a vivacious opportunity for the exchange of effectual stratagems."

Legalist looked at Christian, confused.

"Truth came to visit us," Christian said. "She loaned him a book on pretentious synonyms. He's had little to do during this interrogation, and I think he read the whole thing twice."

"I object!" Zealot said. "Don't you falsely elucidate this situation with your hyperbolic verbiage."

"Your face is a hyperbolic verbiage."

Zealot's face reddened.

"Look, Christian," Legalist said. "I don't see what you're complaining about. We're just trying to help people."

"All you're going to accomplish is raising the people's ire," Christian said.

"My life for ire!" Zealot said.

Legalist stood. "I think this has been a productive chat. I hope to see you at our meeting, Zealot. My aid will give you more details. Please come. As for you, Christian, you're free to go."

Legalist and Zealot left the room. Christian stood to follow, but by the time he stepped out of the room, Zealot and Legalist were far down the hall, leaving Christian alone.

Christian stood in the hall, unsure where to go. Zealot and Mayor Legalist seemed deep in conversation. Christian walked past them. Zealot didn't seem to notice.

Christian walked down several corridors, then reached a large staircase that led down to the lobby and out the main doors of the police station.

It was dark outside the building. Christian sighed and walked over to the park bench. He sat alone.

Zealot had abandoned him. Truth had abandoned him. Some quest this had turned out to be. Christian looked at his hands. He'd like to squeeze Zealot's neck until he couldn't breathe and kick him in the shins. How long would his perky insatiable optimism last when he was choking? No, this wasn't right. That was the burden talking. Had he powered it up to walk out of the police station? Already it filled his mind with murderous thoughts. Zealot was his friend. Why would he want to hurt his friend? With a mental command he forced his burden to power down. Its tendrils reached into his mind, begging him to power back up. Christian felt the desire to walk free again, without the weight of the unpowered burden holding him down.

Christian pulled up his holodisplay and activated the projector. Book appeared, standing over the dead body of a woman and chopping her up into twelve pieces.

"I'm not even going to ask," Christian said.

"You never do," Book said, passive aggression seeping into her voice. "What's the matter? Your new City of Morality not meeting your expectations, and now you've reverted back to little old me?"

"You seem upset," Christian said.

Book looked up from the holographic corpse and scoffed. "Oh, I *seem* upset, do I?"

"Uh . . . yeah."

"Where's Truth and that crazy guy? They left you?"

"Zealot is new best friends with Mayor Legalist. And Truth is on a date with Worldly Wiseman."

Book's expression changed from disappointment to concern. "That's not good. If Zealot throws his lot in with Legalist, then he won't be safe when—Wait, did you say *Worldly Wiseman*?"

"Yes, what were you going to say when you interrupted yourself?"

"Christian, this is very important. You can't let Truth go near Worldly Wiseman."

"Why? What's wrong with Worldly Wiseman?"

"Well, not much more than anyone else, but it's complicated." Book's tone seemed worried, without the sarcastic, sassy tone he expected. "Worldly Wiseman has a lot of good advice, just as the City of Morality has a lot of good rules. But that's not the point. It won't be enough to save them. Something is coming that Worldy Wiseman and Legalist won't be able to stop. You've got to flee from this city and get to the Gateway like I've been telling you."

"Flee?" Christian said. "But there's so much good here. I fled from the realm of sin so I could get this burden on my back removed. I think they have a place around here that can do that. I got so caught up in the excitement, I forgot to ask."

"Christian," Book said, "nothing can remove your burden but the Overseer."

"But the pamphlet said—"

"Oh, I see, now that you've got your new pamphlet, who cares about Book? Guess you can just have that pamphlet and forget me."

"Book, come on. I just thought the pamphlet might help."

"Christian, that suit is fused to your body. Do you think some good living is going to make it magically pop off because some guy on the radio said so? This city can't fix your problem, and it can't save you from what's coming."

"What's coming?"

"I . . . I'm having trouble telling you. I'll have to describe it. If you spent more time with me, you'd understand better."

"Try to explain."

"Ok." Book considered her words. "Christian, you have done evil. The Overseer is perfect and good. What do you think a perfectly good Overseer sends after someone who does evil?"

Christian's heart quickened. Despite the many lights, the street seemed dark. As he looked up, the mountain seemed to loom even higher over the city as if it were about to fall on it. He swallowed, fear seeping into his mind. "Why didn't you say any of this before?"

Book looked incensed. "I'm a *book*. I can't speak up, shout at you, or say anything unless you pay attention to me. Even then, you need to pay *close* attention. I have a lot to say, and you need a lot of that to understand the other stuff I would like to say. If you had put any effort into listening to me, you'd know what's coming. And now I can't properly explain it because you don't understand me."

"What do I do?"

"A lot of things, it's complicated. It will take a little while to explain. You can't rush education. Truth could have told you that. Even Worldly Wiseman could have. Now none of them can save you."

"Are you talking about the impending atomic strike?"

"No, something else. Related and more immediate. Ugh . . . there's no time. This is what you get for ignoring me. It's . . . well, it has to do with that mountain."

"Now you're just being cryptic."

"Oh! Is it always *my* fault that *you* don't understand something? The more you understand me the less cryptic I will be."

"Just tell me who it is," Christian said.

"Not who . . . what."

A scream shook the air. A figure fell from the building and struck the ground, spraying blood across the pavement. It was the interrogator who had questioned Christian and Zealot.

"Oh no," Book said. "You're too late. He's already here."

Christian sprang up. "I thought you said he was a 'what.'"

"It's *complicated!*" Book sounded incensed.

More screams sounded from the police station.

Christian turned toward the building. Zealot was in there and might be in danger. Or more likely, putting others in danger, trying to deal with whatever was causing those screams.

Christian shut off Book, ran across the street, and burst through the front door of the police station. The power in the building flickered, then shut off. Darkness shrouded the lobby.

"What's going on?" Christian turned to Conscience. "Got any ideas, little buddy?"

Conscience wasn't looking at him. He was staring at the main staircase as if in a trance.

"Conscience? Are you ok?"

"It's here." Conscience said in a monotone, as if this was his true voice. "We should never have stayed. It was a trap. This whole city was a trap. And the city didn't know it."

Then Conscience's eyes turned red.

Christian followed the gaze of the tiny robot. In the last flickering flashes of the dying lights, Christian saw something. A figure. Familiar, but Christian couldn't place it. Till he saw the two red eyes. Not eyes, lights. From a machine. Lights shining the same red as Conscience. The flickering lights above illuminated the figure. It was the same figure he had seen back on Mt. Sinai. But now in the fading light, he saw the figure better. In the light, the eyes had only glinted, but in the near darkness, they were like an executioner's pyre.

The figure was a robot. *The* robot. It was dressed in the tattered clothes of a gunslinger, its wide-brimmed hat still drooped over its head. In the light from the robot's eyes, Christian saw a badge pinned upon its chest but couldn't quite make out the writing at that distance.

"You should have left," the figure said, its grating metallic voice now replaced with a low thundering cadence. Its teeth clacked like they were made of stone. A gun hung at his hip.

"And you should have never powered up your burden."

"It was you," Christian said. "You killed those pluralist slavers. You killed that interrogator. Why?"

"Murderers. Tyrants. Slavers. Thieves." The figure recited as if reading from a shopping list. "The list is far too long to recite in total. They thought they could escape the consequence of their crimes and continue their destruction. But consequences always find you out."

"Is that you?" Christian said. "Are you Consequences?"

The robot laughed and a dark smile crossed its vise-like lips. It took a step forward. "No," it muttered in a soft, almost tender voice. "I am far more than that." Its head turned upward, revealing its full face. Rows of twisted metal teeth shimmered in the red glow of its eyes. Its face was that of a metal skeleton, but the eyes, those terrible eyes. They bored through Christian and irradiated a suffocating glow.

Christian took a step back and turned to go. Conscience grabbed him by the ear and turned his chin to face the machine.

Conscience's face had changed. He wore the look of the red-eyed, skeletal monster on the stairs.

"Tell me, Christian." The robot took a step toward Christian. Conscience's mouth moved as if he was speaking, but the words came from the thing on the stairs. "What are your crimes?"

Then Conscience spoke, his voice mimicking that of the red-eyed robot. "Murderer. Tyrant. He took joy in the slaughter of innocents. Mowed them down for pleasure. And pride. He thought some good actions would stop us. Thought a few good deeds would unspill the blood. Also, he kicks old widows in the shins."

"Conscience! Don't rat me out! I've moved on from that. It isn't me anymore." Christian shook the small robot, but it didn't snap out of it. Conscience kept staring into the void.

"Who do you think built that little buddy of yours?" the figure said. "Did you not heed his warnings? Did you not foresee your doom? Did you think you could get away with your evil till the day of total atomic annihilation? You think the Overseer is so void of justice that he would let your depravity run rampant?"

The figure took another step down the stairs. The lights flickered, showing flashes of the police station lobby. The staircase was red. Severed limbs and heads lay strewn about. Darkness. Then another flicker of light. The figure was halfway down the stairs. The face on one of the decapitated heads was pure terror. Eyes swollen, mouth agape, not from pain but from horror.

"Who are you?" Christian said.

"Not who. What," the figure said.

Another flicker of light. The figure was at the base of the stairs.

Christian drew his Gauss rifle. "Don't play semantic games with me. Why did you kill these people? Does your wrath know no bounds?"

The lights flickered again. The figure was gone.

Christian stepped forward, his finger on the trigger of his rifle. Whatever this thing was, it didn't look armored. A few rounds from his rifle would turn it to scrap. But it was too dark. Perhaps Book could illuminate the area with her holographic projection.

Christian turned Book on, but she didn't appear. The image on the holographic projector was of the robot. Unclothed. In its naked metal form, nothing obscured its devouring eyes and monstrous face.

"No," the hologram said. "My wrath is unbounded. My veracity uncorrupted. My hunger insatiable. What am I?" The voice from the holodisplay seemed like Conscience's voice.

Christian tried to shut off the display, but the image wouldn't go away.

"Uh . . . Time. Man. Nothing." Christian recited the stereotypical riddle answers. He pounded on the keypad of the holodisplay, anything to get Book back.

"Do you seek to hide from me within this book?" the figure said. "Fool. I was within the book already, and now that you've seen me, I'm in your mind, your soul. I already was, of course, but now you know it. And now you can never run."

The robot whispered into his ear. Was that Conscience? No, Conscience was on his other shoulder, by his other ear. Christian spun and looked directly into the eyes of the machine, inches away, its breathless mouth dripping oil. He took one step back and fired his Gauss rifle. The shot zipped through the air and struck a window near the entrance to the police station. The robot's head wasn't where it was when Christian fired. Impossible. His sight had been perfectly set on the figure.

Christian fired three more times. The robot moved his head with incredible speed to avoid each shot. One of its robotic hands lashed out and slashed at the gun, which fell from Christian's hands into two pieces. If his claws could do that to Christian's gun, then it'd have little trouble going through Christian's burden and piercing his flesh.

That could not happen.

Christian turned like he was going to run, then at the last second charged the robot, hoping the distraction would catch him off guard. His charge connected, and he knocked the robot into the lobby's main desk.

The robot sprang back onto its feet with unimaginable agility. "You fight hard to resist me," it said. "Admirable. But in the end, irrelevant." It planted its back on the desk and kicked Christian up into the air.

Christian fell on top of the stairs, splashing into a puddle of someone else's blood. He tried to move, but his limbs refused to obey, the weight of his burden holding him down. "Not now," he said, trying to force his burden to move.

"Not now?" the metal monster said. "No. Always." The robot's feet clicked on the stairs. Closer and closer.

"Come on," Christian said. "Move. I don't have time for this."

"I'll say you don't," a voice said. Zealot stepped out of the elevator, pistol in hand.

"Zealot! Thank the Overseer, you're here."

"Okay." Zealot looked upward. "Overseer, thank you that I am here." Then he looked back at Christian. "Now what?"

"That robot. It killed everyone here. This whole city was its trap."

"Trap?" the robot said from the top of the stairs. "I didn't build this city. You puny humans built this city, thinking it could protect you from me. But it is just a—"

A missile struck the robot's arm, blowing it to pieces. Anger flashed across the robot's face, and it snapped its attention toward Zealot.

"Let's see you dodge this." Zealot fired six more missiles.

This time, the robot was ready. It jumped, tucked, and twisted around each missile like it was dancing. As each missile sped past, the robot moved closer and closer to Christian.

Zealot stared in wonder. "Well, I guess I did literally ask for that." Zealot stepped back and looked toward Christian. "Get off your bleep and get to the elevator. This isn't the time to be lazy."

"Right." Christian forced himself up, the exertion tearing muscle and sinew, but he couldn't let the machine get to him. He dragged himself toward the elevator with an occasional glance back.

The robot paused and stopped dodging. A wide, sinister smile slithered across its face.

"That gun. It's a modified conscience, isn't it? Quite a great deal of work you've put into it."

Zealot glanced at his gun, then looked back at the robot. "Indeed." He fired again.

This time, the robot didn't dodge. The missile turned and orbited the robot like a fly.

Zealot kept firing, but the missiles kept turning and orbiting the robot.

The robot motioned with its hand and one of the orbiting missiles sailed toward Zealot, striking him in the chest and sending him sprawling back.

But Zealot kept firing. "You can't possibly stop all these missiles. I have infinite ammo."

Soon, the robot was at the center of a swarm of orbiting missiles. Through the haze of missiles, its glowing eyes never faded from view. "And I have infinite strength. You think you have the will to stand up to me? Do you not know what I am?"

Zealot lowered his gun and squinted. "Wait! I remember you."

"You do?" Christian said.

The robot clapped in a sarcastic motion. "Well done, Zealot. You remember. Few remember. But memory will not save you."

"Who is this monster?" Christian said.

"The one who gave me this gun. The creator of all Consciences."

For the first time, Christian sensed fear in Zealot's voice. Actual fear. In Zealot. Who was this abomination that even Zealot feared him?

Zealot said, "You warned me of the threat of total atomic annihilation," his voice wavered. "I'm on this quest because of you. Why are you attacking me? Why now?"

"You wanted morals forced upon people. As if that would attain a righteousness necessary to protect you from the Overseer's atomic wrath. Now you have it. Morality shall be forced. You first."

Christian reached the elevator. "But what is it Zealot? I don't understand."

The robot raised its arms and smiled. "Just a humble bounty hunter. I am Law."

"Law?" Christian said. If he could keep Law talking, he might have time to get the elevator working. "What is that? One of those robot acronyms?"

Christian pressed the button for the roof several times. "What's that stand for? Legislative Assault Worker?

"No," Law's voice was calm, emotionless, terrifying. "Law stands for law. And you fools thought doing a few good works and moving into a nice city with a pamphlet for better living could satisfy my"— Law's tone escalated to loudness beyond comprehension—"*infinite justice?*"

Pain pounded in Christian's ears. The noise too great for him.

"Zealot," Law said, "you've led many humans down the path to destruction when working for False Religion. Christian, you have murdered so many that only I could keep count. Do you think you can hide from the consequences of those crime? You were given consciences to warn you of the wrath to come. And what did you do? You ignored the voice of your conscience. Turned aside to insufficient morality."

He pointed at Zealot. "You weaponize your conscience. You wish to become me. A condemner, an executer. As if you had the righteousness to justify passing judgment on others. Your self-righteousness knows no bounds. In your pursuit of morality, you have doomed yourselves like everyone who sets foot in this accursed city."

"I understand what you're saying," Zealot said. "But you're forgetting one thing."

"Oh?" Law's voice quieted into an almost amused challenge.

Zealot pointed behind Law. "What the censored is that?"

Law turned to look. "What is what? I don't see anything."

Zealot dove into the elevator.

Christian pressed the button to close the elevator doors.

"What does this have to do with me forgetting something?" Law said, still not turning back around.

Zealot pulled Christian away from the control panel. "That won't work. He's hacked the whole building. Probably the whole city."

Zealot pointed his pistol at the ceiling, pressed a switch on the side of his gun, and covered his head with his hand. "I'm reasonably certain this won't work."

Zealot fired the rockets into the ceiling. This time, they didn't explode. They stuck in the ceiling. After a dozen rockets had stuck into the ceiling, the elevator started to rise. Then it rose faster. Then, even faster than faster. The elevator didn't have a speedometer, and Christian was unaccustomed to measuring the speed of rocket-propelled elevators, but the elevator now seemed to be moving way too fast.

Zealot took a deep breath and shouted over the noise of the rockets. "Running away. What a sensation. I don't like it."

"What are we going to do? That thing is between us and the exit now," Christian said. "Assuming we don't die when this elevator hits the top."

"Don't worry. If anyone can defeat that thing, it's Mayor Legalist. He's a hundred times more powerful than I am. And he mentioned something about Law when I talked with him. He said he'd been trained specifically to deal with him. He was headed to the roof. We just have to get to the roof and tell him what has transpired."

"You're sure Legalist can deal with Law?"

"Of course. Remember, I met Law back when I became a pilgrim. I know a thing or two about it. It's beyond righteous. Law is designed in such a way that its assault protocols are most effective against those who are the most evil. Legalist is the most devout man in the city. What could Law possibly accuse him of? It'll be powerless against Legalist."

"Are you sure?"

"I'm never sure!" Zealot's voice returned to that boisterous over-confident tone that somehow both reassured Christian and made him nervous.

The elevator slammed to a halt sending Christian and Zealot jostling about. If the sudden stop had injured Christian, he didn't have time to notice. As soon as the elevator stopped the opposite door slid open. Law stood before them.

Law held a guard by one hand, anger chiseled across its face. Its fingers were choking the life out him. "There wasn't something to look at. You lied. You said, 'What the censorship is that?' but there wasn't anything."

Christian was too shocked to respond. How did Law get there so fast?

"Lied? Only a little," Zealot said.

Law's anger swelled. It tossed the guard behind its back and off the roof. Wait. Law had both its arms. Hadn't Zealot shot off one of its arms?

Law stepped toward them.

Christian pressed a button on the elevator control pad, but nothing happened.

"Do you think machines can help you?" Law raised a hand.

"Um, yes?" Christian backed against the elevator wall.

"Machines follow subroutines. Rules. As the world does." Law reached for Christian. Its metal fingers were sharp, like blades. They dripped with blood. "But humans, you choose not to follow the rules." The bladed fingers reached Christian's throat.

"But I do," a voice said from beyond Law.

Law turned his head 180 degrees like an owl, its fingers just short of Christian's neck.

Legalist stood in front of an aircraft with two propellors on its wings, parked on the roof's helicopter landing pad. Mayor Legalist walked forward, slinging off his suit coat.

Law pulled away from Christian. "Ah, you must be Mayor Legalist."

Legalist flexed his muscles. "That's what it says on my sash." Without the coat, his physique appeared in peak condition, the kind of figure that sculptors try to emulate.

"Trying to intimidate me?" Law said. "How foolish. Fear is an emotion beyond my comprehension. I have no fear. No love. No hunger." With each word it stepped closer to Legalist. Its feet clattering with thundering reverberation. "In me, there is no feeling but cold hate. Hatred for evil. And I will destroy evil. You're pitiful if you think you can stop me."

"Pitiful?" Legalist's shirt exploded from the force of his flexing muscles. Wisps of energy crackled across his body and his hair stood on end.

Christian and Zealot took advantage of Law's diverted attention and exited the elevator.

Law paced back and forth, eyeing Legalist.

Legalist smiled. "I can stop you, Law."

Law scoffed, the noise sounding like a metallic clatter.

"It's true," Legalist continued. "I'm your greatest nemesis: a good person. I've followed the code of morality since I was young. Brought up others to follow that code as well. I've done more to help the poor and downtrodden than anyone in this city." The crackling energy rippling across Legalist's body grew in power and intensity.

"Oh dear," Zealot said. "I've seen enough Shounen to know this kind of conversation isn't going anywhere fast. Time to commence with unwise heroism." He charged Law from behind but didn't fire his pistol, no doubt suspecting Law would control the missiles like before. He tackled the robot from behind.

"I'll hold him, Legalist. You beat his—"

Before Zealot could finish his sentence, Law knocked him aside, diverting the energy from its charge and knocking him into the air. He sailed over everyone's heads and collided with the aircraft at the far end of the roof.

While Law was distracted, Legalist struck. With super speed that matched the robot, Legalist ran and slammed an electrified fist into Law's chest. Flashes of electricity danced from Legalist's body into Law's chassis.

Law fell forward, but caught itself with one hand, then spun around, kicking at Legalist with both feet.

Legalist blocked both kicks with his hands, backed up, and swung around in a massive roundhouse kick like an expert martial artist. The kick connected with Law's leg.

A resounding metal crack shook the air.

Law pulled itself up, staggering from the injury to its leg. Its eyes flashed with that same red glare. It looked at Legalist and laughed, its voice showing no pain or fear.

Law scoffed. "This is the best you can do? You do what you think is right. But no matter how much you murder, steal, and lie, in the end your excuses to be spared from justice are always the same. You say others are worse than you are. That the good you've done should make up for the evil. And on and on the lies go, belittling your crimes, digging your grave deeper."

Law unleashed a flurry of punches on Legalist, so fast that its movements were a blur. "And as you dig your own grave, I, your undertaker, loom over you ready to seal your fate."

Legalist matched him blow for blow.

As Law increased the ferocity of its attacks, Legalist increased the speed and precision of his blocks.

Legalist smiled in triumph. "Do you care nothing for the good I have done for this city and others? Is moral action meaningless to you? Then you are a poor code." He swatted away Law's attacks like flies.

Law gave a subtle grated growl, a tenor of anger in its metallic voice. Its next attack came so fast, a sonic boom erupted from its fist, sending a shockwave that knocked Christian back.

Christian looked up, expecting to see Law's fist through Legalist's chest.

Legalist held Law's fist mid-strike. Legalist's other hand glowed with power. He struck Law in the chest with his free hand and another sonic boom erupted, this one louder than before. The impact from the strike shook the building. Shook the street below. Shattered windows. And sent Law flying backward, tearing the robot from the arm in Legalist's hand and smashing its torso into the side of the elevator.

Legalist held Law's right arm in his hand.

Law laughed and tore itself out of the wreckage of the elevator. "As if justice could be bribed by activities that you should have done anyway. Instead of justifying your evil, you take away any good that could be said of your righteous actions. You show that you did such actions to save your own worthless soul, not out of any good will."

"Actions are what matter." Legalist pointed with Law's severed arm.

"The heart matters as well," Law said. "To hope good actions will hide your evil heart from my eyes is folly. These eyes pierce through stone, flesh, soul, and lie." Its eyes glowed a deeper red and it moved toward Legalist, dragging its bad leg behind. Half wrecked, dripping oil and sparking electricity, Law somehow looked even more threatening.

"You think good deeds grant you forgiveness?" Law's voice weakened. "You think apathy is man's natural state?" His voice faded, like an audio player low on batteries. "You think, if you come upon an injustice, the natural action is to do nothing and the evil action is to participate?" Law's movements slowed, but it kept coming toward Legalist.

Legalist stood firm, unshaking, immovable.

"You think it is some extra-special action to do good?" Law said. "Is it natural to do nothing? No. The neutral state, the correct and true state is to do good. Thus, doing good does not gain you forgiveness or righteousness. It is simply right. And to do nothing, to be apathetic, that is crime. Your good deeds—they do not justify you. Each good deed is simply you dodging a bullet. But even you, Legalist, even you have more than enough bullets that you have failed to dodge."

Legalist hurled the robot's arm he held, impaling it into one of Law's eyes.

Law lurched back, paused, and righted itself.

Could nothing stop this dreadful machine? Christian had no weapon and could hardly move. Besides, to charge the robot would mean instant defeat as Zealot had shown. He could do nothing but watch and hope Legalist could do enough to stop the death machine.

Law grabbed the arm implanted in its head and wrenched it free. "You wish to use Law against the Law? What a fool." It stuck the arm back onto its torso. Law, now one-eyed, charged Legalist.

Legalist struck his hands together. Energy pulsed from them, then glowed and coalesced into an orb. "My discipline. My strength. My will to do good," Legalist chanted. "My knowledge of right and wrong, my conscience, my morality. I pour all of this into my quest to do what is right. And that will be strong enough to defeat you."

"Ha!" Law said. "Your cliché shounen dialogue is nothing against—"

A stream of solid energy shot out of the orb, around Legalist's hands, and wafted over Law, enveloping it, then blotting out its figure from the night sky. Seconds later, the beam faded away, and all that remained was the twisted metal of what was once Law.

Christian stared at the twisted metal. He should have felt relieved, right? Safe? So why was he more terrified now more than ever?

Legalist gave a long sigh of relief.

"That was incredible," Zealot said. "You actually defeated that malcontent machine."

Legalist turned and bowed. "Simple training and practice will make you a match for Law. For indeed, I fought the law, and the law . . . did not won."

A metal hand burst through Legalist's stomach. Two more hands closed around his neck.

Three metal figures stood behind Legalist, ripping the flesh from his bones. It was Law! It was back! But no, these were different machines. But they all had Law's cold, red eyes.

Legalist turned and hurled one of the Laws off him. A dozen more figures climbed up over the edge of the roof and swarmed Legalist. Two more appeared in the elevator. And one stepped up next to Christian.

"Silly humans," Law said. "You always think there are fewer Laws than there really are."

STAGE 6
THE KNIGHT OF THE BLOOD OATH

"How can this be?" Legalist's face filled with pain and fear.

"Pride in your righteousness," one of the Laws said.

"Leading others in your paths away from salvation," said another.

"Hatred of all who are less moral than you," a third Law said.

"Also," a Law standing by the aircraft said, "you were rude to your mother on seventeen occasions, and thirteen times you did not help the poor when it was in your power to do so."

"But . . . but . . . that's so . . ." Legalist's voice wavered.

"Small?" One of the Laws leaned over Legalist and glared at him with spite. "There are no small Laws."

Christian ran for the tilt-rotor aircraft and dove inside. He heard the sound of ripping and tearing. He couldn't watch. Besides, he was probably next. Christian slid the door closed. The aircraft's propellors started to spin, preparing for a vertical takeoff. Someone else must have had the same idea and gotten to the cockpit before him. The engines whined and almost drowned out the sound of Legalist's screams.

The aircraft hovered off the landing pad.

Christian gave a sigh of relief and settled into a seat.

Zealot poked his head through the door leading to the cockpit. So, he was the one who started the aircraft.

"They tore Legalist to pieces," Zealot said. "Who can defeat Law, if not him?"

"It's impossible," Christian said. "Remember what it said about infinite strength? It's the same technology behind consciences and your infinite missile launcher."

"Infinite Laws?" Zealot said. "That's a lot of laws. At my peak, I could take maybe two." Zealot started counting on his fingers. "How much bigger is infinity?"

"A lot," Christian said. "Maybe Truth can save us. Maybe those Laws are operating incorrectly. Perhaps Truth knows some argument or trick to stop them."

"Perhaps," Zealot said. "But we'd better find her quick. If I'm reading the sensors on this aircraft correctly, then there are hundreds of those Law robots in the city. They're exterminating the populace, block by block. There's no telling when Truth will be next."

"Let's go pick her up and get out of here." Christian slipped through the door and sat in the copilot seat next to Zealot.

Zealot pressed a few buttons on the control panel. "It's fortunate that first Law threw me toward the aircraft so I could start the automatic takeoff protocol and give you an escape."

"And it's a good thing this aircraft was one you knew how to fly," Christian said.

Zealot stared at Christian. "What do you mean?"

"It's good you know how to fly this."

"I just pressed the button to take off. I thought you were driving."

Christian's eyes grew wide. "I just got here. How could I be driving?"

"I don't know how things work. I'm Zealot."

Christian scanned the controls for anything familiar. "Then why were you pushing all those buttons? How did you manage to make it take off?"

"I pressed buttons randomly. Seems I was lucky and pressed the one for automatic takeoff. But don't worry, we will simply hope my luck continues to hold."

Zealot pressed more buttons.

The aircraft took a sharp turn to the left.

Zealot and Christian let out a series of highly non-masculine screams.

————

Truth sipped from her glass and tried to avoid eye contact with Worldly Wiseman. He was charming, smart, and dashing. The last thing she wanted was for him to see her blushing. He'd taken her to a nice restaurant at the top of one of the skyscrapers. They sat at a table that stood on a precipice jutting out from the skyscraper like an arm of an elegant giant. Gardens and fountains stood alongside the tables. Streams flowed along the platform to the edge and fell into a series of aqueducts that connected the skyscraper to the adjoining one. The water flowing into these aqueducts traveled from aqueduct to aqueduct till it finally poured into a fountain on street level.

Truth sighed in delight, contemplating the precise brilliance of the aqueduct's construction. The wine was delicious, the conversation stimulating. There had been some noise from the roof of one of the skyscrapers a few minutes before, but now it was peaceful and quiet. Aircraft sailed about the skyscrapers like bees buzzing around flowers. One was coming close. Really close. In fact, it was flying right toward them.

Laughing, Worldly Wiseman said, "So then I said, 'Water color? Why don't you just say blue like anyone else?'" He looked at Truth and seemed to expect her to laugh. When she didn't his demeaner changed to concern. "What's the matter, my dear?" He followed her gaze and looked over his shoulder.

The aircraft crashed into the edge of the platform. Patrons leapt from their seats. Fire engulfed a patch of garden and a cherubim statue shattered into a dozen pieces.

Fragments of cherubim flew over Truth's head and she ducked under her table.

Two figures crawled from the wreckage of the aircraft. Two familiar figures. Truth did all she could to quell a feeling of elemental rage.

————

"Ha! I live!" cried Zealot. "I knew my luck would hold. Perfect landing." He struck a pose in front of the flaming aircraft just as another explosion vomited forth more bits of statue and metal.

Christian pulled himself farther from the flaming debris and coughed up a cloud of smoke. He looked up at Zealot, incensed.

"Oh, very well," Zealot frowned. "A 6.5 out of 10 landing. But we made it. And that's all that matters." He looked around. "What is this place? Some sort of rooftop incinerator?"

"I think it was supposed to be a garden," Christian said.

"A garden?" He stared at the wreckage. "It's a poor one, isn't it? Look! Here comes Truth to greet us."

Truth wore a shimmering evening gown studded with gemstones. It must have cost an obscene amount of money.

"Greetings, my opal-headed compatriot," Zealot said, waving to Truth. "How fares your romantic expedition?"

Truth slapped Zealot across the cheek.

The force of the slap caused Zealot to spin three times, then stagger back. Truth was about half Zealot's size. How on earth had she—

"Must you ruin my evening?" Truth said. "Worldly Wise Man and I were having a lovely dinner when you came and—"

"Crashed the party?" Zealot said with a smile.

"I wasn't going to say that."

"Well, you should have—top quality pun like that. Not every day you get such a chance to use one."

"Leave us alone," Truth said.

"Hold on." Christian stepped in front of Zealot and pointed. "You two can continue your passive-aggressive flirting later. We're under attack by killer robots. The whole city is in danger."

"Killer robots?" Truth looked confused. "And I do not flirt passive-aggressively."

"Really?" Worldly Wiseman stepped toward them, his face friendly. "Then how *do* you flirt?"

Truth's anger changed to shyness in an instant, and she tried to hide a very immature giggle.

"Christian is right." Zealot said. "Let us ignore Truth's adorable antics and focus on the problem at hand. There's a swarm of evil robots attacking the city."

"Evil robots?" Truth raised an eyebrow. "The only robot swarm in the city I know of is Law. It's not evil."

"Wait," Christian said, "you know about Law?"

Truth gave a condescending glance. "If your question begins with 'Do you know about . . .' then just save yourself the trouble and assume the answer is yes."

"How do we stop it?" Zealot said.

"You can't." Truth walked toward her seat, paying Zealot little attention.

Worldly Wiseman pulled Truth's chair out for her to be seated.

Truth smiled and turned her back on Zealot and Christian. "Now, Worldly Wiseman, earlier you were telling me about how the central interpretive motifs of eastern art in the twentieth century shouldn't be primarily based on cultural context."

Worldly Wiseman started to answer, but Christian interrupted.

"So, we just sit down and die?"

Truth waved a hand in indifference "You do what you want. I'm just a philosophical personification of human reason, knowledge, and wisdom. Law won't attack me."

A finger tapped Christian on the shoulder. Probably Zealot wanting to get his attention. Christian turned around.

Law stood there, tapping its foot. "I appreciate this complex discussion, but I've got a lot of people to kill and a tight schedule."

Christian screamed, staggered back, and tripped over a piece of broken statue before falling on the floor. "Law's here! How did it get here so fast?"

"Laws are almost everywhere," Truth said.

Zealot drew his pistol and aimed at Law. "Truth, assist us. We must commence with violence."

"In a minute," Truth said without looking back at him. "I've got a lot to talk about with Worldly Wiseman here."

"Violence will not save you anyway," Law said. "Don't even try."

"No can do!" Zealot kicked over a table and took cover. He poked his pistol around, and fired in random directions. Various missiles flew about and exploded. None anywhere near Law. "Come, Christian! We can take it."

"No," Christian stood.

Zealot lowered his gun and looked back and forth between Christian and Law. "What? You're sure to die if you don't fight him."

"We can't fight Law," Christian said. "Don't you get it? Legalist couldn't even fight Law. And we are nowhere near as powerful as he was. Truth said Law was not evil, which means we have to be the evil ones."

"No, Christian," Zealot said. "Don't give up. We just need to try harder."

Christian cocked his head back and yelled. "Truth! I'm right, aren't I?"

"Yeah, sure. Whatever." Truth kept her attention on Worldly Wiseman.

Law kept his gun leveled at Christian but wore a look of suspicion. "What's your plan here? Are you trying to trick me? Zealot tried to trick me back in the police lobby and I did not appreciate that."

Christian raised his hands. "No tricks. I confess that I've done horrible evil things. All I can do is ask for mercy."

Law's confusion changed to amusement. "You've asked for mercy and confessed your evil. That's rare. Most try to justify themselves, or say their punishment is unjust, which is only another way of saying that the standards of absolute morality should be dumbed down to their level. But to acknowledge that you're the evil one and choose to allow yourself to be judged. How . . ."

Law's face gave no hint at mercy or forbearance.

". . . refreshing."

Silence.

"So," Christian said, "does that mean you're going to show me mercy?"

Law stared at Christian. "Let me get this straight. You are a murderer."

"Yes."

"You've killed innocent people."

"I did admit to that."

"And you've kicked old widows in the shins."

"Yes."

"And you think you should be shown mercy because . . ."

"Because I confessed?"

"Oh!" Law lowered its gun and shrugged. "Well . . . if you've confessed, I guess that's different."

"Really?"

Law shot Christian in the chest. "No."

Christian fell to his knees. Blood poured from his chest.

The smoke from Law's gun sailed upward and curled around its twisted smile. "There's nothing you can do. No confession, no sorrow, no good work that can satisfy me. You can't un-spill blood. You can't unbreak a law. What's done is done. There is no escape. There is only crime and punishment."

Zealot fired more missiles. Eventually a few flew near Law. But with a wave of Law's hand, the missiles turned aside.

Law pointed its gun at Christian's head. "Now the cliché is to ask for any last words. But honestly, this has gone on long enough. You aren't entitled to anything."

The forcefield protecting Christian's head blipped out of existence.

Law fired.

Christian didn't die, which seemed odd.

The projectile from Law's gun hovered in midair, inches from Christian's face. Law looked at the hovering shot. Then fired again. This shot also hovered midair. "Well . . ." It took a step back and looked around. "This . . . is baffling." Its voice wavered. It fired again. Eight shots in rapid succession. All stopped short of Christian.

A figure appeared between Christian and Law, a woman who seemed clothed in vibrant colorful light.

Christian's eyes adjusted to the brightness. Now he saw her more clearly. Her clothes were obscenely shiny. She wore long white gloves, hip-high boots, a skirt and a blouse bedazzled with various electronic devices. Christian recognized the devices as shield generators of some sort. But he'd never seen ones that shined like that. She had long billowing hair as red as blood, and skin as white as sugar.

She projected a shield in front of herself. The shots from Law's gun crackled against the shield but moved no closer to Christian. As he stared, Christian felt the bleeding from his chest stop, felt the shields form over his chest and knit his heart back together.

Law stared at the woman. "Who, the cuss, are you?"

"Who am I?" The woman's tone seemed happy, as if she expected the question. She was loud like Zealot, but somehow her tone didn't hurt the ears. "Who am I?"

"Yes," Law said

"I am the essence of all virtue."

Law's confusion turned to annoyance. "Oh no. Not you. You're . . . you're . . ."

"I am the inspiration of a trillion songs," the woman said. "The foundation of patience, kindness, trust, hope, the harbinger of all—"

"Her name's Charity," Truth yelled from her table.

Charity showed annoyance for a brief second. "Confound it all, Truth. You ruined my entrance."

"We don't have time for another one of your overly theatrical, quip-filled speeches, Charity." Truth went back to talking with Worldly Wiseman.

"You can't interfere, Charity," Law said. "I have a bounty on this one's head." It pointed at Christian with its gun. "He has done evil."

"Okay, two things," Charity said. "First, Charity is my mother's name. Nobody uses the word Charity anymore, except when talking about giving to the poor, which is only, like, a part of what I do. Call me Love, okay? Charity is like . . . so seventeenth century."

"It does say HELLO, My Name Is Charity on your nametag," Zealot shouted from behind his table.

"It's also what's written on her birth certificate," Truth yelled.

"Oh, you two are no fun," Love said with a voice made of smiles.

"Your name doesn't matter." Law pointed at Christian. "I'm killing this one."

Love waved her hand. A shield pushed Law back and away from Christian. "The Overseer has heard the cry of this poor soul and has given me the authority to forestall his judgement. For now."

"You can't do that," Law said with cold finality.

Love raised her arms and gave a flamboyant pose, her voice

returning to its triumphant tone. "I do not take away your duty to pass judgement. I simply forestall it. Give this one time to choose the correct path. When he dies, you may pass judgment, as is protocol."

Zealot stepped from behind his cover and stood next to Love. "This one's mannerisms amuse me. I'm with her."

Love winked at Zealot, then faced Law.

"But . . . b-but . . ." Law sputtered, not looking nearly as intimidating as before. "But that Zealot one. He wished for true justice to be forced upon people. I am simply granting his wish."

"Put a fork in it, Law." Love rolled her eyes. "What are you, a genie? I'm sure Zealot understands how silly his stupid idea was."

"Hey," Zealot said. "The idea may have been stupid, but it was not silly."

"Yes," Love said. "Very stupid. And silly. Law, ignore the silly man and be gone."

"No." Law leapt at Christian. Its claws flashed but stopped inches from Christian's throat, protected by Love's shield around him.

Love raised her scepter. A beam of blue energy enveloped Law. The scepter sparked, and Love tensed, as if resisting extreme strain. "Don't just stand there," Love said to Christian through gritted teeth. "Run. I can only freeze him for so long."

"Run where?" Christian said. "This city was supposed to be our salvation."

Love slowly looked at Christian like a mother when her child doesn't want to wear pants today. "You poor thing. You forgot already. Ask Book." Strain showed on Love's face. Blood started to drip from her mouth. Was projecting the shields hurting her? "All you need to know is in Book."

"You heard the magical girl," Zealot said. "Book said to flee to the Gateway. Then let's make like a check and bounce." He started toward the door leading to the inside of the skyscraper.

Christian followed, but a hoard of Laws stood blocking their way, frozen like the other one. But who knew for how long?

"I suggest not going that way," Zealot said. "The room beyond appears to be filled with more riotous robots."

"Truth." Christian turned toward the girl, who was still talking with Worldly Wiseman. "We need your help. How do we escape?"

Truth kept talking with Worldly Wiseman.

"Truth!" Christian walked to their table.

Worldly Wiseman sprang up, looking angry. "How dare you interrupt our fine evening? This beautiful, delicious maiden and I have much to talk about."

"Yes," Truth said, sounding as if speaking in her sleep. "Much to talk about."

"I understand you're busy . . ." Christian tried to keep his tone calm. Then he tilted his head in confusion. "Wait, did you just say *delicious*?" Christian looked down at Truth. He waved his hand over her eyes. She didn't react. He shook her. Still no reaction. He turned on Worldly Wiseman "What have you done to her?" Christian grabbed him by the collar and hoisted him over the side of the platform.

Worldly Wiseman had a glinting, self-satisfied smile. "What have I done to Truth?" His voice chilled Christian's heart. "Nothing against her nature. I've simply altered her focus." Worldly Wiseman yawned. "You see, this world has so much knowledge to offer. For instance, did you know that some believe the popularity of rapid-fire projectile weapons only became widespread due to the enlightenment's view of individual freedom and not due to mechanical advances from the industrial revolution?"

Christian looked back at Truth. She didn't seem hurt. "That is really fascinating, and totally irrelevant to our current predicament. We've got to get out of here. Go to the . . . I forgot already." He activated Book.

Book appeared. She was at the head of a massive army of skeletons, dressed in a military commander's uniform.

"The Gateway." Book pointed into the distance toward the glow.

"Right. The Gateway. Besides, how could the enlightenment have resulted in an earlier adaption of rapid-fire weapons given the mechanical constraints of standardized cartridges?"

"Yes, how?" Truth's voice was trancelike.

Christian fell to one knee. Worldly Wiseman's words seemed to eat into Christian's brain, ripping away his will to move.

Worldly Wiseman freed himself from Christian's grasp and leapt back onto the platform. "There are countless examples of ancient rapid-fire weapons of limited use, such as the Chu Ko Nu or its Greek equivalent, the polybolus."

Christian tried to resist, but his hands seemed lifeless.

Worldly Wiseman put a hand on Truth's shoulder in a non-platonic manner. "Granted, the polybolus has only scarce archeological support for its use." He leaned down toward Truth's face. "But writings of its existence detail it with enough precision that we can assume—"

Zealot struck Worldly Wiseman in the face.

Worldly Wiseman went down like the poll numbers of a pro-tax candidate.

"How did you do that?" Christian said, life suddenly returning to his limbs.

"I just did," Zealot said. "Why didn't you? Stop being lazy. Come, we must away." He picked up Truth and shook her lightly. At least, he seemed to *try* to shake her lightly. In reality, he shook the spit out of her.

"Come, Truth," Zealot said. "Wake up from this psychological psychosis."

"No . . . no . . ." Truth said in her trance-like voice. "I want to know about the ancient history of rapid-fire projectile weapons."

"We don't have time," Zealot said.

"But I want to learn things." Truth mumbled like she was living in a dream.

"Truth," Christian said, "you can still learn while going to the Gateway. Whatever you're doing now can't be as important as getting through that Gateway and getting salvation."

"Salvation?" Truth said.

"Yes," Christian said. "Remember? The burden, the Gateway? Total atomic annihilation? If we don't escape, Law is going to kill us super hard. Besides rapid-fire projectile weapons never took off, because they lacked the penetration power necessary to become a counter to decent armor given metallurgy advances at a faster rate than mathematics in ancient times given the written word remained so dispersant in its adaptation."

"That's not the correct use of the word dispersant," Truth said.

Zealot dropped Truth and grabbed Christian. "You're getting caught up in it too."

"Caught up in what? I'm just saying that armor advanced at a faster rate than—"

Zealot slapped Christian.

Christian saw stars for a second.

"We must expunge you from whatever spell or mentalist whatnot Worldly Wiseman has done," Zealot said. "I thought punching him would put an end to his tricks, but it seems this is one of those rare obstacles I cannot punch or shoot my way out of. It's Worldly Wiseman's doing. He has you speaking of minutia instead of fleeing for the Gateway. What good is history? What good is fine art or profound thoughts or understanding if it doesn't cause us to act? If it doesn't cause us to pursue the correct path? Our correct path, which Love and Book have clearly shown us is toward the Gateway."

"Knowledge is its own reward," Truth said.

"Nonsense." Zealot pulled Christian toward the edge of the platform. "Talking of deeper wisdom is fine, but we cannot pursue them instead of pursing the Gateway. Now, where is that pretty, red-haired, female person?"

"Over here," Love said, her voice strained, still frozen in her pose holding back Law. "I can only hold this guy in place for a dramatically nonspecific amount of time. But Zealot is right—knowledge without action is powerless."

Truth blinked and looked horrified. "You're right. Oh no! Zealot said something right, and I was wrong."

"You weren't factually wrong," Zealot said. "That's the most dangerous thing. You were correct, just misplaced in your focus. But that's what I'm here for."

Truth said, "Well . . . thank you."

Zealot smiled. "Any time, beautiful."

Truth blushed. "Aw . . . you're sweet."

"No, I'm Zealot. I thought you knew that."

Truth laughed.

"What a lovely team building moment," Love said. "You know

what? If I get mauled to death by these robots, it's all worth it. I think the shields I'm projecting are reaching their breaking point. Goodbye, Dark Lands. Goodbye, Christian. I'm doomed." Love began to wail in excessive and obviously nonserious tones.

Law lurched forward.

Christian's heart quickened.

Zealot twirled his gun, "Shall we shoot our way through all the rooms leading to the stairwell?" His gun discharged into the ground and he leapt back in surprise, looking embarrassed.

"No time," Love said.

Law moved steadily, with slow but ever-increasing speed.

"The aqueduct waterfall," Truth yelled, "on the side of the building. It's our best chance."

Christian remembered some sort of aqueducts on an adjacent building that water poured into. The far end of the platform had a stream that poured off and fell onto the adjacent aqueducts. However, that edge of the platform was where they had crashed their aircraft.

"Hold on," Christian said. "To get to that aqueduct, we'd have to jump over burning wreckage and fall into the water of the aqueduct as it pours onto lower aqueducts in a glorified freefall down a dozen stories of skyscraper."

Zealot grabbed Christian around the middle and started running. "I fail to see any problem with that route."

"It's going to be dangerous," Christian said. "And hard."

"Perfect!" Zealot ran towards the edge. Truth and Love followed. Zealot leapt from the skyscraper.

Christian screamed in terror, Zealot screamed in delight, and Truth screamed an unconvincing "Whee-e-e" as if she was on a rollercoaster.

Christian shut his eyes.

STAGE 7

THE NEMESIS OF VAN OF THE DAWN

"He's waking up."

"Are you sure? I should probably hit him, just to be safe."

Christian opened his eyes. He was lying on the bank of a small stream. Wilderness surrounded him. Truth and Zealot stood over him, looking down with concern and curiosity.

"Christian! We thought you were out for good." Zealot picked Christian up and squeezed him with a hug that threatened to crack a bone. "There's no time to waste my boy. Let's get walking. The Gateway isn't far off." He plopped Christian down.

Christian looked around, trying to get his bearings. In the distance was a massive rectangular gate. "I didn't know we were that close,"

Truth walked in front of him towards the Gateway. "I told you The City of Morality was on the way to the Gateway. I think that's why it ensnares so many travelers."

"Enough talk. Let's get to it," Zealot pushed Christian forward. "There's no telling when that Law character will show up again. And there is no telling how long that magical girl will be able to—"

A flash of light.

Love materialized in front of them, floating just above the ground. "Did somebody say *Love*?" She flung her arms around, sending flashes of light, hearts, and rainbows, projected from the electronic devices on her clothes.

"No . . ." Truth said.

"Oh." Love looked embarrassed. "Hold on, I'll try again. Go back to saying what you were saying." Love floated off behind a large rock and waited.

Zealot paused. "Uh . . . as I was saying . . . there's no telling how long that magical girl Love will be—"

Another flash of light. Love appeared again and repeated her pose. "Did somebody say *Love?*"

"Sis," Truth said, "can you stop with the gratuitous flamboyance?"

Love gave a friendly smirk. "Truth, you know nobody understands you when you use words with over three syllables."

"Flamboyance only has three syllables, Love."

Christian stepped in front of Love. "Love, how are you here? What happened to Law?"

Love winked at Christian and smiled. "Thank you for asking, darling. It was an epic struggle that wrecked the city and will no doubt be talked about in song and legend. Swarms of his Law bots attacking from all angles. I valiantly held them back with my force field projectors, trying to save all I could from the city."

Zealot looked entranced. "Wonderous!"

Truth looked unconvinced. "He ruthlessly vanquished you, didn't he?"

"No!" Love said. "After a while, I decided I was of better use here. He did get away though. I don't know where he is now."

"Probably after us," Christian glanced around. But there was no sign of the robot. "How long was I out?"

"This is an allegory," Truth said, "so time is really hard to measure as most beings here are incorporeal eternal philosophical concepts and thus not temporally bound."

"Wait. But earlier in the City of Morality you said to meet me in one hour. And you did."

"Yes. Allegories are also known for their wildly inconsistent rules. However, I did say time was *hard* to measure. Not impossible."

"In any event . . ." Christian said with confusion in his voice, ". . . we need to get to the Gate." Christian turned to run in that direction. The rest followed. Zealot's armor clanged with each step, his face forward, focused. Truth walked with her hands behind her and glanced about at the terrain, not looking where she was going yet not missing a single step.

Love floated after Christian, her feet not touching the ground and her attention on him. They continued to travel for several difficult-to-measure, allegorically non-specific time increments. "So . . ." Love said in one of those tones women use when they're interested but are trying to act like they aren't. "How are you doing?" Love smiled, and still hovering above the ground, matched Christian's speed.

Christian glanced at her sideways. "Are you flirting with me? Now?"

"Why? Do you want me to flirt with you?" Her smile deepened.

"Uh . . ."

"I just wanted to ask how you were doing. But romantic pursuits are indeed a noble and useful element that can ease your journey. Not good for man to be alone and all that. Though I should warn you that I'm not actually a representation of a human female but a personification of a series of virtuous concepts using a feminine anthropomorphism. So, dating would be . . . complicated."

"Oh dear," Christian said. "Another Truth."

"Well, we are sisters."

Zealot stepped between them but kept walking. "Now listen here, you well-meaning magus of machinery. We are interested in getting to the Gateway and removing burdens. We don't have time to assess our personal feelings or pursue romance."

"Hey," Love said, "you gotta pursue the Gateway with more than just your mind and strength." She pointed at Truth, then Zealot.

Zealot and Truth exchanged a glance.

"What else is there?" Zealot said.

Love laughed. "Oh, you two are adorable."

"No." Zealot motioned toward Truth. "She is adorable. I am a hard, grizzled ruffian who must get Christian through that Gateway and will not stop for any mere distraction."

"You seemed fine with going to the City of Morality," Truth said, muttering.

"Don't you go putting that on me, Truly," Zealot said. "Going to that city was your idea in the first place."

"It was still beneficial, wasn't it? You still have your upgraded conscience, don't you?"

Zealot checked the weapon. "Yes, but we almost died."

"Well," Truth said, "nothing is perfect."

Love floated over both of them. "But it should be."

"Indeed!" Zealot said. "Why can't things be perfect? That's why we went to the City of Morality. We just wanted to better ourselves. What's wrong with seeking perfection?"

"Besides it being impossible?" Truth said.

"Yes, besides that."

"You're being a homunculi, Zealot." Love said.

Truth and Zealot looked more confused.

Love pointed at Truth. "If you understand all knowledge and all mysteries, is that enough?"

"Uh . . ." Truth seemed to not have a ready answer. Which seemed unusual.

Love pointed at Zealot. "If you give all you have to the poor and are willing to die to do what is right, is that enough?"

Zealot hesitated. "Yes?"

"No!" Love said. "Seeking perfection is inherently selfish in nature. You're wishing to make yourself better."

"And that's bad?" Zealot said.

"It's not *bad*. It's insufficient. So many people try to find the Gateway by keeping a bunch of rules or following a religious code."

"Yes," Zealot said, "that's what False Religion's deal was, saying we just needed to follow some set of bizarre rules and hide under his fallout shelter."

"Kiddie pool," Truth said.

"Wait . . ." Love looked between Truth and Zealot. "He convinced you to do what?"

"Never mind. It's unimportant. What were you saying?" Zealot sounded embarrassed.

Love seemed to notice Zealot's discomfort, and genuine concern filled her face. "False Religion was doubly wrong, not only were his rules wrong, but the very idea of using rules to save yourself was wrong. Legalist was one step better. He had correct and useful rules. But he thought following them would give him the power to match Law's challenge. And well . . . you saw the result."

"So, we shouldn't follow rules?" Zealot said.

Love rolled her eyes but she didn't look angry. More like she found Zealot's statement cute rather than incorrect. "It's always *should* and *should not* with you. That's not a very useful question."

"Yes it is," Truth said. "Knowing right from wrong is important."

"Well, I suppose, but it's incomplete," Love said. "I'm more concerned with why something is done—less with what is actually done. Though that is important. Your heart must be right, and the rest will follow."

"I agree," a voice yelled from somewhere.

Zealot drew his pistol and assumed a combat position.

"Oh, calm down." Love put a hand on Zealot's shoulder. "Who goes there? If you come in the Overseer's name, then by all means, show yourself."

"And if you don't," Zealot said, "then by all means show yourself . . . and DIE."

Love shot Zealot a harsh look then looked at Christian. "Does he ever calm down?"

"No," Christian, Truth, and Zealot all said simultaneously.

A figure stepped from behind a rock. He was short, hunched over, and wore a martial artist's outfit. He held a complicated remote-control device in his hand. "Blessings upon you."

Love beamed. "Look! He's wished blessings upon us. I trust him immediately and will make no effort towards verifying if his intentions are actually noble." She floated to the man and curtsied in the air. "Blessings upon you as well, fellow traveler. What is your name? I am called Love."

"I am called Gnostic."

This earned blank stares from the others.

"Very well." The man laughed. "A more modern name is Spiritualist. Perhaps not completely accurate, but it will do."

"Spiritualist?" Love tilted her head. "That sounds good. I love spiritual things. My name *is* Love, after all. I do love things. Spiritual ones, especially. Don't you guys?"

Christian and Zealot mumbled in half-hearted agreement.

Truth looked cross. "Spiritualist? What *kind* of spirits do you mean?"

"Please forgive my sister's lack of exuberance," Love said. "She can be anti-spiritual sometimes. Are you headed to the Gateway? Come with us."

The man smiled. "I *am* headed to the Gateway. But you are seeking it in the wrong way. For you see, there is a gate within each of us. If we just come into contact with that gate, then we can be freed from our burdens."

There was a long pause.

"What the zooterkins?" Truth said.

Everyone stared at Truth.

Truth folded her arms. "I assure you it's a word. An English one. Though usually it's used as a stand-alone interjection and not part of a sentence as I just—"

"Please forgive *and* ignore Truth." Christian stepped forward. "It's what we all do."

"Hey!" Truth looked shocked.

"You said something about getting rid of my burden? I'm in."

"Yes, yes," Spiritualist said with a smile. "For you see, your burden —the metal prison on your back that drives you to do evil—it is the nature of this carnal and physical world in which we exist. To escape from that, you must escape this physical world and its carnal lusts."

"That makes sense," Love said.

"Not it doesn't," Truth said.

"Oh shut up, Truth." Somehow Love still made the command sound kind.

"It's very simple," Spiritualist said. "The Overseer is spirit. Thus, the spiritual is good. The physical, the source of our evil desires, is bad. Thus, spiritual is good and physical is bad."

"That seems easy to understand," Zealot said. "Therefore, I like it."

"Excellent," Spiritualist said. "Some think physically changing things will save you. You don't need to physically go through the Gateway. Progress spiritually, not physically. Remove yourself from all things physical. Then your burden will lift."

Conscience smacked Christian in the head.

"Ow!" Christian said. "Can you stop doing that?"

"No, I literally cannot," Conscience said. His tone and mannerisms back to his old self.

"Then what is it?"

"I don't know about this Spiritualist guy. Truth might be on to something. Maybe listen to her?"

Spiritualist kept talking. "Like Love was saying, it's the heart that matters. Focus on your thoughts, your mind, your feelings. Gain the necessary knowledge and sensitivity to make your mindset as close to the Overseer's as possible. Then your burden will fall away."

"That's intriguing," Christian said. "But I think Truth was trying to say something."

"Thank you," Truth said, a little annoyed.

"Who is this?" Spiritualist turned toward Truth and gave an untrusting smile.

"My name is Truth. Christian just said that. Now the issue with what you said—"

"Oh, I see. I have one of those too." Spiritualist pressed a few buttons on his remote, and a young girl, about half the size of Truth, hobbled out from the rocks. She looked remarkably similar to Truth. With a few odd differences. She was a child, without Truth's white hair. Her hair was dark, and her school uniform was cobbled together from random clothing scraps. Her movements seemed mechanical.

Truth stared at the girl with confused revulsion. "What is this?"

"This is my Truth." Spiritualist turned to the girl. "Truth, what do you think about what I've said here?" He pressed another button.

"Oh yes, it's all correct," the young girl said in a robotic voice.

"Okay." Truth's face transfigured ever so gradually into a look of abject horror. "Several things are wrong with this."

"What's wrong?" Love drifted over to the young girl. "She seems sweet to me."

"It's not my job to be sweet," Truth said. "It's my job to be correct."

"That may be what your Truth says," Spiritualist said. "My Truth says something else." He pressed more buttons and the younger Truth spoke: "Truth should be sweet to the soul. Otherwise, it's probably false. How could something be true and troubling to the spirit? Things that make you feel bad *are* probably bad. You should try to edify your heart, not fill it with negative thoughts."

"Stop!" Truth raised her voice.

Spiritualist looked at Christian with concern. "Are you going to let your Truth talk like that? You really should keep her under control and not let your Truth go imposing itself on others."

Truth stepped in front of Spiritualist. Closer than he seemed comfortable with. "Listen. You seem like a very intelligent person. So please don't be insulted if I talk slowly. But this is important and I don't want you to misunderstand a word."

She motioned to Christian. "He . . . does not . . ."—she pointed at herself—"own me."

Spiritualist blinked, confused.

"I am my own thing," Truth continued. "I am not controlled by Christian or anyone. Most of the time Christian doesn't even listen to me. He is not my master."

"What a ridiculous thought," Spiritualist said. "Everyone creates their own Truth based on their experiences and observations. I myself cobbled together my Truth from a bunch of discarded android parts. Tell me, what operating system do you run?"

He reached for Truth's hand and looked closely at her. "She's remarkably well constructed. I can't even see the mechanical fusion lines from her construction."

"I'm not an android." Truth pulled her hand away before Spiritualist could grab it.

"Yes, yes, that's what androids always say." Spiritualist gave a dismissive wave.

"I existed long before this fake Truth did," Truth said. "There is only one of me. One of us is the real Truth. Since we conflict, one of us is an impostor—obviously that one. I mean, just look at her hair."

"We will see about that," Spiritualist said. "If you are so certain of your rightness, then what's your problem with my earlier point? Spiritual is good. Physical is bad."

"The Overseer made us physical beings. The Overseer doesn't make bad things. Also, the Overseer became a physical being. You can be spiritual and believe a bunch of stuff that isn't true. But most importantly—" Truth pointed at Love to get her attention. "—Love, you need to listen to this bit." She pointed at Spiritualist. "You're just Legalist in reverse."

Spiritualist scoffed. "That's ridiculous. I am nothing like that pompous mayor. He believed that perfecting one's actions would lead to salvation—not knowing, as Love here pointed out, that the heart is what matters. Your level of spiritual development matters. Simply changing your actions does not change the heart. You must change your heart and seek spiritual enlightenment. Is that right, Truth?" He pressed another button on his remote.

"Yes, quite right. Not like Legalist at all. Spiritual enlightenment is what matters."

"No!" Truth stomped her foot. "This is Legalist all over again. You think you can achieve salvation because you pursue spiritual things *yourself*. Because of a 'truth' *you* invented. At least Legalist followed well-defined and verifiable rules. Or at least tried to."

"That's like, you know, just your opinion, man," Spiritualist said.

"It's also correct," Truth said. "And, I'm not a man. Laws, morals, science—these are absolutes. By definition. And by absolute, I mean that they are the way they are regardless of our opinions about them. As observation of something does not change or define it. It simply brings our attention to what already exists. Morals and laws do not come into existence when we think of them, and they do not cease to exist when we die. Ignorance of a law does not change its nature."

A stern metallic voice came out of nowhere. "How kind of you to mention me."

Law stepped from behind a rock and smiled, its red eyes glinting from below its wide-brimmed hat. "Greetings, everyone. It's me. How cute of you to think running would save you."

Christian bolted. Zealot and Truth followed close behind. Love followed but at a slower pace. Christian looked back as he ran, hoping Law wouldn't catch up.

"Do not worry," Spiritualist shouted after them. "It has no authority here, for I am beyond my carnal lusts and have removed all impure thoughts and desires from my soul."

Law gave a small chuckle. "You humans think making yourself good after the fact will magically remove the previous crimes you committed. You say 'Oh look at me. I killed people. But now I don't. So, I shouldn't have to pay for my many crimes.' How idiotic."

"Not according to my Truth." Spiritualist raised his remote. "Truth. Sic 'em!" He pressed a button.

Truth hobbled toward Law. Then stopped, looked at Law and said, "You are wrong."

Law walked past the android, like she didn't even exist. It loomed over Spiritualist, its red eyes gleaming.

"What can you do?" Spiritualist's voice showed a twinge of fear. "I am a luminous being, not made of this crude matter."

"Indeed?" Law drew its gun and placed it against Spiritualist's head. "Allow me to test your hypothesis." Law fired. Spiritualist's head disintegrated into red mist and Spiritualist's body crumpled to the ground. "Luminous?" Law scoffed. "No. Dust."

Law's head swiveled toward Christian. Christian turned back toward the gate and ran with all his might.

STAGE 8

HACKING INTO THE GATE

Christian and the others ran toward the Gateway. Law was fast. It would catch them soon.

"I'm so sorry," Love said. "Spiritualist's words—they sounded so nice. Hearing them felt so good."

"That's what you get for trusting your feelings and not listening to me," Truth said. "The heart can be deceiving."

"No more distractions," Zealot shouted back at them from the front of the group. "We're almost there."

Christian saw the Gateway. It was large, squarish and seemed out of place in the vast wilderness. There was no wall or fence visible for the Gateway to bridge that Christian could see. It was just a large rectangular building with a massive, closed door on one side. Beside it stood a tall watchtower. On top was a large figure behind a massive machine gun turret. Christian hoped the figure was too far away to notice their approach. At the bottom of the tower, a large barracks stood next to what looked like a giant darkened cage. Whatever was inside, Christian couldn't make out.

The glow that had led Christian there was all around them now. The radiation counter on Christian's suit, once a steady beeping, changed to a frantic fast, constant beeping. He felt the radiation seeping into his burden and nibbling at his flesh. With each step, the Gateway loomed closer, and the radiation burned hotter.

"This whole place is irradiated," Christian said. "We can't stay here for long."

"No can do," Love said. "That radiation is projected down from the Celestial Station onto the Gateway. It will only get worse, the closer we get."

"If I keep going," Christian said, "it's going to destroy my flesh."

"Well duh," Love said without malice or insult. "That's kinda the point."

Zealot slapped Christian on the back. "No worries. We'll muscle through it. Though this path is hard, though it may mean mutilation, pain, and death, if it means the removal of your burden and the vanquishing of your evil nature—well, that makes it worth it, right?"

"If possible," Christian said, "I'd like to get through this without the mutilation and death parts."

Zealot looked at Christian with a disapproving shake of his head. "Your sense of adventure needs nurturing."

Christian stepped forward, but the pain of the radiation was too much. He stepped back. "I can't do it. I'll die."

"If you stay," Zealot said, "then Law will kill you anyway. Now come on. You can do this."

Christian took two more steps forward. His suit grew hot, scalding his flesh like he was showering in molten metal. "I can't do it."

"No, you can't," Truth said. "But you don't have to."

"What?"

Truth walked to Christian and activated Book.

Christian expected another of Book's shocking displays, but she appeared alone, solemnly standing with downcast eyes, adorned as if for a funeral.

Truth pointed at the Gateway, and Christian finally saw it. Atop the Gateway stood a cross. On the cross was nailed a man. The radiation, the presence and judgment of the Overseer, was being drawn into the cross, allowing a narrow path through. The second it appeared Christian rushed forward. He felt his flesh blister from the heat. But there was a path to the Gateway now.

"Not so fast." Law stood before him. "Did you forget I'm everywhere? Your crimes have tainted your soul far too greatly to allow passage through that door."

"You're right." Christian looked up at the cross, into the eyes of the man hanging there.

"So, I reject myself. I reject my path."

"What?" Law's eyes narrowed. He seems to have not expected that response.

"All this time, I've been trying to choose my way, to defeat you with my own power, to flee from you with my own power. Or trick you with my own intelligence. Find my own way. Well, I reject my way. I reject my life. I am evil. You've shown me that. Thus, I reject myself. I choose to fulfill the true meaning of my name." Christian looked again at the cross.

Law drew its gun. "Saying that won't save you, Christian."

Love stepped between them.

Law fired. Like before, the shot reflected off Love's shield.

The shot ricocheted and struck Law between the eyes. Shocked and confused, it fell to the ground. "What is this trickery?"

"Not trickery," Love said. "It is mercy."

The glow from Law's red eyes started to fade. "I can't . . . understand. What is mercy?" Its eyes faded out. It seemed too good to be true. Law had defeated everyone in The City of Morality. Legalist, Zealot, Spiritualist. But now because of Love, Law had defeated itself.

Christian stepped over Law's corpse. Truth grabbed his arm. "Hold on," she said. "Aren't you going to loot the body?"

"Is that customary?" Christian said.

"There is some useful stuff in Law. Just take out its central processor and plug it into Conscience. It will help later. Trust me."

Christian knelt down and did as Truth suggested.

Book projected in front of his face. "Great, now stop wasting time and get through that Gate already,"

Conscience crawled onto Christian's outstretched arm and peered toward the Gateway. "Should be easy sailing from now on."

"I doubt that." Christian took three steps forward.

A flaming bullet struck his chest.

Christian groaned. "Yeah, there it is." Christian didn't feel the bullet pierce his flesh, but it hurt. Was the attack meant only to hurt?

"That's what I get for being optimistic." Conscience looked downcast.

The gunner in the machine-gun tower fired down at him. More flaming bullets struck. Some glanced off his armor. Others tore into him like the others. The creature in the tower was twisted, his skin melted. On his head were sharp horns, and within his face were black eyes, sunken into his skull, looking like black water at the bottom of a well and his mouth was adorned with huge teeth.

"Turn back," the creature yelled, still firing. Round after round struck Christian, rending armor and grazing skin. "It is too hard. Would you give up the comforts and pleasures of seeking your own way? You think this side of the Gateway is difficult? These were but a prelude to what the Dark Lands can bring to bear. Beyond, you will not have the protection of Apollyon. And all my kin shall be upon you."

Christian staggered back. Another bullet struck his suit, sending more of the flaming heat into his sinew, roasting him in pain. He fell to his knees. It felt like blood seeped from his burden. But it had to be in his head, the shots shouldn't kill him. His armor was too thick. As the pain grew, the idea of lying down and dying felt better and better.

The demonic supermutant in the tower laughed in a cosmically horrifying tone. "Have you given up now?"

Christian locked eyes with the demon in the tower, then spotted something behind it. Christian smiled. "No. Because. Uh . . . you're . . . the one who is . . . uh . . . about to be—a person who . . . has become dead. Sorry, catchphrases were never my strong suit."

The demon tilted his head in confusion. "What?"

The demon turned around and looked directly down the double barrels of a gun held by an enormous man in power armor.

"It's pronounced *nani*," Zealot said. "Not '*what*.'"

"Oh, I see," the demon said. "Thanks for the clarification."

There was an awkward pause. Then Zealot blew the demon's head off. A spray of green goo and purplish brains burst into the air and onto the irradiated ground before the Gateway.

"You're the best, Zealot," Christian yelled, tears of happiness streaming down his face.

Zealot looked to the cross. "Hardly. Maybe second best. Sorry it took so long to get into position. Stairs, you know? They're the worst."

The barracks doors flew open. A dozen more demon mutants streamed out with huge guns in hand.

"Excellent! More targets!" Zealot said, half in disgust and half in delightful anticipation. He took his pistol in both hands and fired a steady stream of rockets into the demons coming toward Christian.

"Christian," Zealot said, "get to the Gateway."

"I've been shot."

"Oh, don't be a crybaby."

More demons rushed from the barracks. Some wore power armor. A huge one stepped into Christian's path and looked down with hungry eyes.

"I can hardly move," Christian said. "I can't take this guy."

"You think the guy on the cross doesn't know that?" Zealot said. "Get up. Fight back." He was still firing at demons coming from the barracks. Demon parts flew through the air with each explosion. Yet the demons still came. They reached the base of the tower. Some started up the stairs where Zealot's onslaught of missiles couldn't reach them.

"How can you fight me?" the demon said to Christian. "You don't have a gun."

Christian pulled himself to his feet, his bones cracking, his flesh screaming. But still he pulled himself forward. "Oh yeah? Well . . . uh. So's your mother."

The mutant demon tilted his head. "What? I mean, nani?"

"I told you guys I'm not good at this."

The supermutant charged Christian.

But then, there *was* a gun was in Christian's hand. A bright silver Gauss rifle. Twice as big as the one he had before.

The demon's smile vanished. "Oh, heaven no. Where did you get that? Hacks! I call hacks."

Christian fired.

The demon moved his hand with impossible speed and caught the bullet with his fingers. A spray of green blood shot through the air. The demon roared and leapt at Christian.

Christian took a deep breath, waited for the demon to reach the apex of his jump, and shot him through the neck.

The demon landed, clutching his neck, gasping for air.

Christian ran toward the cross.

The demon grabbed him by the back of his burden. "No, you don't," the demon said, gurgling.

Christian slung his gun backward, shoved it into the demon's mouth. "Yes, I do." He blew the demon's brains out.

"That catchphrase wasn't bad," Zealot shouted over the explosions. "You're getting better!"

A half dozen more demons ran into his path. Bigger than the one he had just killed. "Turn back," they all said.

Christian raised his rifle. "Sounds like you boys needs some exercise."

Silence.

"What?" one of the demons said.

Christian looked up to Zealot, who was wrestling a demon over the machine gun turret. But they stopped and looked at him.

" . . . 'Cause it's time to exercise some demons?" Christian said.

More silence.

"Boo!" one of the demons said.

"Yeah, I fear I'm with the demons on this one," Zealot said. "That was pretty bad."

"Come, Zealot," Christian said. "You know, *exercise*. Exorcism? Demons?"

"No, I get it." Zealot tossed the demon from the tower and blew him to pieces with his rocket pistol. "I simply feel like laughing at said joke would be some sort of criminal violation."

"It was a *little* funny." Christian charged the demons before him. With each step, he felt the crunch of his bones, the snapping of his sinew. His body felt so damaged, it could not withstand the weight of his burden. But none of that mattered. He had to get to the Gateway.

Truth ran alongside him. "These demons are weak in their kneecaps. A single shot to each kneecap should incapacitate them."

"Thanks." Christian pressed a button on his rifle and it transformed into rapid fire mode. He held down the trigger and sprayed three demons' legs with eviscerating gunfire.

"Ok, I said a *single* shot, but whatever works." Truth said.

More demons charged. Christian turned his gun on them but they leapt over his shots and raised their rifles to fire.

"Love!" Christian said. "Shield me."

"On it, boss." Love soared over Christian and projected a shield that absorbed each of the demons' shots.

"I can't act fast enough." Christian turned Book on. "Book, how do I beat them?"

Book coalesced into existence. She knelt over an extremely fat guy who had his belly cut open and his guts were spilled out over the ground. She was reaching into the gore and muttered, "Dang it. I know that sword is in here somewhere."

"Can't hold 'em here forever," Love said, bullets dancing across her shield and ricocheting over the irradiated ground.

"Book. Help. A holographic sword won't help me anyway."

"Wow, you're bossy today," Book said. "Get Conscience to plug directly into your power armor with that processor you got from Law. Conscience can make you react as fast as Law could."

"What?" Conscience said in a timid tone. "I don't know how to do that."

"I'll tell you how." Book projected next to Conscience and they walked up onto Christian's back.

"Hurry it up," Love said. A few bullets pierced the shield and struck her. Her blood dripped onto her skirt and then the sand below, but still she held the shield.

Christian felt Conscience plug into his back. "Okay, how do I do this?" Conscience sounded unsure of himself.

"Plug the processor directly into the suit controls."

"That's it?" Conscience said.

"Oh, I'm sorry. Is my technobabble not obtuse enough for you? Would you rather I require you to reverse the suits quantum polarity matrix?"

"Uh . . ."

"Guys . . ." Love's voice grew worried. "Giving Christian those reflexes would be really good now." Cracks started to appear in Love's shields.

"Yeah," Truth said. "You get a reflex system that good, and you'll be able to do stuff like this." She ran toward the nearest demon.

The demon turned his gun on her. "You can't make it through. This quest is pointless." He fired twice. "We have the power here." He fired again.

"Untrue. Untrue. Untrue." Truth dodged and weaved around each flaming bullet. "Come on, you've gotta think up better lies than that." She flipped backward, kicking the demon in the face, then planted her hands while upside down and spun, kicking the gun from his hand. Then upright, she jabbed him twice in his neck.

The demon gave a croaking sound. He fell to his knees and rolled over in agony.

"Shield almost gone," Love said, another bullet striking her leg. "I can't withstand this assault anymore." She drifted toward the ground and fell in a heap.

"Love is fleeting. Despair is forever." A demon lifted a rocket launcher. "There are millions that must be saved. And you cannot save any of them. Feel the pain of your despair—the powerlessness of your insignificance. Those who love much will feel much pain." The demon fired the rocket.

An explosion enveloped Love.

"Love, no!" Christian reach toward her, a wave of heat from the explosion flooded over him.

More demons poured from the barracks. Laughing. "You do not love the Overseer," a demon said. "You love anime, and video games, and fun. You don't love—"

A rocket flew from the smoke and blew the rocketeer demon's head to pieces.

The smoke drifted away.

Zealot stood in front of Love. Behind him, the ground was untouched by the explosion. Love lay in a heap, bleeding, but alive. Zealot must have jumped from the tower and landed in the path of the rocket, just in time. He was partly on fire. The explosion had blackened his face. He glared at the demons.

The demons took a step back.

"Do ye wish to run that by me again?" Zealot lifted his pistol and twirled it like a cowboy. "You think we don't love the Overseer? Shall we show you how much we're willing to sacrifice for the man on that cross?" He pointed his pistol at one of the smaller demons.

"Wait," Truth yelled. "Don't! It's a premeditated tactical contrivance with the purpose of gaining an advantage against those with the initiative! I mean, a trap."

A millisecond before Zealot could pull the trigger, the demon dashed forward and planted his fist into one of the pistol's barrels. The explosion blew the demon's arm off, but it also knocked Zealot onto his back. The weapon was undamaged. But the explosion so close to Zealot had pushed half its force against Zealot, turning the gun into a sort of rocket.

The little demon leapt onto Zealot's chest and dug his claws into his armor. "By all means," the demon said, "prove how much you are willing to sacrifice for the man on the cross. You must prove yourself. You must kill all of us before you can continue."

"No, Zealot," Truth said. "Don't do what he says."

A demon behind Truth caught her by the hair and hoisted her up. "Little mind. You want to know the mysteries and reality of the universe? Let me show you." He vomited a stream of black light onto her face.

Horror filled Truth's eyes. "So much darkness. So much evil."

"And all true," the demon said. "Focus on this. Can't you see? You have no hope in these Dark Lands."

Now there were so many demons that Christian had lost track of which way to go. Where was the cross? All he could see were demons. "Conscience, Book, I could use that Law program any second now."

"Almost got it," Book said. "There!"

Christian rose and took an over-the-top, action-movie fighting pose.

"Aw, yeah," Conscience said. "I can see each evil act, each temptation, almost before it comes."

"It's about time," Book said. "Now stop with the talk and start with the excessive yet adaptation-accurate violence."

Time seemed to slow, and Christian could see each foe's movement a microsecond before it happened. He calculated the number of targets, readied his gun, and focused.

All eyes turned toward Christian. The rapid fire from Christian's rifle sounded like a single shot. His gun billowed plasma vapor.

A second later, every demon in front of Christian lay dead on the ground, a plasma round between each of their eyes.

Christian stared at the now defeated foes, shocked. "Uh . . . catchphrase?"

More demons charged at them from the barracks.

"Oh, come on!"

Christian looked back toward his friends.

Truth hung motionless from the hand of a demon, darkness filling her face.

Zealot was running around, shooting demon corpses. "I'll show you how much I'm willing to do." His tone was far too frantic, even for him.

Christian shot the demon holding Truth. He fell and Truth fell with him, landing like a discarded bedsheet. She shivered. "The demons . . . so powerful. The world . . . so dark."

Love stepped next to Christian and fell to one knee, bleeding profusely. "I can't move. Too much pain. I feel it all. I see it all. So many I can't help. I'm powerless."

"Don't give me that," Book said. "Love endures all things. You will endure this."

"But . . ."

"No buts. Besides, we can't use that word. This is family friendly fiction. Now get up and let's dismember all these mutant monsters and drench the ground with their blood."

Christian offered Love a hand.

Love rose and looked back and forth between Truth and Zealot. "What's their problem?"

"They've lost sight of the cross," Christian turned and fired at the charging demons from the barracks. "Let's help them out. Hurry. I don't know if I can keep these guys at bay, even with my new reflexes."

Christian and Love ran to Zealot, bullets and plasma bolts striking around them from the attacking demons. The radiation was still burning Christian's flesh, but he couldn't leave his comrades behind. Zealot continued to shoot the dead bodies of the supermutant demons.

"Zealot," Love said. "You don't need to prove yourself. You are loved, regardless of what you do."

Zealot continued firing his missiles into the dead bodies of the demons. "But I can do so much."

The new hoard of demons from the barracks grew closer.

"You do not have to prove yourself to the Overseer," Love said.

"Besides," Book said, "nothing you could do would justify yourself anyway. Don't you remember what Truth said?"

"Truth? Oh, that's right!" Zealot looked around frantically. "Where's Truth?" He found her, shivering. In the heat of the radiation, she gazed into the cold distance with eyes closed as if by invisible locks. Soul rent, mind bleeding.

"You poor thing." Zealot sounded genuinely concerned, not sarcastic or boisterous. "What did they show you?" He spoke with a tenderness beyond compassion.

"I can't . . . I can't say it," Truth said.

"Show me. Do not bear this wound alone. Show me. I will take it."

Tears streamed from Truth's eyes. "It's too evil. The truth of this world. It's too evil. It's hidden in my eyes. Engraved on my being."

"Open your eyes," Zealot said. "Let me see it."

"But I don't want to hurt you." Her tears flowed like blood from an open wound.

"Now you listen here," Zealot said. "I will endure any pain if it means saving you. We cannot go through this journey without you. Reality may be disgusting. It may be evil. But reality is reality. It cannot be ignored or abandoned, no matter how disgusting."

A different type of tear fell from her eyes. Tears of relief. Then she opened her eyes. Black light shot from them.

The black light swarmed about Zealot's head. He rose and roared, as if wrestling with it. Then the darkness coalesced into a form, a demon made of the dark realities from within Truth's eyes. Zealot grabbed it by the neck. "Pick a victim without friends next time." He snapped the demon's neck between his fingers.

Truth gasped for breath. Then cried, "I can't walk."

Zealot gently picked her up as if picking up a ship model made of crystal. "I know. I will carry you. We're not leaving you behind. At least, I'm not. I can't speak for the others. I mean, I can presume they wouldn't, but I know how you do hate it when people assume things."

Truth gave a pitiful attempt at a laugh, as if she had lost the ability to feel comedic mirth and was trying to replicate the sound based on memory.

They continued toward the Gateway, now just a few feet away. The demons had coalesced into a hoard blocking the path.

"What do we do now?" Love said.

Christian looked at Zealot.

Zealot looked at Christian.

They smirked. They raised their guns. "The same thing as before."

"Only more." Zealot grinned.

Zealot and Christian unleashed a crescendo of fire. The demons screamed and tried to charge, but each shot found its mark, each missile its prey, till all lay motionless on the ground before them.

Christian sighed in relief, his flesh broken, his pain immeasurable. His organs leaked their life essence from his body. His wounds felt fatal. He would die soon. But that didn't matter. The path to the Gateway was clear.

"Look," Zealot said, pointing. The sun shone on the wide expanse of the wilderness they had crossed, making the sand illuminate its light. The land around them looked like a sea of sparkling gold coins.

"Wow!" Truth sat up in Zealot's arms and looked out at the Dark Lands.

"Never forget," Zealot said. "The truth can be beautiful too."

Truth looked at Zealot. Zealot looked at Truth.

"Zealot," Truth said, "you're a nice guy, but you heard what Love said. We're both anthropomorphisms of philosophical concepts. It would never work out between us."

"Not all compliments are flirtations, Truth." Zealot had a twinge of annoyance, but mostly mirth, in his voice.

"Yes, they are." Truth seemed too tired to smile, but she tried. "And you can put me down now."

"Oh. Do I have to?"

"Yes."

"Of course, my lady." Zealot lifted her up and planted her onto the ground with sudden speed. His gentleness gone. Truth yelped.

"Sorry! Sorry." Zealot looked embarrassed. "I need to work on that."

They stood before the Gateway. A few more demons rushed from the barracks, but they wouldn't follow Christian and the others up to the threshold of the Gateway. They hissed and bellowed but would not approach or fire.

The Gate was rectangular and made from the same material as the cross. The Gate had no fence. In fact, one could easily walk around it. There was a door inside the Gateway, and it was closed.

Christian walked to the door and knocked.

"Yeah, what?" a voice said from inside the Gateway.

"I need entry through this Gateway. I have a burden on my back that is encouraging me to do all kinds of evil things. I don't want to be evil. I was told this Gateway could take this burden from me and lead me to the Celestial Station."

A small window in the door opened and a face appeared. "Why, yes, it can. Since you have knocked, I am contractually obligated to open this Gateway for you." The man in the door looked ancient and he wore an engineer's coveralls.

"Then it's true?" Christian said. "You can remove my burden?"

"Not me. But it can be removed. Though I warn you, it will not be pleasant."

"I did not choose this path because it was pleasant."

"Is that a fact?" the man said. "Many do. Many are disappointed."

The Gateway opened.

Christian expected the opening of the Gateway to be slow and epic. But it was quick and anticlimactic. Through the Gateway before them was a long tunnel, with several thin metallic arms hanging from the ceiling which looked like force-field projectors.

Christian and the others stepped through the doorway and it shut behind them.

The man in the engineer's clothes turned around and hobbled over to a control terminal at the side of the tunnel. "Welcome to the Gateway. I am called Goodwill. I see you have some companions with you: Zealot, Truth, and Love—all well-chosen companions. Beware their shortcomings. Only the Overseer is perfect. Faith in him should guide you. Not your companions."

"Hold on," Christian said. "Your name is Goodwill? Like the store?"

"Please, this isn't the time."

Laughing, Love said, "Maybe I should have stuck with the name Charity, then—to stay on theme."

"I guess," Zealot said, "we should name our group Salvation's Army—because that's what we are."

"Please, children," Goodwill said. "Focus."

"Yes," Christian said. "We've just been through a very epic battle, and I think we're all happy to be alive."

"Yeah, I saw that," Goodwill said. "Though your spat with Beelzebub's minions hast taken toll on body and mind, I must pray ye not tarry. The path before ye may be thrice as hard as the former."

Everyone looked at Goodwill confused. "What?"

"I pray for thine clemency." Goodwill punched a few buttons on his control panel. "Sorry about that. I've got a translator for you young kids who don't speak proper English. Who'd have thought I'd be here so long that language itself would change? Crazy stuff."

"That's fascinating," Christian said. "But can we move this along? I'm close to death and would kinda like to get this taken care of first. I'm ready to go through." He stepped toward the tunnel.

"Before you go," Goodwill said, "I should instill you with council."

Christian raised an eyebrow.

"What is wrong with this thing?" Goodwill slapped his control panel. "Advice! I mean, advice! Even past the Gateway, there are many who will deceive you—even those claiming to follow the Overseer.

Some actually do. You have chosen good companions, but that is not enough. Do you have a Book?"

Book shimmered into existence. Now she was as big as the rest of them, and instead of her usual crude and ragged clothing, she wore a long white dress. Her hair was done up in a complex braid, and she was adorned with gems. "Yes. What?"

"Oh good," Christian said to Book. "I was afraid you'd appear as some horrifying visage as usual."

Book scowled at Christian.

"What is this?" Goodwill looked Book over. "You kids, with your new-fangled techno gizmos. Back in my day Books were . . . you know . . . books. Like the kind made out of paper."

"That sounds complicated," Christian said. "How do you program a hologram on paper?"

"Hey, don't tease me." Goodwill looked closer at Book, then checked something on his control panel. "Hmm . . . well, she's a Book all right. Sometimes the enemy tries to make false copies to fool people. Always good to check."

"What is the meaning of Book's sudden sprucing up of her superficial visage?" Zealot said. Then he looked to Truth as if expecting her to be impressed. She did actually look impressed. A little.

Book smiled and gave an elaborate curtsy. "You are beginning to overcome your idiotic blindless and see me in my true form. Those who have not entered the Gate think they know me. Even with study and knowledge, I can sometimes seem vulgar or rude. Even cruel. Truth here can help you better understand. But just by entering the Gate, you should have a better understanding of my true nature. So instead of being a brain-dead dolt, you're a . . . semi-brain-dead dolt. So, I should be able to assist you more."

"Will you also be less rude?" Christian said

There was an awkward pause.

"Right? Book? You'll be less rude?"

"Book can help you," Goodwill interrupted, "but many have traveled through these lands without her."

"Travel without Book?" Love said. "That's impossible."

"It is not." Goodwill said. "Who do you think the Overseer got to program Book? Other pilgrims. And they relied on him. Book was just a useful tool. Still is. But ultimately, it's the Overseer who will get you through these Dark Lands. Don't lose sight of that." He pointed at Zealot's pistol. "You've got a nice weapon there."

"Thank you," Zealot said, beaming.

"A weapon given to you by Law, it looks like. And Law was made by the Overseer himself. All tools that we use to help us through these Dark Lands come from the Overseer. Your weapons, Book, even this facility, were all created by the man on that cross outside. Your tools are just tools. They are imperfect. Well, maybe *imperfect* is the wrong term. Incomplete. Only the Overseer is perfect."

"That seems unwise," Truth said. "Why wouldn't the Overseer give us perfect and complete tools? There's so much evil in this world. I've seen it. I wish we could have perfect tools."

"Truth," Love said. "don't question him. And don't question the Overseer. It's not your place."

"What?" Goodwill said. "Where did you get such an egg-brained idea?"

Love blinked. "Egg-brained?"

Goodwill looked back at his control panel and pressed a few buttons. "Confound this machine. Now it's going overboard with the translations."

"You're saying it's all right to question the Overseer?" Love said.

"Course it's all right. If you aren't constantly questioning what the Overseer has done or said, there's a problem. How are you supposed to know if a message or tool is from the Overseer if you aren't questioning? We see through a mirror dimly right now. At one point, we'll see face-to-face and won't have to worry. But until then, question, debate, and disagree. Take every thought captive. Examine yourself constantly to see if you're really on the right path, if you're really in the faith. These are *Dark Lands*. And it's easy as literal Hell to get lost in the dark."

"But what about my question?" Truth said. "About why we can't have perfect tools to fight evil?"

"There are a couple reasons," Goodwill said. "The Overseer could have made a Book that contained all knowledge, but we'd never be able to comprehend it. He could have made our consciences mind-control us into doing the right thing—but that'd be force. And the Overseer isn't going to force anyone to follow his path. But I think the biggest reason we don't get perfect tools is because the Overseer wants us relying on him, not just on the gifts and messages that he sends to us."

"This sermon has been inspiring," Christian said. "In no way is anyone here bored to tears, but I need to get this burden off. Now. I'm dying."

"Oh, you're dying?" Goodwill looked Christian over and didn't seem surprised. "Well, that's a good start. But try to remember what I said. You wouldn't believe how many people come through here, make a beeline for the nearest pit, and throw themselves in. Now, I'll power up the tunnel. Go on through."

Goodwill pressed a few buttons on his control panel, and the tunnel whirred to life. The arms moved about, and the force field projectors danced with electricity.

Christian walked forward. His radiation detector started beeping again. He looked at Goodwill. "If my suit is taken off when the radiation is this high, I'll die."

"Exactly," Goodwill said. "Well . . . it's complicated."

"This radiation is hard enough, even with the suit on."

"Look kid, if you want to turn back—"

"No," Christian yelled. "Burn my flesh away if you have too. Grind me to dust. Just take my evil away."

"That's the spirit." Goodwill slipped a pair of goggles on and pressed more buttons. A force field formed around Goodwill's terminal. "You folks better stand back. And Christian, remember to breath in between screams. It helps."

Christian stepped forward. Then he stopped. Or rather, his burden stopped. He kept trying to move. A force pulled him but didn't pull on the burden. He felt his body press up against the hot metal of his chest piece. Pain shot through his body. There was a sound of tearing metal. Then, with a sudden powerful lurch Christian burst forward out of the burden.

Christian felt the wires and cybertronics pop out of his back, taking bits of flesh with them. But with each gory wrench Christian felt the burden's power weaken. The desires, the thrill, the lust for evil, faded from his mind to a tiny whisper.

It was gone. Christian's burden, the prison fused to his body his whole life, was gone.

Christian continued to fly forward. And then he sailed out the other side of the Gateway into brilliant light.

STAGE 9
PYRRHA NIKOS' FOLLY

Christian flew out the end of the tunnel and hit the ground, his burden left behind. He knelt in the scalding radiation around the Gateway. His flesh melting. Was this the end? So be it.

But Christian didn't die. Which seemed wrong. He'd done evil. He deserved to die. But there Christian was—not dead.

Christian stood up and looked down at himself. From the pain, he felt that his body should be a mash of rotting bones and liquified muscles. But that wasn't what he saw. He saw a body that was strong and powerful. He sat down and stood up again—so easy without the burden. He took a few steps. He felt like he could fly. He cheered and screamed for joy. All those desires and evil natures were now, what? Not gone. He could still feel them in the back of his mind, chained. Under his control.

No, it wasn't him. It was Another.

Someone laughed at him.

Christian looked down to be sure he wasn't naked, which he wasn't. He was wearing white shorts, which he didn't remember putting on. He had Book's holoprojector around his right arm and his new Gauss rifle slung onto his back. He drew the weapon and readied it. He scanned for the source of the laughter, ready for an attack.

Two men sat in lawn chairs just to the side of the Gateway. Both wore burdens but neither seemed threatening.

Christian relaxed his guard.

"Wow!" the first man said. "That's a lot of unnecessary pain you just went through."

"Yeah," the second man said. "I can't believe you were dumb enough to go through with that."

"Who are you guys?" Christian said.

The first man looked at Christian's rifle and laughed harder. "Don't worry, silly boy. We're on the same side."

"Yeah!" the second man said. "We follow the Overseer's way. Ain't that right, False Convert?"

"Sure is, Hypocrisy."

Christian slung his rifle back onto his back. "Doesn't seem like you guys are following anyone's way right now."

"Why need to?" False Convert leaned back in his folding chair and took a long sip from a non-brand-specific beverage. "We saw you fight all those demons and go through that radiation tunnel. What a waste of time. You know, they won't bother you if you go around the Gateway."

Christian folded his arms in disbelief. "Aren't we supposed to go through the Gateway? Reject our evil nature. Give our lives to the Overseer in pursuit of his will for the forgiveness of our evil and furtherance of his kingdom. That way others might be saved and led in the true way?"

Hypocrisy laughed. "Sure, we do all that. But we didn't do it the hard way. We just went around."

"Went around?"

"You know, *around*—like the hokey pokey. Or the German invasion of France in World War II."

"Yes," Christian said, "I'm aware of the concept of circumvention."

"Woah! Let's not get into that. That's an entirely different can of worms."

Christian stared at the two slackers in confusion. "No, no. Circumvention. Not . . . never mind. How exactly do you expect to be saved from the Overseer's wrath? Wouldn't your burdens keep you from being beamed up to the Celestial Station?"

"Nope," False Convert said. "We found a workaround—a way to

be saved from total atomic annihilation, get our evil removed, *and* keep from going through that nasty tunnel."

"Really?" Christian said with distrust in his voice. "What's that?"

"It's a magic incantation," Hypocrisy said. "You just ask Jesus into your heart."

Christian activated Book. "Hey, do you know anything about asking Jesus into your heart?"

Book appeared. She was sitting at a table and before her was a plate of food. She was in the middle of using a salt shaker shaped like a woman. "Nope."

Christian shut her off. "Book says she doesn't know what you're talking about."

"What?" False Convert said. "Don't be silly. Of course, Book knows about it. In order to be saved from total atomic annihilation, you just have to ask Jesus into your heart. Say this magic prayer, and boom! You're good to go."

"Yeah? What do you think?" Hypocrisy folded his arms. "Do you think we gotta do a bunch of works to be saved from total atomic annihilation? I know that's not what Book says. Here, look." Hypocrisy picked up a holoprojector and displayed a figure onto the ground. It was small, and it did look like Book. She had pieces missing, like an empty eye socket and an arm without skin, plus her nose was gone and half of her head was bald.

The zombie Book said, "Not by works of righteousness which we have done, but according to his mercy, he saves us."

Hypocrisy shut the projector off. "See? We don't gotta do anything to get saved from the nukes. We just gotta say that magic prayer and sit here enjoying the scenery." He lifted his bottle of nonspecific liquid, clanked it with False Convert's, then took a long swig.

"What did you do to your Book?" Christian's mouth opened in horror.

Hypocrisy glanced at his Book. "What do you mean? I didn't do anything."

"She has parts missing," Christian said. "That is messed up."

"It's not messed up," Hypocrisy said. "That's scripture. If you've got a problem with it, then maybe you're not really a follower of the Overseer."

"Yeah!" False Convert said. "Sounds like you don't know anything about what it means to follow the Overseer."

"Following implies actually going somewhere," Christian said. "And that's not how Book is supposed to look. Here, look at mine." He activated his holoprojector and displayed Book in front of them. She was in the process of driving a tent peg through the head of some guy.

"Yeah, that's what mine looks like," Hypocrisy motioned towards his holoprojector. "You think my Book said something wrong?"

"No," Book said. "But you're only taking bits and pieces of me and calling it complete."

"I'm not taking bits and pieces," Hypocrisy said. "I got all the files that you got. Maybe I can only understand some of the parts, but you can't expect me to understand every line of code, can you?"

"No, but you can try," Book said.

"There's that works righteousness again," False Convert said.

Christian started to say something but was interrupted by Zealot flying through the air and slamming into the ground next to him. Zealot sprang up. "Haha! Success. Now where's my gun?"

"It's in your hand," Christian said.

Zealot looked at his right hand. It was indeed holding his gun. "Oh yes. That's right. Thank you" He looked down at himself. He wore the same white clothes Christian did.

"What joyous salvation. It makes the incalculable pain from the radiation's searing damage upon my entrails bearable. Now then, let us . . ."

Zealot's voice trailed off when he caught sight of the two men in lawn chairs.

"What's this? Enemies to be done battle with, I hope?" Zealot readied his gun.

"No," Christian put his hand on Zealot's. "Well . . . I'm not sure. Can you help me try to convince these people that they need to go through the tunnel and that just asking Jesus into their hearts won't magically save them from total atomic annihilation?"

Zealot paused. Confused. "Who would want to just say some

magic words? If someone is lazy enough to want to try an 'easy' way to be redeemed I'm not sure I could convince them. Let us not waste our time and find a worthy foe! Or an unworthy foe. I'll take either at this point. I just wish to do battle against evil."

Christian blinked. "You're turning down the opportunity to berate someone you disagree with?"

"Yes. I imagine many of us will act differently after going through that Gateway. Besides, berating them won't do any good. Look, they have no consciences."

Christian looked. Both men didn't seem to have any tiny robots on their shoulders.

"That reminds me." Christian looked around. "Conscience? Where are you?"

"Right here, boss." Conscience climbed from Christian's back onto his shoulder.

"Ah, where were you?"

"I was plugged into one of the ports on your back where your burden was fused to you. It's way easier for me to charge up now that that burden is gone. What do you need?"

Christian walked over to the two men and held out his arm. "Conscience, can you try to convince these people that what they're doing is wrong?"

Conscience climbed out onto Christian's hand and gave a small bow. "Hello."

Hypocrisy and False Convert leapt to their feet. Both drew Gauss rifles and pointed them at Conscience.

"Argh!" Hypocrisy said. "It's a conscience! Kill it. Kill it!"

False Convert pulled the trigger. His Gauss rifle jammed. He screamed in terror and then swung the weapon at Christian, but the man was so fat and clumsy that Christian easily dodged the attack.

"Those things will fill you full of guilt and depression," False Convert said. "You've gotta get rid of it."

"Yeah," Hypocrisy said. "Guilt is not what the Overseer wants." He tried to fire but his gun jammed as well, then he tried reaching for the robot but Christian hoisted Conscience above his head, out of reach.

"You're wasting your time," Zealot said in a cautioning tone. "Now where are Truth and Love? They should be along any—" He looked toward the tunnel.

Truth flew out and collided with Zealot's face, knocking him down and causing him to skid across the ground. She rebounded off of Zealot's face, flipped in the air, and stuck the landing like some sort of Olympic athlete.

Zealot rose from the ground and produced several painful exclamations.

Unlike Christian and Zealot, Truth wore her old outfit, though her hair was whiter. Her eyes seemed to be a deeper shade of blue. She looked around. "What?"

"Christian is being assaulted by large, angry fat men," Zealot said.

"I leave you two alone for ten seconds . . ." Truth muttered to herself.

Christian dodged another swipe from False Convert.

"What do you want me to do?" Truth said.

"Personally," Zealot chuckled, "I find their antics entertaining. But we should not allow ourselves to be distracted from our goal. We must away! The Celestial Station isn't going to walk into itself."

"Then we should follow the King's Highway." Truth pointed at the road that stretched out from the Gateway.

"Ok, let's do it."

Christian avoided another attack and headed toward the road with the others.

False Convert and Hypocrisy darted back to the comfort of their lawn chairs and sat, looking on with distrustful eyes.

As they walked, Love shot out of the tunnel and floated down next to them. "That was delightful! What fun. Let's do it again." She looked at Christian and the others. "Oh, my proclamation! What happened to all of you? You're all shiny now. I mean, I was always shiny, but now you are too. And your burden has been removed, Christian! We must revel in the greatness of this moment."

"We must not tarry," Zealot said. "We've got to go down the path."

"Correct," Truth said. "It's the way to the Celestial Station."

Love folded her arms and frowned. "But I wanna revel." She floated at an angle alongside Zealot. "Besides, I don't know what *tarry* means. Our purpose is not to hurry up and die. We are in relative safety near the Gateway."

Christian glanced back at Hypocrisy and False Convert. "Speak for yourself. I was just attacked by a bunch of angry fat men."

"You went to a conservative Christian publishing house?"

"What? No. It was—"

"Are we desperate to find new problems?"

"Yes," Zealot said. Love stared at him with confused disgust. Zealot looked to Truth and Christian as if for support. "Wait, is that *not* your goal?"

Love's confusion turned to concern. "Ok . . . well I'm glad you can't just summon a problem at will then if your goal is to seek them out."

"Sure I can. Watch this." Zealot cleared his throat. "With our new weapons, powers, and skills given to us by the Overseer, what could possibly stand against us?"

The ground rumbled and a noise shook the dust from the air.

Christian reached for his gun. "Oh curse. Zealot what did you do? Summon an earthquake?"

"No," Truth said. "That noise isn't the shifting of tectonic plates. It's a growl."

"Ha!" Zealot said in triumph. "I knew trope rules would dictate that if I said, 'What could possibly stand against us?' those words would summon some great evil for us to do battle with."

"Wait, how do you know that?" Truth studied Zealot's face like trying to comprehend some scientific experiment. "You aren't related to Omniscience."

"Oh please, you don't have to have metacosmic intelligence to know how tropes work."

"Metacosmic isn't a word, Zealot."

"What?" Zealot drew his pamphlet on pretentious synonyms and started leafing through it. "I could have sworn . . ."

"This isn't the time, you two," Christian said.

The shaking changed to steady, pounding notes. They grew louder and louder till the noise was as deafening as it was constant. Footsteps.

Love floated behind Zealot and looked around. "Upon further

reflection, I have been persuaded. Let's make like a lumber mill and log out."

"I concur," Truth said.

Truth, Christian, and Love started down the path.

"Oh, come on!" Zealot twirled his gun. "Let's stay and fight this evil. It'll be fun. Are we not to face evil wherever it rears its ugly head?"

Before anyone could answer, a cyclopean horror of impossible size and eldritch form slunk over the top of the Gateway and howled down at them with mind-shattering cadence. A tentacled tongue burst from its teeth and licked its lips.

"Oh French!" Christian turned and ran harder. "How could you, Zealot?"

"Oh," Truth said in realization, as if finding the answer to a difficult crossword puzzle. "That large cage that we passed coming in—this must be the creature that was kept there."

Zealot pointed his pistol at the sky-blotting monstrosity and fired missiles into its gesticulating hide.

"What the execration is that thing?" Christian said.

"It's a spiritual attack dog." Truth's tone remained devoid of fear or concern. "Sometimes they are sent after newcomers through the Gateway."

"Spiritual Attack Dog? They really gave the creature the acronym SAD?"

"I don't think that's the intended interpretation of this allegory," Truth said. "But yes."

The creature slid off the Gateway and trampled toward them in slow, yet unstoppable, steps.

Hypocrisy and False Covert cowered under their lawn chairs, but the creature paid no attention to them. It just slid right past, its many eyes locked on Christian.

Christian slid to a halt and shouldered his Gauss rifle. He couldn't leave Zealot behind. Zealot's missiles struck the creature with little effect. What good would his Gauss rifle do? Could even a hundred men with rifles slow the Spiritual Attack Dog?

"I don't know what to do." Christian turned from the monster to Truth. "It's almost on us. Any ideas?"

Truth pulled out a nail file and started filing her nails. "Nah, I got nothing."

"Just ask the Overseer for help," Love said.

Christian blinked. "We can do that?"

Love tilted her head. "Obviously. Just radio him."

"What's his channel?"

"He's the guy who made Omniscient. Just speak. He'll listen. But be careful when you hear him talk back. Make sure it's really him. Book can help with that."

"Okay." Christian looked around. "I don't have a radio transmitter."

"Try using Conscience."

"Oh." Christian grabbed Conscience and held him up to his ear like a telephone. Conscience gave a surprised squeal.

"Hello?" Christian said with an unsure tone.

"Hey, what's up?" a voice said, but it wasn't Conscience's voice.

"Uh . . . we're being attacked by a giant, tentacled kaiju dog. Can you help?"

"Yeah, ok."

"Oh. Uh, thanks."

A massive metal object fell through the clouds like a missile, leaving a trail of brilliant white. The object struck the ground and sent a shockwave through the earth a hundred times louder, stronger, and deeper than the footfalls of the Spiritual Attack Dog.

The dust settled, revealing a towering humanoid shape made of white and gold metal. It knelt in front of Love, Christian, and Truth. A hand reached out to Christian.

"How cool!" Love bounced up and down in the air, clapping her hands. "Quick. Let's get in."

"Wait. Stop." Conscience grabbed Christian by the ear who gave an annoyed cry of pain. "You can't just climb into any random spirit from the sky. What if it's a fake?"

"Oh, come on," Love said. "This came down right after Christian asked for it. It has to be from the Overseer."

The monster's growls grew louder. It snapped at Zealot's missiles. Zealot gave shouts of joy like he was having the time of his life.

"No, I agree," Truth said. "We should check."

"Let's just get inside," Love said. "Is anyone not seeing the giant unholy abomination of twisted flesh charging toward us? Do you have any idea how little time we have?"

No one answered.

"That wasn't a rhetorical question," Love said. "I actually would like to know. Time really is hard to measure in these allegories."

"Don't be such a scaredy virtue," Truth said.

Love looked angry. "I'm just saying that Zealot won't distract him for long."

"I dunno. You may be underestimating how annoying Zealot can be." Christian's remark was immediately punctuated by several explosions, screams, and bellowing growls.

"We'll work fast." Conscience tapped the holoprojector on Christian's arm. "Hey, Book, we gotta check a spirit for authenticity."

Book materialized in front of them. She appeared to be trying to put on contacts using a bottle that said *Fish Scale Brand Eyedrops*.

"All right, but you don't have to be so bossy about it. So, what's this spirit you want to . . ." Book looked at the towering figure. "Oh, fun. A mech. Yeah, give me a sec." Book projected over to the mech and started looking it over.

Zealot kept shooting at the Spiritual Attack Dog. One of its tentacles grabbed him by the leg and swung him in the air like a flyswatter. Despite this, Zealot kept firing missiles at the beast.

"You're doing great, Zealot," Christian shouted. "Keep it up." Christian smiled at Love. "See? Zealot's got us covered."

"Uh . . ." Love looked more worried. "Conscience, how long did you say that scan was going to take?"

Christian looked down and saw Book and Conscience both sat playing cards with each other.

"Hey! You're supposed to be scanning that mech!" Christian said.

"Oh, we finished a while ago," Book said. "But as I'm a philosophical personification of an inanimate object. I can't take initiative."

"Well?" Christian said. "Is the mech legit?"

"Oh no." Book played a card. "It's fake as hell. Well . . . not 'fake as hell' as Hell is, in fact, quite real."

"What?" Christian shuddered and the thundering grew closer. "Where's the real Mech then?"

"It's over there." Conscience pointed over his shoulder then played a card from his hand. "Wow, this twilight denial strategy of yours is really strong, Book."

"Thank you, Conscience. Though with all your minions still roaming, it's not exactly hard."

Christian followed Conscience's direction and noticed another Mech, right next to the first. It looked far less flashy and obvious.

"That's the real one?"

"I'm not moving on," Book said. "Your turn."

"Book!"

"What?" Book looked up from her game. "Oh, yeah. It's real. Anyway, I'll discard this card . . ."

"Then, let's go. Come on, everyone." Christian turned off Book, scooped up Conscience, and ran toward the Mech.

The Mech reached out, gently grabbed Christian, Love, and Truth, and hoisted them up. Then its chest opened and the Mech placed the three inside.

Christian found himself in a massive control room with two chairs, a half dozen display screens, and countless control panels.

Truth slipped into one of the chairs and began typing Initiating startup sequence into a console. She grabbed a communication headset from a drawer. "Love, get to the engine core. It's in a room below us. You should be able to supercharge this thing with your magic girl powers."

"I should be able to do what?" Love said.

Truth rolled her eyes. "Increase the effectiveness of our defense from spiritual attack by creating a foundation of Love, securing our identity in Christ so no spiritual evil can convince us that we have no authority over evil spirits."

"Now that's more like it." Love ran through the door at the rear of the control room.

"Ok, now what?" Christian looked over his controls.

"Let's ask Book." Truth reached for his projector.

"You don't know yourself?" Christian said.

"Just 'cause I know things doesn't mean we shouldn't consult Book."

"Ok." Christian activated his holoprojector.

Book appeared, still playing her game. "Why'd you shut me off? I was winning!"

"After stopping at site four? I doubt it," Conscience said.

Book sent Conscience a condescending glance. Then looked back at Christian. "I'll need your access code to get this thing started up."

"My access code?"

"You need to ask for spiritual assistance or the Overseer won't grant it. The Overseer will not force himself on you."

Christian sat in the central chair, looked at the controls, found the input terminal for his passcode, and entered his name.

A screen appeared saying, Initializing Holy Ghost startup.

"Holy Ghost startup," Christian said. "What's that?"

Book looked at his screen. "Oh, this thing is running on an older OS, back when this thing was called *ghost*, not *spirit*. Shouldn't matter though."

A series of complex UI popups appeared on the screens.

"I don't know what any of these screens mean," Christian said. "How do I drive this thing?"

"Of course, you don't," Book said. "It's beyond your pitiful attempt at comprehension. But the Overseer has a built-in assistance program that will give you guidance on how to operate the UI."

"The *what* is going to *what*?" Christian said.

"The Overseer will guide you. Don't be afraid of not knowing what to say or do. He will give you the words to speak."

"Oh, I understand now," Christian paused. "Uh . . . how do I do that?"

"Input the command angelicassistance.exe."

"Huh?"

"*Pray.*" Book's tone grew in annoyance.

"Why didn't you say that?"

"Because we are about to enter another contrived allegorical combat sequence and it's really hard to stay consistent with all the allegorical verbification."

"We're going to fight that thing?"

Book looked shocked. "What did you think we were going to do? Hide in here?"

Christian exchanged a glance with Truth. "Uh. No?"

Book scoffed. "We need Zealot back here to return your pitiful excuse for a spine."

"Hey, Truth." Christian leaned over toward her. "Does this thing come equipped with *chill* dispensers? I think Book could use one."

"*Christian!*" Book put her hands on her hips.

A robotic voice came from the speakers. "Enemy SAD approaching."

Truth slid over to another console. "Love—report. How's that power core coming?"

No response.

Truth sighed. "The green button on the control panel. Near the door controls. That is the com system." Truth's voice was understanding, gentle. But Christian could see annoyance in her face.

Still no response.

"Hold down the green button to talk to us," Truth said.

Love's voice came in over the intercom. "This green button?"

"No, the one next to it," Christian said with a sarcastic tone.

"Oh, okay."

There was a long pause.

"Oh, my third commandment violation," Christian said. "She fell for that. I'm so sorry. It was a joke."

"Oh dear." Truth ran to the doorway. "I'll have to walk her through it. Get that assistance program running."

"Sure." Christian typed in the command that Book had given to him.

A figure appeared on the monitor—a young man in a military uniform, with a headset on. "Celestial Station Tactical Assistance. This is Angel. How may I direct your call?"

Christian started to answer.

Angel cut him off. "Trick question. We already know what you need. An assistance program? Yeah, running those things can seem overwhelming at first. You better act quickly too. Your friend is about to get eaten by that Spiritual Attack Dog. Here, I'm downloading a User Interface directly into your brain."

"You can do that?" Christian said.

"You kidding? We could make waifus real if we wanted to."

"Wait, really?" Christian sounded a little too enthusiastic.

Angel stared at him with no emotion. "No. Prep for the UI program."

Christian felt new information in his mind, and he could now understand the displays on the control screens.

Truth appeared. "I have successfully explained the interface to Love."

"You taught her to press a button?" Christian said.

"Yes. It was harder than it sounds." Truth saw the screen. "Oh, who's this?"

"Guy named Angel."

Truth gasped. "It's an angel!"

A voice piped in over the com.

"What are you waiting for?" It was Zealot.

"Zealot!" Truth sounded relieved. "I'm happy at least you understand how to use a com system."

"Can you assist me? This tentacled tetrarch of terror seems only moderately mortified by my missiles."

"Hey, Zealot," Christian said. "Hold on. We're working on it."

"You've been working on it for many minutes. Or is it hours? Truth was right—time is quite hard to measure. No matter. I can take him."

There were more explosions followed by infernal screaming.

"Don't do anything rash," Truth said. "We are checking in with Angel to see how to operate the Mech."

"We're trying to hurry, Zealot," Christian said. "Just hold on. How do things look on your end?"

"Very, uh, stomachy."

"Zealot . . . were you eaten?"

"Only a little. Plus, from the inside I have far less chance of missing with my rocket pistol."

"He'll find a way," Truth said.

"Keep that optimism, Zealot." Christian examined a nearby control panel. "How much longer before you're digested?"

"Some assortment of seconds. Hold on. I'm going to try something."

"Uh-oh," Truth said.

An alert came onto a screen.

"We've got an object approaching at a fast speed," Truth said. "It will strike us unless we—"

Zealot struck the main window to the mech and stuck to it. He was covered in slime and was bleeding all over. He was unconscious.

"Oh no." Christian typed several commands. "Seems the SAD doesn't like the taste of missiles. We've got to get Zealot in here."

One of the mech's hands closed around Zealot and pulled him away from the main window.

Christian pressed a com button.

"Love, I'm sending Zealot directly to your chamber. He's been hurt. Can you help him?"

The response over the com was mostly static.

Truth shook her head. "Love can be so difficult when it comes to communication."

"On that note," Christian said. "I recall from the information Angel downloaded into my head that this thing has tactical nukes. Normally, in this kind of fight, we'd start with smaller, less effective weapons and work our way up to the big ones but that sounds dumb so let's nuke this thing first." He entered a command into the controls.

Nothing happened.

He tried it again. "Angel, I'm having trouble activating our tactical nukes."

"Yeah," Angel said. "Rules of engagement. You haven't been authorized. That Spiritual Attack Dog attacked Zealot. Until he gives you permission to help, you don't have the authority to engage it."

"He did ask for help," Christian said. "Earlier, he was complaining that we weren't doing anything."

Angel looked off-screen. "Stand by. Let me check if that's enough."

The Mech lurched back.

Christian checked the monitors. A massive set of tentacles wrapped around the Mech's torso. The creature latched onto the Mech's face with two enormous sets of jaws and bit into the metal.

"I'm reasonably sure this qualifies as an attack," Truth said.

Christian looked back to the monitors. Every restriction on the combat capabilities of the Mech lifted immediately.

"You've been attacked," Angel said. "Full authorization for maximum usage of all combat abilities authorized. Happy nuking! Thank you and have a nice day."

STAGE 10
ERECH

The massive arms of the Mech closed around the thrashing tendrils of the Spiritual Attack Dog. The Mech pulled on the tentacles, ripping them from the hide of the creature like pedals from a flower.

The beast roared and clamped down harder on the Mech's chest with its jaws, its acidic saliva eating into the white metal.

"It's squirming too much." Christian's hands danced across his control panel, inputting dozens of commands at once. "I can't get a solid grasp on it."

"I'll try to find its weaknesses." Truth changed the view on her screen to a technical readout of the beast. "Its form is difficult to scan, but I'll do my best."

The Mech wrestled with the beast, tearing into its flesh with its fists, but it could not break free. The beast's tentacles dug deeper into the Mech.

Truth enhanced a section of data on her screen and pondered it for several seconds. Then she sat up. "Its flesh is getting crushed in between our internal mechanisms."

The room shifted and Christian lurched back. "That's it. I'm nuking it."

"No," Truth said. "Our ability to maneuver is being compromised. We'd nuke ourselves."

Christian looked at another screen listing all the technical specifications of the Mech. "What else does this thing have . . ."

Love's voice came in over the intercom. "You've got to do a self-diagnostic. You need to understand your true nature, the true nature of this machine, and its connection to you. From that position, you can vanquish the SAD."

"Okay." Truth turned around in her chair. "I appreciate that Love has figured out how a single button on her com pad works, but I'd just like to take this opportunity to remind everyone that the Spiritual Attack Dog is not an allegory for being literally sad. That's just a random fluke of the acronym. It's a symbol for spiritual attack."

"Can you quit it with your omniscient ramblings?" Christian tumbled out of his chair from another lurch.

Love's voice piped in over the coms again. "Christian, use the authority protocol."

Christian pulled himself back up onto his control panel, trying to remember the information Angel had given him.

A tentacle squirmed through the ceiling and drooped down toward him, dripping ooze that hissed and crackled when it touched the floor, burning holes into the metal.

"It's inside the Mech," Christian yelled. "I need help here!"

"I'm on it." Truth rose from her control panel, leapt onto the back of her chair on one foot, and sprang toward the tentacle, cartwheeling through the air. She struck the tentacle aside, screamed, and fell to the floor. "It burns," Truth said, clutching her leg.

More tentacles crept into the room.

Truth tried to get up and away from the writhing fetid appendages, but her leg failed her. One wrapped around Truth, hoisted her up, and swung her at Christian like a flail, knocking him from his station again.

Christian skidded across the floor and hit the wall. "Love, Truth tried to fight the tentacles and couldn't. Now it's swinging her around like a flail."

"I know. The narrator just said that."

"The what?"

"Never mind. The enemy sometimes likes to twist Truth against us, they're actually really good at it."

Christian crawled back toward his console. He had to save Truth, but he also had to pilot the Mech. If he stopped fighting the monster, more tentacles would get in.

The tentacle swung Truth toward Christian again. Christian ducked under the blow. The smell of burning flesh mixed with Truth's screams.

Christian looked at the display screens. The monster sunk its teeth and tentacles into the Mech.

He reached for his Gauss rifle, but a hand stopped him.

"Oh, look. I have to do everything myself. As usual." Zealot stood smiling, rocket pistol in hand. Half of Zealot's flesh was burned beyond recognition. Part of his head was missing its hair and skin, revealing his skull underneath. Part of his lower lips were gone, and his muscles and sinew were visible over much of his torso. He was missing a few toes on one of his feet, and his non-gun hand was badly swollen. If not for the vibrant smile, he would have been quite terrifying.

Nope. Still terrifying.

"Oh, my salty language." Christian jumped out of his chair. "Zealot, are you okay?"

Zealot shot the tentacle holding Truth. It blew apart and Truth fell to the floor. "On the contrary," Zealot cried with delight. He shot two more tentacles. "I'm in unimaginable pain." The smile never left his half-destroyed lips. He shot indiscriminately all over the control room, hitting mostly tentacles, and only one or two control panels.

"Let's not dwell on the negative." Zealot laughed. "We've got an unspeakable horror to annihilate."

Truth freed herself from the pile of tentacles. "Zealot, you're the best. I could just kiss you if you still had all your lips."

Zealot sighed. "It's always some excuse like that with woman."

"How are you even walking?" Truth's tone was full of shock and concern.

"Love cast a protective shield over me that is binding my various limbs and organs together. Isn't that something? What will she think of next?"

Truth pulled herself toward her chair.

"I was being hyperbolic, Zealot." Truth took her seat. "You should get back to Love so she can fix you."

"Nonsense. I can't be distracted from the objective. Let's thrash this evil creature and thrust ourselves into the next adventure." Zealot gave a flourish, tripped over one of the dismembered tentacles, and fell onto his back. "I'm all right. I'm all right," Zealot said in a reassuring tone.

Love piped in over the coms. "I've established full power. Nothing is stopping you from wrecking this thing but your own fear. You have the authority. He attacked us. You have the power. You are walking within the Holy Spirit/Holy Ghost."

"Excellent!" Zealot leapt up, ran to Christian's console, and pressed a large red button labeled Fire All the Nukes.

A dozen rockets shot into the air from the Mech's back.

Christian and Truth stared at Zealot.

Zealot looked around as if confused. "What?"

"You've just targeted this spot with nukes!" Christian said. "Even I knew that was a bad idea. And I'm an idiot."

Zealot looked over at Truth.

She shrugged. "That is correct. He is an idiot."

The creature ripped out a chunk of the Mech with its teeth, leaving nothing but air between Christian and its gaping jaws. The lights flickered.

"Oh no." Christian punched a command into the keyboard.

The Mech unleashed a torrent of punches into the beast's hide at speeds so fast, each blow created a mini sonic boom that erupted across the creature's flesh.

"What's going on up there?" Love said from the coms.

"Zealot just targeted us with a nuclear strike."

"Why?"

"He's Zealot!"

"Oh, yeah. I keep forgetting."

"Twenty seconds to impact," Truth said. "We don't have time to reposition or change the direction of the missile strike."

"That means he can't dodge either." Zealot showed a triumphant smile.

"So, your plan is suicide?" Christian said.

"If you call it *martyrdom* it sounds more spiritual."

"That doesn't make us any less dead."

Zealot shook his head and gave a disapproving snicker. "That kind of thinking will never get you a sainthood."

The Mech reared back and delivered a final blow, knocking the beast far from them, tentacles billowing behind it like ribbons in a girl's hair.

Christian typed in a command, and the Mech grabbed the beast by one of the tentacles and swung it around.

"Ten seconds to impact," Truth said.

"Zealot,"—Christian's hands moved across the controls with a speed he didn't know he had—"I need you to shut up and focus on thinking up a catchy one-liner. That should keep you out of trouble."

"Finally! A task perfectly suited for my skills."

The Mech flung the entire beast into the air. The beast sailed upward. High into the stratosphere. A few seconds passed. Then there was a massive explosion that sent a shockwave of brilliant light and fire across the skies. Wreckage and gore fell and drenched the Mech in fiery waves, radiation, and eldritch viscera.

The Mech wavered but stood strong, then walked out of the ocean of atomic fire, a shield protecting the inside of the Mech from the radiation.

"You threw it into the nukes? Well done," Truth said.

"Thank you, Truth. But I was just following the protocols Angel gave me. Now Zealot,"—Christian turned in his chair—"about that one-liner?"

Zealot handed Christian a small data pad.

"Christian, we did it," Love said. "You see, with faith in the Overseer we can—"

"Hold on." Christian stared at the data pad and cleared his throat. "Is this a kill streak? Because we just got a tentakill."

Silence.

Truth stared at Zealot.

Christian stared at Zealot.

Zealot looked embarrassed. "I was on the spot and given little time. Forgive me for my lack of poetic aptitude."

Christian turned back to his control panel and went back to typing. "Zealot, go down to the Reactor Room. Let Love patch you up, and think about better catchphrases."

"Aw." Zealot looked dejected. He walked out, dragging an injured leg behind him.

———

Christian and the others exited the Holy Spirit. The Mech transformed into a rocket, then blasted into space from whence it came. Christian didn't see the Mech return to the Celestial Station. It was beyond what his eyes could see. Nor did he remember when he started using words like *whence*. Weird.

Christian and Zealot wore power suits they had found in the armory of the Holy Spirit. Zealot still looked like a ravaged husk of a human being, even after Love had healed him to the best of her ability. His new suit of power armor helped hold his body together, so Love no longer needed to use her shields to keep him from falling apart.

"That was intense! I've heard there are people who can walk around in their spirits almost all the time," Love said. "Maybe someday I'll have enough energy to do that."

"The Holy Spirit will follow us in orbit," Truth said, "ready to come to our aid when we are in need."

"At least we have obtained these glorious power suits," Zealot said. "And they have the added benefit of not instilling within us the desire to mercilessly slaughter innocent people. What a useful feature."

Christian grimaced. "Can we not talk about that?"

"I'm still worried"—Love floated closer to Zealot—"going around outside of the Holy Spirit. I feel much safer inside its protection."

"We're always under the protection of the Overseer," Truth said. "Some people don't even believe in getting inside the Holy Spirit."

"What?" Zealot said. "That's absurd. How would we have defeated that SAD if not with the help of the Holy Spirit?"

"Some people just ask the Overseer for orbital strikes. They say it's dangerous to get inside spirits, because it's too easy to be fooled by a spirit not from the Overseer."

"Well, that's just silly."

Truth raised an eyebrow. "What's so different between asking the Overseer for orbital strikes and asking for a Mech to climb inside and pilot? Both are asking for assistance from the Overseer and relying on his strength."

"Well . . ." Zealot stroked his chin. "Doesn't just asking the Overseer for help quench the spirit or something?"

Truth sent Zealot a blank stare. "You think you can limit the Overseer because you didn't ask for help the *right* way?"

"Well, I don't *know*; since you asked in such a condescending manner."

"Oh good, that was my intent. The Overseer is far more powerful than our mistakes."

"Hey, look." Love floated down between them and pointed toward the horizon. "It's Palace Beautiful, one of the few resting spots for pilgrims. This place has been here for ages."

Christian looked over the horizon and saw the minarets of a tall palace. The King's Highway headed straight toward it. As they got closer, it looked less beautiful and more dilapidated. Maybe it once was a beautiful palace with shining towers and strong parapets, bright flags and colorful banners, but now the banners were faded and the towers were crumbling.

A huge crowd of people were near the entrance.

"Look," Love said, "fellow pilgrims. Oh, thank the Overseer." She floated ahead toward the people around the entrance.

Zealot stroked his chin. "Maybe they'll have somewhere I can get some more healing. Or at least where I can grow back a couple of toes. Not that it matters. That's why the Overseer gave me extras."

Zealot and Truth walked toward the palace.

Christian could almost feel Conscience staring at him from his shoulder. "What's the problem?" Christian said.

"I don't know," Conscience said. "Isn't that scary? This is indeed a good group, one that we should pursue and hang out with. Book was telling me there's all kinds of edification you can get from fellow pilgrims."

"As Truth, Love, and Zealot have already proven."

"But something about this place gives me foreboding."

"Last time you felt that way, we ran into a blood-thirsty bounty-hunting robot that nearly killed us."

"I'm still here, by the way," Law said.

Christian nearly leapt out of his power armor.

Law stood less than a foot from Christian. Christian stumbled back and fell. Law leaned down and its glowing red eyes bored into him. Christian studied his sharp metallic smile and wondered what painful evisceration the robot had planned.

"Don't worry, little man," Law said in slow, terrifying tones. "The bounty on you has been collected. I have no authority to ice you or your friends." Law sounded disdainful. Angry. As if every line of code in its programming begged him to slaughter Christian but something held it back.

Christian's heart raced. "You've gotta stop sneaking up on people like that."

The robot's eyes glinted that same terrifying red. "No."

"You must have been why Conscience was worried." Christian rose. The feeling of not being attacked after talking with Law so long was weird. Christian didn't know if he should talk or flee. "What are you doing here, Law?"

Law gave a gentle growl. "I live here. Though some of these pilgrims try to ignore me. I'm always here."

"Do you . . . you know . . ."

"Kill them? No. There are no bounties on pilgrims."

Christian relaxed. But Law lost no intensity in his gaze. "Don't get comfortable, Christian. I exist for a reason. And even if you aren't doomed for breaking the law, there will still be"—it paused, its face full of subtle rage—"consequences. Every one of me, every Law, exists for a good reason, Christian."

Christian gave a nervous chuckle. "Is this supposed to be a helpful warning? Or an ominous threat?"

"A helpful threat. But if you want a warning, I'll say to watch out in that palace." It motioned toward Palace Beautiful. "Pilgrims usually fall into two camps—the first are folks who pretend I don't exist. You already met a couple of those on the way over here."

"Hypocrisy and False Convert?"

"Yes. Their ilk is getting more common these days. And a lot of people refuse to become pilgrims, because they think it's as hollow and vapid as the lives those two live."

"What's the other group?"

Law paused, then, somehow its tone grew more serious. "The other group is dangerous. Though, they aren't as bad as they used to be. They won't burn you at the stake, just talk about you behind your back because you read books with the word *magic* in them. Or kiss your girl-friend before you're married. Then they try to use their religious authority to *encourage* you to do things their way. Passive-aggressive-ness is their strategy and guilt is their weapon. Their heart is in the right place, but ultimately, they find trying to fix other pilgrims easier than fixing themselves."

"Which camp should I listen to?"

Law showed no change in expression. "Neither. But that doesn't mean either are devoid of value. No human is going to obey me perfectly, or even remotely perfectly. I'd like to turn all you pilgrims to ash for that. But I can't." It sounded sincerely sad. "Remember, if you could have defeated me without help, you'd have never needed the Gateway."

Christian saw death in its eyes. Yet despite its ominous presence, Law hadn't attacked him. It must have been true—Law was no threat anymore. Christian expected relief, but for some reason, Christian still felt fear.

"Well, I'll be careful." Christian turned to follow the path.

"Looks like someone needs to tell your friend that." Law motioned past Christian toward Palace Beautiful.

Christian tried to see what Law was motioning toward. To enter the courtyard, they had to pass through a gate. Presumably, the small man out front was there to greet people. Presumably, because at the moment, he was not greeting people. He was being hoisted into the air. By Zealot.

"Oh, what the billingsgate." Christian went over to Zealot.

"What do you mean I cannot get in?" Zealot said, loud enough that it seemed he intended for everyone on the continent to hear.

"Well, sir, it's your outfit," the man said in a fearful, timid voice.

"Outfit? This is power armor given by the Overseer himself. I believe it is my scarred face and my bleeding joints that bother you."

Blood leaked from the joints in Zealot's armor—quite disgusting. Probably more so for someone who hadn't been walking around with Zealot for a long time and gotten used to his antics.

"Is this not a haven for pilgrims?" Zealot said.

"Yes, but we expect a certain level of decorum," the man stared into Zealot's fist.

"I am sorry," Zealot said, "that my injuries are so offensive to you. By all means, let us only allow people who are untouched by the enemy to enter your haven. I'm sure *they* are most in need of your healing and comfort."

"Well . . . um . . . ."

"Are you hearing the sarcastic tone in my voice, tiny man?" Zealot yelled directly into the man's face. "In case it was not obvious, I'd like to establish that I was being sarcastic."

"Zealot," Love yelled from another crowd, "you can't go attacking the greeters."

"But this greeter has done violence upon my honor."

Love floated over and put a hand on Zealot's arm that was holding the greeter by the collar.

Christian approached the altercation. "Zealot, put the man down. What the bad word were you thinking?"

Everyone gasped and turned toward Christian.

He took a step backward, broadsided with embarrassment.

"You can't say *bad word*," one of the pilgrims whispered, compassion in her voice.

"Hey!" one pilgrim said. "*You* can't say *bad word*."

"I didn't say *bad word*. I was just saying—"

"You just said it again."

"Said what?"

"*Bad word*."

More gasps. "You just said it!"

"I did not!"

After that, several more shouts and accusations sounded from all around. So much so that Christian couldn't understand anyone.

After some time, the shouting died down and a tall old lady walked up to Zealot and the greeter. "What's the matter here?" The lady's voice was calm and controlled.

Christian pushed through the crowd to hear better.

"My friend here"—Love motioned towards Zealot, who still had not put the poor greeter down—"simply wishes access to your great palace. He has been through the Gateway. He gave up his life to follow the Overseer and has been inflicted with many injuries by those who would dissuade him from this path."

"We can't let him in," the greeter said from Zealot's grip. "Look at all those wounds and blood. It would get all over the carpet and tapestries. Our palace has deteriorated enough as it is."

Zealot gripped the man tighter. "Is this your minion?" Zealot said to the lady. "He wrongs me."

"I'm sorry," the lady said. "Of course, you'll be allowed entry. Allow me to introduce myself. I'm this man's Superficialvisor. His *supervisor*, if you will."

"Superficialvisor?" Love looked around. "What happened to Watchful? He used to be in charge of this place."

Superficialvisor gave an uncomfortable smile. "Oh, yes. He's still around here somewhere. But I'm managing our public image."

"I see," Love said.

"Enough of this." Zealot loomed over Superficialvisor. "Will you let us enter your sanctuary?"

"Of course. The Palace Beautiful is open to all pilgrims. We'll just need to paint over the blood stains on your armor."

Zealot narrowed his eyes. "What do you mean?"

"Just keep Palace Beautiful clean. Pretend you don't have any of your wounds, and everything will be fine. We don't want to draw attention away from the speakers. We must consider the plight of others above ourselves."

Zealot stroked his chin with his free hand. "I suppose. Will you assist in the healing of my injuries? I have suffered greatly at the hands of the enemy. Even now, I must strain myself to avoid collapse from the mind-shattering pain that envelops every sinew of my rotting flesh." He smiled as if his statement was a proclamation of triumph.

"Sure, why not?" Superficialvisor turned to another pilgrim. Apparently, their conversation was now over.

Zealot released the greeter and shouldered his way into the courtyard. He kept eyeing the greeter, whitening the poor man's face with terror.

Truth walked into the courtyard with Christian. "Zealot always has to make a scene."

"He was just eaten by a giant devil dog and then regurgitated," Christian said. "Plus, he saved your life. Show some thanks."

"I'm sorry," Truth said. "It's just that Zealot doesn't think through his actions, which gets him into a lot of trouble. Then we pay the consequences. He tries to do the right thing, but he never tries to do it with the rest of us. We could have gotten past a lot of our problems if he had just conferred with the team first."

"You should tell him that." They walked through the courtyard towards the main entrance.

"I can't tell him that. He's so . . . big."

Love floated over to them and stuck her smiling face into the conversation. "Zealot would never hurt you."

Truth raised an eyebrow.

Love looked upward as if thinking, then looked back at Truth. "Zealot would never *intentionally* hurt you."

"That sounds more accurate," Truth said.

Love didn't seem sure what to say. Then her face brightened as if remembering something. "Here's something that will cheer you up. Look!" She held up a small basket, adorned with flowers, holographic banners, and decorations. "Look at these lovely gift baskets the greeters here were handing out."

Christian looked unimpressed.

Love reached into the basket. "Here, we have some cryogenic Gauss rifle rounds for Christian."

Christian's eyes brightened.

"What is this?" Love drew a small chip from the basket. "Some sort of dust jacket program for Book." She handed the chip to Christian and he plugged it into Book's holoprojector.

Book materialized in her normal outfit, then changed to a long flowing duster. "Ooh . . . I like." She twirled, letting the long jacket flow behind her. "It doesn't change any of my programming, but it sure looks nice."

Zealot shouldered his way through the crowd back to the group. "Can you believe these trogdorites tried to deny me entrance?"

"It's pronounced *troglodytes*," Truth said.

"No . . . I'm rather sure it's *trogdorite*. Anyway, I got through. All I have to do is cover up my wounds and pretend I have no problems. I'll fit right in. Since I do that anyway, it's an easy ask."

"Are you sure that's a good idea?" Christian sounded unsure of himself.

"Why wouldn't it be? Going to this palace will fix all my problems and heal all my wounds. Why make a big deal about my problems now, since they'll be taken care of soon enough? If you'll excuse me, I'm going to see if I can load some of these cryogenic Gauss rifle rounds into my rocket pistol." Zealot laughed and limped back into the crowd. As Christian watched him go, he thought he spied a hint of blood leaking from one of the creases in Zealot's armor. Would paint really be enough?

STAGE 11
THE ISLAND'S MYSTERY BOX

C hristian crossed the courtyard to the main entrance to the palace. An old sign above the entrance said PALACE BEAUTIFUL with the words crossed out. A newer sign underneath read GRACE CHURCH OF LOVING FAITHFULNESS. Then the words blurred and changed to CHRIST'S LOVING HOPE CHAPEL OF CENTRAL LOCATIONSVILLE. The sign blurred again and changed to ST. HOLY PERSON'S CHURCH. Again, it changed, this time to FIRST DENOMINATION'S CHURCH OF VARIOUS VIRTUES, then to SECOND DENOMINATION'S CHURCH OF VARIOUS VIRTUES, finally to 387TH DENOMINATION'S CHURCH OF VARIOUS VIRTUES.

Love floated to Christian and looked at the sign. "Don't let the sign confuse you. Many rooms are within Palace Beautiful, with many different congregations. Though there are many more rooms outside it."

Truth popped over. Her face brightened. "Which one is right?"

"None of them," Love said.

"What?" Truth folded her arms and looked disappointed. "Then what's the point of being here?"

"Well, they are *less* wrong than the ones outside these walls. Much less. Palace Beautiful at least gets the basics correct. Not like False Religion."

Truth narrowed her gaze.

Love shrugged. "If you're seeking infallibility, you won't find it here. Or anywhere on this planet for that matter. This place attracts the most lost, morally bankrupt, and disgusting people. I think that's sort of the point."

"But . . . b-but . . ." Truth sputtered, not getting the words out.

"Please, Truth, not now. I want to talk with Christian. Leave us alone, but stay close. We'll probably need you soon."

"Fine. I'll go make sure Zealot isn't causing another scene." Truth marched off into the crowd.

Christian watched her go then turned to Love. "What were you saying?"

"Ah, yes. Everyone here was once lost like you. These people are the criminals, the evil, the shameful and disgusting."

"Regular people, then?"

"Aw . . . You're catching on. That's cute. You're cute. Have I mentioned that?"

"Uh . . ."

"Never mind. Don't let your guard down though. Even around fellow pilgrims. Ultimately, we should only trust the Overseer."

"Even you?"

Love blushed and looked away.

Book appeared from Christian's holoprojector. She was standing at an intersection and wore a crossing guard uniform. At one end of the intersection was the sun and Book held a large stop sign in her hand which she held up, keeping the sun in place. "The heart is deceitfully wicked above all things. Who can know it?" Book dissipated back into the projector.

Love's blush vanished and she frowned. Then gave a sigh of defeat. "Yes. Even me. It is true. Though Truth will, no doubt, regale you with the fact that I represent not just the heart but all positive emotions, feelings, desires, and needs to show and be shown love. Ultimately, those feelings, even as important and moral as *agape* love, come from the heart. That's why we should always keep Truth close."

"Because she can sense oncoming danger?"

"No, that's what Conscience is for. Truth is more able to identify danger when it is already present. Some deceptions sneak past Conscience's senses. Even Zealot's Conscience is imperfect."

Christian paused to consider Love's words. "That's what Goodwill said. Imperfect tools, so we might rely on a perfect Overseer, not on his gifts."

"Goodwill is a wise man. It is smart to listen to his council. But again, all humans are fallible."

"Sounds like the danger isn't worth the reward." Christian looked around at the other pilgrims with suspicion. "Couldn't we just avoid places like this and not risk it?"

"No," Love said, "for three reasons. First, there is much in this place that can edify and assist you. Second, it is easy to be led astray when you retreat solely into your own thinking. And third, it isn't about you. Maybe you can help others by coming here. Since this is such a large assortment of broken and hurting people, it is the perfect opportunity to show some love."

"Hey, that's your name."

"Uh-huh." Love winked at Christian.

"You need to tell Zealot that last part. If you're not careful, he's going to get into a fist fight with the first person who says anything theologically dubious."

Love gave a sudden look of fear. "Oh dear, you're right. Where is he? I should probably assist Truth to keep him from terrorizing this place." She floated just above the crowd and looked around for Zealot.

———

Christian waited for several minutes. Everyone shuffled into a large auditorium. Christian followed. He found a seat next to Love, Truth, and Zealot.

Nothing happened for a while. The crowd murmured.

Christian glanced at Zealot. Either he had stopped bleeding, or he had repainted the parts of his armor that seeped blood. Hopefully, pretending no damage existed within his armor didn't have any long-term consequences.

As Christian was pondering, a musical group got up on stage called the Vain Repetitions. They performed a few songs that sounded good —but the songs mostly repeated one or two lines over and over.

Christian shouted over the noise, "Didn't we already sing this?"

"Repetition makes it easier for everyone to sing along," Love shouted back.

"Nobody is singing along," Christian said. "The music is too loud."

"What?"

"The music! It's too loud."

"No, thank you. I've already had one."

Christian stared in confusion. "What?"

"Stop it, you two," Truth said. "This comedic bit is entirely overdone."

"What?" Love said.

"Ok, now you're doing that on purpose," Truth said.

Love gave a guilty smile.

The music stopped. Christian's ears rang, recovering from the noise.

A man walked onstage. He had a frantic face, darting eyes, and hair that looked like it was electrified. He walked to the lectern, slammed his hands down, and gripped the sides hard enough for his fingers to bleed.

"Oh, good," Love said, "a sermon. This will be most edifying for us on our journey."

"Be afraid!" the man said. "Be very afraid."

"Oh no!" Love's face filled with terror. "What do we have to be afraid about?" She looked to Truth in concern.

Truth showed no fear. She looked at the speaker with distrust, but said nothing.

The speaker pounded his hand on the lectern again. "Outside the walls of this sanctuary is . . . the world." His last words sounded like he was talking about some monster in a fireside ghost story.

Zealot scoffed. "What madness is this? Fear is for ninnies. Does this ostentatious orator think this crowd appears ninniesque?"

"Zealot," Truth sent Zealot a sideways glance, "we agreed that every time you make up a non-existent word, you're supposed to give me a dollar, remember?"

"I don't remember that," Christian said.

"It happened off-screen," Truth said.

"So, it did." Zealot reached into a compartment of his armor and removed his wallet. It was soaked in blood.

Truth looked at the blood-soaked wallet. Then at Zealot. "You know what? You can owe me. Just stop talking over the speaker."

"But he speaks of the world like it's some unspeakable evil."

"What? How can you speak of something if it's unspeakable?"

"Precisely!"

The man onstage kept talking. "My name is Fear Monger. Let me tell you, the world is full of unimaginably evil things. People will attack you. They don't like our lifestyle. They want to indoctrinate your children to be evil like them. You must be afraid of the world. Avoid it at all costs. Don't listen to their news, read their books, or watch their anime."

The crowd gasped. Someone from the back said, "Not the anime!"

"Yes!" Fear Monger said. "Even the anime. You see, the world is run by the enemy. Therefore, everything the world does is bad since the enemy is bad. And therefore, it should be avoided."

"Hold on a second," Zealot shouted.

Fear Monger turned toward Zealot with an acidic glare. Figuratively though. He didn't actually spray acid from his eyes. Though with all the crazy stuff Christian had seen in his travels, it wouldn't have been surprising.

"I'll acknowledge your interruption," Fear Monger said, "since apparently responding to hecklers has inexplicably become socially acceptable."

"Wondrous!" Zealot smiled. "Wouldn't it be horrible if people could just preach for hours on end and not be cross-examined for theological accuracy?"

There was an awkward pause. Fear Monger broke the silence. "What is your inquiry?"

"I was just wondering . . . Why should we care?" Zealot's curiosity sounded genuine.

A murmur of confusion ran through the crowd.

"Why should we care?" Fear Monger's tone rose. "The world is bigger than us, more powerful. They could burn this palace to the ground if wanted. They've tried before. Countless pilgrims have been slaughtered by Apollyon and his minions."

"It's true," Christian said. "I used to be one of those minions. I can't remember how many I've killed."

"You see?" Fear Monger said. "We must cherish and protect those who come to this citadel, especially those such as your friend, so the world does not wrench them from our counsel."

Murmurs of acknowledgment passed through the crowd. A few people placed hands on Christian and blessed him. Some said how brave he was to come to Palace Beautiful even though others might chase after him. How horrible it must have been having to come so far to reach the safety of this palace. The words of affirmation made Christian's heart swell. He who had slaughtered these people and their kind was so easily accepted, despite confessing to his evil. Such forgiveness seemed impossible.

"I am not afraid of the world," Zealot said. "The Overseer is bigger than anything the Dark Lands have to offer. If I am to die or be oppressed, which is likely if the dangers you speak of are true, then I shall be twice blessed for the opportunity to die for my Overseer and to hasten the day when I shall see him face-to-face."

More murmuring came from the crowd.

"You don't understand the power of the enemy," Fear Monger said. "People need to understand how persecuted we are by the world."

"Why?" Zealot said.

"Because that proves we are in the right. Obviously, the world will be converted to our way of thinking if they realize how much they are treating us unfairly."

"That doesn't make any sense," Truth said. "The lost are convinced by our message, not out of sympathy for our situation. If they were, then they would become like False Convert, choosing to follow the path of the Overseer simply because they don't want to be part of the group that hurts us, not because they believe our message."

Fear Monger scoffed. "How else are we supposed to convert people to follow the Overseer if not by the use of guilt trips? Do you expect us to actually go into the Dark Lands and convert the lost to our way of thinking? That's far too much work. It's far easier to complain about all the things the world does than to do anything about it. Just condemning their activity as evil should be enough."

"This seems wrong," Love said. "Are we not called to love the world? My name's Love, by the way. That's why I asked."

"Yes," Fear Monger said. "We should love the people in the world. But not the world itself."

"Certainly," Love said. "But how can we love the people of the world if we are afraid of them?"

A bell rang, indicating Fear Monger's time was up. He gathered his papers and left the stage.

"That's convenient," Christian said. "Good thing these preachers have limited time so they don't drone on and on with an unfocused speech, which belittles their message and numbs people's minds to the Overseer's teachings."

"Right," Truth said. "Can you imagine if all sermons were required to fill an arbitrary hour and a half time slot?"

"As for that Fear Monger guy," Christian said, "he's just wrong. Wanting to be afraid of non-pilgrims and avoid everything they have to offer? Should we not use any technology not invented by a pilgrim? Are we pilgrims so holy that everything we put our hand to is pure?"

Another figure walked onstage wearing a brightly colored daredevil's jersey with an open vest that revealed a chest so hairy it looked like it could deflect bullets.

"I hope this guy isn't like the last one," Truth said.

"Hello, everyone," the man said in a wildly over-the-top voice. "I am called Secularist. I couldn't disagree more with the last speaker."

"Great!" Christian said.

"We can't go locking ourselves up in this palace," Secularist said.

"Exactly," Christian said

"How are we to reach the lost if we are hiding?"

"Right! This guy gets it."

"We've got to be relatable to the lost."

"I guess. Yeah."

"So, we need to experience what they experience. Do what they do."

"Hold on."

"We're under grace after all. So, let's just do whatever the lost do, and that way they'll be more likely to hear what we have to say."

"Uh-oh . . ."

"On that note,"—Secularist drew a massive Gauss rifle—"in order to get the lost to really listen to us, let's murder some children, just to prove that we're relatable to folks who murder children."

A missile struck Secularist in his chest hair and exploded, sending him flying through the back wall.

Everyone looked at Zealot who held his pistol outstretched, smoke gushing from one of its barrels.

"What?" Zealot said. "He was obviously an imposter, attempting to persuade us to murder children. I'm not the only one who heard that right?"

"Don't be so hostile," someone said. "We don't do that here. We have to be kind to everyone."

"Oh, he'll be fine," Zealot holstered his pistol. "Did you see his chest hair?"

Murmured agreement sounded through the crowd mixed with shouts of disapproval.

A screech sounded from the hole and Secularist appeared again. The torso of Secularist, at least. The torso was connected to a mass of writhing tentacles. Tentacles that ended in mouths filled with sharp teeth.

A dozen other pilgrims drew weapons and sent a volley of shots into the beast. Zealot joined in with a stream of missiles of his own. After several seconds of sustained fire, the beast that was Secularist was nothing more than smoldering goo.

Christian stared in shock. Unsure if what he'd seen had really happened.

"It was a mutant imposter," shouted one pilgrim. "That's the third time this week."

Another pilgrim said, "This is what happens when we get too much into extremism. We've got to get back to basics. Talk about what all pilgrims agree on."

Zealot grumbled and slunk back into his chair. "If we all agree, then what's there to talk about?"

Superficialvisor walked onto the stage and talked with a few other people who looked important. Then she went to the lectern. "Clearly, we have had too many extremists proclaiming their ideologies tonight. We must find balance between these extremes."

"Yeah," Christian said, "that sounds right. Those last guys were extremists. We should be more balanced."

"In order to avoid any more theological gunfights, we'll have someone preach who is not an extremist in any way." A drumroll started. Superficialvisor's tone rose as if announcing some famed celebrity. "Everyone's favorite. You know him and love him."

Two spotlights danced across the stage. A roar came up out of the crowd with cries of anticipation.

Love squealed in delight and floated toward the ceiling, buzzing about like a horsefly with caffeine injections. "It's him. It's him!" she kept saying.

"Ladies and gentlemen . . ." Superficialvisor motioned towards the center of the stage. "Let's give a Palace Beautiful welcome to the Platitude Platypus."

The two spotlights focused on center stage and a platform rose up from the floor. The spotlights froze on the platform.

On the platform, was a platypus. The platypus wore a fine suit, specifically tailored for his semiaquatic topology. A torrent of cheers and screams of delight came from the crowd.

"What the vulgarity is that?" Christian said.

Love floated down next to Christian. "This is great. You'll really like him. His words are so encouraging." She turned to Zealot. "And elegant. You can't help but be inspired."

"Okay," Truth said, "but is he theologically accurate?"

"Is he accurate? Why there's not a false word that comes out of his bill."

The Platitude Platypus wiggled his way up to the lectern, hoisted himself up on his back haunches, and lowered the lectern down to his height. He cleared his throat and gave an odd chattering noise. "We've got to come together as a cohesive and effective embodiment of Christ."

The crowd cheered.

"We must embrace purposeful living through meaningful action."

Zealot cheered this time. "Action? I like that. This small terrifying creature understands me."

"We must live out what it means to be pilgrims. After all, are we not all the Overseer's children?"

More cheers from both Zealot and Love.

Truth seemed to be the only person not getting excited.

"If we are to be followers of Christ," the Platitude Platypus said, "are we not to follow Christ? Answer me that. Are we not?"

"Yeah," Zealot yelled. "I mean, no! They should have brought this nightmare creature up ages ago. I can see why the crowd is so taken with so wise a theologian."

"Remember,"—the Platitude Platypus raised a flipper—"only through the cross can our true redemption be made manifest in our daily walk. Love is the fuel that powers the walk of the pilgrim. Never let your engine run empty on love."

"That's me," Love said with a fan-girlish squeal. "He said my name."

"We must prioritize the facilitation of a spiritual furtherance," the Platitude Platypus said.

"What?" Truth shouted.

"Do not let the enemy conquer your mind with his lies."

"Yeah," someone yelled. "Don't believe lies. I agree with that. Who would want to believe lies?"

"Yes," Truth said, "but what does that mean?"

Zealot glared at Truth. "I would think you of all people would be against lies."

"I am. But . . . but . . ."

"Sin cannot be allowed to flourish in our lives," the Platitude Platypus shouted.

"Which sins?" Truth said. "How do we keep them from flourishing?"

"I'm certain he will get into more specifics." Zealot gave a reassuring nod.

Truth did not look reassured.

"We must respect those in spiritual authority over us," the Platitude Platypus said.

"Yeah, but what does that mean?" Truth muttered.

"With a peaceful acceptance of the Overseer's missional living, we will be able to intentionally fulfill the calling to mercy and grace that the Overseer has put on all our lives. But only after we pursue a lifestyle that is in step with the calling that the Overseer has put upon each and every one of you."

"All right, that's it." Truth walked to the aisle and started toward the exit. "I'm tired of this meaningless talk. I going to find a denomination that actually cares about me."

Zealot turned to face Truth, shock on his face. "Are you saying this is false? Are we not supposed to have peaceful pursuit of the Overseer's missional living?"

"What? No, that's not . . . ugh . . . you don't understand." She tossed her hair and stormed out with a huff.

After an awkward silence, the platypus continued. Christian wanted to run after Truth, but the platypus's words were so soothing. He wanted to stay for just a few more minutes.

Several hours later, Christian turned to Zealot. "Isn't this great? I don't know what Truth's problem was."

"Indeed." Zealot winced briefly in pain but then looked normal. "This small duck-rabbit's words are so kind, so reassuring."

Christian listened a bit longer, then grew a bit confused and leaned over to Zealot. "Do you understand what having a Christ-centered attitude means?"

"I think so," Zealot said. "It means . . . having an attitude . . . centered around Christ. You know, like thinking about Christ, in how our attitude is. Not having it focused on other, uh . . . non-Christ things." He shrugged. "I'm sorry, I am endeavoring to understand. This tiny egg-laying bear's wisdom is beyond me. Also, the searing pain of my previous injuries is making cognitive functions difficult."

Christian turned to Love. "Are you getting this?"

Love looked up from a well-accosted notepad, her hand still scrawling with frantic erraticism. "Yes, you can tell because I'm taking notes. That's the sign of a *real* pilgrim. We have to be quick. He has a lot to say." Ink flew from her pen as if from an arterial wound.

Christian looked over her shoulder at her writing. One section said *find your identity not in this world but in the identity Christ has for you.* All of the words were underlined. As if that would make their meaning more apparent.

Christian looked back toward Platypus. "He is certainly saying a lot of words."

"And that's how we know he's smart." Love looked back to her notes. "All sermons are supposed to be long. What do you think—that sin is not ended by multiplying words, but the prudent hold their tongues? That's just crazy talk."

Book appeared from Christian's holoprojector. She held a soda can in her hand called Golden Calf and seemed to be saying something. But so many Book holograms were already being projected from other pilgrims and saying various things that nobody listened to Book. In fact, no one seemed to be listening to the other Books either. They were all saying a lot. Book got annoyed and flickered back off.

Christian felt a pang of guilt. "I'm going to go see if I can find Truth."

"Are you sure?" Love said. "There are like seven more hours of this. He hasn't even gotten to the best part. I think he's going to do a section on 'Choosing to Walk in the Name of the Overseer.' That's my favorite."

"Uh-huh." Christian rose. "I'll be at the power armor recharge station if you need me."

————

Christian took a deep breath when he exited and tried to wrap his head around what the Platitude Platypus had said. No use. As he left, his memory of the sermon evaporated. What was the topic? What had he learned? Was this why Love took notes? Would that have even helped? The chamber outside the auditorium was mostly empty. Along one side of the chamber was a series of power armor charging stations. Christian walked toward them. The clank of his metal boots echoed off the walls and stained-glass windows. He plugged into the charging station and stared at the high, vaulted ceilings.

"Pretty great place, isn't it?" a voice said.

Christian looked to his right, expecting to see Law. Of course, he'd be the one to show up and bother him during a quiet moment. But instead, an older man in power armor was in the charging station next to him.

"What is? The palace?" Christian said.

"Oh, yes," the man said. "Sometimes, I just come out here, look at the largeness of the place, and contemplate how small I am in relation to the universe. Really makes you appreciate the significance of the Overseer setting up that Gateway for us. Did you know it's his own son who is nailed to that cross above the Gateway?"

"Yes, I heard Book explain that. Crazy stuff. I'm Christian, by the way."

The man shook Christian's hand. "I'm Interpreter. Though most people these days call me Pastor."

"Pastor? So, you must run this place."

"No, I'm afraid that Palace Beautiful is more in the market for speakers than pastors. But I do speak sometimes."

"Some of those speakers are crazy." Christian pointed toward the auditorium door. "You aren't one of the crazy ones, are you?"

"Sure am. Better check what I say. Could be wrong."

Christian tilted his head. "That was not the answer I was expecting."

"Always check what you hear against Book. That doesn't change when you're listening to a smart person. Only the Overseer can really be trusted. That's why it's good to listen to a lot of different folks. It's like Book always says." He activated a holoprojector on his arm.

A life-sized version of Book displayed on the floor. This one wore a zookeeper's outfit and was in front of a menagerie with several different animals, each had way too many heads. "Plans fail for lack of counsel, but with many advisors they succeed."

"How'd you get your Book to display so large?" Christian said.

"Mine mostly only appears as a small figure. She's cute but easy to ignore." Christian activated his holoprojector.

Book displayed on the floor, wearing the same outfit as the previous Book. She was larger than when Christian first met her, but still a fraction of the size of Interpreter's Book.

"What?" Book said. "You expecting me to get annoyed because you called me cute? I am cute. Get over it." She flickered back into the holoprojector.

"Is something wrong with her?" Christian said.

Interpreter laughed. "She's fine. Though I think you might be picking and choosing which parts of her code you're paying attention to. We all do it. Some people read only the parts about the Overseer's love, some only the parts about his truth or wrath, or just the history, or everything but Song of Solomon. Even when we don't try to, we often have bias." He detached from his charging station and started toward the main entrance to Palace Beautiful.

"Hey, where are you going?" Christian said.

Interpreter stopped and turned around. "What do you mean? There's lots of work to do. This place is great to recharge and edify yourself—maybe share some knowledge and teaching with others. But the road is out there. The real fight, the real pilgrimage is beyond these walls. Don't forget that." He tipped a nonexistent hat and then left.

Christian pondered Interpreter's words. Indeed, many were still back in the land of sin, facing total atomic annihilation. He would need to leave soon to help those who did not understand the gravity of their situation. Or rather the physics of their situation as atomic bombs were not powered by gravity. His thoughts were interrupted by a loud noise.

A half dozen motorcycles careened into the chamber. The riders whooped and hollered, swinging chains over their heads and leaving tire tracks across the floor.

Christian detached from his charging station and reached for his Gauss rifle. Then he stopped. One of the riders was Truth.

STAGE 12
ZUKO'S QUEST

Christian stared. Then stared again. Yes. Truth was riding the motorcycle. He couldn't believe it. Her hair was all ratted and crazy like she had purposely messed it up to get attention. Her schoolgirl uniform was replaced with black leather. She had a bunch of piercings in her ears. The other riders of various ages had dark sunglasses, long beards and obviously temporary tattoos.

"Yeah, that's right," one of the bikers yelled in thick slang. "We're here now. What are you going to do about it?"

They went circling around one of the pilgrims in the chamber, jeering and swinging chains in the air.

"You call yourself a real pilgrim?" the lead biker yelled.

"Yeah," another biker said. "You're just a lazy half-baked pilgrim who hides in your palace and preaches false doctrine."

"Yeah, false doctrine," Truth said. "That mess is straight crazy, bro."

"Straight crazy," a biker echoed.

Christian approached the circling bikers. "Hey! Leave that pilgrim alone. He hasn't done anything to you."

"We won't hurt him," the lead biker said. Christian guessed he was the lead biker as he had the longest beard.

"Yeah! Who do you think we are?" shouted another biker.

"Yeah," Truth said. "We ain't gonna ice no squares. We're the elect. You know what that means, punks? Means we're predestined to wreck face and spray mace. You know what I'm saying . . . uh . . . Ace?"

"Truth, what the four-letter word?" Christian stepped into the path of the bikers but they just went around. The other pilgrim saw how slowly the bikers were driving and ran off. The bikers diverted their attention toward Christian.

"Run off, little heretic," the lead biker yelled. "You can't resist what's irresistible."

"That's right!" Another biker did a high five while circling.

"Truth, snap out of it." Christian ran after Truth's motorcycle. "Who are these guys?"

"These are my new crew," Truth said. The sound of her atrocious attempt to emulate the biker's accent caused Christian's ears physical pain.

"They're correct. And they care about me. Unlike that Platitude Platypus. They won't let people spit false theology without spitting fire back."

"Truth be straight dope, boys," the lead biker yelled. The other bikers gave more cries of approval and some started chanting, "Truth. Truth. Truth."

Christian looked from Truth to the bikers and back. "And these people are . . . who, exactly?"

Truth dropped her accent. "I think the author is using this opportunity to criticize any agonistical theologians and isn't brave enough to call out any specific denomination as he wants to avoid controversy."

"We're the Calvinists," the lead biker said. "And we don't care who knows it."

"Oh." Truth showed a twinge of surprise. "Never mind then."

The Calvinists gave more shouts of affirmation. Truth smiled, tried to do a gang sign, and almost fell off her motorcycle.

"Do they have to be so destructive?" Christian said. "This can't be helpful for these pilgrims." He motioned to the pilgrims at the edges of the room, cowering from the bikers.

"Man, we don't care about those silly consequences," the lead Calvinist said. "Overseer be in control. So ain't nothing go down that he ain't got sorted."

"What?" Christian said.

"Yeah," Truth said, her accent returning. "Peeps be straight wicked. So, the Overseer sends his boi down to get whacked, but only for the bros he wants. Not because of any shine they got, but because the Overseer be straight merciful."

"Straight positive merciful, bro," a biker said.

Christian blinked again. "What?"

Truth kept talking, "But we ain't got no dog in the fight of choosing to turning to the Overseer 'cause he got dat sitch on rails. And since the Overseer got dat on rails and his gears don't go in reverse, dat means dat once we get clear with the Overseer, we ain't ever getting non-clear again. 'Cause salvation keeps on truckin' bros."

Christian's expression made no change. "What?"

Truth stopped her motorcycle and got out. "Look, it just makes sense. The Overseer is all-powerful, so everything he does is his will. It must be predestined."

"Okay. That does actually make a lot of sense, metaphysically, but do you have to act so—"

"Rebellious?" Truth swung a chain over her head, emulating her fellow bikers. Then she accidentally smacked herself in the face. And stopped. "Rebellion is duty in the empire of lies."

The bikers looked at her strangely.

Truth looked embarrassed. "Uh, I mean, gotta scrape when squares be shredding wack theology . . . uh . . . bro?"

The Calvinist biker gang hooted their approval. Truth smiled at the affirmation.

"What's all this?" a voice said from the entrance to the auditorium. Zealot and Love stood near the door, ready for battle.

"We were alerted by the sound of hijinks." Zealot saw Truth and shock filled his face. "Truth! What did they do to your hair? Was it this one?" He pointed at one of the bikers. "I'll hang him by his own beard."

The lead biker pulled in front of Truth and scowled at them. "You got it all wrong, lie spouter. Truth is hanging with our crew. We're the Calvinists, and we don't care who knows it."

Christian stepped next to Love and Zealot and faced the bikers. "Sounds like you care a lot that people know it."

"Quiet you," the lead biker shouted. "Calvinism rocks."

Love winced. "Oh no. Not these guys again."

"What?" One of the bikers drove up to Love, pushed forward, forcing her back. "What? What, what, what? You got a problem? Huh? Do you? Don't you like our theology? You think we're wrong? Prove me wrong. Do it, punk. I dare you. You think the Overseer ain't all-powerful? That what you think, cherry picker? Say it. Say that you don't think the Overseer is all-powerful."

Zealot stepped between the biker and Love. "Do you wish for me to disembowel this rambunctious motorman?"

"You wanna go, big chin?" The biker drew a flamethrower from a pouch on his bike. "We'll show you what we do with heretics in the Republic of Geneva."

"Wait." Truth drove her motorcycle between Zealot and the Calvinist. "Don't go burning people you disagree with. What kind of Calvinist would ever do that?"

There was an awkward silence.

Two of the bikers grabbed Christian by the arms before he could raise his Gauss rifle. They stuck flamethrower spouts to his head.

"You wish to commence with violence?" Zealot said. "That I can abide."

"Yeah," the biker leader said, "but don't forget that you started it."

"Stop," Love said. "We're all pilgrims here. There's no reason to fight."

"We don't wanna fight," the biker in front of Zealot said. "We'll do it if you start flicking lead at us."

"No one is flicking lead,'" Love said.

"Indeed," Zealot said. "My gun shoots missiles."

"No way," the lead Calvinist said. "That's sick!"

"Oh." Zealot smiled. "Then thank you. These boisterous brigands seem to appreciate the finer points of excessive firepower. Surely, we can talk out our differences."

"Sounds fly to me," said the lead Calvinist.

The Calvinists lowered their flamethrowers and released Christian.

The lead Calvinist's tone softened, "So you don't think the Overseer is all-powerful?"

"No. Obviously he's all-powerful," Love said. "But this isn't about—"

"Then predestination is the word, bois."

"Straight word." Truth revved the engine of her bike. She lost control, and the bike shot out from her, skidding across the floor. "Sorry, sorry," she said, running after the bike.

"Looky what we have here," another voice said.

Everyone turned. A half dozen men in suits, trench coats, and fedoras walked out from a side hallway. They held tommy guns, and the world seemed to turn black-and-white around them.

"Oh no," one of the bikers said. "It's the Arminians. Those boys is wack."

Zealot leaned down next to Love and whispered, which for Zealot meant everyone in the room still heard him easily. "What do these Calvinists have against people from Armenia?"

"No, no. Not Armenians. Arminians," Love said.

"Yeah," the lead Arminian said. "We're Arminians. Not the Armenians. Well, except our man Armand in da back there, who's our Arminian Armenian." He motioned toward someone in the back of the crowd. "Regardless, we ain't scared of no heretics. Any of you step out of line and our ill-tempered gun-slinging lady named Ann will take you all out." He motioned toward a lady to the side of the crowd who held two tommy guns.

"Ah," Zealot said with understanding. "So that makes her an 'armed meanie Ann.'"

Everyone stared at Zealot.

He sent back a bemused glance. "Oh, come now. Everyone saw that pun coming, right? It was a quite obvious setup."

"You have stolen the punchline of our pun," the lead Arminian said. "For this, we must kill you."

The Arminians raised their weapons.

"Oh, very well, I apologize," Zealot said.

"Oh, ok."

All the Arminians lowered their weapons.

One of the Arminians in front stepped toward the Calvinist. "You got a lot of nerve coming into our turf, Calvinists. Are you trying to violate our right to free will again? We don't take kindly to that. Hurts our feelings, you see."

"Hurts 'em real bad." Armand, the Armenian Arminian in the back slowly ran his hand across his tommy gun. "What kinda flowers you want on your grave? Tulips, I guess." This earned a chuckle from the other non-Armenian Arminians.

"You wanna dance, Arminians?" one of the Calvinists said bursting forward and thrusting a finger toward the face of the lead Arminian.

"Any time, anywhere," said the lead Arminian. "As long as it's metaphorical, 'cause we don't actually like dancing."

"It's a recipe for temptation, capische?" the armed meanie named Ann said.

"How about right now?" Truth said. "We can take some heresy spitters."

"Sounds good to me," the lead Arminian said, "'cept the weekly potluck starts in ten minutes. We don't want to miss out. That's the only time it's socially acceptable to talk to the opposite sex."

"Armies is right," one of the Calvinists said. "We can't miss out on the potluck. How are we supposed to show how holy we are without choosing not to talk to women during the one time of the week when it's okay to talk to women?"

"Yeah, I got ya," the lead Arminian said. "I don't want to be late to the potluck and miss all the good casseroles. So, we dance after the potluck. Capische?"

"Don't be late," the lead Calvinist said.

"Now you believe we have the choice to be late," Armand said. "What? You believe in free will now?"

The other Arminians laughed.

The lead Calvinist raised his flamethrower and moved toward the lead Arminian. Another biker stopped him. "Cool it, man. He ain't worth it. We'll get him later."

"Yeah," the lead biker said. "Come on, guys. Let's make like folks confronting sexual temptation and flee."

The Calvinists revved their bikes and took off toward the exit.

Truth tried to get back on her bike and follow them, but she was still having trouble. "Hang on, guys. I'll be right there."

The lead Arminian snapped his fingers, and they walked out in unison. The world where they stood returned to color.

Christian, Zealot, and Love walked in front of Truth, who was still trying to get her motorcycle started.

"Truth, what are you doing?" Love said. "Why have you joined up with those disrespectful reprobates?"

"Because they're correct. And don't . . . uh . . . talk smack about my homies like that."

"Okay, listen . . ." Christian put a hand on Truth's shoulder. "You're making a mockery of punk accents everywhere. Please stop."

"Fine." Truth returned to her normal accent of overt pretentiousness. "But you are mistaken about my new comrades. They care about me."

"They're just using you to go after people who believe things different from them," Love said. "They're doing it in a most unkindly way."

"We haven't hurt anybody," Truth said. "What we believe does matter. Plus, it's factual."

"Why does that matter?" Love said. "Why does it matter if everything we do was predestined?"

"Why does it matter?" Truth said. "It's a discussion on what is real and what isn't. Of course it matters."

"We can't know everything, Truth."

"Don't say that." Truth's face seemed to grow heated. "You know I hate it when you say that."

Love put a hand on Truth's shoulder. "I'm on your side Truth. I care about you. You're my sister."

Truth looked away, but her face grew less angry. "Yeah, well, that doesn't make you right."

Truth revved her motorcycle and took off toward the exit.

———

The weekly pilgrim's potluck was larger than Christian expected. Several long tables in the courtyard had way more food than any of them could eat. The Calvinists and Arminians were there with the other pilgrims, but they made sure to stay on opposite ends of the courtyard and eat at their own tables.

Christian was in the middle of eating his pomegranate casserole when a young lady walked up.

"Hello, miss," Christian said.

"Hello," the lady said. "Do you wanna . . . not hang out?"

"What?"

The girl ran away, giggling.

Love and Zealot walked up and sat at his table.

Zealot winked at Christian. "Conversing with the local beautiful women, are we?"

"That was the weirdest thing." Christian went back to eating his casserole. "She just asked if we wanted to not hang out. Then she ran away. Love, do you have any idea what's going on here?"

Before Love could answer, an overweight man in a police officer's uniform walked up. "What's going on here? We can't have women and men sitting at the same table. Look around you."

Christian and Zealot looked around. It was true. Every table either had all men or all women. Even the Arminians and Calvinists had segregated.

"Is there a rule that women and men can't sit together?" Christian said.

"No, that'd be legalistic," the man said. "But you still shouldn't do it."

"Who are you who demands such authority?" Zealot said.

"I'm called Officer Courtship. You should sit with your own kind. If you go hanging around women too much, who knows what could happen?"

"Friendship?" Christian said. "Edification? Maybe romance?"

"Or sex!" Courtship said. "That's how it works, you know. Stand around women too long, and sex happens."

"What? No. That's not how . . ." Christian turned to Love. "That isn't how sex works, is it?"

"No," Love said.

"What's this?" Officer Courtship pulled a whistle from his pocket for a long blast. "Are you talking about sex with the opposite sex?"

"Technically, I'm just a feminine representation of the virtue of—"

"Now listen here . . ." Officer Courtship produced a chalkboard with a graph out of seemingly nowhere. Courtship pointed at the graph—"You have the orthodox." He pointed higher—"The unorthodox." He pointed at the top of the graph—"And the most unorthodox." He paused for effect. "You are in the *most* territory. Most, I say."

Zealot turned to Christian. "Ortho . . . ducks?"

"Like an orthodontist for ducks?"

"Does he know ducks don't have teeth?"

"Maybe he means cartoon ducks. Those often have teeth."

"Oh yes. Quite terrifying."

"You said it, Zealot."

Officer Courtship groaned and stamped his foot. "No, no, no! What I mean is its dangerous! Spending too much time with the opposite sex."

Christian stared at officer courtship. "I think Zealot and I won't die if we have lunch with our friend Love."

"But you are not guarding her heart."

Zealot rose. "Guarding her heart? From what? Are we under attack?" He drew his pistol. "Don't worry, Love. Before they get to you, they'll have to walk over my already decaying and blood-leeched corpse."

"Yeah, me too." Christian echoed Zealot's motions. Then paused. "Wait, what?"

"You don't understand," Officer Courtship yelled. "You go giving your heart away, and it will cause irreversible damage. Whenever you spend time with someone of the opposite sex, you give a piece of your heart away."

Christian scoffed. "How can spending time with someone be giving my heart away? And even if it did, I have a big Overseer. Nothing is irreversible. Now beat it. You're scaring my friend here. If we aren't careful, he's going to open fire on the chili station."

"It could be a heart attacker in disguise." Zealot aimed his pistol at the end of the table where a large pot of chili stood. "Officer Courtship said to guard our hearts. Well, the cardiovascular buildup from such food would be quite a threat to our hearts."

"What? No, that's not what I mean by guarding your heart."

"Well, you should." Zealot twirled his pistol. "Have you seen how overweight everyone in this palace is? I'd say they need to guard their hearts."

Officer Courtship scoffed and hobbled off. "We'll see what Superficialvisor has to say about this. Most unorthodox, I say. Most!"

Christian watched the officer leave. Then shook his head. "What's his problem?"

"Oh, he's just been upset recently," Love said. "He used to be a lot more popular and have more influence. But so few people have been getting married. Because of him, a lot of people don't listen anymore."

Conscience jabbed Christian in the cheek. "Psst. Hey, Christian."

Christian ignored him. "Does he want people of the opposite sex not to spend time alone with each other?"

"Sometimes. Other times he demands relationships be organized by parents."

"Won't that just lead to plummeting marriage rates and immaturity in romantic relationships and thus numerous post-marriage problems?"

"Yes," Love said.

Christian waited for Love to elaborate but she didn't.

Conscience pestered Christian again but he was too busy eating.

Zealot pointed toward the Calvinists. "It would seem that a thing is about to . . . go down, as the kids say these days."

Christian looked up. The Calvinist leader walked toward the Arminians. "Yo! Armeanies. Let's dance, bois."

The Arminian leader approached the Calvinist. "We accept your challenge." He turned to face the crowd. "We'll be having the fight in the usual place. Everyone who wants to watch may attend."

The two leaders eyed each other and walked back to their sides of the courtyard.

"Well," Love said, "this is the nicest gang war I've ever seen. That's to be commended."

"We must observe this contest of violence," Zealot said.

Conscience poked Christian again. "We gotta go."

"Huh?" Christian jolted as if being freed from a trance. "Oh, right. We got work to do. The lost need saving. Impending atomic doom and all that."

"Quite right," Zealot looked thoughtful, then his expression returned to his usual energized frenzy. "But we should watch this fight first."

"We need to support Truth," Love said. "We can't leave her behind."

Christian shifted his weight. "I suppose."

Conscience looked at him with concern in his tiny eyes, as if some major mistake had just been made.

STAGE 13
CALVIN BALL

"Welcome," the announcer shouted, "to the four hundredth meeting between the Calvinists and the Arminians." The fans in the stadium roared. It had taken Christian and the others almost an hour to find seats. The stadium was the biggest Christian had ever seen. It seemed designed to hold every single pilgrim on earth. The dome above covered the sky, completely enclosing the stadium, and the stands stretched for miles.

"This seems a most organized commencement of violence," Zealot said with distrust in his voice. "It seems amiss."

The Calvinists and Arminians walked onto the field. Various pilgrims in the stands whooped, hollered, and booed. Truth stood among the Calvinists. The two leaders of the respective gangs walked up to each other and shook hands.

"Hold a minute," Zealot said in disappointment. "This is not a fight. It's a sporting event."

A figure in a ref's uniform walked up and said something to the two captains. After flipping a coin, he addressed the crowd. "The Calvinists have elected to receive."

The Calvinists and Arminians lined up across from each other and one player from each team approached the other.

The lead Calvinist reached into his coat and pulled out a holo-projector.

"John 6:44, I choose you!" The lead Calvinist threw the holoprojector onto the field. An image of Book appeared. She stood there on the field, looking confused. She looked normal except that her hair seemed to be made up of several small goats.

The Arminian leader scoffed, then shouted, "Go Psalm 119," and threw another holoprojector, which fell near the other one. Another Book image appeared identical to the first.

The two looked at each other. "Oh, hello," said the first Book.

"Hello yourself," said the second Book.

Nothing happened.

"Fight!" the Calvinist and Arminian said in unison.

The two Books looked at each other then back at their respective sides. "Why?" They both said.

The Calvinist leader walked up to his holodisplay and shoved it toward the Arminian's. The Books bumped into the other. "Oh. Excuse me," said the first Book.

"Oh, it's ok," said the second Book with extreme politeness. "I love your dust jacket."

"Oh, thank you. I just got it. And I love all your maps. They're very pretty."

The crowd booed.

The Calvinist and the Arminians pressed buttons on their holoprojectors. The Books' expressions changed from cordiality to rage.

"Looks like we got a strong showing from each team today," an announcer said over the speaker.

The first Book projection dove forward and smacked the other Book in the face.

"Ooh! The Calvinists open with a strong reference to John 6:44 and 45."

The other Book grabbed the first's arm and twisted it then started punching the other Book with her free hand.

"But look at that. The Arminians counter with a flurry of blows from Psalm 119. Look! Verse 30, 111, and a devastating final shot from 173."

"John 6:44," the Calvinist shouted. "Return!" His hand glowed with magnetic energy, the holoprojector flew back and he caught it midair.

The lead Calvinist grabbed another holoprojector from his belt and threw it. "Go, Romans 9:15."

The crowd roared.

The announcer continued his play-by-play commentary. "Now the Calvinists are falling back to their old standby, Romans 9:15 to 18, staving off the Arminian blows. But what's this?"

The Arminian threw another holoprojector onto the field.

"The Arminians are using their fundamentals as well, switching to Ezekiel 18:23. Now a shot from Ezekiel 33:11."

Zealot's distrust changed to excitement, and he cheered the Books wrestling on the field.

"This just feels wrong," Love said. "Theological discussions shouldn't be wrestling matches."

The Calvinist looked angry and shouted something at the ref, which Christian couldn't hear.

The announcer said, "Looks like the Calvinists are accusing the Arminians of overly focusing on Old Testament verses. Seems they think that is a penalty for some reason. But wait, the Arminians came back with a reference to Hebrews 6:4 to 6 and 1 John 2:2. Now the Calvinists are recovering with another blow from John 6:44 and 65. Absolutely devastating. Ah, but the Arminians are saying that verse reference ignores the context of verses 29, 35, and also 40. And they're saying it was offsides. Oh, my potty language. A massive hit from a John 15:16. I don't see the Arminians overcoming that one."

Christian looked around. "What's the deal with this announcer?"

"I don't know," Love said.

The crowd roared. One of the Books had the other in a headlock.

Zealot cheered.

"Zealot, how could you?" Love glared at Zealot, who looked confused.

"Easily. This is fun."

"It's barbaric, making Book fight herself."

"I'm cheering for Truth's side to win." Zealot looked back to the field. "Yes! That's it, Book. Uppercut!"

Love huffed in disapproval.

Conscience poked Christian. "Hey, I think Love has a point. This doesn't feel right. Book shouldn't be fighting herself."

Christian looked down at Conscience. "You think one of those aren't the real Book?"

"I don't think so. It might be worse. Did you see how they pressed those buttons? They're making Book fight herself."

"Precisely!" Zealot said. "I wonder who will win. Book or Book?"

"Zealot, the Books are all using the same operating system," Love said. "Neither one will win."

Christian looked at the announcer's box. The windows were tinted too dark to see inside. "Meaning this will keep going until . . . when?"

The crowd roared again. Louder this time.

Zealot's glee turned to concern.

Love gave Zealot an I-told-you-so look in return.

Conscience poked Christian again.

Christian swatted at Conscience. "Hey, quit it."

"Christian, if they can start making Book do whatever they want . . ."

Christian looked around the stands. "Oh no."

The crowd's energy was now out of control. Dozens of fights had broken out. Holoprojections of Book appeared everywhere, attacking one another. Some people were coming to blows.

Zealot's face grew serious. "It's like . . . It's like . . ."

"Like how things were back in the land of sin." Love's expression echoed Zealot's concern. "I've seen this before. Long ago a man named Inquisition came. Encouraged people to fix errors in others instead of themselves. Split palaces all across the Dark Lands. We didn't expect it. No one expected it."

"But hold on," Zealot said. "I have heard of others who split palaces. What about the man named Reformation. Did he not reveal demons who infiltrated the palaces? Or when Secularist tried to infiltrate. We rightly fought him off. Do you wish for us to avoid conflict like what Superficialvisor wanted?"

"No," Love said. "But not all conflict is useful."

"So, some conflict can be good and some can be bad?" Zealot sounded perplexed by the idea. "How can we tell the difference?"

Christian considered that. "Truth is on one side here. So, this must be an important conflict. Right?"

"Truth takes sides in literally every conflict, Christian," Love said. "Whether it's the path to salvation from atomic doom or proper grammar."

Zealot and Christian shared a glance. Zealot shrugged. "She does often correct my grammar."

"And would you fight a fellow pilgrim over such a thing?" Love said.

"Well, yes. Fighting is fun."

"No!" Love stamped her foot. "We shouldn't fight over things so trivial unless it's done in a kindly way."

"And this isn't kindly?"

The crowd roared as one of the Books roundhouse kicked the other across the stadium.

"I see your point," Zealot said. "This *may* be something not justifying such violence. But how are we to know?"

Love snapped her fingers and sparkled. "I have a plan. Christian, Zealot, get into the announcer booth. Get him to tone down the vitriol, see how he responds. I shall confront those on the field."

Zealot smiled. "Confronting the announcer. Sounds confrontational. I'm in. Come, Christian. Let us see what danger lurks in that mysterious announcer's box."

"You make it sound like some epic adventure."

"To follow the Overseer is the most epic of adventures. Now forth with us." Zealot headed down the aisle to the steps leading to the announcer's box. His progression was slow, having to step over spectators. Thus, the inspirational nature of his statement lost most of its luster.

Christian stumbled after Zealot. He paused, doubt in his heart. He looked back at Love. "You're sure you can get to the bottom of this?"

Love floated into the air then flew down toward the field and looked back at Christian with a smile. "Leave it to me. As long as they listen to me, then this won't go too far."

"And if they don't?"

Love continued floating down toward the field.

Christian cupped his hands over his mouth and shouted, "Love, what happens if they don't listen to you?"

"Just keep your weapons loaded," Love shouted back. "It will be fine."

The sound of violence continued to rise.

———

When Love reached the field, the two Books were strangling each other, hatred in their eyes. She landed onto the holographic projections of the two battling Book images.

The images dissipated.

"Stop this mockery of reason." Love faced off against the two groups. Truth stepped out from the crowd of Calvinists.

"Love," Truth said, "what are you doing here?" She caught herself. "Uh . . . I mean, what you on about, punk? Quit hogging the limelight. Make tracks or get flacks."

"You have forgotten what it is to be a pilgrim," Love shouted above the din. "You have forgotten about me. Love. You tear into one another with the ferocity of predators, not with the kindness of brothers and sisters."

"Hey, beat it, floaty," said the referee.

Love ignored him.

"Why you wanna ice our debate, doll?" the Arminian leader said. "We just trying to figure out who's right. Be good pilgrims, capische?"

"I want you to be *loving* pilgrims," Love said. "You should be both. What does it matter which of you is right?"

Truth pushed her way past the other Calvinists. "Of course it matters."

"But is it worth tearing this place apart?" Love pointed at the stands. Arguments and fights raged amongst the spectators, filling the stadium with a cacophony of noise. "Look what's happening."

"Right and wrong matter," Truth said. "Right and wrong are worth fighting for, no matter the cost."

"This is a discussion on nonimportant metaphysical concepts that are beyond human understanding. You're talking about the very nature of the cosmos. Whether it's predestined or if we have free will, it is a question too large for us to answer."

"Try me," Truth said. "If we work hard enough. we can understand all mysteries and all knowledge."

"Even if you do," Love said, "what is it worth if it means rejection of me?"

After a moment, all of the Book holograms popped into existence, one after another. All took turns speaking: "Nothing. Zilch. Nada. None. Nothing."

One Book said to the other, "You already said *nothing*."

"No, I didn't say *nothing*," the other Book said.

"Who said *nothing*?"

"No one. We all said something."

"One of us said *nothing*."

All the little Books formed a circle and argued with one another about the proper usage of the word *nothing*.

One of the Books stepped forward and raised her hands. "Ladies, please. The correct term is 'void of cosmic essence.'"

The other Books stared at her.

"Who is this lunatic?" one Book said. "The Message?"

"No. No," the Book said with a friendly smile. "I'm the Passion Translation."

The other Books gasped. "Kill it with fire!" they all shouted. The Books swarmed over to the Passion Translation and started beating her with sticks.

Confused by the whole sequence of events, Truth turned back to Love. "See? Now that's an issue worth getting contentious about."

———

Christian and Zealot reached the announcer's box. They tried the door. Locked.

"Allow me." Zealot ripped the handle off the door. "Oops." He tried again, but the door still wouldn't budge.

"This guy has a lot of locks on his door," Christian said. "Why?"

———

Love watched the little holographic Books pelt the Passion Translation with holographic stones. As they did, the Passion Translation shifted and twisted into a holographic monster. The other Books kept up their assault, resulting in an epic, though tiny, battle whose description would damage the pacing of this scene.

Love resisted the urge to laugh at the visage of all the tiny angry holograms then turned back to Truth. "Like I was saying, if this were a discussion on the nature of sin, the divinity of Christ, or the requirements for salvation, this divisiveness would be justified. But look, everyone is using Books, and you all agree on the fundamentals."

"How can we be sure?" Truth said. "They could be secret imposters like Secularist was."

Love rolled her eyes. "That's Fear Monger's way of thinking." She pointed at the Calvinist leader. "You, Calvinist. Do you believe in God the Father, Creator of heaven and earth and the Holy Spirit? Is the Lord Jesus Christ the Son of God, who was crucified for our sins and rose again? Do you believe that only through Christ can we be saved and all scripture is inspired by God?"

"Woah, sis," Truth said before Calvinist could answer. "This is an allegory. You have to stick with all the allegorical terminology. Say the Overseer, not 'God.'"

Love rolled her eyes. "Truth, this isn't time for you to flaunt your semi-omniscience."

"For the last time," Truth said, "something can't be a semi *and* an omni."

"This is important," Love said. "Truly, I don't want to confuse people with the allegorical terms."

"You said you wouldn't call me Truly, *Charity*." Truth put extra emphasis on the last word.

"Fine. I'm sorry. I'm trying to make a point here." She pointed at the lead Calvinist. "Do you agree with my last statement?" Then she pointed at the lead Arminian. "And you. Do you believe the same?"

The Calvinist stroked his beard. "I dunno nothing about no allegories."

"No, I mean the statements about God. I mean, the Overseer."

"Yes," the Calvinist said. "But—"

"Hey, stop it. You agree. Now, Arminian. What about you?"

The Arminian leader crossed his arms and scowled. "Yes, I agree. But there's a lot more to the Overseer than just that. This Calvin boy thinks the Overseer forces us to do evil. Says we don't choose anything cause the universe is all preset and stuff. That ain't capische. Capische?"

"I ain't never say the Overseer forces us to do evil," the Calvinist said.

Love stepped between them. "Stop it!"

"Hey, you can't stop them from discussing theology." The referee walked up to Love. "That's an important part of being a pilgrim. Also, it's a five-yard penalty."

Love glanced at the ref for a brief moment. She turned back toward Truth. "If your goal is to combat, degrade, or show how spiritual you are through debate, then your discussions are counter-productive. These kinds of discussions should have the goal of edifying, not the goal of . . ." She paused for a closer look at the referee. He was wearing a large ball cap that covered his face. She hadn't actually seen his face during the whole conversation.

———

Zealot fired a half dozen missiles into the door. Its few remaining components blew apart.

"Have you never heard of subtlety?" Christian walked through the doorway.

"Subtlety? No. Is it a good technique for knocking down doors? I assure you I am already skilled at that." Zealot followed Christian across the door's subatomic dust and looked into the announcer's box.

At first, the smoke from the explosions clouded Christian's eyes. He waved the smoke away to get a better look. Demonic writing and occult sigils covered every inch of the room. At the controls sat a disfigured, snarling demon.

The demon twisted its head around and peered at Zealot and

Christian. "Hello," the demon said in the announcer's voice. "I know this looks bad. But let me assure you, it is much worse than it appears." The voice was so natural, so exuberant and wholesome.

Christian wondered if it would be less terrifying if some guttural snarl had come from the demon's maw instead of the natural-sounding voice.

Everyone looked at the speaker attached to the control panel which controlled what everyone in the stadium heard.

They all dove for it.

———

The referee leapt at Love. Before she could fly, he slammed into her and forced her down and pinned her to the ground. His claws flashed and sparks flew from Love's shields. The talons froze, just micrometers from her flesh. "That's enough talking for you." He closed his fists around her throat. "Those shields can protect you from a lot, but can you breathe when your windpipe is crushed?"

Love gasped for air. She looked for Truth, the Calvinists, anyone. They were all around her, but they didn't seem to notice the ref's true form.

"I know what you're thinking," the referee said. "You're wondering why your friends won't help. I'm afraid they're far too busy fighting among themselves to see your need."

Love felt pressure on her chest from the referee's knees digging into her and the lack of air. She tried to speak.

"What's that?" The referee put a hand to his ear in mockery. "I won't get away with this? Don't make me laugh. My work here is already complete. You can't hear them, but I can. Let me show you. Listen to how much you've failed. They were too busy listening to that absurd Platypus to recognize our plan." He put a hand over Love's face, and dark light flooded her ears. She heard the crowd, their arguments, their words, their thoughts.

———

"I'm a better pilgrim than you, because I don't date."

"Oh yeah? I'm a better pilgrim than you, because I don't kiss."

"Oh yeah? I'm better, because I read my Book every day."

"Oh yeah? I pray every day."

"Oh yeah? I don't play *Dungeons and Dragons*."

"Oh yeah? I don't play video games."

"I don't watch R-rated movies."

"I don't watch movies, period."

"Oh yeah? I'm more spiritual than you, because I don't judge people for what they watch or play. I love everyone equally."

"Yeah? I'm not a glutton who eats too much at potlucks."

"Yes, you are."

"Fair enough. We all are. But I don't spread gossip. That makes me more spiritual."

"I've never had sex. That makes me the most spiritual."

"I've never even had romantic feelings. That makes me maximum spiritual."

"I was a pilgrim all my life. So there."

"I wasn't a pilgrim all my life. I repented from some *real* sins, not *little* sins like you've got."

"I'm poor. So there."

"I give money to the poor. So there."

"Oh, thank you."

"You're welcome. But I'm more spiritual than you, because I don't get caught up in pointless theological debates."

"I homeschool my children."

"That's nothing. I eat only certain foods. That makes me more spiritual."

"Yeah? I tell the lost about their impending doom, so that makes me more spiritual."

"I write overly pop-cultural-referencing sci-fi allegory novels, so I'm the most spiritual!"

"Nobody thinks that's spiritual, David."

"Aw . . ."

The voices grew faster and louder till Love could hardly comprehend them all.

The referee whispered into Love's ear.

Her vision started to fade.

"You see?" The ref said. "They use good and bad teaching alike, to oppress, to justify, to show off. They do not pursue the path. They hide in these palaces, so fearful that they think they must separate themselves from everything, even one another, for fear of being corrupted. Their faith in the Overseer's power to protect is laughable. You have no power here, little heart." He continued squeezing Love's neck.

With no air, Love felt her shields waver.

A whine sounded from the stadium speakers.

"Hello?" Christian's voice boomed over the speakers. "Is this thing on? Wow! That was close. He almost destroyed the controls before we could stop him."

A sound of infernal screeching could be heard in the background.

"Uh, listen," Christian yelped and a crash sounded. "I don't want people to panic but—"

More scuffling noises, gunfire, and screeches sounded.

Zealot's voice broke in. "Come now, Christian. You're doing it all wrong. Allow me. Ahem . . ."

Another cacophony of explosions.

"Panic! Everyone, panic. Demons have infiltrated this stadium. They have tried to set us against one another through vitriolic theological debates with no end or resolution. The announcer is an unspeakable writhing horror that defies description. Just look at how indescribable he is. I can't even begin to properly describe him. For all that is good and holy you must—" The referee drew a communication device from his pocket and pressed a button. Zealot's voice cut out.

"That's enough of that." The referee turned back to Love and smiled through rotting teeth. "A bit longer and our illusion might have been—"

A kick sent the referee flying backward. He turned end-over-end and slid across the field. Truth stepped over Love and struck a fighting pose. Her leather jacker fell to the ground, showing her old schoolgirl's uniform. "Stay away from my sister."

The ref's uniform melted away, revealing a body of powerful muscles and sharp protruding spikes. Several long fleshy tendrils jutted out of his head like hair. He took a fighting stance as well.

One of the Calvinists stepped next to Truth and pointed his flamethrower at the demon. "Dumb move, sucker. We got you outnumbered."

"Outnumbered?" The referee laughed, his voice twisted a tone no natural creature could make. "No one can outnumber me. For I am Dogmatism, and Dogmatism always has allies." His tendrils lashed out and stuck into the nearest pilgrim.

The pilgrim's demeanor changed, his eyes glazed over and his skin faded to match the color of Dogmatism's.

More tendrils sprouted from Dogmatism with incredible speed, grabbing and changing more pilgrims.

The pilgrims shambled toward Love and Truth, muttering. "You're a heretic. Apostates must be purged. Shun the nonbeliever. Shun—" More tendrils sprouted from the newly corrupted pilgrims, seeking out uncorrupted flesh. Pilgrim after pilgrim joined Dogmatism's web.

Love raised her hands to project a shield. "Over here. I'll shield us."

A half dozen Calvinists and Arminians leapt to Love's side and the protection of her shield. The tendrils slammed against the barrier.

Love took a deep breath and tried to rally her strength. The shield crackled and the tendrils slammed into it again and again.

"Well," the Calvinist leader said, "I never thought I'd die fighting *with* an Arminian."

"What about dying next to a friend?" one of the Arminians said, shouldering his tommy gun.

"No, don't be ridiculous," the Calvinists said. "But next to a fellow *Lord of the Rings* fan. Now *that* I could do."

The barrier weakened. "Well, we have to start somewhere," Love said.

The shield dissipated for a second.

"We can't just wait here." Truth started at the writhing tentacles. "We have to confront Dogmatism."

"I agree." Love turned to the other pilgrims within her shield. "All right, everyone. Listen, I'm going to drop this shield."

"What? We'll be Dogmafied," a Calvinist said.

"We'll be what?" an Arminian said.

"Dogmafied?" another Arminian said. "I think it's the process by which one is turned into a dog."

"No, it's not that," Truth said.

"Focus," Love said. "Don't be afraid. I'm altering my shields so they'll be around each of you individually. The tendrils shouldn't be able to corrupt you, but you've got to remove all hateful thoughts. Dogmatism will try to make you hate one another. He will do his best to fill your heads with hate and a desire to correct even the most trivial of theological points in hopes it will fill you with more rage. You've got to love through it. Or we don't leave the stadium alive."

"Those are our buddies out there, doll," Armand, the Armenian Arminian said. "We can't go icing 'em."

"Right. Attack the tendrils, not the people themselves. The people aren't your enemies, just Dogmatism. But aim carefully. You don't want to destroy Truth either. That would be . . . very bad."

"That ain't going to be easy," the lead Armininan said. "We've got tommy guns and flamethrowers, which aren't very precise weapons."

"Do your best," Love said. "Now as for Dogmatism himself—"

More tentacles slammed against the shield. Love strained against the force.

Truth put a hand on Love's shoulder.

Love looked back and saw Truth, her old complexion back, staring at the masses of tentacles.

"Get me to Dogmatism," Truth said. "If I close the distance, I can take him down."

"Are you sure?" Love looked concerned. "He's like you. He isn't using lies to do this like Gnostic, False Religion or a demon. He's using real actual teachings like Worldly Wiseman did. Only many of his teachings are actually correct. You could be the easiest to corrupt."

"That's why I'll beat him." Truth's eyes blazed with energy. "You can't defeat him, Love. He was specifically trained to fight you. I have to take him."

The shield started to crack.

"Party is about to start." The lead Calvinist issued a small stream of fire from his flamethrower in preparation of the shattering shield.

"Trust me," Truth said. "Dogmatism doesn't really understand me. He just thinks he does. That will be his downfall. I'll need a holoprojector with Book on it. Anybody got—"

All the Calvinists and Arminians offered projectors.

Truth smiled and took one. "These are my people."

Truth readied to strike. The shield shattered, and the tentacles swarmed in.

Bullets flew, and flames spouted.

STAGE 14

MERRY ST. BARTHOLOMEW'S EVE, MR. PINCHER

The mass of tentacles stretched out from the center of the stadium. Each tendril grabbed a pilgrim, infected them, and then more tentacles spouted from the pilgrim, reaching out for more prey.

Christian pulled away from the broken window. The announcer's body still smoldered from Zealot's missiles. "Great work, Zealot. Now let's get back on the speaker and—"

Zealot fired missile after missile into the remains of the announcer. "Die, foul fiend of fiendish foulness." Several missiles struck the control panels. Zealot ceased fire.

Christian stared at the control panels in disbelief. "Zealot, you destroyed our only way to communicate with the stadium."

Zealot matched Christian's glare and fired one more missile at the announcer's remains. "Oops?"

"We've got to warn them. They may have not heard our first message." Christian surveyed the controls, desperate to find anything functional. Then he paused. "Wait . . . the Holy Spirit." Christian activated the radio transmitter on his arm. "Some sort of tentacle beast is possessing a bunch of pilgrims. We need your help."

"Yeah, ok." the voice on the radio said.

Something huge hit the ceiling of the stadium.

Christian looked up and saw a massive dent. "Oh no. The stadium ceiling is keeping the Spirit out."

"How strange," Zealot said. "The Holy Spirit will not force its way in. As if each pilgrim is ignoring the Overseer's guidance and is basing their debate on their own logic, reason, and self-created ideology and that self-centered devotion has been allegorically manifested in this domed ceiling keeping the Mech from coming and assisting us."

Christian blinked. "Since when did you take to allegorical fourth wall breaking in an omniscient tone?"

"Oh, I was just guessing." Zealot twirled his pistol in his hand. "No omniscience here. Not that I know of, at least. Which I assume would be part of omniscience. I don't know, I've never met the man."

Christian turned back to his radio. "We have a ceiling that looks like it can prevent the Mech from getting to us forever."

"Confirm. Commencing conviction protocol," the voice said. "This may take a while."

Something struck the ceiling again. Then again and again. But still the Mech did not break through.

The tentacles worked their way up the stands toward the announcer's box.

"Commencing with 'shooting them' protocol." Zealot took a firing position and opened a window.

"Hurry up!" Christian yelled into the radio.

"Forcible conviction not possible," came the response.

The tentacles reached the announcer's box. Each sprouted from a corrupted pilgrim. "They're at point blank range!" Zealot bellowed. "Excellent! Even I cannot miss." Zealot fired two streams of missiles at the advancing tentacles. Pilgrims flew back from the explosions. Pieces of infernal sinew flew through the air and splashed onto the remaining glass windows and other pilgrims.

"Stop it." Christian grabbed Zealot's arm. "Look what you're doing."

"I'm shooting the enemy." Zealot looked confused by Christian's revulsion.

"No, look. Those aren't monsters you are shooting at. Those are fellow pilgrims who have been led astray by the enemy's trickery."

Zealot followed Christian's gaze. Many pilgrims writhed on the ground, burned from the missile explosions. "I'm trying to hit only the tentacles."

"But the splash damage is still hurting pilgrims. Since the tentacles are fused with the pilgrims, you're hitting both."

Zealot paused, uncertainty on his face. "How am I to assault the enemy without harming our comrades?"

One of the tentacles reached through the door to the announcer's box.

Christian shot it. "I don't know. Aim?"

"Of course. Brilliant!"

The pounding on the dome continued.

Christian scanned the field for the source of the tentacles. Several tentacles were reaching up from the field and sliding across the dome above them. "What the . . . They're strengthening the ceiling. Closing everyone off from the Holy Spirit Mechs."

"The Holy Spirit will not force itself into the heart of one who chooses not to listen," the voice from Christian's radio said.

"Of course." Zealot stroked his chin and looked thoughtful. "That's what Legalist did. But without our mechanized muscle how are we to do battle with these writhing wretches?"

"I don't know. But those are excellent band names."

"Ah, so they are."

The tentacles reached the window and slithered through. Each one had a mouth on the end that snapped at Zealot and Christian.

"Any ideas?" Christian fired at the tentacles.

"One." Zealot reached into his belt and produced a handful of cryogenic rounds. The ones given to them when they first entered Palace Beautiful. "Never got a chance to test these properly. Seems an ideal opportunity." He slammed the rounds into his rocket pistol.

Christian dove backward, away from the snapping jaws and Zealot's field of fire.

A bolt of white energy shot from Zealot's gun. It struck the tentacles and enveloped them, then coalesced into a giant block of ice. He turned and did the same to the door, stopping the tentacles intrusion.

"These cryogenic rounds are wondrous. That's the power of gift bags I suppose. Now we'll just—"

A tentacle grabbed Zealot's hand. He'd missed one. He considered the gestating barb. "Oh no," Zealot said in an even tone. The tentacle burrowed into his suit. He fell to his knees.

Christian ran forward. "Zealot! No, you have to fight it."

Zealot's eyes glossed over and gained a purple tint. "No, they wouldn't help me."

Christian shot the tentacle attached to Zealot's hand.

A tendril broke off farther down, reattached to Zealot, and thickened. It plunged deeper into his armor.

"None of the pilgrims would help me." Zealot hobbled forward. "They hide in their palaces, doing no work. I've fought demons, robots, and giant mutant sloths. I've saved people from death and damnation. What have they done? Even now, I bleed, and they do nothing. I'm not good enough for them."

Blood seeped from the cracks in Zealot's armor. Seeped from where his armor had been painted. The tentacles enveloped him and wiped away the paint, revealing the blood.

Zealot stared at Christian with purple eyes. "No, they're not good enough for me."

Christian shook Zealot by the shoulders. "Snap out of it, Zealot."

"They're so self-righteous. They think I'm disgusting, because I bleed from my wounds. They make me cover my wounds. And you,"— Zealot shoved Christian back, knocking him onto the ground "—you're one of them now. You're lazy. Grown soft. You think I . . . that I . . ." a tentacle sprouted from his armor and turned toward Christian. Zealot winced and grabbed the tentacle, pulling it back. "No, you're my friend. We've been through the Dark Lands together. We've been through so much they don't acknowledge. They judge us. Revile us. They—"

"They're us, Zealot."

Zealot paused, and for a moment, his eyes cleared.

"Everyone one of them,"—Christian rose and faced his old friend— "with all their evil and shortcomings. They're no better than us. We're all evil."

"You think that justifies it?" Zealot shambled over toward Christian and swung his arms up to grasp him.

Christian dodged away. The announcer's box was small, with little room to escape. He couldn't avoid Zealot for long. More tentacles sprouted from Zealot's suit and sprang toward Christian. Christian raised his rifle and fired at the tentacles, taking a step back with every shot. "No, don't give in, Zealot."

"Do you think excuses will save you from the Overseer's wrath? Now that we've passed through the Gateway, do you think we can revert to our evil ways?"

"I don't." Christian pointed his rifle at Zealot's chest, tears in his eyes.

Zealot raised his pistol. "All heretics . . . must burn."

————

The tentacles slunk through the broken shield. Instead of standing still, Truth, Love, and the other pilgrims burst forth with a blaze of fire and a torrent of gunshots. Fire sprayed out into the masses from the Calvinist's flamethrowers. Arminian tommy guns shot laser bullets through the jungle of snapping jaws. The tentacles shrieked and fell back before the onslaught.

"Watch where you aim," Love yelled. "Don't hit the other pilgrims."

Truth dashed past the others, ducking and weaving through the writhing tentacles like a dancer on a crowded floor. Each time a tentacle reached for her, she struck it aside. Her reflexes too strong and her speed too fast for the clumsy tendrils.

She found her target.

Dogmatism stood near the stands, the tendrils all flowing from the back of his head. He looked over his shoulder at Truth and smiled, a shimmer reflecting off his rotten teeth. "Oh look. The little mind. You think I've said something untrue? Try me."

Truth took a deep breath. "Though the voracity of your words is an important question. It is not the core issue here." The words seemed to make her mouth bleed.

"What?" Anger rose in Dogmatism's voice. "Don't be ridiculous. Is not the purpose of religion to know what we should do and say? How can you ignore the very foundation of what it means to be a pilgrim?" He dove at her.

She leapt backward, backflipped, and landed on the bleacher railing. "You're wrong. Law showed me that to follow a path of moralistic living is impossible. And while we should pursue that goal, we must never forget the ultimate futility of our efforts. You are like Legalism, but with a pilgrim's veneer."

A tentacle caught Truth off guard and pressed her into the stadium ground. Dogmatism loomed over her, darkness radiating from his twisted eyes. "Do you think Law will save you? He has no place here. All my victims are pilgrims. No bounties on their heads. Law will not help you. That's the beauty of my Dogmatismic shackles. Without the solidity of the law, each pilgrim can craft a set of morals that suits them so they may look down on others. There's a little of you in every one of their shackles. A little Truth." Dogmatism tightened his grip. "Which is what you are. A little girl powerless to stop me. But still useful to my ends. I must thank you for participating in this competition." His tentacle wrapped around her neck and squeezed. Dogmatism's eyes flashed with purple light again. "I couldn't have done it without your help."

Truth grabbed the tentacle and smiled. Dogmatism took a step back. She ripped the tentacle in half, freeing herself, then leapt toward Dogmatism. Truth slammed her fist into his face. A concussive wave erupted from her fist, shaking the stadium and sending Dogmatism into the air.

Dogmatism hit the turf and sent a shockwave through the field, knocking the Calvinists and Arminians to the ground. Truth leapt over the shockwave and alighted on the ground with dainty agility.

"I may be little"—Truth strode forward retaining her fighting stance. Energy crackled across her body and made her hair ripple behind her like a flag—"but I'm at least correct. You aren't."

A dozen more tentacles sprouted from the back of Dogmatism's head and shot toward her. "What have I said that's wrong? Which teaching? Which doctrine?"

Truth spun and kicked with a speed so fast a sonic boom erupted from her foot, sending the tentacles away before the kick even connected. "Wrong? No. Incomplete—which is no different than a lie."

She leapt at Dogmatism and slammed her hand into his neck. Then again. And again. Each blow sent a micro sonic boom across her knuckles on impact, reverberating across his skin and into his throat. His eyes bulged, and his arms went to his neck, trying to block Truth's attack.

Truth struck again.

This time, Dogmatism grabbed her hand mid-strike. He reached for her other hand. "To do wrong is wrong. To do good is good. What else is there? How can that be incomplete?"

Truth pulled out of his reach and activated the holoprojector. "Theology is true. But so is Love." She hit a button.

Book appeared. She was setting up some sort of castle defense board game. Book looked up from her game and glanced around at the chaos. "Hey," she said. "I see you people are getting into trouble as usual."

Dogmatism squeezed Truth's wrist, then threw her to the turf.

Truth, face half-pressed into the dirt, looked up. "Book, say the thing."

"Fine." Book stood from her game and cleared her throat. "There is now therefore no condemnation for those who are in Christ Jesus." Book blurred and changed to a different outfit. "All things are permissible for me, but not everything is beneficial. All things are lawful for me, but I will not be dominated by anything."

"But are we not to persuade?" Dogmatism swung Truth in an arc and slammed her into the ground again.

Truth spat blood.

Dogmatism lifted her, then slammed her into the turf once more. "To turn others to the light?" The impact sent a sound of cracked bones through the air. "Is this entire allegory not an attempt to point the finger at others?"

"Conviction is the job of the Overseer." Truth coughed up blood. "But you wish not to build up or convict. You build yourself up by tearing others down. And this allegory attacks ideas, not individuals."

Dogmatism put his foot on Truth's neck. "Face it, little mind. As long as you exist, so will I. As long as things are true, people will stand against truth. Shall heresy not be resisted?" He kicked Truth in the chest, and the air burst from her lungs.

Gasping for breath, Truth's words sounded weak. "No person can fulfill all truth. That is the point of the law. And even if they could,"—she swung her leg to kick the back of Dogmatism's knees and sent him sprawling onto the field, then flipped up onto her feet—"even if they could, if they had not Love . . ."

Light shone from the hologram, and Dogmatism covered his eyes.

Truth's hand shot into Dogmatism's chest and returned with a pulsating heart. "Then you are nothing." She crushed the heart in her hand.

Dogmatism fell to the stadium ground, and his tentacles went limp.

Truth looked down at the still-writhing corpse. "The problem with you is"—Truth panted—"you're too heartless."

The writhing stopped.

Several Calvinists and Armininans started lightly clapping. Armand said "Now dats a good one-liner."

Book looked at Truth with concern. "Wasn't that a little violent?"

"Like you're one to talk." Truth snickered, then collapsed.

The Book hologram shrugged and vanished into the holoprojector.

The tentacles broke off from the pilgrims, and when they did, the pilgrims stopped their zombiesque mannerisms, their glares replaced with confusion.

Still lying on the turf, Truth grabbed the device Dogmatism has used to control the stadium speakers. She pressed a few buttons and then spoke into it. "It's all right, everyone. You're safe now. Seems the enemy was trying to set us against one another."

Confused murmurs echoed through the crowd.

Truth looked at Love. "They don't understand?"

Love helped Truth to her feet and took the device. "We must come together, pilgrims. Though we may disagree, we must do so in the love of Christ."

More confused murmuring.

Another voice cut in over the intercom—Fear Monger. "Yes, agreed.

Your fear and hatred are misplaced. The sinful world is out to oppress. The sin and evil of your fellow pilgrims is nothing compared to the sin and evil of outsiders. We must band together. Hide from the sinful world so it may never influence us again."

This gained a cry of agreement from the crowd.

Truth smacked her face with her palm. "What the gratuitous vulgarity!"

"Don't listen to him," Love said. "Fear is not the answer. Dogmatism managed to turn us against one another because we were too afraid to leave Palace Beautiful. Our fear of the outside led us to believe it had infiltrated our sanctum."

"Nonsense," Fear Monger said. "We must fight all things the world has to offer, lest they corrupt us as Dogmatism did. Remember, Christ is weak, and the world is strong. We must make up for this difference by our own vigilance."

"What? No." Love sounded exasperated. "Zealot! Christian! Get down here. Fear Monger is trying to make everyone lazy again."

Truth and Love looked up at the announcer's box.

Christian burst from the window, riding on a large block of ice. He skidded down a stairway to the field, then slid over to Truth and Love. Inside the block of ice was Zealot.

"Hey, girls," Christian said. "Did you take care of all those tentacles? Nice! Good job."

"Thank you," Love said. "It was mostly Truth." Love looked at the block of ice, then at Christian. "Uh, why is Zealot frozen in ice?"

"I've heard of icing people," the lead Arminian said, "but this is ridiculous."

"He got infected."

"So, you *froze* him?" Love sounded shocked. "How?"

"Those cryogenic rounds they were handing out in the gift baskets. Great stuff."

"Oh, I see." Truth said with admiration. "The cryogenic rounds from the gift basket represent the friendly culture of modern pilgrim groups which, while often leading to vapid timidity also can ensure the fire of contentious dissentient be quelled in a gentle manner to prevent division."

Christian stared at Truth. "Uh . . . yes . . ."

Christian stepped off the block of ice and glanced around the stadium. "So . . . how have your calamities been?"

Truth hobbled to her feet, wincing in pain. "Fear Monger is back to his old tricks. He's trying to turn the pilgrims into cowards again. We need Zealot."

"He's gonna need awhile to thaw out."

Truth grabbed a Calvinist flamethrower and fired a stream of flame at the block of ice.

Christian yelped and jumped away. "Or we could do that."

Zealot rose from the melting ice, his tentacles still sprouted from the joints and cracks in his armor. He shambled toward Truth.

"Why would you do that?" Zealot groaned. "You know the plight I have been inflicted with. Yet you burn me like I am an expendable sack of putrid flesh?" He loomed over her, hatred in his eyes.

Truth slapped him in the face.

Zealot spun and stepped back, the force putting confusion and wonder on his face.

"Quit it, Zealot. We don't have time for your bellyaching. We need your help."

Zealot blinked, and his demeanor changed. Purple oozing tentacles dripped out of the pores in his skin, and he rubbed his head as if awakening from a trance. The tentacles in his armor fell away. "Right. Very well, my lady. What is required of me?"

"Wait . . ." Christian said. "That's it? He's cured? That was easy."

"Yeah." Truth looked bemused. "That feels anti-climactic given all the narrative buildup for this subplot."

Love shrugged. "People tend to have less time to attack one another when they're busy helping one another."

Fear Monger's voice came through the speakers again. "We pilgrims are the light to the dark world."

Zealot looked around, bewildered. "What? He seems to have the right idea."

"Therefore," Fear Monger continued, "we must hide from the world, lest that light be corrupted by the world as this fiend has tried now. We must double our efforts to cut ourselves off from the world's culture, society, and fellowship. Our light must be preserved."

Zealot's eyes seemed to change to a form which seemed more akin to a type that would shoot fire. He grabbed the com device out of Truth's hand. "Cease your heresy you atrocious apostate."

Love touched his arm. "Zealot, please don't be so—"

"Do you have such little faith in the Overseer to think the power of darkness can overcome the power of light? What is the point of staying in the safety of our palace if we can't confront the Dark Lands and try to lead people away from their impending atomic doom?"

"Hey now," said the lead Calvinist. "Technically, we don't save people from atomic doom. Only the Overseer does the—"

"Oh, shut up. I said lead not save." Zealot snapped at the lead Calvinist.

"I agree, we must fight against the Dark Lands to defend ourselves from their attacks," Fear Monger said over the intercom.

Zealot scoffed. "Ridiculous, our job is not to lighten our load by keeping the world from oppressing us. Let them revile us. Let them hate, defame, and kill us. Is our mission to have an easy life or to be pilgrims? These are the *Dark Lands*. What did you think? That going through the Gateway would lead to a life of pleasure and laziness? We are sluggards. All of us, sitting around, thinking of ways we are better than others, better than the world—only so we can feel better about ourselves."

"But we are better," Fear Monger said. "We are the redeemed. The world is full of sin, evil, and crime."

"If not for the grace of the Overseer, we would be too. If you think the Overseer's grace is so weak that the world can conquer it, then you are poor pilgrims." Zealot turned to address each section of the stadium. "I will not continue to stagnate in this festering white-washed tomb while my brothers and sisters live under the threat of total atomic annihilation. Now who is with me? I shall venture forth from this place and confront evil where it lurks."

"You cannot leave Palace Beautiful," Fear Monger said. "What of the edification and fellowship of fellow pilgrims?"

"We are the palace." Zealot motioned toward Christian, the Calvinists, and the Arminians. "Wherever we go, Palace Beautiful shall be there as well."

"But edification," Fear Monger cried.

Truth took the headset from Zealot. "Edification? Your Platitude Platypus is rich in words but poor in edification. When you aren't listening to that egg-laying mosaic rambler, you are turning on one another with loveless assaults on mostly meaningless topics."

Zealot took the intercom. "Yes, Palace Beautiful is a useful haven for pilgrims. Now I fear that too often it's a trap—a trap better than the City of Morality. Edification is good. Fellowship is good. Palace Beautiful is good. But you should not seek edification at the expense of our work as pilgrims. To reach the lost. You hate and fear the lost instead of engaging them. That makes you worse than the Land of Sin where there are few readings of Books or donning of Holy Spirits to guide and protect. Here, with all your wisdom and holiness, you do as much to save the lost from the Dark Lands as the lost do."

"Why shouldn't we be afraid?" Fear Monger said. "Even now while we have argued, the Dark Lands have sent their Persecutrons to assault us while we are weak. Look!"

A sound of clattering footsteps sounded outside the stadium. Everyone looked toward the sound.

An explosion.

Christian raised his Gauss rifle in one hand and a discarded laser tommy gun in the other.

Zealot's hand went to his pistol.

Love projected a shield.

Truth stood there, looking disinterested.

Several large figures burst through the stadium walls, weapons blazing.

The crowd screamed, and people ran for the exits.

Christian tightened his grip on his weapons. "Oh, come on. If it's not one thing, it's another."

The stadium echoed with a raucous, ear-shredding scream of terror. Everyone seated in the stands ran for the exits.

STAGE 15
MATT HOPPER'S FOLLY

The Persecutrons were enormous.

The Persecutrons were metallic.

The Persecutrons were . . . fake?

The second they stepped into the stadium Christian realized they were fake. He'd seen real Persecutrons in action. These . . . were not them. These Persecutrons fired enormous terrifying lasers from their eyes that, while looking frightening, did almost no damage to even an unarmored target. But the pilgrims didn't seem to understand that.

One beam cut across Christian and left only a slight singe on his armor and skin. Yet the pilgrims screamed and fled from the automatons anyway, as if they had just mutilated Christian.

More Persecutrons poured into the stadium. Two of them combined their lasers and shot Zealot in the chest. Zealot looked down at his chest, then up at the robots. "Are you attempting to damage me?" He looked more confused than injured. He raised his rocket pistol and aimed at the Persecutrons. Then he lowered it. "It seems a waste of missiles."

"Zealot, your pistol has infinite missiles," Truth said.

"And yet it still seems like a waste."

A Persecutron walked up and looked down over them like an ancient titan. "You are dumb." Then it fired into Truth. The laser didn't even singe her skin. Behind them, the stadium had lost control. Thousands swarmed for the exits, and Fear Monger yelled over the speakers to evacuate to the fallout shelters.

"I don't understand," Christian said. "These things are little more than an inconvenience."

"I'm afraid it is worse than you think," a voice said.

Truth, Zealot, Christian, Love and a few of the Calvinists and Arminians turned toward the voice.

It was Interpreter.

Truth waved in greeting.

"What do you mean?" Christian said. "These things are harmless."

"Exactly," Interpreter said with a grim smile. "That's what makes them so dangerous."

Pilgrims continued to scream.

Christian and the others just stood around.

Interpreter leaned against a Persecutron as if it were a watercooler. "You see, long ago the Dark Lands used to send large and destructive Persecutrons that slaughtered many a poor pilgrim. They are still used a couple places far away. But here, Apollyon learned he didn't need that effort. The Persecutrons were rallying the pilgrims to fight harder against Apollyon's forces and showed the lost that their allies were not moral. Apollyon then developed these fake Persecutrons, because he knew that was enough to scare the pilgrims into apathy and avoidance of the Dark Lands. If anyone acted out against the Persecutrons, the Dark Lands would see it as an overreaction to a mostly harmless force and damage the reputation of pilgrims."

"Then how do we defeat such an enemy?" Zealot said. "They keep coming. There are far too many to eliminate all on our own. Though I could certainly try." He glanced at his pistol.

"Another symptom of their design," Interpreter said. "Being cheap and mostly harmless, they are easily mass-produced and sent against any pilgrim. They usually focus on those who dare step outside the boundaries of Palace Beautiful or those who want to." He sent a knowing glance at Christian. "Within these walls, we are of limited threat to the Dark Lands. They occasionally burst in here like this, leaving everything in chaos for weeks."

"Then what do we do?" Christian said.

"It's very complicated, so pay attention." Interpreter turned toward one of the holes that the Persecutrons had made in the stadium. "We do nothing."

Everyone stared at Interpreter.

Zealot's mouth dropped open. "We do . . . *what?*"

"Of course!" Christian nodded in in understanding. "These things are just a distraction."

"But they're so large and shootable." Zealot gave a look of shocked dejection. "How can the solution to their presence not be violence related?"

"They're just trying to bait out violence from us, don't you see?" Christian said.

A Persecutron walked up to Truth and stared down at her. "Religion is anti-science."

Truth's face slowly took on a cartoonish look of horror and rage. "You mother knower."

Truth leapt at the Persecutron and spun, landing a perfect roundhouse kick into the machine's torso.

The Persecutron exploded into tiny pieces. A dozen others turned toward Truth, raised a hand, and shouted, "Hey!" They trundled up to her and kept pointing and shouting. "Hey. Hey. Hey."

Truth gave a yelp and backed away from the approaching automata.

Interpreter put his hand on Truth's shoulder. "What did you just learn from fighting Dogmatism? That we must disagree with love."

"What?" Love looked worried.

"No, no. I mean when you disagree you must do so with love."

"Why do you have to disagree with me?" Love pouted. "Am I . . . disagreeable?"

"You aren't. Maybe I should use a different word. We must disagree *in love.*"

Love's pout turned to disgust. "Ew."

Behind them, the Persecutrons continued their rampage.

"Shouldn't we . . . uh . . . worry about that?" Zealot motioned towards the chaos.

Love and Interpreter looked at it, then back at Zealot. "No, just muscle through it," Interpreter said.

"Ah, that I can understand." Zealot smiled.

"So then about this people disagreeing in love thing," Love said. "Do I need to be cut open? And what about someone bigger than me like Zealot? How is he supposed to—"

Truth scoffed. "Love, as objectively comedic as this exchange is, you know what Interpreter means. But I don't see why I have to be kind to a bunch of robots from the Dark Lands. They aren't like fellow pilgrims. And what's more, they're *wrong*."

"Of course, they're wrong," Interpreter said with a smile. "But you have to ask yourself, are you going to confront them because you think you can persuade them to a correct way of thinking? Or is it because you want to feel better about yourself by arguing with someone wrong?"

"There's a difference?" Truth said with genuine confusion in her voice.

"Yes!" Love's tone held a twinge of shock.

"Besides," Christian said, "how exactly does one persuade a robot?"

Zealot looked thoughtful. "By shooting it?"

"Ok. You can try that." Interpreter gave a fatherly laugh.

Zealot shot one of the Persecutrons. It exploded. Zealot looked at the wreckage.

"Fascinating. It did not work. But it was fun . . ." Zealot aimed at another robot.

"Cool it, Mr. Missile," Christian said.

"Oh, very well." Zealot holstered his pistol. "But only out of appreciation for that nickname. I still fail to understand. When persecutors are embarrassed and attacked for their wrongful acts, they are more prone to changing their ways. Right Love?"

Zealot looked at Love.

Love looked at Truth.

Truth looked frustrated. "Not quite."

"Then what are we to do?" Christian looked at the chaos. No one seemed to be getting hurt, but they were all quite terrorized. "Ignore the world entirely until atomic annihilation?"

"Certainly not," Zealot cried. "It is better to face these malicious machinations than do nothing."

"No, stop." Interpreter put a hand on Zealot's shoulder. "It is not our duty to fight Persecution. If these automatons were a large threat, we might have to avoid or confront them, but this is not a worthy distraction from the true goal."

"Hold on," Zealot said. "What was our true goal again?"

Interpreter walked toward the hole the Persecutrons had come through. Multiple Persecutrons faced him and fired their lasers into his flesh, again with no effect. He turned and shouted over his shoulder, "Have you forgotten those who are still under threat of total atomic annihilation? There are greater fights beyond these walls. This place is good, but it is only a rest stop for the true fight." He walked through the hole in the wall.

"Of course!" Christian said. "The lost! Why do I keep forgetting?"

"Because remembering is hard?" Zealot said.

"Because we're being selfish?" Love said.

"Because the underlying temporal non-specificity of this allegorical plane makes ongoing action difficult to portray due to the chronological nature of the portrayal of events?" Truth said.

Everyone stared at Truth.

Truth looked shy. "What?"

The Persecutrons continued their rampage.

Christian and the others stood there, waiting.

Zealot broke the silence. "Well, I'm bored. Let's follow Interpreter. Didn't he mention something about a greater fight than this? Wondrous. These artificial hoodlums are poor opponents anyway." He strode up to the hole. Paused, then shot another Persecutron, chuckled to himself, and disappeared into the hole.

Truth stepped forward next. "Very well, shall we follow?"

Christian looked back at the other pilgrims on the field. "Who is with us?"

A few of the Calvinists, Arminians and one or two others looked about then shouted their approval.

Christian tossed one his laser tommy gun and marched toward the exit. "Then forward we go, into the Dark Lands."

Persecutrons stepped into his path.

Christian swallowed and approached the machines. He didn't want to say anything, but the beings terrified him. He had seen what real Persecutrons could do to pilgrims. But these were fake. So, he had little to fear, right? He started toward the hole where Interpreter exited.

The Persecutrons focused their lasers on him. "You puritanical theocrat," one Persecutron said.

"You wish to impose your will on others," said another.

"Happy Holidays," said a third.

"You believe in the Overseer? You must hate the gays."

"Oh no," Truth said with an eye roll. "How are we to stand against such irrefutable logic?"

Christian kept walking. This wasn't so bad. He had faced mutant demons, killer-robot swarms, and eldritch abominations from beyond his worst nightmares. By the grace of the Overseer, he had made it through. This was nothing compared to that. He pushed through the Persecutrons with little effort and stepped out of the stadium into the blasted wastes of the Dark Land. "Through here," he said. "You can make it. It's easy."

Not everyone made it through. Truth and Love did. But only some of the Calvinists and Arminians who had said they would follow appeared on the other side.

Now past the breach, Christian peered at the horizon. The Dark Lands stretched before him like an animal's skin on a tanner's bench. Dry, bleached, and dead. These festering irradiated lands looked no different from those that he and his friends had fought through before. Yet now, with his new suit of armor from the Overseer and with his burden removed, the lands somehow looked hungry for his flesh.

A fear crept into Christian's heart. Before, he had been one of the lost, walking through those Dark Lands. He was at home in that infinite blackness. But now, the lands were not his home. They were his enemy.

He thought of those he had slaughtered, those who likely just wanted to help him, to warn him of the impending threat of total atomic annihilation. Would he meet the same fate? That seemed poetically just—to die in the manner that he had killed so many.

Christian stepped toward the Dark Lands, rifle in hand, friends at his side, and Palace Beautiful behind him. Let others cower in the safety of their homes. Even if death faced him in the Dark Lands, he would do for the lost what Evangelist had done for him.

"I'm scared," Christian said.

"Irrelevant!" Zealot strode ahead of him. "Shall we let something as immaterial as fear keep us from saving those under threat of total atomic annihilation?"

"Uh—"

"No! That was a rhetorical question."

"But I could make things worse, there is so much hatred toward pilgrims. Sometimes for good reason. Just look at what went on in Palace Beautiful."

Love took his hand.

Christian looked into Love's eyes. She sparkled with compassion. Literally. The colors of her magical girl clothes became more vibrant, as if she had turned into a beautiful animation.

"Keep close to me," Love said, "and their hatred will seem as foolishness to them."

Christian turned to Truth. "I'm afraid of saying the wrong thing when talking to the lost—that I will lead people astray."

"Good. You should be," Truth said.

Christian blinked. "What? Did we not just have a big battle involving a guy trying to spread fear? Isn't fear bad?"

"It's more complicated than that." Truth tilted her head as if pondering something. "You should be afraid of leading people astray. You've got to study. Listen to what Book says. And constantly radio the Overseer. Always check his transmissions with what Book says. Sometimes the enemy will send us transmissions as if they're from the Overseer."

"This isn't reassuring." Christian shifted his weight.

Truth nodded. "If you wanted reassurance, you should have kept talking with Love. What is real and false is incredibly important. Distinguishing lies from reality is difficult. It requires study and hard work. There isn't a shortcut or trick that will make that easier or any less time-consuming. You must be vigilant in your—"

"Don't overestimate your power to stand against the Overseer," Zealot said.

"Hey," Truth said. "Let me finish."

"In a minute," Zealot said. "You will most likely lead folks astray. You will say things that are false, despite your efforts to speak otherwise. But if you do, then the lost will still be no worse off when it comes to eternity. So do not let fear of failure keep you from engaging the lost."

"Don't use that as an excuse not to study," Truth said.

"Yes, yes." Zealot gave a dismissive wave of his hand which almost knocked Truth over. "I'm simply trying to keep you from scaring yourself into a life of apathetic study like those Calvinists and Arminians over there." Zealot pointed at the crowd of fellow pilgrims who followed behind Christian.

"Hey!" an Arminian said. "We're here, aren't we?"

"The point is," Truth said, "don't say what is wrong."

"But also, don't worry," Love said. "We're under grace. The Overseer has forgiven your past as well as your future sins."

"Which is really cosmically fascinating when you think about it," Truth interrupted.

"Regardless," Love continued, "While you should avoid sinning, you should also not be surprised when you mess up. You *will* mess up. After all, being a pilgrim is not about being perfect. Though you should try to, anyway. If we were perfect, we wouldn't need the Overseer. He oversees us, comes alongside us, and helps us to face the infinite terrors and pains of venturing through"—she paused for dramatic effect—"the Dark Lands."

STAGE 16
ECCLESIASTIC BOOGALOO

Stage 16: Ecclesiastic Boogaloo

"There it is," Interpreter said, "the Mobile Fair of Futility." He passed the binoculars to Christian.

Christian peered through them. In the distance he saw a massive assortment of vehicles, hover platforms, and floating structures—connected by suspended walkways. Each platform seemed to try to move in its own direction conveyed by either wheels, hoverprojectors, or mechanical legs. Yet the whole tangle of platforms ended up moving in the same direction, despite each platform's apparent individuality.

"Finally." Zealot snatched the binoculars from Christian's hand. "It has been too long since we experienced conflict with our true enemy. Why is this place so insidiously difficult to locate?"

"The Great Mobile Fair of Futility constantly moves." Christian took the binoculars back from Zealot. "Hence the name. I've never been to it myself."

"Why are we here again?" Truth said taking the binoculars and examining the city herself.

Christian snatched the binoculars back. "We've gone over that for the past several days. Why are you asking now?"

"Because all that other stuff wasn't on-screen and the audience needs expositional establishment of intent."

"Oh, well why didn't you say so. We're here because it's the closest place I know the lost congregate."

"Still . . ." Zealot reached for the binoculars "Why would someone enter such a congregation of concrete congestion?"

Before Zealot could grab them, Truth jerked away and looked back at the city. "The lost within are constantly seeking new enjoyments, new diversions, and new philosophies, vainly trying to feel safe from total atomic annihilation."

Interpreter took the binoculars from Truth and hid them behind his back as if to stop the constant snatching. "That is why this was once called Vanity Fair. But after an unfortunate copyright suit by some obscure magazine, they were forced to change the name."

Christian glanced at Zealot, confused. "What on earth is a magazine?"

Zealot shrugged.

Interpreter sighed and shook his head. "Kids these days."

Love snuck up behind Interpreter and grabbed the binoculars, but didn't look through them. "These poor lost folks must be told of the evils they have done. They're totally going to get nuked if they keep it up."

Truth snatched the binoculars from Love's hands. "Why did you take the binoculars if you weren't going to use them?"

"I thought we were using it as a speaking stick." Love grabbed the binoculars back. "You can only talk if you're holding the binoculars."

"What? No," Truth said, as she instinctively reached for the binoculars.

"Enough of this talk," Zealot said but not before first grabbing the binoculars. "We must engage the denizens of this mechanical festival in rhetoric, lest their doom go undissuaded."

"Dollar." Truth said.

"What?" Zealot's tone rose.

"Undissuaded isn't a word."

Zealot frowned in confusion and anger. "Dissuaded is a word. Thus, undissuaded should be as well."

"It isn't. You owe me a dollar."

"Oh, very well." Zealot handed Truth a dollar and scowled.

"I gave you that collection of pretentious synonyms so you would stop making up words."

"But how else shall I elucidate my verbiage?"

"I'm going to elucidate your verbiage if you don't stop it." Truth put her hands on her hips and returned Zealot's glare.

"Ha! You may try! You can't force me to do anything I don't want to do."

"Yeah, that's not a good thing," Love said.

"Oh?" Zealot loomed over Love, staring with his best intimidating glare. "Well, your f-face isn't a good t-thing." The insult came with the eloquence of a stuttering child.

Love's mouth hung open, and tears welled in her eyes. "Why would you say that? What's wrong with my face? Has it always been so revolting to you?"

"Zealot," Christian said, "what have you done? You can't talk to Love the way you talk to Truth." He put an arm around Love's shoulder. "It's okay, Love. He didn't mean it."

"Is it true?" Love grabbed Christian by the armor and peered into his eyes. "Am I really hideous?"

"Uh . . ." The sudden assault left Christian speechless.

"If you were, it wouldn't matter," Truth said. "The aesthetic quality of our exterior forms has little value in the grand scheme of things. Especially for allegories like us."

"Yeah," Christian said. "What Truth said."

This didn't seem to have any effect on Love. She burst into tears.

Christian looked worried. "Love, you are a very lovely and charming, magical girl." He looked around, searching. "Where's Zealot?"

Truth raised the binoculars, then swore. "Running. Like any sane man would do in this situation. He's heading to the city. After him!"

————

Christian woke up with his head feeling like it had taken a job as a crash test dummy. He sat up and looked around. What had happened? The last thing he remembered was walking toward the Mobile Fair of Futility. Everything afterward was a blur.

"You're awake. Finally," Conscience said.

Christian put a hand to his head, a sharp pain reverberating across his skull. "Argh! My head. Why does it hurt so much?"

He looked down at Conscience. Conscience held a small hammer in his hand. Conscience looked at the hammer, gave a nervous chuckle, then tossed the hammer out of sight. "Never mind about that. We've got to get going. It took me days to wake you up from your trance."

"Trance? You mean I went back to my old ways?" The thought brought horror back to Christian's heart.

"Not quite that far. You didn't kill anybody. And it was easier to wake you up this time."

Christian looked around. He was in a gutter on the side of a large walkway on top of one of the hover platforms that made up the Mobile Fair of Futility.

Hordes of people rushed past him, their destinations unclear.

Christian rose, clutching his head, like a hangover from heavy drinking. But he didn't remember consuming any alcohol.

"Where are the others?" Christian said.

Conscience hopped up onto his shoulder. "Heaven if I know."

"You're a big help."

"Aw," Conscience said in a sad tone. His robotic eye slits drooped.

Zealot, Love, and Truth were nowhere to be seen. When was the last time he had been without his friends? A cold feeling of fear wormed its way into his mind. This fear was different than the horror of returning to his evil. More pronounced. Much worse if all his friends had left him. He picked a random direction and started walking.

"What's your plan to find the others?" Conscience said.

"I figure someone as loud and boisterous as Zealot won't be so hard to—"

"How dare you exclaim such obvious nonsense toward me, you foul-brained ruffian," a voice shouted from across the street.

"Ah," Christian said, "there he is."

Zealot stood in the distance, a good head and shoulders taller than the others around him. He stood in a small clearing between two walkways, confronting some sort of street preacher in a priest's outfit.

Christian ran up to Zealot, which left him short of breath. "Zealot? Why are you berating this well-dressed man?"

"Don't be ridiculous," Zealot said.

"Impossible." Christian caught his breath. "But I'll try."

"I berate everyone."

"I know, but I was wondering why this man in particular."

Zealot pointed at the priest. "This man has the gall to say my gun here came about by random chance and was not intelligently designed." He waved his gun around and fired a few shots into the air.

"It's simple science," the priest said. "If you have not met the designer or the designer's name isn't on the item, then it must have come together through random chance."

"How is that scientific?" Christian said.

The priest raised his hands as if about to pray. "It has been decreed as science from on high by the Holy Order of Smart People. Blessed be their name."

Christian folded his arms. "That isn't how science works. At least, I don't think so. Where's Truth?" Christian looked around, but she was nowhere to be seen. "Anyway, I'm pretty sure science is based on evidence, observation, and logic—not decrees from on high by some people who claim to be smart."

"You deny science?" The priest looked shocked. "The very idea of denying what the Holy Order of Smart People has decreed is beyond ignorance. Or my name isn't Atheist."

"Your name isn't Atheist." Zealot pointed at the man's chest. "Your name tag says HELLO, My Name Is Agnostic."

"What?" Atheist looked down at his priest's outfit with surprise.

Christian followed his gaze. The man did indeed have a nametag labeling him as Agnostic.

"Exclamations of disgust! I thought I had that fixed." Atheist rubbed the writing on his nametag as if attempting to alter the words. They did not change.

Christian scoffed. "You can't possibly believe that something as complex and intricate as Zealot's conscience pistol came about randomly and wasn't designed. Just look at it—far too interactive and systematic. Ordered systems require intelligent intervention to be made. You wouldn't believe a robot was made randomly."

"I don't have to believe. I know because that is what has been decreed by the Holy Order of Smart People, blessed be their name. For they are never wrong, and all human knowledge flows through them."

"Now hold on a minute," a voice said from the crowd. A tall man in a lab coat walked forward. "I am part of the Holy Order of Smart People, blessed be their name. I assure you that ordered systems cannot be formed through disorder."

"What?" Atheist said. "Excommunicate him! He has spoken against the true gospel of smartness."

Several people in priest's robes burst from the crowd, grabbed the man in the lab coat, and pulled him out of sight.

Zealot and Christian glanced at each other. Zealot looked at a loss for words. Almost. "You intellectual tyrant." Zealot aimed his pistol at Atheist. "Taste justice."

"Ha!" Atheist said with a grin. "Justice is a philosophical concept and thus has no taste. Making your threat only illustrates your lack of intelligence."

"How dare you—"

Christian cut him off. "Knock it off Zealot. Shooting him will not further this discussion in any meaningful way."

"Very well." Zealot holstered his pistol.

"We aren't getting anywhere with this guy. Let's go. We've got to find the others." Christian pulled on Zealot's arm.

"But I must stay." Zealot stayed in place. "This man says things that are false."

"Maybe Truth can talk some sense into him. Let's go find her."

"Truth?" Atheist said. "I have Truth right here. Don't be fooled, ladies and gentlemen. This is the real, genuine Truth." He waved toward an android woman who looked nothing like Truth. She was old, with the white hair of Truth, but her eyes were faded and dull, with little of that rambunctious curiosity that was so infectious.

The haggish woman lifted a claw toward Atheist and said in an obviously robotic voice, "What he says is accurate—"

"You see?" Atheist didn't wait for her to finish. "What I say is true.

Believe in the power of the Holy Order of Smart People, blessed be their name. For only they can interpret the sacred text of scientific evidence or make the logical decisions necessary to know what is and is not science. Shun these unbelievers. Shuuuun them." Atheist pointed at Zealot and waved his finger like pointing at a witch.

Zealot shook his head in disbelief at the man's antics. "But what about the complexities of—"

"Shunn," Atheist said.

"But . . . but . . ." Christian sputtered, wondering what argument would persuade the priest. "Energy and matter cannot come from nothing within a temporal system because of the requirement for all things to have a beginning unless forces outside the system—"

"Shunn," Atheist shouted.

Christian threw up his hands "We're wasting our time. He's a religious fanatic. We're not going to get anywhere with him unless we can show him Truth. Not through passion at least. Seems he has passion to match."

"All right." Zealot turned to go. "I suppose I should have ceased my attempts weeks ago."

Christian followed Zealot. "What was that? Weeks? How long ago did we enter the Mobile Fair of Futility?" They made their way past the crowd. Atheist went back to his preaching.

"I do not remember how long we've been in the Mobile Fair of Futility." Zealot slowed his pace and stroked his chin. "Time seems weird here."

"If that's the case, then how long have we been walking?"

Zealot and Christian stopped and looked around. They were in an entirely different part of the fair. A far less-populated part. Just a few yards away was a small gathering of people watching a man in a magician's outfit.

"Look!" Zealot said. "There's Truth."

Sure enough, there was Truth, standing in the crowd, watching the magician.

"She seems perturbed," Zealot said. "More so than usual, I mean."

"Yeah, he must have said something slightly incorrect. She hates that." Christian raised his voice to shout, "Hey, Truth! Over here."

Truth didn't respond.

The magician did a trick, pulling a rabbit out of a hat.

Truth jumped up and down and pointed. "There! See? There's Argument."

The moment she said those words, the rabbit climbed up the magician's sleeve and disappeared.

The crowd laughed.

"Silly little girl," the magician said. "There is no Argument. For I am Art, not Argument. I am here to dazzle you with my powers of elation."

Fireworks shot out of the man's sleeves, and the eyes of the rabbit poked out for a second.

"There he is again." Truth pointed. "You said at the beginning of this act to watch for your rabbit named Argument. I'm just pointing out where he is."

"Stop spoiling the show," someone from the audience said. "It's like the man said, there is no rabbit named Argument."

The rabbit climbed out of the magician's sleeve and hurried up his arm and into the magician's hat.

"But he's right there." Truth pointed again.

"My poor little girl." The magician gave a condescending smile. "This type of magic is called satire. And my pet Argument is not a part of any of that."

"But I see him."

"Nonsense." The magician spun with a flourish, and Argument disappeared. "I am the amazing magician, Art, who bedazzles and befuddles without the use of a pet rabbit assistant named Argument. Look, it's on my business card."

Cards shot out of the magician's sleeves and sprayed all over the crowd.

Christian picked one up. Sure enough, it said, *Art: magician who bedazzles and befuddles without the use of a pet rabbit assistant named 'Argument.' Lost items found. I don't do birthday parties.*"

The rabbit tucked his head over Art's shoulder and whispered into his ear. "What's that, Argument?" Art said. "So, you want to do the trick where I saw you in half to illustrate the dual nature of mankind. Well, only because you say so."

Truth turned to the crowd "How are you people not seeing this? He's literally saying that Argument is there."

"Hey, Truth." Christian waved at Truth.

Again, Truth didn't respond.

"Truly! How goes it?" Zealot said, louder than Christian.

Still no answer.

"What is this?" Zealot's eyes opened wide in fear. "She's been so entranced by this magician and his long-eared raccoon that she does not even notice when I misuse her name. This calls for drastic measures."

"Truth, snap out of it." Christian ran in front of her to get her attention. "You're being distracted by a small inaccuracy. You've got to focus on the task at hand. Hurry, before Zealot takes drastic measures. Whatever that means. It can't be good."

Truth stood on tiptoes to look over Christian.

"Down in front," somebody yelled.

"Yeah, let us watch the magician who doesn't have a pet rabbit named Argument," another said.

Christian tried to block Truth's gaze, but she looked around him.

"We have to get her attention somehow," Christian said. "Quick! Zealot! Yell something objectively false."

"Uh . . ." Zealot pondered a few moments. "Code Geass is an anime of only marginally above-average quality," Zealot yelled.

Truth spun and glared at Zealot. "What? Why would you say that? Everyone knows Code Geass is objectively the greatest . . ." Her voice trailed off and she stared blankly for a moment. "Wait, what was I doing? Where am I? And what's the deal with all these sudden pop culture references?"

Christian took Truth by the hand and pulled her away from the crowd. "I think it's that Art guy."

"Oh yes. Of course. He represents not only ancient human culture but modern pop culture as well. Thus, he's infected us with an aura of pop cultural referential tendencies. Oh dear, we should get out of here before we continue spouting topical references that damage this allegory's attempts at timeless appeal."

"Uh, ok."

They continued walking away from the crowd.

"Anyway. What's happened? I seem to have just awoken from a trance illustrating the passivity that everyday human life brings upon a person when they consume culture so much it distracts from their vocational pursuits."

"You were being distracted by a magician attempting to hide his Argument behind illusion and trickery," Christian said.

"I was not," Art yelled after them then he addressed the crowd. "For my next trick, I will pull a hat out of this rabbit."

The crowd gave a collective mutter of wonder.

"Oh, my dirty word," Truth looked shocked. "I've been standing here for so long, trying to explain to these people the Argument that Art was hiding. How could I waste so much time on something so mundane?"

Christian and Zealot looked at Truth. Christian raised his eyebrows. "You mean . . . how could you do that *again*?"

Truth looked embarrassed, then defiant. "In my defense it has been months since our adventure at Palace Beautiful."

"Months?" Christian narrowed his gaze. "Just how catawampus is time here? And where is Love? We better find her before a year passes."

"Love," Truth said, as if suddenly remembering something. "I left her back in the Rock-Banging Club."

"The what?"

"There's no telling what happened to her in all that time." Truth ran toward one of the walkways leading to the adjoining platform. "Quick, follow me."

Zealot trudged after her with Christian close behind.

STAGE 17
THE THREE COWARDLY LIONS

Truth, Zealot, and Christian stood outside the entrance to the Rock-Banging Club. The building seemed unremarkable, with no paint or signs indicating what the nature of the club was. If Truth hadn't pointed out the door, they would have likely run right by it.

"All right, everyone," Truth said. "There's no telling what we're going to face in there."

Christian loaded his Gauss rifle. "Didn't you go here already? What exactly is this place?"

Truth tilted her head to the side and thought for several seconds. "It's difficult to explain. It's best if you just see for yourself."

Zealot twirled his pistol. "I am ready for anything. Let the enemy throw its fiercest foes upon us so we may test our metal in glorious combat." Zealot twirled his pistol too hard and it fell out of his hands. In an instant he snatched it back up as if hoping they didn't see the blunder.

Truth looked uninspired by Zealot's antics.

"Don't worry, Truth," Christian said. "I'm pretty sure Book mentioned something about the Overseer helping us face any foe. That also includes things we won't have to shoot. This might be one of those situations."

Zealot paused, as if caught off guard. "I had not considered that."

"You never do," Christian said.

Truth reached for the door and stopped. She looked back at Christian and Zealot with caution in her face. "Let's go in on the count of three, all right?"

"Three!" Zealot yelled. And he charged into the building.

"Oh, Oath," Truth shouted. "Zealot, get back here."

Zealot did not get back here.

Truth and Christian charged after Zealot, crossed the threshold, and stepped into darkness.

For several seconds Christian could hardly see. Nothing perilous happened, at least, so far. Christian walked farther in. His eyes slowly adjusted to the darkness. He saw the nightclub with a bunch of nonthreatening folks sitting around scattered tables.

"This isn't as bad as I thought," Christian said, but didn't relax the grip on his gun.

Zealot looked around the room. "Where is Love? If she has been pirated away then we must commit all necessary violence with which to—"

Truth put her hand over Zealot's mouth and pointed. "There she is."

Even with Truth's hand over his mouth, Zealot attempted to shout, with limited success.

Love sat in a corner booth with a few other individuals. A very dim light illuminating her profile.

Christian and the others approached slowly, ready for danger.

"So then, he's all like 'What are you?'" Love said. "And I'm all 'Baby don't hurt me. Don't hurt me. No more.'"

The people at the table laughed. Love joined in, her bubbling song-like laughter annihilating any fear or dread in Christian. He slung his Gauss rifle onto his back and relaxed.

Zealot put a hand in front of Christian, blocking him. "Take care, my little friend. She may be entranced like Truth was by Worldly Wiseman."

"Hi, guys!" Love rose and beckoned them over. "Come meet my friends. This is Atheist, Pagan, and Satanist." She motioned toward the others seated at the table.

Christian recognized Atheist as the same priest who preached at them just a few minutes ago. Or was it hours? Days?

Zealot blinked. "Atheist? Weren't you just . . ." He looked back at the door. "What the revilement? Time certainly does work strange here."

"Ah, yes!" Atheist rose and offered Zealot his hand. "My old nemesis. Well, a friend of Love is a friend of mine. Come sit. Love was just telling us one of her hilarious stories."

Zealot looked at Atheist in confusion, likely because it was not immediately apparent how the situation could be progressed with gunfire.

Love sat back down with a relaxed sigh. "Did I tell you about the time that one guy thought my last name was *Me Do*?"

"Yes," Pagan said, "but it's worth hearing again."

"Wait, stop." Truth raised a hand and looked at Love, confused. "What in the name of taking the Lord's name in vain is going on here?"

"I'm just chillin'." Love folded her hands and smiled.

"You're doing what?"

"Sorry," Love said. "I'm just chilling. I forget, you get confused by when I abrev things."

"When you do what?"

Everyone at the table laughed.

"I have a question." Christian raised a hand. "Why is this place called the Rock-Banging Club?"

"That reminds me,"—Satanist pulled a rock from her pocket—"it's time again." Everyone at the table, except Love, pulled rocks from their pockets and slammed them into their faces. Blood trickled down their faces and dripped onto the table, joining the stains already there.

Truth, Zealot, and Christian stared.

"I have several questions," Christian said.

"What the Purgatory?" Zealot said.

"Don't you mean what the Hell?" Truth said.

"Certainly not. I can't say 'What the Hell.' That would be swearing. I choose to use made-up nations to swear by. Like Purgatory, or Narnia, or Palestine."

"About the rocks," Christian said, trying to ignore Zealot's overtly political but objectively correct statement.

"I've been trying to get them to stop with the rock banging." Love shook her head and laughed. "Apparently they're super into smashing rocks against their heads and causing irreversible brain damage."

"Yeah, I love smashing rocks into my face," Pagan said. "It feels great."

Truth's mouth hung open for several seconds, then as if to use the involuntary movement toward a constructive end, words started coming out, "Have you tried explaining to them the dangerous of doing this activity?"

"No," Love's voice filled with realization. "I didn't think of that. I just made friends with them and hoped that would get them to stop. For some reason that didn't work."

"Are you being sarcastic? I can never tell with you." Truth slipped into the seat next to Love. "Listen up friends, my sister and I care about you, so we would be bad friends if we didn't let you know that you are hurting yourselves by smashing rocks into your heads."

"Hey, don't go judging us," Satanist said.

"Yeah, that's mean," Pagan said.

"If you think this is bad," Christian said, "you should have seen what I used to do. Trust me, we aren't any better than you. But listen to what my friends have to say. Truth is pretty smart."

Truth blushed.

"Love has been a good friend," Atheist said, "not a jerk like Zealot was."

"Hey!" Zealot said without denial.

"Zealot, please." Truth sent Zealot a dismissive glance. "The sane people are talking. And I hate to agree with Atheist but you are often quantifiably a jerk."

"Well, yes, but you don't have to be a jerk about calling me a jerk."

"Anyway . . . about the rock smashing . . . The human body simply wasn't designed to have rocks smashed into it."

"But it feels so good," Satanist said. "Things that feel good can't possibly be bad, right?"

Truth grimaced. "If damage to your body and soul makes you feel good, then that is a sign you have even worse problems."

Satanist, Pagan, and Atheist looked offended.

Love, seeing the offense, cut in. "We say this because we care about you."

"We aren't hurting anybody," Atheist said. "As long as our actions don't hurt other people, can't we just do what we want?"

"You shouldn't hurt yourself," Truth said in an even tone. "Just as it's wrong to hurt other people, it's also wrong to hurt yourself."

"Why?" Pagan said. "They're our bodies, aren't they? Shouldn't we be able to do what we want to them?"

Truth and Love exchanged glances, confused.

"Certainly." Zealot stepped forward and pounded his fist on the table. "You should be allowed to damage yourself. Limit your potential. Hinder your ability to help others. It is not our place to force you to change. But look at yourselves. It is as my friend Truth said. You were not made to smash rocks into your face. It damages the brain and the mind. It has twisted your nature into liking the pain. We must endeavor to be our best so we can help the most. Think of all the people you could have helped, were your minds not damaged by multiple concussions. Those people's blood is on your hands, because you chose to damage yourself so you could not do good. Besides, you are making yourselves into beings you were not meant to be. Enjoying pain is the opposite of what pain is intended for."

Truth stared at Zealot.

Zealot caught her gaze and then looked confused. "What?"

"Since when were you so reasonable and articulate?"

Zealot looked from side to side. "Uh . . . Tuesday?"

After this answer, Truth looked more confused.

Satanist considered Zealot's words. "You mean it's not enough to not do bad, but we have to constantly try to do good?"

"Is it wrong to limit our ability to do good," Pagan said, "just as much as doing bad?"

Small metallic Conscience figures crawled onto the shoulders of Satanist, Pagan, and Atheist.

"That seems an impossible task," Pagan said. "How could a mere mortal do such a thing? We can't possibly stop smashing rocks into our faces." Pagan smashed another rock into his face.

"Correct," Truth said. "For mere mortals it is impossible to resist immoral urges, but with the Overseer, all things are possible. It is not a task to take lightly."

"But I like smashing rocks against my head," Satanist said. "It's who I am. I don't want to change who I am,"

"But it's not who you are meant to be," Truth said. "You are so much more than that."

Pagan and the others looked thoughtfully at the blood on the table.

The door burst open.

A crowd of people in officer's uniforms swarmed into the night-club. In seconds, they surrounded the table with raised weapons.

Zealot drew his pistol.

Guns fired. Missiles flew. Furniture exploded.

A canister bomb detonated and caustic gas filled the room.

Christian fell to the ground, choking. His eyes faded. He saw Truth roundhouse kick three attackers out the door, then, choking she fell next to him. Love fell too.

Zealot stayed on his feet, firing missile after missile, undeterred by the caustic gas. Zealot grabbed Love, who was nearest to him, slung her over his shoulder and ran for the exit, bullets and lasers zipping around him. Christian saw Atheist run for the exit. Pagan and Satanist also tried to run but the officers caught them and threw them to the ground. Then the gas overcame Christian and everything went black.

———

Christian awoke upside down. He dangled above a giant vat of what looked like boiling tar.

Truth was tied next to him in the same position.

They hung in a large courtroom with windows on all sides. Below the windows were seats. Half looked like bleachers for a fight ring, the other half like the seats for a jury. The seats looked like they could hold several hundred, but only a couple of dozen people were seated. Looking through the windows Christian saw they were in a room at the top of a tall skyscraper. Beyond the windows stretched The Mobile Fair of Futility.

Christian stared at the vat of tar below them. "What in tarnation is going on here?"

Truth and Christian looked at each other in silence.

"Get it? Tarnation?" Christian said. "Because of the tar?"

"Oh, I get it." Truth's voice held no emotion. "I'm just not going to laugh. This is a serious situation. Also, it wasn't funny."

"Hey," Christian sounded dejected, "if I'm going to get boiled in tar, I should at least joke about it."

"No, you shouldn't. This is exactly when one should not joke about things."

A figure strode to the judge's seat and sat down. The figure was large, bigger than anybody else sitting around the courtroom. The figure was also a lion. He had a name tag that said HELLO, My Name Is Fascism.

Another lion walked in front of the judge's seat. He was smaller and dressed in a bailiff's uniform. "All rise for the Honorable Judge Tolerance," the bailiff lion said, motioning toward Fascism.

Nobody rose. "Very good," Tolerance said. "Never let anyone tell you what to do."

Christian checked the nametag of the judge lion again. He whispered to Truth. "Why is he called Tolerance if his nametag says HELLO, My Name Is Fascism?"

Fascism growled at Christian, apparently hearing his words.

Foam dripped from the lion's mouth, and anger flashed in his eyes. "I am Tolerance, as my good friend Tyranny here has said." He motioned toward the lion in the bailiff's uniform. "You stand accused of the highest crime that we have in the Mobile Fair of Futility."

"Your name isn't Tolerance," Truth said. "It's Fascism."

Tolerance leapt up onto the rim of the judge's box and redirected his growl toward Truth. "Projecting, are we? Fascism is exactly what you are accused of today. You are forcing your beliefs on another, in defiance of the rules in the Mobile Fair of Futility. The first rule: That all must accept all philosophies as equal."

"How can all philosophies be equal if they aren't the same?" Christian said with genuine confusion in his voice.

"And your name tag says HELLO, My Name Is Fascism." Truth motioned toward the nametag with her head.

"Enough." Tolerance pounded a gavel. "Officer Tyranny, read the charges."

Tyranny lifted a small electronic tablet and started reading. "Conspiracy to force your beliefs upon others through threat of violence. Holding a belief that you are superior to others due to your beliefs and thus are allowed to rule over people who disagree with you. Being in league with the City of Morality with intent to force your views upon others through violence and coercion."

Gasps and murmurs sounded through the crowd of spectators.

"That's ridiculous," Christian said. "I've done none of those things."

"Oh no?" Tolerance growled again, looking at Christian like he was a prospective dinner. "We have written testimony saying that you said someone's beliefs were wrong. Pagan and Satanist say you told them the act of smashing rocks into their faces was wrong."

The crowd's murmurs grew into shouts of shock.

"What?" Tyranny turned and looked up at Tolerance. "Surely no person would do such an immoral thing. It is unheard of."

"No, it's true," Christian said. "They really were smashing rocks against their heads. It was really weird."

More gasps of shock. One or two old ladies fainted.

Christian looked at Truth. "What? What did I say?"

"Only accurate things," Truth echoed his confusion, "as far as I can ascertain."

"Then you admit it," Tolerance said. "You forced your beliefs upon others."

"No," Christian said. "I did no such thing. I would never force somebody to follow my beliefs. Force should only be used to stop other people from using force. People should be free to do what they want, especially in regard to what they believe."

The crowd's shock transformed into confusion.

"Wait. Slow down." Tolerance put his lion paws into a timeout signal. "You said you think the act of smashing rocks against one's head for pleasure is immoral."

"Not to mention unnatural."

The courtroom erupted into screams and shouting again.

Tolerance slid back into his chair and pounded his gavel. "Louder, louder, show more outrage, everyone. This isn't enough. Disorder! We must have disorder in the court."

After several minutes, people tired, and the noise reduced enough to talk.

"The convicted admit to forcing their beliefs on others," the lion Tolerance said, "thus, being intolerant."

"No," Truth said, "we don't. When did we force our beliefs on others?"

Tolerance snarled at Truth. "When you said what they were doing was wrong,"

"That isn't force," Truth said. "We didn't threaten, coerce, or trick them into doing anything they didn't choose to. We just said words to them."

"But you believe everyone should be forced not to smash rocks against their heads," Tolerance said.

"No, we don't." Anger rose in Christian's voice. Why couldn't the lion understand? "That won't solve the problem and will take away the ability for that person to choose to do the right thing of their own free will."

"Good," Tolerance said. "Then we are in agreement. Smashing rocks against one's head for fun is indeed a moral and good activity."

"No, I never said that."

"But you said people should be allowed to do it."

"Yes, but I don't think they should do it."

"You don't think they should do it,"—the lion strained as if trying very hard to comprehend Christian's words—"meaning you think they should not be allowed to do it! How dare you. People should do whatever they want as long as it doesn't hurt people."

"They should be allowed to do whatever they want as long as it doesn't hurt people. But that doesn't make every activity right."

"Well, of course. Some activities harm other people. Murder and theft, for example. All these, we can agree, are immoral activities."

"Yes, but some activities that don't hurt other people are also wrong. Holding hatred in your heart for example, or doing activities that hurt yourself. Not helping people when it is in your power to do so. That is also wrong."

"You think some activity should be illegal because you think they cause people to hurt themselves?" Tolerance growled in hatred. "What evil. You do not control other people's actions or have a right to make them do what you think is right."

"I don't think I have a right to make people do what I think is right. People have to choose to follow the Overseer. They can't be forced to become pilgrims."

"Yet that's what you're doing now, trying to force your beliefs on everyone in this courtroom."

Christian gave a confused look. "I'm chained up and dangling over a vat of tar. How am I using force on anyone? How?"

"That's it. Tyranny, do the thing." Tolerance ordered.

Tyranny walked over to a control panel next to the giant vat. He pressed some buttons. "You have no respect for other people's beliefs." Tolerance continued. "You think all must convert to your way of thinking or suffer the consequences. For this you must suffer the gravest punishment this court can issue."

Christian gasped.

Truth gasped.

The crowd gasped.

"That's right!" Tolerance said with triumph in his voice. "Public ridicule."

Silence.

"That's it?" Christian said with confusion and relief. "I was thinking it was going to be something worse than that."

"And of course, the stereotypical way to do this, is via tar and feathering. Which we have boiled to the heat of an active volcano."

"Oh." Christian grimaced. "That's more what I was expecting." The chains started moving. Truth and Christian descended toward the boiling tar.

Christian wiggled in the chains, trying to get free. "This isn't public humiliation. This is torture."

"Stop complaining," Tyranny said from below.

They descended closer and closer to the tar. Christian felt the heat from the boiling mass. Bubbles popped and flicks of tar struck his cheek, burning the flesh.

"Stop!" a voice cried.

The chains stopped. Christian's head dangled just a few inches above the boiling tar.

A figure strode into the courtroom that Christian didn't recognize. She was an older woman in plain, tattered clothes that looked like a cheap cosplay of Law's outfit. She had a briefcase in one hand and wore a look of stern determination.

"Who are you?" Tolerance said. "What gives you the right to intrude into my courtroom at such a dramatic last-minute moment?"

"Wait," Tyranny looked at the woman, then terror struck his face. "Oh no! It's Puritan!" He ran away from the vat and ducked behind the judge's box, tail between his legs.

The newcomer pointed at Tolerance and stood like an imposing statue. "Your honor, you have condemned this man without aid from his court-appointed legal counsel."

"Curse it all, Puritan." Tolerance leaned back in his chair and groaned. "How do you keep getting back in here? This is . . . what? The fourth time this week you've broken in?"

Puritan gave a wicked smirk. "As if anything can stop me. I laugh at your pitiful attempts to bar my entry. I laugh at them, I say. I do not literally laugh, as I am a serious attorney. But I do make the statement that 'I laugh.' Meaning, said *laugh* is figurative. But still laughter."

Christian laughed—literally, not figuratively—despite the impending doom. "Finally! Someone to help us. Puritan is good, right?"

Truth looked at the newcomer. Truth seemed unchanged in her emotion. "I don't know. I've heard of Puritan. This woman seems . . . different than what I've heard."

Puritan opened her briefcase and fumbled through papers as if consulting notes. "You've condemned these good people without a proper defense. As their appointed counsel, I must make my argument."

"Guards," Tolerance said, his voice cracking, "take this crazy woman away."

He poked his head over the side of his judge's box. "We do have guards, right Tyranny?"

Tyranny poked his head out and looked embarrassed. "Our policy of not telling people what to do has proved . . . complicated when it comes to training guards."

Tolerance growled, exasperated. "All right, then. Tyranny, go get her."

Tyranny stepped toward Puritan. The second he did Puritan gave a sudden and seemingly animal like snarl. Tyranny yelped and ran back to cower next to the judge's box.

Tolerance glared down at the cowardly lion and hissed like an overweight cat hissing at an enemy it is too lazy to confront.

Tolerance shook his head. "Look at you, Tyranny. You used to be so powerful. Now you can't even viscously maul to death an old woman. Honestly, I'm embarrassed for you."

"But she scares me." Tyranny sounded more like a baby than a lion.

"As I should," Puritan said. "Now, then. As I understand it, these poor delicious souls have been accused of forcing their beliefs on others."

"Yes," Tolerance said. "A crime they have confessed to committing."

"No, we haven't," Truth said. Then her expression changed. "Wait, did she just say *delicious*? Why do so many people find me delicious?"

"Is no one going to mention the fact those lions can talk?" Christian said. "What's up with that?"

Truth sent him a quizzical look. "The talking Platypus was normal but talking lions is what confuses you?"

"Well duh, of course Platypuses can talk. Don't be silly, Truth."

Truth's mouth hung open in shock. "I would *never*."

"Yeah, I guess that's not fair of me. I'm sorry."

"I forgive you. But don't ever call me silly unless you have a good reason."

"Shush." Puritan looked condescending toward Truth. "Let the adults talk." She looked back toward the judge's seat. "Why shouldn't these fine people force their beliefs upon others? Their beliefs are correct are they not?"

"Wait," Christian said, "we haven't forced anyone—"

A look from Puritan silenced him. There was a power in the woman's eyes, an authority that wouldn't let him say more.

"They are not correct beliefs." Tolerance slammed his paws on the judge's box and rose. "They think smashing rocks against your head is wrong and should be banned."

"We never said it should be banned," Truth said.

Puritan silenced her with a gaze then turned back toward Tolerance. "Isn't smashing your head against a rock damaging to one's body and soul?"

"Not in our opinion," Tolerance said.

"Opinions are irrelevant," Puritans said. "Rules are what matter."

"Yeah," Truth said. "You see, what we believe is—"

"I'm not going to warn you again, young lady," Puritan said with another piercing glare.

"I'm not young," Truth said without emotion.

Puritan ignored Truth. "As I was saying, to damage one's self is wrong. Therefore, the belief that rock head-smashing should be banned is justified."

"Not, it isn't," Christian said. "We don't want to ban anything. If we did, then people would be doing good for selfish self-preservation reasons, not moral conviction."

Puritan looked up at Christian and folded her arms, looking like a teacher who had just heard a child try to explain why three plus five is ten. "You think that smashing rocks against your head for fun is good?"

"No, I don't."

"Then you agree it should be banned," Puritan said, as if that settled things. "We cannot allow people to do bad things."

"But then we take away their ability to choose the right thing of their own free will," Christian said.

"Don't be naive," Puritan said in a tone full of condescension. "The point of morality is for people to do the right thing, not to change people's hearts."

"It's a lot more complicated than that," Truth said. "You see, regarding human action, the intent—"

"That's it." Puritan's gentle tone turned suddenly harsh. "I won't represent these pro-evil people. Tar and feather them, for all I care."

"Oh, come on," Christian said.

Tyranny ran to the control panel for the vat Christian and Truth were suspended over. "You don't have to tell me twice."

"I will anyway," Puritan said with a little too much enjoyment in her voice. "Tar and feather the scoundrels."

Tyranny reached for the control panel.

A wall exploded. Debris and dust burst through the room.

Truth and Christian swung back and forth from the force of the explosion, still mere inches from the tar.

"Never fear," a familiar voice yelled. "Zealot is here."

Sure enough, Zealot sprang from the smoke, rockets flying from his pistol. Love walked close behind projecting defensive shields, followed by a few other people Christian couldn't make out in the dust and smoke.

"Zealot! Thank the Overseer," Christian shouted. "Shoot at us!"

Truth sent Christian a confused look.

"He'll miss and hit the lions," Christian explained.

"Ah. Very smart."

Tyranny turned away from the controls. His expression and manner changed. His fear evaporated. He roared an impossible, soul-annihilating roar. It bypassed the ear, as if such a crude sensory device was not designed to ascertain such a noise. The windows shattered. Tyranny twisted and grew. His arms extended, his snout elongated, and the once timid-looking lion was now a thrashing eldritch abomination of impossible ferocity and writhing form. His bailiff's uniform twisted and grew along with him, as if it were part of his body.

"Oh faun. I mean, oh deer." The voice was Love, one of the figures in the smoke. "It's the twin lions that used to deter the entrants to Palace Beautiful. Seems they changed venue since that place is less of a threat to them."

"Silence the intolerant tyrants," Tyranny yelled in a voice now wreathed in emanations of demonic tenor.

Tyranny bounded toward Zealot and Love with a speed that defied his size.

Love screamed and jumped away from Tyranny.

Puritan slid an arm around Love's neck and grabbed her from behind.

Zealot sidestepped Tyranny's charge, then swung his pistol down and pointed it at Puritan.

"Wait, stop!" Puritan released Love from her grasp.

Zealot blew her head off. Puritan's head, that is. Not Love's. Though it would make sense to think otherwise, given Zealot's penchant for bad aim.

Puritan staggered back, headless. Then slowly, tendrils of flesh wound together where Puritan's head once was, and re-formed into a . . .

Love gasped.

Christian gasped.

Zealot gasped, then started choking on the dust and smoke from the exploded wall which was still surrounded him. Gasping in such a circumstance was evidently a bad idea. "Just"—he coughed—"as I"—another cough—"suspected."

Puritan's head had indeed re-formed, but not as a human head. It was the head of a lion.

Tyranny snatched at Zealot, taking advantage of his weakened state.

Zealot leapt out of the way of the first paw, but the second grabbed him by the leg and hoisted him into the air.

Tyranny's mouth opened impossibly wide revealing rows of teeth, teeth made of guns, not bone. The mouth opened wider, so wide his jaw was perpendicular with the floor and the gun teeth pointed directly at Zealot.

"Cool!" Zealot said. "Look at this. He has guns for teeth." The sound of a dozen guns readying to fire echoed from the lion's mouth.

"Oh no," Zealot said in a less enthusiastic tone. "He has guns for teeth."

Zealot fired into Tyranny's face before the lion could fire.

Tyranny flailed from the explosions and roared in pain. Zealot flew from the lion's grasp and fell near the judge's box. Tyranny turned on Zealot and fired a stream of bullets and lasers from his gun teeth. Zealot dove for cover behind the judge's box. A shot from the cloud of smoke burst through one of Tyranny's eyes. Tyranny grabbed his face. Purple blood trickled through Tyranny's paw. He stayed on his feet, his single, remaining unblinking eye filled with rage.

Puritan leapt at Love.

Love tried to deploy a shield.

Once again, Puritan was too fast. Her hands now twisted into massive lion's paws. She grabbed Love by the neck. "To love those who do evil is to love evil."

"No." Love writhed and gasped, her shields doing little to slow the lion's crushing grip.

"To punish the wicked is to show them love." Puritan's voice was a growl—inhuman, and beyond anything a real lion would produce. "You must punish the wicked."

Out of the smoke, a bullet struck Puritan.

The figures Christian had seen in the dust and smoke emerged revealing their forms. They were Priests.

"Wait a minute," Christian said. "The Holy Order of Smart People?"

Atheist ran from the dust toward Puritan, firing a Gauss rifle, sending round after round into her flesh. "Need help?" He knocked Puritan away with the butt of his rifle.

Love gasped for breath and started to fall.

Atheist grabbed her by the hand. "We heard Tolerance, or 'Fascism' as he's actually called, was oppressing some people just for what they believe, and we couldn't stand idly by and let that happen."

"I don't understand," Truth said. "You disagree with us."

"Doesn't mean you should be persecuted for it." Atheist called back to his comrades. "All right men, lay down fire on Tyranny. Keep him at bay, and I'll cut loose those two heretics dangling above the tar. Just because they're heretics doesn't mean we want them tarred and feathered."

The Holy Order of Smart people opened fire on Tyranny.

Atheist ran toward the control for the vat of tar.

Tyranny turned toward it and fired from his gun teeth. In a second, the control panel exploded into bits.

"Oh no. I should have shielded that." Love's voice sounded distraught.

Bullets and lasers flew toward Atheist. A shield coalesced just before the projectiles struck home and they bounced off. Atheist glanced at Love. "Why thank you. Can you get me to the top of the vat?"

"Yeah, give me a second." Love waved, and a forcefield appeared in front of Atheist in the form a stairway up to Christian and Truth.

"Many thanks." Atheist ran up the stairs, shot the chains holding Christian and Truth, and then grabbed the two captives as they fell. He leapt from the vat.

"This is heresy," Puritan growled and sprang at Love.

Love's shield went up.

Puritan's claws raked against the barrier, leaving deep tears in the shield. "You can't accept help from Atheist. He's evil."

Christian looked at Atheist. Then back at Puritan. "Why not? He's against Tyranny and Fascism as much as we are. Just because he believes something wrong doesn't mean he can't help us."

Truth nodded. "And just because he's wrong in some areas doesn't mean he can't believe something else that's correct."

"Nonsense!" Puritan struck the shield again and again. With each blow, her claws broke off and new ones grew back. "There are only two sides. Us and them. You are consorting with them. They are the enemy."

"Our enemy isn't people." Love's voice grew weaker with each blow from Puritan. "Our enemy is evil spirits and evil philosophies."

"Consorting with the enemy," Puritan said, "makes you vulnerable to their influence. You must be stopped."

Love's shield shattered and she fell to the ground.

Puritan crouched, then pounced toward Love.

Truth jumped into the air, then dive-kicked Puritan, blocking her attack on Love.

Puritan landed on her feet. "Fool," Puritan said, snarling. "Cat's always land on their—"

Truth spun and landed a kick upward into the bottom of the lion's snout.

Puritan went flying up and crashed deep into the ceiling, stuck there for a moment, then fell into the vat of tar.

Truth brought her foot down and struck a fighting pose. "The spirit within me is greater than the spirit that is within the world. I will not be influenced by the lost. Instead, the lost will be influenced by me."

A few of the people in the stands clapped. Most yelled or screamed obscenities at her.

"This conversation has been compelling." Atheist rushed toward the exit then slid to a stop and beckoned to the others. "But I think we should make like a dog and flee."

Atheist, Christian, Truth, and Love turned toward the hole blown in the wall.

Tyranny was too fast for them. Tyranny raised one arm to block the gunfire from Atheist's compatriots and charged for the hole. He knocked the entire Holy Order of Smart People through the hole, then stood, barring the escape of Christian, Zealot, Truth, Love, and Atheist.

Blood poured from a hundred wounds in Tyranny's body, but they seemed to have little effect on the beast. "Who shall be the first to die?" Tyranny said.

"Oh, pick me!" Zealot said.

Christian turned and looked toward the sound of Zealot's voice.

Zealot was standing in the judge's seat. He grabbed Tolerance with one hand and put his gun to the lion's head. "Alternate suggestion. I paint the walls with your commander's brains, and then I turn my righteous fury upon you with all the wrath and justice my Conscience can muster."

Tyranny leapt toward Zealot, jaws open, eyes red.

Just as the beast leapt, Zealot released Tolerance and jumped up and over Tyranny. He stepped on the lion's head midair, then jumped for the exit.

Tyranny smashed into the judge's seat.

Zealot, flipped for no apparent reason, then landed with a crash, pistol in hand.

Zealot struck a pose and twirled his gun. "Their plan is foiled. And I ain't lion."

Atheist, Christian, Love and Truth stared at Zealot.

"Boo," came Puritan's voice from inside the vat.

"This is the kind of thing that keeps us from becoming pilgrims," Atheist said

"Oh?" Zealot said. "And what of your dog-and-flee pun you said earlier?"

"That was tasteful," Atheist said, a smile betraying his feigned revulsion.

Tyranny howled again and twisted his snout around to glare at them. He had Tolerance in his mouth. Blood gushed from his teeth and nostrils like the monster had blood instead of snot.

"Wait, Tyranny, don't," Tolerance cried from within Tyranny's jaws.

Tyranny swallowed Tolerance in one gulp.

"Let's run for it," Christian said.

"We can't possibly outrun a giant lion." Truth pulled out a nail file and started filing her nails.

"Everyone,"—Zealot raised his gun toward Tyranny, who seemed to still be growing in size—"I have a plan. Before, our tactic was to shoot him. Now hear me out. What if, instead, we shoot him *more*?"

There was a brief moment of contemplative silence.

"Works for me." Atheist tossed Christian his old Gauss rifle.

Christian raised the rifle to his shoulder. "All right, you overgrown feline. Prepare to eat our collective violence."

Tyranny opened his mouth. His gun teeth were . . . different.

They were now all rocket launchers.

"Christian, what are you doing?" Truth put down her nail file and glared at Christian. "We talked about this with Zealot. According to trope law, overconfident taunting always worsens your circumstances to an extreme degree."

"Oh no. I'm sorry, Truth. I forgot," Christian said with embarrassment and fear in his voice. "But Love, you can protect us, right?" He glanced at Love. She was passed out on the floor. Presumably being choked, knocked about by a monster lion, and then having to project shields constantly was not conducive to perpetual cognizance, and something about the lion's attacks did seem to be extra effective against Love's defenses.

The rocket launchers readied to fire.

"What do we do?" Terror filled Christian's voice.

"Shoot him more. We talked about this." Zealot opened fire. As did the others.

Tyranny fired. The missiles flew toward Christian.

Truth stepped in front of him. Then in a blur of punches and kicks, Truth knocked aside each missile as it flew. The missiles, trajectory altered, then smashed into the walls and floors and exploded, sending concussive blasts that rattled Christian, but he remained standing.

"Tyranny is based on lies," Truth said, still kicking and punching over the din of gunfire and missile explosions. "And defeating lies is my specialty."

Zealot fired missile after missile into Tyranny's flesh. Chunks of lion flew through the air, and purple blood gushed from the beast like he was a giant grape-juice fountain. But the creature shrugged the wounds off and continued firing back.

Christian felt his body weaken from the constant nearby explosions.

"This isn't working at all," Zealot said. "Clearly, we aren't shooting enough."

Tyranny climbed down to the floor from the judge's seat.

"He's going to pounce on us," Truth said, still kicking the missiles. "And I can't stop that. Because when tyrannical regimes use force to crack down on those who speak the truth, simply speaking the truth will not stop their forceful onslaught."

Tyranny rolled on his heels toward Christian and crouched, preparing to leap at them.

"Then what do we do?" Christian said.

"Usually this is when pilgrims get martyred," Truth said.

"That seems like a bad plan."

"Don't worry, I have a better one." Zealot pressed a button on the side of his pistol, a small control panel appeared and he pressed several more buttons.

"You?" Truth said. "But you never have good plans."

"Trust me, Truly. Against Tyranny there is only one remedy: Action!"

Zealot fired a single missile.

It missed Tyranny entirely.

Truth looked at Zealot with confusion and disappointment. Yet still she kicked aside every one of Tyranny's missiles, even without looking.

Zealot smiled "Wait for it . . ."

The missile sailed around the room, striking nothing, then struck the vat of tar on the far end.

The vat tipped over toward Tyranny and a wall of tar gushed out of the vat and flowed onto the giant lion.

"Be entangled in the chaos of your own vitriol," Zealot said with a triumphant bellow.

The boiling tar flooded around Tyranny's ankles, stuck Puritan against him, and bathed both of them in the sticky burning goo.

Tyranny scooped up the female lion and placed her on his shoulder like a parrot. He stepped toward them, but stumbled. The tar slowing his progress.

"Oh brilliant," Truth said. "The culture's system of oppressing those who disagree can be turned against their very creators, as any system of imposed tolerance is inherently self-defeating."

"Uh . . . yes," Zealot said.

Truth sighed. "I mean . . . you trapped him in the tar. Good job."

Christian picked up Love and slung her over his shoulder. "That tar isn't going to slow him long. Time to . . . uh . . . make like a baby and head out."

"We don't have to." Zealot fired more missiles into Tyranny.

"But we should," Truth said. "Tyranny can never be fully defeated. We can only do what we can and then move on to the important work of following the Overseer."

"Ah yes, following the Overseer. How could I constantly forget?"

Zealot ran for the exit alongside Truth, Atheist, and Christian who carried Love on his shoulder.

They all leapt from the tower and the whole party fell through the air to the street below.

The street *very* far below.

"Oh dear," Truth said as they fell. "I don't think we thought this through."

STAGE 18
RAILGUN'S CRUSADE

"So, then this guy says, 'and I ain't lion.'" Atheist raised a glass from the table. "I almost started shooting him on principle."

Everyone at the table laughed. Atheist, Christian, Zealot and Truth sat in a large corner booth along with a few members of the Holy Order of Smart People.

"A fight devoid of zingy one-liners is poor tactics, I say." Zealot took a long drink from his mug.

"How about that escape?" Christian said. "Everything that happened after we jumped from the skyscraper. I thought we would die from the fall. What a momentous and crazy sequence of humorous and epic events that caused us to not die. It was all so incredible. I can't imagine how anyone could put it into words and portray it accurately. Especially in text form."

"Agreed," Atheist said.

Christian smiled. "This is so surreal. Earlier, we were adversaries. Now we're swapping war stories of how we stuck it to some anthropomorphic lions."

"It is a small victory," Atheist said. "Just wait. In a couple of days, Tyranny will puke out that little kitty, Fascism, and he'll rename him to something else to hide his motives. Something like Multiculturalism or Diversity."

"Or maybe Anti-Fascism," Truth said with a laugh.

Everyone looked at Truth. They didn't laugh.

"What?" Truth said.

"Don't be ridiculous," Atheist said. "Fascism would never be crazy enough to call himself Anti-Fascism. What is he going to say? That free speech is actually tyrannical? That in order to have freedom, we have to limit what people can say? Nobody would be that crazy."

They kept talking.

Christian's gaze drifted over to the booth at the far end of the room. Love sat alone, staring at a glass of something vaguely nonalcoholic.

"Excuse me." Christian left the table, and walked over to Love. "Mind if I sit here?"

Love shrugged.

"That was quite the battle back there."

Love shrugged again.

"Thanks for getting all those guys to come to our rescue."

"That was mostly Zealot and Atheist," Love said.

"I find that hard to believe." Christian tried to catch Love's gaze.

Love just stared at her drink. "Then don't."

Silence.

Christian drummed his fingers on the table.

Love looked off into the distance.

"Truth has convinced a few people to join our journey to the Celestial Station." Christian nodded toward the corner table. "Now that we've fought together against the lions, a few of The Holy Order of Smart People are willing to hear about the threat of total atomic annihilation."

"Great," Love said without any discernable emotion that Christian could identify.

"I think, maybe they're more willing to listen ever since you talked to them."

Love picked up her drink and studied it for a few seconds. "If you say so."

"What's the matter?" Christian sent Love a look of concern.

"Nothing."

"Not true," Truth yelled from across the room without leaving her conversation.

Love glared at Truth.

"Thanks, Truth," Christian shouted, "but I could figure that out on my own."

"Oh, dear. Am I that easy to read?" Love said.

"You neglected to drink your vague non-brand-specific beverage."

"Oh?" Love said. "Because vague non-brand-specific beverages are my favorite."

Christian laughed in a friendly way. "Is this about your fight with Puritan?"

"Not exactly. I felt so useless back there. No one was listening to what I had to say. They just threw it back in my face. All I could do was convince a bunch of Overseer-deniers and a crazy gunslinging loudmouth to come help. They did far more than I did. Puritan had me at her mercy."

"Hey, you shielded us."

"Puritan made my shields useless."

"Hey, don't be hyperbolic. I'd say *almost* useless."

Love rolled her eyes at Christian in a way that seemed to be communicating something but Christian couldn't figure it out.

"You helped Atheist get to us."

Love scoffed. "That's me. The great and powerful magical girl and conjurer of stairs. Flee before my power, and despair as you face stairs."

"Don't go beating yourself over the fight. Each of us has a strength and a weakness."

Love slouched in her chair. "Is it because I wasn't articulate enough? Did I say something wrong? Am I wrong?"

"What's this?" a voice bellowed. Somehow, Zealot was now standing at the end of the table, peering down at Love with indignant rage.

Love gave a quiet high-pitched squeaking noise and slid toward the wall, away from Zealot's sudden and inexplicable appearance.

"Zealot," Christian said. "Stop sneaking up on us like that."

"Never!" Zealot slammed his fist on the table, causing Love's non-brand-specific drink to spill. "Do I understand that this great young lady is reviling herself after a successful and glorious day of righteous combat? For shame! Shame on you for feeling shame. You must not feel shame that others did not listen to you. Such feelings are shameful."

Love started to say something, then stopped to think. "Wait . . . so should I feel shame, or not?"

"Not," Zealot said. "In times of great conflict, few have the wisdom to listen to you. The lions were too blinded by their rage, so I was needed to thwart their evil schemes."

"I just felt so useless," Love said.

"What?" Zealot grabbed Christian's arm and pressed buttons on Book's holodisplay control panel.

Book projected onto the table. She was asleep in a holographic bed. There was a nightstand next to the bed with a digital alarm clock.

"Book," Zealot said, "set this poor wonderful woman's mind right."

"Book!" Zealot swung his hand as if to smack Book awake but his hand just passed through her. "Awaken!"

The alarm went off.

Book cracked her eyes open very slightly then pressed the snooze button on the alarm clock. "Shut up, Samuel, go back to sleep." Book said, muttering.

"Book," Christian shouted.

Book opened one eye and yawned. "Oh? You guys are actually consulting me for something? And here I was, hoping I could sleep forever, hoping you had achieved moral perfection not needing me. I'm merely the divinely-inspired AI built by the one and only eternal Creator of all cosmic reality."

"Can we skip the sass this time, Book?" Christian said. "Love is feeling guilty for her lack of help in our most recent battle with Tyranny, Fascism, and Puritan."

"So, stop." Book pulled the covers over her head.

"Oh, come on," Christian said. "It can't be that simple."

Book groaned and poked her head out of her holographic covers. Then she looked at Love. "For everything there is a season, a time to kill, a time to heal, a time to tank, a time to peel, a time to break down, a time to build up, a time to say bye, and a time to say, 'What's up?' A time to mourn, a time to dance, a time to be dressed, and a time to not wear pants. A time to love, and a time to hate. A time to be Australian and use the word *mate*. The Overseer has made everything beautiful in its time. Something, something, this last part has to rhyme."

Christian sent Book a suspicious glare. "You made that up."

"I made half of that up." Book pulled the covers back over her head. "I'm too out-of-practice for a proper verse. Or rather, you are too out-of-practice. You get the idea. Maybe if you consulted me more, you'd get better advice that is closer to what my author intended. You consult me this little, and to you I will sound like bad poetry."

"I think," Zealot said, "this small shiny woman is trying to say different circumstances require different approaches. You cannot expect kind words and actions to be sufficient every time."

Love cracked a smile. "I see. That does cheer me up a bit." She sipped her drink, what little was left after it had spilled. "Oh dear, I need another one." She raised a hand to summon a passing waiter.

The waiter replaced Love's drink with unusual speed, as if anticipating the spill before it happened. "Can I get you anything else?" the waiter said.

"No, we're good," Christian said.

Truth walked over and sat next to her sister.

"Are you sure?" the waiter said. "Ice cream? Pizza? Dream job? Comprehensive dubbed anime streaming service?"

Zealot laughed. "This small food-servant assaults us with humor. As if such a wonderous thing could ever exist."

"Exactly," Love said.

"Forgive me," Truth said, "but I take hyperbole very seriously."

"Yeah," Christian said. "To her, hyperbole is the most important thing in the world."

Truth scowled at Christian.

"Sorry." Christian gave a sheepish smile.

"Regardless," Truth said, "I'm not certain anyone would want a comprehensive anime streaming service. It would include horrid stories."

The waiter smiled. "If you want a world where those things don't exist, I can get that for you."

Everyone stared blankly at the waiter.

He looked uncomfortable. "All I have to do is erase your memory of those things, anything to have our customers content."

Zealot grabbed the waiter by the scruff of the shirt and hoisted him into the air. "Are you saying you can make me forget any work of fiction I don't like?"

"Well, uh . . ." The waiter was perturbed by being hoisted into the air. "Sure, I could even make it good."

Zealot dropped the waiter and turned toward the table. "Do you all understand what this means?"

"We could make *Pilgrim's Progress: Reloaded* good?" Truth said.

"Well, even I have my limits." The waiter straightened his shirt.

"Cease your omniscient banter." Zealot turned back toward the waiter. "This drink fairy can bestow upon us whatever we want, no matter how impossible."

"Wait, really?" Love sprang to her feet and stepped in front of the waiter. "You mean you could create for me a four-versus-one hunting game involving monster tracking and tactical map presence?"

The waiter considered the question. "Well . . . that seems oddly specific. As if you are mourning the cancelation of a particular obscure game. But yes."

Love made a shrill noise like a mixture between a bird's cry for help and a hyperventilating Valley girl.

"Hey, everyone," a voice said from the doorway. It was Interpreter, along with a gaggle of Armininans and Calvinists. "I've been looking all over for you. What have you been up to Christian?"

"We've been fighting lions and fascists with stairs."

"Oh my." Interpreter paused and looked around. "A pop culture reference? Without Art nearby? Then this place must be the Restaurant of Culture."

Christian paused as if waiting for Interpreter to make some sort of ominous inference. He did not.

"Is that bad?" Christian said.

"Eh," Interpreter said with a nonchalant tone. "In any event. We're about to head out to the next city. Are you coming with us?"

"Yes, in a minute," Love said. "These waiters were going to grant our every possible desire."

Interpreter raised an eyebrow.

"Is *that* bad?" Christian said. This time with more emphasis. Which is what the italics is for.

Interpreter considered this for several seconds. "Well . . . not necessarily."

"Great!" Christian turned to the waiter. "Now about that video game . . ."

Interpreter shrugged and stepped outside, the Arminians and Calvinists followed.

The waiter walked to a large screen at the far end of the restaurant, pressed a few buttons, and the title screen for a video game appeared.

Love ran to the screen and pressed her hand against the pixels. "You did it!" Love said with a squeal of delight.

Christian looked at Truth, questioning. "What's her deal?"

"It's too complicated to explain," Truth said. "But that won't stop me. So, there's this studio called Turtle Rock—"

"No, not that," Christian said. "Love never struck me as much of an aficionado of fine art."

"Aficionado. Nice word, Christian. I approve. And yes, Love is best-suited for appreciating fine art. Especially well-designed ones like that game seems to be, objectively."

"You know, guys,"—Love turned and faced the group with a smile that seemed huge even for Love—"this is a five-player game."

"I can get you four other players," the waiter said.

Four holographic people materialized next to Love, with their own computer consoles.

"Sweet," Love clapped her hands together in joy.

Interpreter appeared again at the door. "Hey, it's been awhile. Are you coming?"

"Oh, dear," Zealot said. "The confounding chronology of this concrete collective has befuddled us. We should indeed set about assisting Interpreter with his efforts to warn others of the threat of total atomic annihilation." Zealot started toward the door.

"Wait, I want to try something." Truth walked up to the bar at the end of the restaurant. "Waiter! I need an answer to a question."

The waiter said, "Will this make you more content?"

"Yes," Truth said. "How many angels can dance on the head of a pin? I must know."

"Fourteen."

Truth paused, as if surprised by the sudden precise answer. Then she produced a datapad and typed in something. "Fascinating. Does that vary depending on the dance?"

"Yes. Fourteen is both the Mean and the Mode of how many angels can dance on the head of a pin but with other dances the actual number is higher or lower."

"Does it vary based on the type of pin?"

"No."

"Ah! Due to the incorporeality. Very fascinating. Can you stick around? I have so many questions I need answers to."

"If it will make you more content," the waiter said.

"Great! Now regarding the number of angels that can dance on a *pen* . . ."

Zealot walked up to Truth, and interrupted. "Truth, we must begone."

Christian walked up next to Zealot. "I think we've earned a little time off."

Zealot looked to Interpreter.

"Rest is important." Interpreter sound as if he was unsure of the statement. "Just meet me outside of town tomorrow." He ducked back outside.

"Right," Truth said, still typing on her datapad. "Atlantis. Is it the Eye of Africa or just some myth the Greeks made up to make people try harder to be upstanding?"

"This is great," Christian said. "Can we wish for anything? I would like some ice cream."

The waiter blinked. "You can wish for anything. And your wish is for ice cream?"

"Hey, get off my back. I'm a simple man. Have you ever had ice cream?"

"I have not." The waiter turned to the back of the bar and rifled through some compartments. "But anything to make you content." He glanced back at Zealot. "What will it be for you?"

Stroking his chin, Zealot didn't answer.

"I can get whatever you want."

"Please, silence," Zealot said. "You are interrupting my chin stroking. Such is a vital activity for proper thinking."

"I guess I'll get back to you." The waiter handed Christian his ice cream. After which Christian didn't pay much attention to anything else.

———

Zealot sat in a corner booth, surveying the rest of his comrades. Love was now playing through some game called *Fifty Percent Death 3*. Truth was at the bar, asking questions about various mythological creatures. Christian was just sitting there, eating ice cream.

"Anything we can do to make you feel more content?" the waiter said.

Zealot leapt from his seat. His hand went to his pistol on instinct. "How did you get there so fast? Are you a teleporting waiter person?"

The waiter raised his hands and backed away. "All right, I get that you don't need anything. Just let us know."

Zealot glared at the waiter as he walked away. His hand never left his pistol holster. "I believe we must away," he said, loud enough for the others to hear.

"I can't yet," Christian said. "The waiters said they'd get me a high-paying job here. I need that." He took another bite of the ice cream.

"A job? Working for who?" Zealot said with skepticism.

"The owner of this restaurant," a waiter said, who was now suddenly next to Zealot.

Zealot sprang back away from the waiter. "How do you keep doing that? Is this how other people feel when I sneak up on them?"

"Don't worry," the waiter said. "We only want you to be content. The manager demands it."

"Manager?" Zealot said, his eyes narrowing. "Who's your manager?"

"You know," the waiter said with a shrug. "Just some guy. A normal person. Who is definitely not a giant."

"I didn't claim he was a giant," Zealot said with a growing tone of distrust.

"Oh. Well . . . good, 'cause he isn't one. He made this place so weary pilgrims could be content and find fulfillment. Whether that be through art, work, food, or obscure asymmetric video games."

"I think me and my friends are sufficiently content," Zealot said. "We really must be going."

"But we can't leave," Love said. "*Fifty Percent Death 4* is coming out in just a few days."

"That does excite me." Zealot paused, a twinge of excitement in his voice, "But we must find Interpreter. No doubt, he is worried about us. It has been a day, hasn't it? Or has it been longer?"

"But I'm learning so much," Truth said. "For example, did you know Bigfoot is actually a hoax? I mean, I'd suspected but now I know for sure."

"Ok . . . but what use is that?"

Truth blinked. "I don't understand the question. I'm learning things. That's probably good."

"Probably? Since when do you not give straight answers?"

"Get off my back." Truth's tone was unusually harsh.

"Yeah," Christian said. "Besides, we aren't just having fun. I got a job. I'm being productive. I start in just a few minutes."

"How did you get the job already?" Zealot said. "We've only been here—" He checked his wrist computer. The chronometer seemed to be malfunctioning. He struck it a few times to see if that remedied its malfunction, then he struck it a few more times for fun.

"We will help Interpreter," Love said, "eventually. We're just taking a break."

"This cannot be healthy," Zealot said.

"Sure, it is," Truth said. "I'm learning a lot. Christian is starting a big important job, and Love is having a good time. You're the only one complaining, Zealot."

"Because we have a mission to pursue."

"What is wrong with being content?" Christian said through a mouthful of ice cream.

"Anything is wrong if it keeps you from doing the work which we set out to do. Outside those doors, people are in need of our help. They are under threat of total atomic annihilation. We must do our part."

"You want me to quit my job?" Christian said.

Zealot sputtered, unsure what to say. "Not . . . necessarily."

"You think video games are bad?" Love said.

"Of course not."

"You think I shouldn't learn?" Truth said.

"Listen to yourselves. You sound just like—" Zealot looked around. Several waiters were walking toward him. He inched his hand closer to his pistol. "Just like the lions."

"Can we get you anything?" a waiter whispered into Zealot's ear.

Zealot leapt away from the waiter. Almost a dozen waiters were in the room now. How were there so many? Just before, there had been only one or two. Hadn't there?

"We just want you to be content," another waiter said.

"I know what I want," Zealot said. "I want my friends to come with me and fight the good fight."

"Certainly," a waiter said. "How about a nice game of *Rebellion* first? Or a complete viewing of *Code Geass*? Maybe to satisfy your desire to contribute, we could get you a job testing firing railguns?"

"Language!" Zealot said. "It's everything I could have ever wanted. And I can't find anything wrong with saying yes."

"Because there isn't anything wrong with saying yes," Truth said. "Those railguns aren't going to test fire themselves."

The waiters surrounded Zealot.

Zealot shook. "I can't understand it, none of what is being asked of me is wrong. But why do I feel that something is wrong?"

"Maybe it's just you," Love said, her eyes still on her game.

Zealot looked down at his pistol, then up at Christian's Conscience.

But Conscience was no longer on Christian's shoulder. He dangled from the grip of one of the waiters. Conscience tried to speak, but the waiter squeezed his neck which seemed to silence the robot.

Zealot's grip on his pistol tightened. "Christian, we are in peril. These waiters are strangling your Conscience." He ran forward, grabbed Christian, and tried to pull him away. But Christian was chained to the bar.

"Christian!" Zealot tried wrenching the chains free from the bar. "You're in chains. Help me free you."

"Don't worry. I've got the key. I can free myself."

"So do it."

"In a minute. I need to file some TPS reports."

A waiter grabbed Zealot by the arm. "Please, just let us take your weapon. You'll be more content." He placed a hand on Zealot's pistol.

Zealot glared at the waiter with rage beyond his comprehension.

The waiter's face went white.

"Sir. I must inform you"—Zealot pointed the weapon at the waiter's head—"that you have dun goofed."

The waiter hissed, bearing a mouth full of fangs and sharp teeth. The skin parted, revealing the face of a mutant demon.

Zealot fired, and the waiter's head exploded into a cloud of red mist.

The other waiters charged at him.

Zealot spun, firing missiles into each of the fanged waiters.

A laser blast struck Zealot's back. Zealot turned around. Three waiters arose from behind the counter with laser rifles.

Zealot kicked over a table and dove for cover.

Lasers danced across the restaurant floor and shredded the walls and other tables. Scraps of paper napkins, salt and pepper shaker contents, and bits of silverware flew through the air and burst into flame. Lasers riddled the restaurant.

Zealot poked his head over the table to get a vantage of the gunmen.

A laser struck Zealot's shielded head.

He ducked back down. His invisible shielded helmet would withstand many such strikes. But the gunmen were firing very many lasers. And very many was more than many. Plus, the gunmen didn't seem to be running out of ammunition.

Zealot looked at Christian, still on the barstool, looking at a pile of documents and eating ice cream. None of the lasers touched him. He seemed oblivious to the attack.

"Christian," Zealot said, "assist me. These waiters are not what they seem."

"I've got to focus on my work." Christian didn't look up from the documents. "Besides, I wouldn't do much good."

"What?" Zealot said.

"Yeah," Love said. "We've been fighting these forces of evil for so long, and what do we have to show for it? Nobody will listen."

Zealot sent a missile in the general direction of his attackers. "All the more reason for us to fight harder."

The gunfire from the waiters sent chips of wood flying from the table, eating away at Zealot's cover, bit by bit.

"I can do something with my work," Christian said. "Fighting these forces of darkness doesn't seem to get us anywhere. I'm content to let skilled people handle it, like Interpreter."

"Skill is an illusion." Zealot's cover was now half the size as before. He crouched lower to avoid the laser blasts and sent missile after missile back at his attackers. "I need your help. Those still under the threat of total atomic annihilation need your help. We must help." The waiters seemed undeterred by Zealot's counterattack.

"Sorry," Christian said. "Don't have time." He yawned and returned to his paperwork.

Zealot looked toward Truth, then Love. They were as enraptured with their contentment as Christian, which left only one option.

"This is going to hurt." Zealot tensed, preparing his mind for the pain. With his eyes wide open, he jumped over the table. Lasers ripped into his armor, some bouncing off, some melting bits of metal. He felt the melting metal burn his skin. He raised his pistol and fired three times.

Christian's paperwork, Love's screen, and the waiter talking to Truth all blew up.

"Zealot!" Love turned on Zealot, anger in her eyes. "Why would you do that?"

Christian threw up his hands in exasperation. "How am I supposed to make a living now?"

"Are you some sort of anti-intellectual hack?" Truth yelled.

More laser blasts burned into Zealot, and he crumpled to the ground. Blood seeped from the wreckage of his armor.

"No matter," Love said. "There are always other ways to have fun." She walked to a shelf that materialized out of nowhere, full of board games.

"I will find other work." Christian turned back to the counter and a waiter placed more paperwork in front of him.

"The world has no shortage of useless information," Truth said.

Zealot groaned and fell forward onto his face. A pool of blood seeped outward from his body.

"Finally," a waiter said. "I thought he'd never go down."

"Look at this." Love pointed to the shelf of games. "How about a nice quick game of *Twilight Imperium: eighty-seventh edition*?"

"Not yet," a voice said.

"What was that?" a waiter said.

Something in the center of the restaurant moved.

"What? How?" a waiter said.

More gunshots.

Zealot shambled forward, his armor turned red from his blood.

The waiters turned their guns on him and fired. Blood and metal flew from Zealot's chest.

Zealot continued forward. He raised his gun.

The waiters ducked for cover.

Then Zealot stopped.

"There's only one way to stop this." Tears fell from Zealot's face, mixing with the blood. He turned his pistol toward Love.

STAGE 19

WHAT THE GIRL IN THE YELLOW CARDIGAN SAID

Love walked forward, looking at the box art of her board game.

A missile struck her in the chest. The box flew from her hand. Shields crackled around her, and she skidded backward.

Love looked shocked. "Zealot, why?"

Another missile struck Love, knocking her back. Then another missile and another.

With each missile, a tear fell from Zealot's eyes.

Love flew back into the wall, but the missiles kept flying, her shields fighting against the successive explosions. With each strike, the shields grew weaker. Then she fell, blood flying from her mouth.

Zealot trudged over to Love, each step sending a sound of cracking bone echoing through the restaurant. He pointed his gun into Love's face.

Love's eyes pleaded. She tried to speak, but she choked and her blood mixed with her red hair till you couldn't tell what was and was not bloodied.

"Zealot," Truth yelled.

Truth and Christian left their seats at the bar then stared at him in shock.

"Love has been corrupted," Zealot said. "All passion, all zeal has been diverted toward mundane things."

"So you're going to destroy her?" Christian said with fear and confusion in his voice.

"I can't let you all be trapped in this place. If I remove all ability to love—"

"Then you'll take away someone the Overseer sent us," Christian said.

"What else can I do? You have all succumbed to contentment."

"You're becoming like Puritan." Christian took a step toward Zealot. "You're becoming like Legalist. Nothing we are doing here is wrong."

The gun shook in Zealot's hand. "Then it is not what you are doing. It's what you are *not* doing."

"Why do we need to do more good things? Is this not enough?" Christian said.

"No, it is never enough, not while there are still those who . . ." Zealot fell to one knee and clutched his chest. "Those who . . ." He collapsed, and fired another missile at Love. Red blood and red hair flew through the air.

———

Christian looked down at Zealot and Love, both immobile, bleeding husks. "I don't understand." His brain refused to process what had happened. "What have we done?"

"We have let Zealot and Love fade away." Truth fell to her knees, tears streaming from her face.

Christian looked back at the bar where two waiters were reloading their laser rifles. He grabbed one of them by the collar. "What did you do to Zealot?"

"Hey, we just do what the manager tells us."

"Then I demand to speak to your manager," Christian said.

The waiters exchanged looks, then snickered at Christian.

The restaurant shook. Glasses fell from the counter, shattering and adding to the salt, wood splinters, and blood puddles across the floor.

Christian scanned the room. His heart quickened. "That . . . uh . . .

may have been a mistake." He released the waiter and backed away from the bar toward Truth. He went for his rifle.

Dust shook from the ceiling. Then, the ceiling cracked and rose above the restaurant. Two huge hands hoisted the ceiling into the air and moved it aside, as if they were opening a giant cylindrical container of non-brand-specific chips.

"Fee, Fi, Fo, Fum," a bellowing voice said. "I smell the blood of a Christian man."

"Hey," Truth perked up. "That's the original line."

Above them, where the ceiling used to be, stood an enormous giant. The giant was dressed in a well-tailored bathrobe and had a pipe in his mouth.

The giant reached down and snatched up Christian in one hand.

Truth tried to dodge but the giant scooped her up as well in his other hand.

"Can't believe you let me grab you." The giant looked down at Christian and smirked. "You might have dodged me if you had used that Law Protocol you have plugged into your suit."

Christian winced. He'd forgotten Conscience had been given him that ability. In fact, Christian seemed to remember there was some other powerful ability he had been given. Christian couldn't put his finger on it. What was it again?

"What do you want with us?" Truth said, squirming in the giant's grip.

"What do I want?" the giant said. "Nothing but to serve you. To give you contentment. After all, I am the Giant Contentment. Your happiness is my only desire." He motioned toward a name tag on his bathrobe that said HELLO, My Name Is Giant Contentment.

"If that's all you want," Christian said, "why did Zealot and Love go crazy? What did you do to them? Are they still alive?"

"Hard to say." Contentment's voice was so loud, Christian's teeth rattled. "Zealot wasn't the type to be satisfied by contentment. His conflict with Love was inevitable."

"Put us down." Christian struggling to get loose. "We have to help them."

"I'm afraid I can't let you help Zealot. He means to ruin your contentment, always demanding you do more and more. You must rest."

"What about Love?" Truth said. "That's my sister down there bleeding out."

"I think you'll find it easier to be content with her out of the picture. She, like Zealot, kept wanting more and more, perhaps even more than I could provide. With her gone, you'll find your desires far more subdued and easier to quench. So, just stay put and enjoy yourself."

"But I need to leave here and help Interpreter," Christian said. "There are so many who are lost."

"Have I not given you jobs that will fulfill your desire to have purpose? Why do ye need to leave this restaurant?"

Truth twisted, then with surprising strength, popped out of the giant's hand.

The giant looked shocked.

Truth ran up Contentment's arm to his shoulder and slid down toward the giant's name tag, which was the size of a small billboard. She grabbed one end of the name tag and ripped it off before Contentment could stop her.

Contentment roared a guttural inhuman roar and grabbed Truth with his free hand.

"Ha! I knew it." Truth pointed at the giant's chest, where another name tag stood underneath the original. It said HELLO, My Name Is Giant Despair.

Truth looked at the name and shuddered, as if it brough back a horrific memory. "You're not Contentment. You're the Giant Despair."

The giant looked down at the new name tag. "As a matter of fact, it does say Giant Despair on my uniform, but that is a mistake. I changed my name long ago. I used to waylay travelers and toss them into my dungeon to be eaten, but I don't work that way much anymore. Now, pilgrims are more than happy to chain themselves in my dungeon so long as they have contentment. That usually gets them out of the way, and I get to sit back and relax. Before, I had to work hard to capture pilgrims and hold them in my dungeon. Now, it is quite easy."

Christian looked down at his hands. He still wore his chains. The chain went all the way down to the desk below in the restaurant.

"I don't understand." Christian wrestled against the giant's grip but to no avail. "Nothing you offered in the restaurant was sinful. How can it trap pilgrims?"

"They don't have to be sinful," Truth said in sudden realization. "These things he offered us—they make us content but do little else. They've corrupted Love's desires and tried to stifled Zealot's passion. That can only lead to despair. We were never meant to remain fully content, we were meant to strive to do more, unsatisfied with the imperfect nature of this world."

The giant grinned. "It seems you are wise to my shenanigans."

"Let us go," Christian said.

The giant chuckled. "Very well. If you do not wish to pursue contentment, then we shall be forced to inflict upon you our greatest weapon."

"You don't scare me." Christian voice cracked.

Despair smiled. "Good." He grabbed Truth, picked both of them up in one hand, whipped them around his head and flung them into the distance.

———

Christian gasped and opened his eyes. He tried to get up. Something was pushing down on his chest. Pain sang from almost every sinew of his body. He felt like he had several broken bones or ruptured organs. He felt the medical protocols in his suit trying to kick in. They seemed ill-suited for the extent of his damage.

"So, it was Contentment who did you in." The voice came from just above his chest.

Christian looked up. A short figure with crossed arms stood over Christian wearing a baker's apron, and leaning down on him with one foot.

"I must say, my minions thought you'd get stopped by my boys at Palace Beautiful. Who knew Giant Contentment would win the bet? Another golden fiddle lost. Oh well."

Christian groaned and tried to move, but the figure held him in place.

"Personally, I thought Fascist would get you. Never thought the Atheists would turn on me like that. Pretty clever, ya'll, to use them as compatriots against your common foe."

"Who are—" Christian tried to speak but the pressure on his chest was too great.

"Who am I? You don't recognize me? I'm hurt." The figure made an overly dramatic gesticulation with his hands, then leaned in closer. Though he wore the garb of a baker, he didn't look human. To say the face was ugly, demonic, or like the supermutant monsters Christian had faced before would be to miss the point. Those horrors did not compare to this phobic, monstrosity.

"Apollyon," Christian said.

"Yeah, that's the name used in this allegory. I got a ton of 'em though." With a twisted smile through his mangled teeth, Apollyon handed Christian a tray of chocolate cupcakes. "Cupcake?" Apollyon said with bizarre normality.

Christian looked at the cupcakes, then back at the lord of all evil, who was dressed as a baker.

"They're poisoned," Christian said.

"Of course, they're poisonous." Apollyon grabbed one and took a bite. "Given your circumstances, I figured you might consider suicide. You'd be surprised how many suckers take the easy way out. Does my job for me. It's amazing how little I have to do for folks to go astray. Most folks look at me as some constant cosmic evil, but I'm just a baker. A little levin, a little heat, and the little muffins do most of the work for me."

Christian looked around for help, but there was only sand in every direction.

"I'm afraid you won't find much assistance in the Desert of Emptiness." Apollyon yawned and dug his boot heel deeper into Christian's chest plate, cracking a rib. The armor was the only thing keeping Apollyon's foot from grinding him to mush.

"Let's see." Apollyon counted on his fingers. "Zealot bled out back at Despair's restaurant. What's left of Love is getting cooked into pies that Despair's waiters are serving to unsuspecting guests, and that leaves"—Apollyon smiled with feigned indifference—"Truly. Wasn't that what you called her?" He snapped his fingers. Two supermutant demons walked up, holding Truth above the ground.

Truth wrestled with the brutes, but they were too strong for her.

"You—" Christian tried to cough out an insult.

Apollyon smirked down at him, stopping the words in Christian's throat. "What? I what? Please, Christian, you did this to yourself. You want to blame me for all your problems, go ahead—makes it harder to repent when you think your problems are caused by an outside force."

"Christian," Truth said, "don't listen to him."

Apollyon snapped his fingers, and one of the demons clamped his hand over Truth's mouth.

"I don't believe you," Christian said. "Any second now, Zealot and Love will show up and beat your muffin man's behind."

"Yes." Apollyon hissed, a forked tongue appearing for a moment between the baker's teeth. "Rely on your own power to get out of this mess. That's a great plan. Now then, as for Truth." He stepped off Christian and walked to Truth.

"Stop." Christian tried to get up, but his leg gave a loud snap and he fell to the ground, screaming in pain.

Apollyon looked Truth up and down. "You've been a real pain. You know that, Truth?"

Truth could only glare at the baker, her mouth still covered by the demon's hand.

"You shouldn't be too difficult to deal with. Love and Zealot dealt with each other. Now that Christian here has had so many misguided desires, I doubt he'll ever want to love anything. Contentment has sapped him of any passion to do more than the mundane. But you—" He ran a taloned finger across Truth's cheek, leaving burned flesh in its wake. "—you might prove a problem. Fortunately, Christian has done everything we need, for we are in the Desert of Emptiness. When one is empty of passion, drive, and love, the mind slowly follows. Without the will to learn, little knowledge is gained. Without the drive to understand, little wisdom is nurtured. Lies will eventually creep in."

Apollyon motioned to the two demons, and they dropped Truth.

Truth screamed and punched Apollyon in the face before he could say anything.

Apollyon's head snapped back with a sickening crack. He pulled his head back into place. "Oh no." His tone was wreathed in sarcasm. "Never saw that coming." He rolled his eyes and struck her to the ground with one blow. "Not so fast and powerful now, are you? Now that Zealot isn't around." He knelt and whispered into her ear. "You get the slowest death. Have fun." He started to walk away with his two demonic goons.

"That's right," Truth said, rising slower this time. Her skin seemed whiter, and her white hair had grayed. "You better run." Truth fell again, then turned toward Christian.

Christian tried moving toward her with little success. "You're not going to finish us off?" he said to Apollyon. "Classic evil overlord mistake."

"Afraid I can't," Apollyon shouted over his shoulder. "Overseer would atomize me if I tried. Not that I've ever needed to do much. You've managed to cause more damage than I ever could have hoped. What else would I suspect from such a homicidal maniac? You are welcome to help yourself to those cupcakes if you want. They're fresh and will result in a mostly painless death."

Truth crawled over to Christian, looking older now. Weak. Frail.

Christian just lay there. Movement hurt. Not like before, under the weight of his burden, but from the pain in his flesh, and in his heart.

"Truth," Christian said. "Help me out of this. Zealot and Love are gone. What can I do without them? What can I do without you?"

Truth paused as if considering her answer. "Even without us . . ." Each word sounded painful. "You won't be alone. Your chains are unlocked. You can . . . You can . . ." Her hair turned to dust, and she collapsed.

"Truth, no!" Christian reached for her. "Don't you leave me too. I won't give up. I won't." He tried rising, but collapsed. His damage was beyond pain, his horror beyond grief. He could not move. After ten minutes of trying, he said, "I can't."

Apollyon was long gone.

Truth was almost motionless.

"I can't move," Christian said. "I can't make myself help you. I can't make myself do anything. All I have is emptiness. Zealot is gone. Love is gone. There is only emptiness. What do I do, Truth?"

Truth gave no answer.

Christian groaned, closed his eyes, and waited for the end.

STAGE 20
ANODOS' LIBRARY

Christian gasped and opened his eyes. How was he in a new place? This time he felt no pain. He sat up. It was night. He was lying on the sidewalk of a high school campus. A few feet away, a set of steps led down to a large plaza.

Next to the steps sat a purple-haired girl. The girl was looking toward the plaza and didn't seem to take any notice of Christian. She was looking through the scope of an enormous sniper rifle, a weapon that seemed far too large for her. "Finally, you're awake," the girl said without moving from the rifle.

Awake? How had he gotten there?

"Hey, this may sound sudden," the girl said, still looking through the rifle. "But would you join up with us?"

"Join up with you? I don't understand. Where am I?"

"You died, right? This is the afterlife. You have to fight. You'll get obliterated if you don't."

"The afterlife?" Christian folded his arms and looked at her, suspiciously. "This doesn't look like the Celestial Station."

"Celestial Station?" She looked over at Christian with an amused look. "Why would we be there? What are you, some kind of moron?"

"Maybe a little. Who are you?" Christian said with a tone full of distrust.

She smirked. "We are The Not Dead Yet Battlefront."

Christian stared at her. "I'm sorry, what?"

"We used to be called Afterlife Battlefront. Then 'I Want to Be Dead Battlefront.' That name lasted about a day. Man, were people upset about that one. We're still open to new name ideas. You got any?"

"Uh, no." Christian looked closer at her rifle. "Is that thing real?"

"It wouldn't be much good if it weren't. We have to be on our guard to fight the enemy. Look, here she comes."

Christian followed the point of the sniper rifle down to the plaza. A small girl with white hair walked across the plaza. She looked like a younger version of Truth. "Who's that?"

"That's Change. She's been fighting us since before I can remember. She may look like a sweet innocent girl, but she'll obliterate you if you're not careful."

"Okay." Christian moved away from the girl with the rifle. "I think I'm done here. I'll go talk to her." He walked down the stairs.

"What! You can't do that. You'll be obliterated. Ugh. What the expletive, I used to be such a great recruiter."

Christian ignored the purple-haired girl's protests. This had to be some kind of dream, so he didn't care too much about dying. Not that dying would matter anyway. How different was that from his past existence? He reached the bottom of the stairs and approached the young girl with the white hair. "Hey, I should probably tell you that there's a girl up there pointing a sniper rifle at you."

She didn't look concerned. "That's all right." Her voice sounded almost monotone. Not robotic, just weary.

"That's all right?"

"It's not as if anyone can die here."

"Why can't they die?"

"Because everyone is dead."

Christian raised an eyebrow. This was a dream. So, it's not as if he expected a logical conclusion. Still, it seemed odd. "Already dead? That's impossible. This can't be the afterlife. What about final judgment?"

The girl cocked her head and looked at Christian as if studying some strange species of animal. "Oh, I see." She wasn't smiling. "You think this is the afterlife for those who have physically died. It is not. This is the afterlife for those who have died spiritually."

"What's the difference?"

"Not much. Usually, those who have died physically have a greater impact on the living though."

"Ouch. Anyway, that girl back there with the sniper rifle said she was part of something called The Not Dead Yet Battlefront. She says you're their enemy."

"I'm just trying to get them to act. To cure their apathy. They think, if they can defeat me, they won't have to do anything anymore. It's quite sad, really. They wish to find validity in their inaction."

"That sounds dumb."

"Perhaps, but it is easy. And that makes it attractive."

"Then what should I do?" Christian said, pleading. "I don't want to be spiritually dead."

"Really?" The girl looked surprised. "You wish to be awakened from your apathetic slumber?"

"Yes!"

"Okay." She stretched out a hand. "Guard skill: Hand sonic." An energy blade coalesced into existence out of her wrist and before Christian could even think, she stabbed him in the chest.

Christian gasped and opened his eyes. He really had to stop doing that. He sat up and looked around. This time he was in a small old-timey dormitory, reminiscent of a renaissance university. The room was a mess. Clothes and detritus lay strewn about all over. The only clean part was a large mirror at the far end of the room which reflected the entire room.

"What now? Am I really dead this time? Is this supposed to be Hell?"

"Nope," a voice said.

Christian looked toward the sound of the voice.

A skeleton sat chained near the mirror.

Christian jumped back from the skeleton. "Talking skeletons?

Really?"

"I'm not the skeleton," the voice said. "I'm back here."

Christian turned around. Behind a stack of papers was a woman sitting on a bed. She was dressed in the finest garments Christian had ever seen. Even greater than anything Truth or Love had worn. She seemed completely out of place in the trashed room. She looked like Love but with brighter hair, and more sunken, depressed eyes.

Christian said, "Where in the name of George MacDonald am I?"

"I don't know," she said. "I've been trapped here for weeks."

"And you haven't cleaned the place up?"

"I can't. Look." She reached down to pick up a pair of dirty undergarments, but they wouldn't move.

Christian reached for a book, but it also was immovable. "This doesn't make sense."

"I think I've figured it out," she said. "Look." She pointed at the mirror.

"What? I don't get it?"

"Look closer."

As far as Christian could tell, the room was the same in the mirror. A man walked into the room in the mirror. Christian looked around, but the man wasn't present in the room he was in. Only in the mirror. The man picked up a book and set it on a shelf before sitting on the bed and going to sleep.

Christian looked back around the room. The book was now indeed on the shelf. The shelves had been empty just a moment ago. "How is this possible?"

"I think," the woman said, "the more important question is, *what does it mean*? This man in the mirror is leading a disheveled and disgusting life. He thinks it is only affecting him. He doesn't know about us. He doesn't know the effect that his depravity is having on others. We would like to improve things, but without help, it is impossible."

"Do you think the man in the mirror will change?"

"Let us hope he can, and it won't take a monumental sacrifice. Perhaps if he could see us, then he would have hope."

Christian walked to the mirror. "I'm not waiting for somebody else to change their life to fix things for us. Looks like this mirror is binding us to him. So, if we can break it . . ." He pulled back his fist.

"Wait, no!" the woman shouted.

Christian punched the mirror.

The sound of shattering glass.

Then darkness.

––––––––

Christian gasped and opened his eyes. He now stood on a massive flying machine, high in the upper atmosphere of a planet he didn't recognize. Below him was a rotor for the flying machine, but it wasn't moving. The rotor on the opposite end of the flying machine was moving, but that seemed insufficient to keep it aloft as the flying machine slowly drifted toward the planet. At one end of the vessel several people climbed a ladder into an escape craft. At the rate the vessel was drifting downward, they wouldn't have time to escape. He looked closer at the immobile rotor. Why had it stopped?

The rotor was jammed. One man was crammed into each of the three blades. Each wore identical clothing and had the same face and body type. Clones, perhaps? They looked a little like Zealot, but without his fiery passion and a little shorter. The men appeared unharmed from being jammed into the rotors, and each spoke with varied levels of concern at the predicament.

Christian couldn't make out what they were saying, so he moved closer.

"Now we are all in the same boat again," one of the men said.

"I think I can free myself," another man said. When the man moved, the propellor started spinning again.

The three men became a blur of movement. Then the rotor stopped, and the three men were trapped just as before.

"Don't," the first man stuck in the rotors said. "The rotor is only stuck because we're all in between. As soon as one of us moves, it will start running again. Then we all die."

"But," the second man said, "if we continue blocking the rotor, then the highboat will crash. One way or another, we're dead."

"Just how did we manage to end up in this stupid situation?" the third man said.

"I'm sure it's the culmination of a fascinating and well-designed German adventure game that details the events leading up to this moment."

"What?" the other two said.

"Don't look at me. You two messed it up this time."

"What? Can't come up with a cunning plan for once?" the third man said.

"Let me think." The first man paused. "Nah . . . it's completely hopeless."

"So, we can relax then," the second man said, with an edge of sarcasm in his voice.

"Self!" A female's voice cried from nearby.

"Goal!" the three men said together.

A tall, thin auburn-haired woman in a white jumpsuit walked up to the rotor and looked down at the three men. "What's happened here?"

"Doesn't matter," the second man said.

"You have to get us out of here," the first man said.

"Preferably before the highboat crashes," the third said.

"It's a little too late for that," the woman said. "All these rotor failures have damaged the engines. We're able to hold the highboat in position for now. But evacuation has already started. We've only got minutes."

"Get me out of here." The second man looked up at the woman above the rotor, pleading. "You can only save one of us before the rotor starts turning again."

"Come on, make a decision," the third man said.

"How can I decide that?" she said. "I don't even know who's who."

"I am Self," the first man said.

"He's lying," the second man said. "I am Self."

"They're both bold-faced liars," the third man said. "I am Self."

"Oh, great," she said. "Can the real Self give me some sort of proof?"

"Of course, I can," first Self said. "Simply trust your heart."

The woman looked deeply into first Self's eyes. An eternity of memories seemed to flash between the two—times of struggle, chaos, triumph and love.

"My heart says . . ." She sounded uncertain. "Um . . . perhaps the one in front?" She pointed at second Self.

"What? No!" the first Self said. "Forget the bit about your heart. There are more reliable methods. Look carefully. I'm much better looking than those two scarecrows."

The woman scowled at the first Self. "You all look the same."

Christian called for help, but the four people could not hear him, either because he was too far away, or this illusion was not meant to be tampered with—as if this image was sent to send a message.

"Who cares which of us is Self?" the first Self said. "Just leave us here, and save yourself. The most important thing is that you survive."

"Ha! He just gave himself away," the second Self said.

"Exactly," the third Self said. "The real Self—that's me—would never say such a thing."

"You're right." The woman sounded sad. "That really didn't sound like Self. Could you have changed that much?" She peered into the first Self's eyes.

"The real Self will never change. You know that." The third Self sounded sadistically triumphant.

"Then perhaps it's just another trick to look good." The woman's look changed from sadness to uncertainty.

"No!" The first Self looked down at the long fall to the planet below. "It's true. I'm not Self." He pointed at the second Self. "He is."

The other two Selfs looked shocked.

"What?" Collecting himself, the second Self's demeanor changed. "Um . . . yes. Yeah, sure. He's right. I am Self."

The woman looked at the first Self, then the second. "Is this a trick? A last desperate maneuver?" She looked back at the first Self. "If I help him, it's too late to change your mind. You're going to fall—and die."

"Definitely." The first Self started to move. "Just think: How can I be the real Self? The real Self is never going to give up. He'll never change. And he'll never"—he pried himself free from the rotor—"let go."

"Stop!" the woman said.

The first Self, the true Self, fell from the rotor.

With the first Self no longer blocking the rotor, the second Self pulled himself out of the rotor with the help of Goal. The blades spun, lifting the highboat up and away from the planet below.

"No!" The woman reached down toward the image of the real Self, falling toward the planet. "No . . ."

The platform lurched upward, and Christian fell. Screaming, he sailed down toward the planet after Self.

Christian fell for a minute. The planet grew closer and closer.

"Hello, Christian," a familiar voice said. Interpreter was just a few feet away, falling with him.

"Interpreter? What are you doing here?"

"Do you understand, Christian? About Self?"

"This is a dream. A vision."

"Actually, it's a scene irreverently stolen from a masterpiece of interactive storytelling. But, yes. Do you understand?"

"Sort of. Explain it to me anyway, so there's no confusion. This seems very contrived."

"Self was a scoundrel who would sacrifice anything to get what he wanted. But his true goal was the heart of that woman, Goal."

"Her name was Goal?"

"Turns out old-timey theological epic fantasy isn't the only work of fiction that uses overly obvious allegorical personifications. Ultimately Self's plan was brilliant, really. It was the only thing he could do—a genius plan from a philosophical point of view, the ultimate altruistic deed. Granted, you didn't see everything leading up to this point. But Self—the oh-so-selfishly-resolute Self—finally changed at last. Not only was Goal saved, but so was everyone trying to escape on the highboat. A bunch of other people too, but I don't have time to explain all that."

Christian didn't respond.

"Christian?"

Christian tried speaking, but his throat had grown dry.

"Oh no, I think I've kept you under too long," Interpreter said.

In an instant light filled Christian's vision, he gasped, and actually opened his eyes.

STAGE 21
THE KISS OF C.C

"Christian," Interpreter said, "you're awake. Thank the Overseer."

Christian squinted, then looked around. He was back in the Desert of Emptiness. Interpreter stood next to him, and Truth lay just a few feet away, withered and possibly asleep. A few of the Calvinists and Arminians stood around Truth. In the distance, a massive hovervehicle had a few other pilgrims around it.

"How did you like my allegories?" Interpreter said.

"Your what?" Christian rubbed his head.

"The visions."

"You gave me those visions? How?"

"I plugged an artificial reality hard drive into your suit and accessed your subconscious to create a series of synthesized dream states via a cultural zeitgeist matrix. You know, it doesn't matter. The point is, did you understand the message?"

Christian stared at Interpreter, puzzled.

Interpreter gave a kindly but disappointed look at Christian "The visions were all from famous works of fiction. Surely you saw their meaning."

"Famous . . . right."

"Okay, obscure works. But philosophically poignant."

Christian tried to stand, but his legs sent familiar pain from the crunching bones. He fell back on his back. "It looks like I'm back where I started. So no. I didn't catch the message."

"Don't you appreciate fine art?"

"No, I don't know any of the works you were referencing."

Interpreter sighed and rubbed his forehead. "Look, just go read *Phantastes*, and watch *Angel Beats*. The *Deponia Trilogy* has some bad content, so maybe stay away from that, but the point . . ." He trailed off.

"The point?" Christian said.

"Right, the point. The first vision had to do with those who fight against change. Those who fear their ultimate demise instead of using it as inspiration to do good. This causes, or is the result of, spiritual death. The complete lack of willpower. They see the truth of their powerlessness and thus, lose all zealotry. To do nothing, to be without purpose, is to die. All The Not Dead Yet Battlefront could find to fight was the concept of change, for they saw change as beyond their control and thus it terrified them. And to reject change is one of the main signs of spiritual death. Though it's more complicated than that."

"That's why Apollyon didn't seem too concerned with me dying."

"Exactly," Interpreter said. "You weren't much threat to him either way."

"And the second vision, with the room and the mirror? You were trying to show the effects of my actions on others?"

"You're close," Interpreter said. "The man in the mirror world and his inaction led to the woman's discomfort. When he cleaned the room, the mirror room became clean. In that story, at first, the man, one Cosmo by name if you care about the lore, didn't even see it. The lesson is that we can do all manner of good, but we are often blind to it and its effects. In our love of ourselves, our incomplete love, we refuse to see the truth of our situation. We do not see what we could do, those we could help, for we are too content in our inaction."

"And the final vision?" Christian said. "A message that the self can be redeemed?"

"Yes, sort of. Self can be pulled up from even the most depraved selfishness. The message is more hopeful—that ultimately, redemption is the only way out. Self tried all manner of verbal tricks to escape his conundrum. He thought if he tried hard enough, had enough zeal for his cause of escape, that he would triumph. He thought all puzzles could be solved, and all evils were avoidable, simply with enough hard work. Which in the game that allegory came from had always been the case up until that point. There was always a solution, a trick that resulted in triumph, though often also in the downfall of others— whom Self cared little for. Though he isn't called Self in the original. The lesson seemed to be that through enough zealotry any barrier could be overcome. But in that final test, no matter how close Self got to convincing Goal of his identity, the impostors could have made the rotor spin, mixing them up again. Self-sacrifice, in this case, a redemptive action and the ultimate expression of love, was his only choice. And ultimately, it is our only choice. To let Self die so that our Goal may be saved."

"Wait, are you getting into predestination stuff here?"

The lead Calvinist ran up, looking excited. "Did someone say, *predestination*?"

"No, none of that, now." Interpreter shooed the Calvinist back. "Go away. Work on the hoverbase or something."

"Aw . . ." The Calvinist walked toward the large vehicle with the other pilgrims.

"That hoverbase is ours?" Christian motioned toward the vehicle.

"Yes, I won it in a long-windedness competition, but back to the point. Redemption is our only choice, not in a predestination sense, but in a moral sense. As our minds become more like Christ, doing good becomes more of a reflex and less of a choice. That is ultimately our goal. Back in the Restaurant of Contentment, you were all hung up on choice, doing good or doing bad. You correctly saw that the diversions and enjoyments of the restaurant were not bad things. But following the Overseer isn't just about not doing bad, just as Self's ultimate choice wasn't to convince Goal of his identity but to save her through a selfless act. He had to do good, not simply prevent a bad thing."

"The man in the mirror," Christian said, "he didn't do bad. But not doing good had ramifications beyond what he could see."

"Yes," Interpreter said. "When all you focus on is not doing bad, you end up empty, easily diverted by the soul-crushing nature of contentment."

Christian's face hardened. "Then I think I know what I must do. But what about Love and Zealot? Are they really dead?"

Interpreter's face grew solemn. "Zealotry and Love are the first to go when one is empty. I'm afraid that is what has happened to them. They're trapped."

"They're not dead?" Christian sat up, ignoring the pain. "But Apollyon said—"

"Apollyon is the baker of lies and father of pies. Or wait, maybe I have that backward. The point is, don't trust him. Love and Zealot are philosophical personifications of specific virtues. You think they can physically die? Didn't Truth tell you this was an allegory?"

"Yeah,"—Christian scratched his head—"I still can't comprehend what exactly that means. But what I can comprehend is that we've got to save Love and Zealot. Where are they trapped?"

Interpreter stared at Christian, as if pondering something. Then grimaced. "You're not really in any condition to go attacking one of Apollyon's strongholds."

"But you just said I needed to do something. I can't just lie here."

"You shouldn't," Interpreter said.

Christian grumbled. "What do I do? I can't stay here, and I can't go. What you're asking of me is impossible."

Interpreter clapped and smiled. "That's it! You're very close to understanding."

"That what I need to do is impossible?"

Interpreter pointed at Christian like a teacher singling out a student in his class. "Yes, and?"

"And what? I can't do it. So, I do nothing?"

"No, you shouldn't do nothing. Didn't you pay attention to everything I just said? Doing nothing is quitter talk."

"But it's impossible," Christian said. "I can't even move my legs."

"Yes! Impossible!"

Christian stared at Interpreter. "Is there some law that old mentors have to be overly cryptic?"

"Yes. It's a union rule for the Old Mentor Union. But besides that, it's the law of 'people learn better when they figure things out themselves.' I think it's the reason for a great deal of the misery the Overseer lets us get ourselves into." Interpreter's expectant look turned to a frown. "That was a clue."

"The Overseer?"

"Yes!"

"That sounds simplistic."

"Oh, I guess you think simple answers are always wrong?"

"Uh . . ."

"Well, as with most things, it's a bit more complicated than that. Who do you think is most equipped for doing the impossible? The Overseer."

"But it's impossible."

"For you!"

"Oh," Christian said with realization.

"When was the last time you called for the Holy Ghost Mech? Or used the Law Protocol to give yourself infinite reflexes?"

"I think that was back at Palace Beautiful—"

"Have you forgotten what you've done that was supposedly impossible? You walked all the way to the Gateway in an unpowered burden through seas of radiation. You could hardly move two feet at the beginning, right?"

Christian nodded.

"Sounds to me like the Overseer has already helped you do an impossible thing or two. Ask him for help."

"What if he doesn't help?"

"You mean: What if he doesn't do exactly what you command him to do? Then you'll know that to do what he wants, you don't need whatever you asked for. And that is a comforting thought."

"How so?"

"If you go into battle," Interpreter said, "and you ask for body armor, but your commander, who is an expert in all things martial, says you won't need it, isn't that more comforting than being piled high with armor and weapons?"

"Either way, I guess I'd feel reassured."

"Exactly!"

"Wow!" Christian said. "This whole time, I've just been sitting here. I must have looked so foolish."

"If it's any consolation, no one could see how foolish you looked. At least as far as I know."

"Thanks," Christian said, "that's *so* comforting. Wow, it's amazing the things we can forget when we lose focus. I hope there's nothing else I'm forgetting."

"Like, say, a wife and children you left back at the City of Destruction?"

Christian considered that. Then shrugged. "Nah, I'm about seventy percent sure I'd remember if I left a wife and children back at the City of Destruction."

"Oh good. You'd be surprised. There was this one guy—"

"Tell me about it later. I need to focus." Christian lifted his wrist computer up and opened a frequency to the Celestial Station.

Mr. Angel appeared on the screen. "Celestial Station. How can I direct your call?"

"Wow, that was easy," Christian said in relief.

Mr. Angel raised an eyebrow.

"Well, it was uncomplicated. Listen, I can't walk. I've gotten all jacked up by Giant Contentment. I need to rescue Zealot and Love, but they are far from me. I can't get to them."

"Confirmed," Mr. Angel said. "Standby for Spirit Fall."

"Wait, I just need medical treatment. No need to summon a—"

A massive object struck the ground a few yards away, billowing sand far from its epicenter.

Dust covered Christian and Interpreter.

The same massive Mech from before, at the Gateway, walked forward and reached down toward Christian.

"Ooh!" Conscience said, "another Mech spirit."

Christian had forgotten the little machine was on his shoulder. When had he last talked to it? That was a frightening thought. "You and Book, give it a check."

Conscience grabbed Book's projector and clambered over to the machine to check its authenticity.

Conscience scanned the Mech with Book. After a thumbs up from

Conscience and Book, Christian let the machine pick him up and put him into its chest.

The Mech placed Christian in a seat, then retracted its hand and closed the opening to the Control Room. The chair locked Christian in place and dropped through the floor to a chamber below. The room was dark and had several medical apparatuses, which Christian couldn't identify.

Mr. Angel appeared on a screen. "Greetings, Christian. We're initiating medical protocols. Fair warning. This will hurt."

"Is there, maybe, a way not to have it hurt?"

"I'm afraid not. Your inability to hurt is part of the problem. Pain exists for a reason. To remove or ignore pain leads to contentment, which can lead to apathy, and that can lead to despair and ultimately, suffering. Which is ironic, I suppose."

"Contentment isn't good?" Christian's chair moved near a set of robotic arms that dangled from the ceiling. They had various needles and clamps in their hands.

Mr. Angel looked up, as if trying to decide how strongly he should shoot down Christian's statement. "Like all emotions, contentment is good if it's for the right reason and in the right quantities." He paused, thinking. "Well, it's not a matter of quantities as much as it is of ratios. People try to deal with too much contentment or too much passion by reducing their passion or contentment, which can lead to the problem of apathy. Often, the solution is to increase something instead, like more respect or more understanding. Sometimes more sensitivity is needed, which is the ability to feel pain. But the ability to feel pain without the will to do something about that pain leads to other problems. After I turn on your pain receptors, you need to free Zealot and Love as quickly as you can. Otherwise, the pain might make you relapse into further apathy. Or you might go mad."

"Wait, go mad?"

"Right. But, you know, just don't."

"Oh. Ok. I won't then."

"Good. You ready to start?"

"Uh, no."

"That's the spirit. Here we go."

———

Christian sailed out of the front of the Mech. Pain swam through every fiber of his being—pain for every wasted second and misspent passion.

He landed on the sand, screaming. Eventually his voice tired, and he staggered to his feet, shaking in fear.

The Mech shot back into the air and toward the Celestial Station.

"You feeing any better?" Interpreter said.

"Nope. Much worse. But that isn't important now. Didn't you say you had a hoverbase?"

"Yes. We won it in an off-screen tournament arc that the Calvinists and Arminians signed me up for as a prank."

"Don't distract me with your unnecessary subplots. I've got to save Zealot and Love."

"Are you sure you don't want to hear about it? A lot of interesting things happened. Like Armand, the Arminian Armenian and our meanie Ann got married. Now the meanie Ann is Armand's Arminian meanie Ann, though she's still not Armenian until the immigration paperwork makes it through the system."

Christian stared at Interpreter. "Yes, I'm sure I don't want to hear about it."

"Okay, I have Love and Zealot's location marked on my map." Interpreter pressed a button on his wrist. A holomap of the Dark Lands projected above his arm.

"Excellent." Christian looked around as if he had lost his keys. "Now, Truth. Where is she?"

"Right here," Truth said from behind Christian's ear.

Christian spun and almost smacked Truth with the butt of his Gauss rifle.

Truth looked much better than before, though still withered. She stood filing her nails which seemed to have grown long. How much time had passed?

"Truth, are you like Zealot now? Since when do you sneak up on people?"

Truth didn't look up from her nails. "You will often find me where you least expect."

"We've got to rescue Zealot and Love."

"Yes." Truth said no more.

Christian waited for Truth to say more. When she didn't, he followed Interpreter to the large mobile hoverbase.

Truth walked at Christian's side. She was older, but each step seemed to take her a bit back toward her usual age.

"Why," Christian said, "weren't you adversely effected by Giant Contentment's restaurant?"

"You can thank Book for that." Interpreter pointed behind himself without looking. "Had you not been so equipped, Truth might have been corrupted into Conspiracy, Occultism, or any number of falsehoods. Book does a good job of repelling those maladies."

"It was close though," Truth said, avoiding eye contact with Christian. "I was wasting away. But not from falsehood. From despair."

"Despair?" Christian said. "How would that affect you?"

"It wouldn't, technically. I was at no risk of dying, but my power was diminished. Zealot is the fuel that feeds us. Or to use another analogy, Love is the gun that directs the bullets, but Zealot is the trigger. Without that, nothing happens. After all, how can a young man keep his way pure? By keeping it according to the Overseer's word."

"Hey, that's my line." Book suddenly projected from Christian's wrist, scowling at Truth.

Truth said, "You realize that other people can say things that are accurate, right? You aren't the only one."

"But I'm divinely inspired." Book stamped her foot.

"That doesn't give you a monopoly on accurate statements. Or an exhaustive list of all things that are accurate."

"Still," Interpreter said, "there is no other source of reliable accuracy like Book."

"Of course, there isn't." Book looked insulted. "I'm the divinely inspired word of the eternal Creator of all existence."

"Wow," Christian said. "Who knew the divinely inspired word of the eternal Creator of all existence would be such a tsundere?"

"Hey," Book said, acquiring a red blush on her holographic cheeks. "How am I a tsundere?"

"Let's see." Christian counted on his fingers. "You sit around, expecting people to pursue you, but when they do, they mostly read a bunch of stuff that punches them in the gut. They feel conviction and pain about their depravity, but you're really a sweet love letter on the inside—despite a lot of violent tendencies."

There was an awkward pause.

Book sputtered, "That . . . that . . . that doesn't mean . . ." Book looked at Truth. "Truth, help me out here."

Truth's usually controlled face showed shock. "Oh, my shazbot. She's totally a tsundere."

Book glanced back and forth from Truth to Christian, her blush deepening. "I am not!" Then she looked toward Conscience. "Conscience, you don't think I'm a tsundere, do you?"

Conscience shrugged. "You do kinda have an entire section devoted to calling people *idiots*."

"That is not what Proverbs is about," Book said. "Not entirely."

"Proverbs?" Conscience blinked. "I was talking about Judges."

Christian tried to laugh, but it was difficult. His thoughts went back to Zealot and Love. He had to rescue them. Or die trying.

———

Interpreter looked out the main observation window of the hoverbase and pointed. "There it is. That's where they're holding Zealot and Love."

The hoverbase rumbled to a stop.

Christian looked where Interpreter was pointing. In the vast stretch of desert stood a single circular hole. The bottom was either too dark or too deep to be seen from their position.

"That," Interpreter said, "is the Pit of—"

"Despair?" Christian's eyes brightened with excitement.

The Interpreter shook his head. "Christian, try to pay attention."

"Can't we call it the Pit of Despair? You know, 'Don't even think about trying to escape. The chains are far too thick'?

"No."

"Does it have a machine that slowly sucks the life force out of people?"

"Well, sort of, but it's called the Pit of Humiliation."

"Pit of Despair sounds cooler."

"Christian," Truth said in a threatening tone.

"All right, but if we see an albino with a wheelbarrow, I'm going to be very disappointed."

"Pay attention." Interpreter gave a friendly smile. "This is serious. Zealot and Love are trapped in a series of virtual reality chambers. You have to jack in and get them out."

Interpreter pressed a control panel button, and a door opened to the outside of the hoverbase. "There is little time. The longer we wait, the harder it will be to rescue them. Take a grapple gun from the armory, and get into that pit. I can advise you further over the coms here."

"Fine, but in my mind, it's the Pit of Despair.

———

Christian stood at the edge of the Pit of Humiliation. If the pit had a bottom, he couldn't see it. The only light came from dozens of green cylinders lining the walls. Unconscious people were in some of the cylinders hooked up to wires and tubes. Some cylinders had names: Hope, Courage, Ambition, and more.

Christian held a grapple gun. It felt light and insignificant in his hands. But if he were to rappel down, it would be the only thing keeping him from plunging into the abyss below. He pointed the gun at Truth and she grabbed the grappling hook. "You won't drop me, will you?" Christian said.

Truth smiled. "Don't worry. I may not look it, but I am quite strong. I'll keep you from falling into that bottomless pit. As long as you don't let go."

"Bottomless? Wait, what?" With one kick from Truth, Christian fell in. The grapple gun released its coil and Christian plunged downwards. Christian activated the Emergency Stop and the cable went taut.

Christian swung and planted his feet on one of the cylinders. The only thing keeping him from falling endlessly was his lifeline to Truth.

Christian touched his ear to activate his com system. "All right. I'm descending. The kick was unnecessary, by the way."

"I know." Truth's voice responded in his ear.

Christian pressed a button on his grapple gun, causing the line to slowly unwind. He descended further.

Minutes passed. The rows and rows of human-sized cylinders were mind-boggling. Many contained individuals. Others were empty. Soon the only light he could see was from the vats around him. The top of the hole was a distant pinprick of light. Christian looked over the vats, trying to find Zealot or Love. "What about all these other people?"

"They are the companions of other pilgrims," Interpreter said from the com. "I'm afraid only their pilgrim companion may free them from the Pit of Humiliation."

"Right, so who are we going for first?"

"Zealot should be easier to free than Love."

Christian kept examining the vats. None of their occupants seemed familiar. "Where is Zealot? He's not at the bottom, is he? Because of his name?"

"No. Don't worry," Truth said. "The Pit is not alphabetized."

Christian stepped down to the next level. And there he was. Zealot floated suspended in a vat directly before him.

"Found him!" Christian said. "I must have missed Love. I'll have to check again on the way up."

"That will probably not be necessary," Interpreter said. "Zealot will assist you in locating Love."

Christian checked the cylinder for buttons or controls to release its prisoner. There was a control pad, but it seemed related to a series of plugs along the bottom of the vat. Nothing appeared to be an open switch.

"Truth, what do I do? Just shine light on him, and he'll wake up?"

Interpreter answered instead. "It's more complicated than that. No, you'll have to jack in—similar to how I got you out of your slump in the Desert of Emptiness. But be careful. I know it's all a simulation. But if you die in the simulation—"

"I die in real life?" Christian said.

"What? No," Interpreter said. "It will just be very painful and a huge hassle to jack you back in. Why would dying in a simulation make you die in real life? That makes no sense."

"All right," Christian said. "How do I jack in?"

"I'll walk you through it," Truth said.

"It's just a simulation," Interpreter said. "All it can do is send your brain information. How could that kill you?"

"First, grab Conscience," Truth continued as if Interpreter wasn't speaking.

"Ok."

"Wait what?" Conscience sounded from Christian's shoulder, concern in his voice.

"Sure," Interpreter said, "the program could tell your brain to kill itself. But why would your brain do that? That's expecting somebody to die only because they're told to. Even if you wanted to die you can't just make yourself die by wanting to."

Christian grabbed Conscience by the neck. The little robot started to chatter and beep in an annoyed tone. "Ok, I have him by the neck. Now what?"

"The neck?" Truth said in horror. "You're not trying to kill him, you idiot. The opposite of that!"

"Oh, right."

"I'm just saying that," Interpreter continued, "just because it would be more dramatic if dying in a simulation resulted in dying in real life, that doesn't make it any more realistic. When you die in a dream, do you die in real life? I don't."

"Now, do you see a connection port at the base of the cylinder?" Truth said, no annoyance in her voice from Interpreter's tirade.

Christian scanned the cylinder till he found it. "Yes."

"Sure, this is an allegory so you could argue that realism isn't important. But that doesn't mean a digitized simulation can—"

"Interpreter," Truth said in a firm but calm voice.

"Oh, sorry," Interpreter said. "I had you all on mute. How are things going down there? Have you freed Zealot yet?"

"No. I haven't even jacked in yet. I was wanting some advice first since you're the expert, apparently. What should I expect?"

"I have no idea," Interpreter said. "What gave you the idea I was an expert?"

"Your unceasing rant about digitized mortality?"

"Oh, that. Well, I haven't the faintest idea what you can expect."

"This was your idea!" Christian inadvertently squeezed Conscience tighter and the robot made more annoyed beeping sounds.

"You're about to hack into a subconscious mindscape for a philosophical personification of human will that has become corrupted and is unique to your psyche. Your guess is as good as mine on what you'll see."

"But can't I control the simulation," Christian said, "like you did?"

"Not unless you have the experience and training that I have."

"Then why can't you do it?" Christian's tone turned accusatory. "Like how you helped me?"

"Zealot and Love are elements of you, not me," Interpreter said. "I will say this: the only thing keeping Zealot in that tank is Zealot. He needs to want to escape."

"He also has to believe he can escape," Truth said. "One of Apollyon's common tricks is to make his victims think they can't escape. So they don't try. A cage with unlocked doors can work just as well a one with locks."

"What do I do?"

"First of all, stop choking Conscience," Interpreter said. "I can hear his pained beeps over the com."

"Oh right." Christian relaxed his grip on Conscience. Conscience gasped for breath.

"Oh, get over yourself," Christian said. "You're a robot. You don't need air."

"Still . . ." Conscience muttered. "Rude."

"Now slam Conscience against the plug at the base of cylinder as hard as you can," Truth said.

"Oh no," Conscience groaned.

Christian did as he was told.

Everything went black.

STAGE 22

MUSASHI'S NAIL

Christian gasped and opened his eyes. "If I keep doing this, I'm going to hyperventilate." He rose and rubbed his head.

"Stop. Who goes there?" Zealot's hands closed around Christian's armor.

Hoisted into the air in Zealot's firm grip, Christian glanced around the room—a small apartment covered in trash, clothes, and various detritus. He couldn't even see the floor.

Zealot shook Christian. "How did you get in here?" Zealot was thin, almost decrepit. Not old, but withered. Like he hadn't seen the sun in a month. His voice rose. "Well?" He sounded frantic. Angry. Fearful? Impossible!

Christian put a hand on Zealot's arm. "I'm jacked into your virtual simulator. I've come to rescue you. Put me down."

"Rescue me? Indeed!" Zealot leaned in as if sniffing Christian. He pulled back as if he had detected something. "You're in league with the enemy. I know it. You're all in league with the enemy. I'm the only one who sees it. None of you are to be trusted."

"Yes, you are correct," Christian said. "I was distracted by the Giant Contentment who was actually the Giant Despair in disguise. But I'm better now."

"Ha!" Zealot hoisted Christian even higher. "Then you admit it. I should throw you out my window."

A window materialized in a wall where no window had existed before.

"Yes," a voice said.

Christian looked toward the voice, but all he saw was a refrigerator.

"He can't be trusted," another voice said.

Christian looked for that voice but only saw a rice maker.

"He's evil. You can only trust yourself." The voice came from the television.

Christian looked back at Zealot. "Your appliances can talk?"

"No, appliances can't talk," the refrigerator said.

"Oh, yes," Zealot said. "They do that. You spend enough time alone in a room and all the major appliances gain sentience and communicate with you."

"Really? I've never experienced that."

"You have to be alone for a *long* time. Long enough to . . ." Zealot's voice trailed off. "Wait! You're distracting me. I was going to eject you." He pulled Christian back, ready to throw him through the window.

"Zealot," Christian yelled, "Love is in danger."

Zealot stared at Christian and relaxed his grip, still looking suspicious.

"Love is dead." Zealot's voice cracked, and tears filled his eyes. "I know she's dead. I saw . . . I . . ."

"You're wrong. Love is still alive." Christian scanned Zealot's face for any sign of acceptance, any crack in his frantic resistance.

"There is no Love," Zealot screamed as he dropped Christian to the floor. Zealot collapsed, his hands covering his face. "All that exists for me is this room. I can't go out and risk getting corrupted by you and your weak-willed ways. What if I hurt another person?"

"Such a sad existence," the rice maker said. The appliance did indeed have eyes, a mouth, and other general features of anthropomorphism that Christian had not noticed before.

"This is a horrible way to spend your days," the television said.

"It's true." Zealot lowered his hands and looked toward the television. "Simply staying in here is a useless existence. I must be useful."

For a moment, he sounded like his old self. Then he groaned and covered his face again. "But no, it's too risky."

"No, it's not." Christian put a reassuring hand on Zealot's shoulder. "Listen to the talking appliances."

"You could kill yourself," the refrigerator said. "Eliminate your sin and shame. Hide yourself from the world completely."

"Okay," Christian said. "Stop listening to the talking appliances."

"I can't go out," Zealot said. "What else is there to do?"

"You have wasted your life," the coffee maker said. "You are a failure."

"It is true," Zealot said. "I have failed."

"Wait! No!" Christian activated his com link. "Truth, quick, tell Zealot he isn't a failure."

Christian raised the volume for Zealot to hear. There was static.

Truth's voice came through. "Zealot *is* a failure," she said. "I mean, objectively speaking. He failed to stop the Giant Contentment, though he was the first to realize something was wrong. He got fooled by Platitude Platypus, and—"

Christian muted her. "Truth! You're not helping."

"You see?" the television said. "Truth agrees. Through death, maybe you can atone for your crimes."

"That's just crazy talk," Christian said. "You can't atone for anything through your death. That's why death is eternal. It will never be enough to make up for your evil."

"Then what?" Zealot looked up from the floor and stared into Christians eyes. Zealot looked like he was pleading with Christian. But his tone sounded demanding.

Christian took a deep breath. "You just have to leave this room."

"No! I'll be corrupted. The outside is dangerous."

"Is that the Zealot I know? A coward?"

"How dare you." Zealot stepped toward the window, which enlarged and twisted into a balcony with no railing. Far below was a river of icy water. He stepped toward the edge.

Christian reached out to pull Zealot back. Zealot's size and strength made such an effort seem silly. But Christian did have power armor, and Zealot wasn't wearing his.

"I have no purpose here." Zealot pushed toward the edge. Even without power armor, he was unimaginably strong. "It would be no different if I were dead."

Christian thought back to the images Interpreter had shown him. "Zealot! Remember when I was trapped by The Sloth of Despond?"

"When I arrived too late to save Open-Minded? Yes, I do remember that."

"But you helped me." Christian pulled, but Zealot inched closer to the edge. "In the City of Morality, remember that hotel? You tried to save those slaves while Truth and I sat around talking about metaphysics with the secretary."

"And I saved no one." Zealot reached the edge.

Christian pulled harder, but he lost his grip and fell back.

One foot stepped out over the long drop below.

There was one trick left. Christian ran past Zealot and dove off the balcony.

"Help," Christian shouted as he was falling.

A hand grabbed his wrist. It was Zealot. The real Zealot. He no longer looked weary or scared. His body no longer looked weak and frail. "Christian! You must be more careful. You could hurt yourself being so . . ." His voice trailed off. "Wait. Where are we? Why am I not wearing my power armor? And why am I not currently in the process of annihilating some evil fiend?"

"We're trapped in the Pit of Humiliation. This is all a simulation."

"Why was I acting all nonzealous?" Zealot had a twinge of distrust in his voice.

"It's this place. It twists you."

Zealot leaned closer, still distrustful. "How were you able to snap me out of it?"

"I used the old Clarence Trick. Apparently, all these artificial dream states use pop culture references for their base programming so I thought it would work. I appealed to your instinctual desire to help others. Your problem was selfishness. So, I figured a little selfless act could help you out."

Zealot put Christian down on the balcony. "Ah, very clever. But risky. I might not have caught you."

"Not really." Christian adjusted his armor. "Interpreter said that if we die in the simulation, we don't die in real life. Seems this is a low-quality simulation."

"What? There's no risk of death? Then we must escape. What fun is life without peril?"

Suddenly, Christian was back in the Pit of Humiliation.

Zealot stood inside his cylinder. The glass was smashed out from the inside, and the green fluid had drained out into the pit.

"Well, that was easy," Christian said.

"As I predicted," Interpreter said over the com. "Get Zealot going in the right direction, and he will do the rest of the work."

"Indeed!" Zealot ripped out the wires and tubes that connected him to the inside of the cylinder. "Now come! Let us go forth and find Love. I remember now where they imprisoned her and feel responsible for getting her into this predicament. But even if I hadn't, it is my fortune to be given a chance to assist another. Forward!" He looked around. "Or rather, upward!" He clambered out of the cylinder, unaware of the sharp glass, then clambered up several rows of cylinders.

Christian watched him for a while then spotted Love in a cylinder that Zealot blindly clambered past. "Zealot, you passed her three levels ago."

"Oh, right." Zealot reversed course. "Downward!"

With his grapple gun, Christian pulled himself up to Love's level and reach it just as Zealot did.

Love hung suspended in a cylinder of green fluid, just like Zealot's. But she seemed more graceful, more at home. Her eyelids fluttered as if she was in a vivid dream.

"Conscience?" Christian said. "Will you do the honors?"

Conscience pouted, then clambered down Christian's shoulder and into his hand.

Zealot drew his pistol. "Can we not simply destroy her cage with a comically excessive use of force?" He fired a few missiles into the glass. The explosions shook the shaft, and rocks fell around them. But there was no effect on the glass.

"No such luck," Interpreter said. "Those cages are virtually indestructible."

"Zealot was able to break it earlier," Christian said.

"That was from the inside," Interpreter said. "From the inside, this glass is as feeble as paper. But from the outside, it is among the strongest materials ever made."

"You don't mean . . ." Christian's voice trailed off for dramatic effect.

"That's right. Video game cutscene glass."

Zealot and Christian gasped.

"Then it is settled." Zealot slapped Christian on the back. "Nothing can break through video game cutscene glass. We must commence with these cyberpunk shenanigans."

Zealot reached for the top of the cylinder. "What do we do?"

"We hit it with our Consciences as hard as we can."

"Actually," Truth's voice broke in, "you can try to just lightly touch the port with Conscience. You don't need to—"

"As hard as we can!" Christian hoisted Conscience up. Conscience gave a terrified squeal.

Christian and Zealot struck the cylinder.

Christian closed his eyes and waited for whatever chaos lived inside Love's mind.

———

Someone smacked Christian in the face, and he woke up. Zealot was standing over him smiling.

"Ouch! Zealot. Why did you do that?"

"It looked like you were about to gasp and open your eyes. I decided to wake you up before that happened."

"Thanks." Christian stood and brushed himself off. They were in a long, empty corridor, completely dark except for a few flickering glows from broken electronics in the walls and ceiling. "So, this is Love's subconsciousness?"

"More like Love's mindscape prison," Truth said over the com, "crafted for her by Apollyon."

"It's so quiet," Christian said.

"This seems ominous," Zealot said.

"Indeed." Christian raised his Gauss rifle.

"That's my line." Zealot gave a friendly shove.

Christian almost went to the floor, but he regained his balance and looked behind him, weapon ready.

"A little jumpy, aren't you?" Zealot followed Christian's gaze. Nothing in the corridor—but it was so dark, could they be sure?

Christian shrugged and headed down the corridor. "Don't scare me like that."

"It was unintentional," Zealot said.

"It always is," Christian said under his breath.

Zealot looked at Christian and a twinge of concern crossed his face. "What manner of gratuitous terror has caused you to feel such general aversion?"

"Something about this place seems familiar." As Christian walked down the corridor studying the walls, strange sounds came from the end of the hall.

"This seems to be a vessel of some kind," Zealot said. "I recognize its various aesthetics."

They reached a large blast door. It seemed like an entrance to a bridge. As they approached, the door opened. Before them stood a dimly lit room. To one side stood a large holographic display of a globe. Sides of the room were filled with dozens of control stations and screens displaying a myriad of tactical information. A red, humanoid-shaped blob of bleeding flesh stood in front of the main control panel.

Zealot and Christian pointed their weapons at the humanoid shape.

"Wait!" Christian looked closer at the figure. "Oh, my flowerbed. It's Love."

The figure turned its head and surveyed them. The look on the figure's face seemed disinterested. Almost distant. But there was no mistake. This was Love. She wore her old outfit, and her hands moved lazily over several control panels in weariness.

Zealot holstered his pistol. "Love, what has been done to you? Who did it? How might I best damage them?"

Love looked back at the screens and typed onto a keypad. "What do you mean?"

"Oh no," Zealot shouted, much louder than before. His normal talking voice could be interpreted as a shout. "She's attempting passive-aggression, given my previous misdeeds against her." He looked worried.

Something beeped on the screen.

Love looked closely. "No! Another soldier has died because of me." She raised her remote. More lines of blood appeared on her flesh, and she winced in pain.

"Love, stop!" Christian stepped toward her, but her shield pushed him back.

"I must pay for my failures." Love lowered her remote and turned to another screen. "Grapple the snipers up onto the high ground. They should be able to clear this pod. But open with the heavy's grenade to shred the enemy armor and remove their cover."

"Wait a minute." Zealot took a step back and looked around. "This control panel. That hologlobe. Truth, where are we?"

Truth's voice came in over the com. "It looks like you're in a squad-based tactical rouge-lite game whose specificity can't be stipulated due to copyright reasons."

"Of course," Christian said. "It all makes sense. A simulated squad-based game with permadeath and procedural generation. It's the ultimate expression of empathetic masochism!"

Zealot stroked his chin. "Then Love is trapped within this prison of empathetic masochism. We must free her." He pointed his pistol at Love. Then hesitated. "Hold on. Is this one of those problems I can fix by shooting?"

"That seems unlikely given shooting her is what precipitated her malady," Truth said.

"Shooting her again won't undo being shot?"

"No. This isn't like head-trauma-induced memory loss which for some reason always undoes itself with another blow to the head. Shooting Love again will not free her from her masochistic emotional isolation."

"Phooey."

Christian studied the screen which displayed a squad of soldiers moving through an abandoned neighborhood.

"These names seem significant." Christian pointed at the soldiers' name tags: Dream, Hope, Ambition, Calling . . .

A warning flashed across the screen. Squad member Dream fell into a puddle of his own blood.

"Another one dead." Love struck a monitor. More lines of red flashed across her flesh. Tears fell from her face, whether from pain of heart or pain of body was unclear.

Zealot winced. "Love, you have to cease this mockery of justice. You cannot punish yourself for these squad members dying."

Love waved a dismissive hand. "It is my duty to escort these people to safety. If I cannot, then I must be punished."

"It isn't your place to punish yourself," Christian said.

Love's look at Christian was venomous. "Are you trying to take away my one solace in this hard time? Tough. If I can't do good, at least I can punish myself for my failures. It's the only source of satisfaction I have left. None of those squad members will make it to the end of the mission. So, I deserve it."

Zealot walked forward into Love's shield. He didn't back away. Her shield crackled against his face and torso. He glared into Love's face, looking down at her with contempt. "Now you listen to me, small woman. Nothing you do can make up for any evil you have done or good you failed to do. Those hopes, dreams, and goals that are dying on that screen—you can't undo their deaths by slicing up your own flesh. Do you think the Overseer is so poor a judge that he would be bribed by your self-destructive efforts? For shame, Love. For shame, I say. Thrice more, I say, for shame."

"Don't talk to me," Love said. "You shot me."

"Yes," Zealot said, embarrassed. "I am sorry about that. That was my bad. I believed you had been corrupted beyond salvation. I thought all desire had been twisted into a distraction. But now I understand that it was a twist of something good. Stifling or destroying you was not the solution. That led me to imprison myself in a self-centered prison of paranoia. You must be brought under control, not destroyed."

Love's eyes filled with an anger that mirrored Zealot's. She floated upward so she could look down at Christian and Zealot. "You wanna control me—Love? Try it."

A bright purple flash blinded Christian. When his eyes readjusted, he and Zealot were standing in a clearing in some vague cityscape. In front of them stood a series of specifically waist-high walls.

Zealot looked around at the conveniently placed cover. "Uh-oh."

Four soldiers ran toward them from an alley at the far end of the clearing. They opened fire.

Zealot and Christian dove for cover.

Love's voice sounded from atop one of the buildings. She looked down at her troops below and shouted orders. "Stay behind full cover. Flank them."

Christian glanced up at Love. She stood on the top of a two-story building next to the clearing. Christian scanned the assailants. "Okay, there are four of them and two of us. We should probably wait for them to flank us and focus on defending one of those flanks, moving forward to avoid the opposite flank. Then it's two against two. We could probably ignore the other flankers and go straight for—"

Zealot was gone. Christian looked around. Zealot charged toward the four assailants, shouting and firing rockets.

"Manmade lake obstructions," Christian swore, then vaulted over his cover. Two bullets struck his armor and he rolled toward the next set of cover. "Zealot, wait! Let's talk about this."

An explosion. One of the soldiers flew over Christian's head.

Christian saw the glint of a sniper rifle at the end of a clearing. A bullet whizzed past his head, and he pulled back behind cover.

"I am Doubt," a voice shouted from the sniper's direction. "You will not advance. You will stay where you are." Another shot.

"No, I won't." Christian leapt over the wall and ran for another piece of cover. The sniper's rifle barked and bullets ripped into Christian's armor. Christian fell to the asphalt, out of view from the sniper. He crawled through the cover toward the building Love was at.

A soldier stepped into his way. "I am Pain. I say you cannot confront Love." Pain leveled a shotgun at Christian. Christian rolled away, avoiding a shotgun blast.

Christian raised his rifle to fire at Pain.

A small flying robot flew over to Pain and projected a defense matrix over the figure.

A soldier far in the back of the clearing had a control pad in his hand. "I am Fear. I say you cannot confront Pain."

Christian fired at Pain, but the defense matrix turned the bullets aside.

A grenade landed at Christian's feet. He jumped away, but it was too late. The grenade exploded and tossed Christian against a wall. He hit the ground. Blood dripped from cracks in his armor.

A figure stepped out of the smoke, grenade launcher in hand. "I am called Thrill. You must go where I say."

"Zealot, help," Christian said, coughing. "They've got me surrounded." He looked around. "Zealot? Where are you?"

Zealot landed in the center of the clearing with an impact that knocked all the soldiers to the ground. In one hand he held his pistol. In the other, he held Love.

"Zealot!" Christian staggered toward him. "You got to Love. How?"

Zealot looked like he didn't understand the question. "I just did. Her protective shields were a bit rough to overcome, but I just gritted my teeth and muscled through them."

"But how did you make it past Doubt, Pain, Fear and Thrill?"

Zealot looked around at the battlefield, confusion on his face. "I just ignored them."

"You can do that?"

Zealot tilted his head and raised an eyebrow. "Yes. Why didn't you?"

"They were shooting at me."

"And this means you had to let them stop you?"

"How could I not?" Christian looked around at his assailants. They hadn't moved from being knocked down by the shockwave from Zealot's fall. "I still don't understand how you made it through."

"I just did. Saving Love was my priority."

"But didn't they shoot at you?"

"Maybe. I honestly don't remember. It's possible I was struck a few—"

"You think you've won?" Love shouted from Zealot's back. "Do your worst. I won't break."

Zealot redirected his confusion toward Love. "Love, I do not wish to hurt you."

"Oh, I see," Love said. "You think I'm too weak to withstand your torture."

"We aren't going to torture you, Love," Christian said. "We are trying to rescue you."

"Ha! Like I'm going to fall for that." Love scowled at Zealot. "This one tried to destroy me."

"I said I was sorry. What more do you want?" Zealot scoffed. "Women are so complicated."

Love's scowl deepened.

"Maybe try apologizing better," Christian said.

"Very well." Zealot grabbed Love and set her down with such force that she gave a small yelp. He fell to one knee and bowed as if in shame. "Words are such a futile medium to properly convey my sorrow and pain at the thought that I would willingly do you harm. Yet the facts are worse than mere thought. It was action, multiplying such pain and sorrow to such an extent that I would join you in self-destructive damage toward myself in hope that it would one day atone for my incomprehensible evil. But to do so would be futile. No action I may take could possibly atone, even in part, for the cowardly, distasteful, evil, and just plain rude actions that I took back in the Restaurant of Contentment."

Love stared at Zealot. Her expression unchanged. "Did Truth dictate that to you?"

Zealot looked ashamed and pressed a hand to his ear, deactivating his com link.

"Love, cut him a break," Christian said. "He's trying to say he's sorry."

"Well, I'm not sorry." Love looked away and turned up her nose. "I wasn't doing anything wrong in the Restaurant of Contentment."

"Then why were you damaging yourself earlier?" Zealot said, looking confused.

"Because I feel guilty."

"For what?"

"Uh . . ." Love looked from side to side, avoiding Zealot's gaze. "I don't know. I just did."

"This isn't getting anywhere," Christian looked around for an exit. How could he get out of the simulation? "We need to go. We need you to come with us."

"I'm staying."

"No, you aren't." Zealot pinched the back of Love's head.

Love screamed, and the whole virtual realm shook.

THE BLOOD OF QUINCY MORRIS

Christian awoke in the Pit of Humiliation. Zealot was still next to him.

Love still floated in her cylinder. But her eyes were open. And she did not look happy. She banged against the glass. "You woke me up!" Her voice echoed oddly through the fluid inside the cylinder.

"Yeah." Christian looked at Zealot, surprised. "How did you wake her up so easily? I thought it'd be hard."

"Pure willpower," Zealot said. "If I put my mind to it, I, Zealot, can be stronger than Love." He climbed above Love's cylinder, reached down, and pried the entire thing from the wall with one hand.

"All right then. Up we go." Zealot started climbing out of the Pit of Humiliation, dragging the cylinder behind him. Love floated in the middle of the cylinder, arms folded and nose turned up.

Christian pressed a button on his grapple gun and started his ascent. "How long are we going to keep her in there?"

Zealot continued his one-handed climbing with incredible speed given the cylinder he carried. "Given enough time, she'll get over herself and wish to rejoin us. It will be difficult. I shall have to make us follow the path, but I am certain Love will eventually return to her old self as the poison of humiliation drips from her."

Christian touched his ear and activated his com system. "Truth, Interpreter, we're on our way out."

"How was the mission?" Interpreter said.

"Uh . . . we're sort of one and a half out of two."

"What does that mean?" Truth said.

"It means we rescued 75 percent of two people."

"Ew . . ."

"What? No. Not like that. Look it will make sense when we get to the top."

They continued upward. Their ascent didn't feel significantly delayed due to Zealot having to lug Love with them. After several more minutes of climbing, they reached the top.

Christian put down his grapple gun and collapsed on the sand, exhausted.

Zealot put down Love's tank and kicked Christian in the ribs. "Come now. That's no way to act. We've got a pilgrimage to progress."

"Leave him alone," Love said from her vat. "He wants to rest."

"What is there to even do?" Christian said.

"What is there to do?" Zealot said with a scoff. "Follow the path, of course. Look, there it is now, stretching out before us."

Christian sat up. Sure enough, the King's Road, the one they had followed from the Gateway, shot out in front of them. "That's weird. I didn't see it before."

"Perhaps," Zealot said, "because I was not here to point it out to you. But hark, here I am. Now let's get moving." He started down the road, walked past Interpreter and Truth, and gave them a quick nod, inviting them to come along.

Christian watched Zealot go, then looked toward Truth and Interpreter. "Did he just say *hark*?"

Interpreter gave a nostalgic smile. "It's enough to make this old man cry." He wiped a tear from his eye. "But we must be going."

"What about me?" Love tried to give a look of disinterest.

"Right. We can't leave you behind." Christian tipped her cylinder over and started rolling it down the road, behind Zealot. Truth walked alongside them.

Love hovered in the center without turning around, but she still looked annoyed by the situation.

The moment Christian set foot on the path, he felt a kick in his step.

Cracks appeared on Love's cylinder. His happiness waned a bit when he saw where the path led them. "It's taking us back to the City of Destruction."

———

"It looks so different," Christian said.

The City of Destruction spread out before them in the distance. Skyscrapers, factories, and military bases filled the horizon. Between them, the stony wilderness where this had all started.

Zealot looked toward the City of Destruction. "Yes, I see what you mean."

"I don't," Truth said. "The city is the same as before."

"Truth is correct," Interpreter said. "Christian's eyes have changed, not the city."

Christian looked up. The City of Destruction was massive. Its skyscrapers went into the clouds, casting shadows that stretched like fangs across the countryside.

"I never noticed before. But it looks very similar to the City of Morality."

"That's on purpose," Interpreter said, "to trick people into diverting into that death trap."

Christian thought back to his misadventures in the City of Morality. His entrapment by the Sloth of Despond. His battle at the Gateway. It felt so long ago.

"So, it has come to a full circle." Christian tightened his gaze on the city. "I return to the place of my depravity. As a proclaimer of redemption. As one who I once wished to annihilate."

Everyone looked at Christian for an uncomfortable amount of time.

"What?" Christian said, his eyes darting from person to person.

"When did you become so poetic?" Truth said.

"Twenty minutes ago. Why?"

"Your tone is far too pessimistic for my liking." Zealot slid his arm around Christian and motioned toward the city. "Out there is a land rife with those who need the Overseer's help. You are uniquely suited toward conversing with these people to inform them of their state, given your shared heritage, so I don't like this negative outlook."

"Yes, I understand all that." Christian tried to shirk away from Zealot with little success. "I just wanted to sound more poetic."

"Poetry isn't pessimism," Zealot said.

"Of course it is. Poetry is pain but put in rhyme."

"Being more poetic doesn't make you right," Truth said, "no matter what every contemporary worship band thinks."

Zealot raised his hand for the others to stop.

"What's the matter?" Christian said.

"Someone is approaching—"

A bullet struck the ground a few feet from where the group stood.

Christian raised his weapon. "Home sweet home."

Truth seemed unperturbed by the disturbance.

"Who goes there?" an unfamiliar voice shouted. "State your business or be fired upon." The voice was far away.

Christian couldn't see the speaker. "We have already been fired upon."

"What?" the voice said. In a quieter tone, and seemingly not in their direction, the voice said, "Dangarnam it! We talked about this." The voice sounded like it was berating a fellow before returning to its former intensity.

A figure appeared on a nearby hill and walked forward, rifle raised above his head. He had camo paint across his face and was dressed in an army uniform, like something out of a cartoonish boardgame set in World War II. "Who are you?"

Zealot gave an ostentatious bow. "We are but poor lost circus performers."

Truth elbowed Zealot in the chest. Zealot winced and stepped away with an annoyed look.

"Pay no attention to my friend here," Christian said. "We are pilgrims following the King's Highway. It has led us back to the beginning of our journey. Though how, I do not know, for the highway is straight and narrow."

"Yes, it is a most perplexing road," the figure on the hill shouted. "Lots of non-euclidean hijinks."

"Most things are non-euclidean," Truth said. "Euclidean geometry only refers to—"

Christian stepped in front of Truth. "Please. Ignore my other friend here as well. She doesn't know when people don't want to discuss theoretical mathematics."

"It's not theoretical," Truth said in an even tone.

The mysterious soldier turned around and shouted down toward the other side of the hill. "Have no fear. These strangers are our reinforcements."

He turned back to Christian. "Well, don't just stand there, pilgrim. We need you at the front." He turned and started up the hill.

Christian followed.

"Are you sure that is wise?" Zealot said. "He may be untrustworthy."

"Don't worry," Interpreter said, following far behind. "I know this man. He is one of the evangelisms."

Christian paused and looked back at Interpreter. "Don't you mean one of the evangelists?"

"No," Truth said before Interpreter could respond. "This is an evangelism, not an evangelist."

"What's the difference?"

"One is a philosophical personification evangelical action by persons, this is a philosophical personification of a cohesive strategic worldview regarding evangelical action. Understand?"

"Yeah. Uh huh. Those are words."

Truth looked downcast. "The point is . . . this is one of the good guys. I'm sure he's harmless, though. The difference between the various evangelisms is their efficaciousness."

"What the efficacious does that mean?" Christian looked back at Truth.

"What am I, a thesaurus?"

Christian, Interpreter, and Zealot exchanged an awkward glance.

Christian gave an awkward cough. "Did you . . . uh . . . think you weren't?"

"I wasn't going to *say* it," Interpreter said, muttering.

Truth's mouth dropped open, and her eyes glared in shock.

Zealot leaned over to Christian and whispered, "What kind of dinosaur is a thesaurus?"

"I think it's the one with the long neck."

"That makes sense." Zealot gave a nod of understanding. "Truth does have an abnormally long neck."

Instead of fiery rage, Truth's gaze turned cold. "That is true. Statistically speaking, my neck is above average by one half inch."

There was an awkward pause.

Interpreter cleared his throat. "Well, now that we have that settled, shall we see what aid we may render to this evangelism?" Interpreter continued up the hill. The rest followed. Rolling Love's Cylinder up the hill proved a slow process.

As they approached the crest of the hill the City of Destruction loomed closer.

Christian looked down the hill. A small military base lay on this side of the hill. Evangelism stood at one of the gates to the base, motioning for them to come down.

"Come on, come on," Evangelism said. "We don't have a second to lose."

Christian followed Evangelism and looked around. Another military base, just like the one before them, stood just a few hundred yards away.

"What about that base over there?" Christian said.

"Don't worry about that base," Evangelism said. "This is the base of Judgmental Evangelism. Our job is to protect pilgrims from City of Destruction assaults." He raised a bullhorn to his mouth and shouted, "All right, boys. Fire another judgement barrage."

A series of artillery guns fired, and a few explosions echoed in the city.

"Ha! That will teach those scumbag sinners to be sinners."

Zealot smiled. "Oh, this seems a wondrous group to compatriot ourselves with. We *must* investigate."

Christian looked at Interpreter and raised an eyebrow.

Interpreter looked concerned.

Christian turned back to Evangelism. "Do you people save many of the lost with this tactic?"

"Hey, it's not about saving the lost. Only the Overseer does that. We just got to do our job and keep the enemy at bay. If they come out and attack us again, who knows how many pilgrims will be lost. We must protect our people from the enemy."

They reached the gates to the base.

Evangelism slid a card through a card reader and the gate opened. They walked through into the base.

Everyone but Truth. She froze and snapped her fingers. "Guys, we are forgetting someone."

Zealot and Christian looked around.

They said in unison, "Love!"

"We left her back at the base of the hill," Christian said.

"Oh, dear," Zealot said. "Leaving her alone in a vat of green liquid will not be conducive to rebuilding our relationship I expect."

"Don't worry," Evangelism said. "You don't need Love here. As long as you have Truth and Zealot, that will be enough."

"No," Christian said, "we can't leave Love all alone in her vat."

"I shall fetch her." Interpreter started up the hill.

"I'm telling you, old man," Evangelism said, "that's not necessary."

"That's Mister Old Man to you," Interpreter shouted back as he continued up the hill.

Evangelism scoffed.

"Trust me," Christian said. "I've noticed that bad things happen when I don't have all my companions."

Evangelism gave a dismissive shake of his head but protested no further.

"While we are waiting," Christian said. "What can we do to help?"

"Yes," Zealot said. "How soon shall we be able to operate those lovely cannons? I wish to fire all of them."

Evangelism smiled. "Hold your horses there, pilgrim. You've got to pass our background check, just to make sure you are who you say you are. You'd be surprised how many fake pilgrims try to infiltrate our ranks. It's insidious, I tell you. They will stop at nothing to destroy us. We must fight them in any way we can."

"Yes! Fight!" Zealot made various excited gesticulations.

"Don't you mean *save* them?" Christian kept his focus on Evangelism. "We must save them any way we can, right?"

"Yes," Evangelism said, "of course. That's what I meant. Now then, on to the test." He ushered them into a large military tent with several bizarre mechanical devices that Christian didn't recognize.

"All right then," Evangelism said. "Let me just take this scanner here." He waved one of the machines toward Christian. "Yes, you do seem to be a repentant sinner who has given his life to the Overseer. Everything seems to be in order."

"What is that thing?" Christian said. "Some kind of fancy tricorder?"

Evangelism looked confused. "A what?"

"A tricorder. You know, from *Star Trek*?"

"What?" Evangelism looked shocked. "You can't go referencing secular media."

Christian looked from side to side, confused by Evangelism's sudden shock. "I can't?"

"The world is evil. Thus, anything the world makes is evil. We can't go using or ingesting anything the world makes. It would corrupt us. We don't allow any worldly things into this camp. The world is bad. We must fight the world and everything it stands for. They are pure evil. Anything the world does is evil." He stuck his head out of the tent flap and yelled, "Fire the guilt cannons. See if you can hit any children this time. Let's try to make them feel evil for liking anything worldly."

The sound of artillery echoed through the tent.

Truth shook her head with a frown.

"Guys," Christian said, "I don't think this is a good group for us."

"Nonsense." Evangelism pulled back into the tent. "This is the only way to combat the City of Destruction." He stuck his head back out. "Yes! Keep the guilt cannons firing."

Christian looked around, feeling out of place. "Don't we want conviction, not guilt? Won't guilt just make them hate us?"

Evangelism looked confused. "What's the difference?"

"Guilt make you feel hopeless," Truth said. "Conviction makes you feel inspired to do good."

"Nah," Evangelism said. "That doesn't sound right."

"That's it, we're out of here." Christian walked out of the tent and headed toward the exit.

"But we haven't fired the cannons yet," Zealot said with a disappointed whine.

"Wouldn't you prefer a more up-close and personal confrontation?" Christian said. "This is just aggravation from afar."

"But cannons!" Zealot motioned toward the thundering machines.

"Listen to your friend," Evangelism yelled. "What are you going to do, go to the neighboring base? They are just lazy folks who accomplish nothing."

"How is that different from your camp?" Christian said.

"What?" Evangelism said. "How dare you."

"You simply assault the City of Destruction, ensuring that those within will hate and despise those who would lead them to salvation."

"You underestimate the power of the dark side. It is too powerful. We must do everything we can to stop it."

"Hold on," Truth said. "Now you're quoting secular media. You said you didn't like that."

Evangelism looked concerned. "I didn't quote secular media. That's not true. That's impossible."

"Search your feelings," Christian said. "You know it to be true."

Evangelism roared in horror and ran into the tent.

Christian and the others left the base and waited several minutes for Interpreter to return.

Interpreter appeared at the crest of the hill, rolling Love's cylinder, which was cracked and leaking green fluid. But she still floated suspended in the center of the cylinder. Interpreter paused and looked down at them, considering everyone's expressions. "So . . . things went poorly?"

"Sort of," Christian said.

"What a shame," Love said passively. "Wish I had been there to take part in your escapades."

"Well," Christian said, "I wouldn't exactly call them—"

"Because I've had a great time lying in place, staring at nothing. It was a rollicking adventure."

Truth rolled her eyes. "We've very sorry we left you behind."

"Indeed," Zealot said. "We simply forgot about you."

Truth elbowed Zealot in the chest again.

"What?" Zealot said.

"Oh, well," Love said. "I'm sorry my presence isn't more memorable."

"Yes, we are all very sorry," Christian said. "You could have broken yourself out of that vat you know."

Love folded her arms and glared at Christian. "I'm not Zealot, okay? I'm not going to do all the work for you."

"She's right," Truth said. "Love is a big baby. Requires a lot of care and effort. She'll fade away if you don't constantly attend to her."

"You don't have to make it sound so negative," Love said.

"It is what it is," Truth said. "I can't make anything sound negative or positive that's just inference based on your own incomplete understanding."

"Enough of this talk." Zealot walked to Love's cylinder. "I say we investigate that alternate base and commence with our campaign against evil. Now then, let's see if this cage of yours has weakened enough." He smashed his fist through the glass, grabbed Love by the arm, and pulled her out.

Love flopped onto the ground, coughing out the cylinder's green liquid. She floated above them "Argh! Look at me. I'm a mess." She wiped the green out of her hair. "Why didn't I notice how icky this stuff was when I was in the cylinder?"

"You're welcome," Zealot said.

"I'm still mad about you shooting me, but thank you, Zealot."

"Aha! Progress." Zealot smiled and marched forward toward the other camp.

Love shook her head and sighed.

"Now then," Zealot said, "that other camp that does battle with evil. Let us accost them with our assistance."

Truth walked after Zealot with the rest close behind. "I don't think *accost* is the most accurate word for what you're trying to communicate."

"Quiet, Truth. Your speakage is annoying my walkage."

"Neither of those are words. That's two dollars, Zealot."

"Dollars well paid!" Zealot slapped two dollars into Truth's hand with a smile.

"The point of that game was to deter you from making up words."

Zealot started to respond but was interrupted by a woman in front of them.

The woman wore a nice suit and walked toward the party with outstretched arms. "Greetings, friends. Welcome to our military base. Come in, come in." She waved them toward the gate of the camp. "We are so glad you could make it. We get so few reinforcements these days."

"Hello." Christian walked past the woman and looked at the base. "I'm Christian, the big guy is Zealot, the old guy is Interpreter, the quiet girl is Truth and the woman combing the green slime out of her hair is Love."

"Hey!" Love said. "Don't draw attention to it."

Christian rolled his eyes and turned back to the woman.

She bowed. "I am called Evangelism."

Interpreter chuckled. "Ah, but which one?"

Evangelism raised an eyebrow as if she didn't understand. "I'm just Evangelism."

"Uh huh," Interpreter said in a tone that suggested that this conversation had been repeated many times before.

"Wasn't that previous guy also called Evangelism?" Christian said.

"That's correct," Truth said. "They can't both be Evangelism. We should call her Evangelism Two or something." She turned to Interpreter. "What are they, variations on evangelism? But they both think they're the real one?"

"Something like that," Interpreter said. "She probably thinks the other Evangelism is an imposter."

Evangelism folded her arms, her expression becoming less friendly. "That man in the adjoining camp is called Judgmental Evangelism. He's an imposter, I assure you. I'm normal unadulterated Evangelism."

"Your nametag says HELLO, My Name Is Lifestyle Evangelism." Truth pointed.

Evangelism looked down and then looked shocked as if this was new information.

"See?" Interpreter said.

"I do see," Truth said. "Each variation sees the other as imposters.

"Does that mean each is wrong?" Christian said.

"Nonsense," Zealot said. "Just because each one disagrees with the others doesn't mean all of them are incorrect. A correct variation would disagree with all the incorrect ones."

"But that's just theoretical, Zealot." Truth put her hand to her chin and looked more thoughtful than usual. "It's possible each is wrong. Or similarly correct."

"I am the correct Evangelism." Evangelism motioned toward herself. "You don't have to talk about me like I'm some specimen."

Truth smirked. "How cute. She doesn't know she's an allegorical personification."

"You're also an allegorical personification, Truth," Interpreter said.

"Yeah, but I *know* I am one."

Evangelism took a step back, looking shocked. Her eyes welled up with tears, and she cried.

"Truth," Love said in a shrill, shocked voice. She floated over to Evangelism and gave her a hug. "Look what you've done. You made Evangelism Two cry. Just because she's an allegorical personification doesn't mean she doesn't have feelings." She hugged Evangelism tighter and both women started to cry.

Truth looked at Interpreter, then back at Love. "But I'm right."

Christian folded his arms. "That *was* kinda a mean thing to say."

"Indeed," Zealot said. "Most unbecoming. I feel we must hear out this lady, out of obligation alone."

"Oh, come on!" Looking desperate, Truth turned to Interpreter.

"You shouldn't flaunt your semi-omniscience," Interpreter said

"Fine." Truth stepped toward the weeping woman. "All right, Evangelism Two, go ahead and give us your pitch."

"Wow, Truth," Christian said, "I'd expect that sarcastic tone from Book, but not you."

"Indeed," Zealot said. "Could you sound any more sarcastic?"

"Yes," Truth said, as if answering a perfectly normal question.

Love released Evangelism from her hug but stood near her, still with a disapproving look toward Truth.

Evangelism dried her eyes. "At the Lifestyle Evangelism camp"—her voice cracked a bit, but eventually her words came with an eloquence that suggested memorized repetition—"we believe in non-intervention. We avoid confrontation at all costs. We never attack the City of Destruction, not ever. We simply lead good lives and hope the lost will come to our camp because of how great our lives are." She wiped her eyes and took a deep breath then looked toward the group as if awaiting a response.

"That's the most ridiculous thing I've ever heard," Zealot said.

Evangelism Two burst into tears again.

"Zealot!" Love redirected her ire toward the big man.

"What? Only Truth is allowed to be rude?"

Evangelism buried her face in Love's shoulder.

"My criticism is legitimate," Zealot said. "Not personal. How are we to fight the forces of evil unless we—you know—fight the forces of evil?"

Love held Evangelism close, and her gaze darkened toward Zealot. "You're just complaining because these people don't have any big guns for you to shoot."

"Yes, that's exactly why I am complaining. The other camp had cannons. Cannons, Love! And you wish to gallivant around with a cadre of cowardly converteers?"

"*Converteers* isn't a word," Truth said with subtle anger. "That's another dollar."

"No, it works—like *musketeer*. But for those who convert, not those who musket."

"*Musket*'s not a verb, Zealot. That's another dollar."

"Hold on, the deal was for made-up words. Not incorrect grammar. And you're telling me *table* can be a verb, but *musket* can't be? They're both inanimate objects."

"Can we get back to the task at hand?" Interpreter said with gentle sternness.

Zealot smiled. "But Truth and I are bickering. *Good* bickering is so hard to come by."

Evangelism looked over Love's shoulder, confused. "Why would you like bickering?"

"Bickering," Zealot said, "is how we determine what is and what isn't. It is how falsehood is revealed and reality is clarified."

Truth smiled. "Correct. Argumentation is vital to the pursuit of knowledge and determining what is correct. If a theory can't stand up to argumentation, then it is flawed."

"But argumentation is so—nasty." Evangelism walked toward Zealot. "At the Lifestyle Evangelism camp, we are kind to people so our friendship may show them the glory of the Overseer."

Truth burst out laughing.

Everyone looked toward her.

Christian raised an eyebrow.

Truth continued laughing.

Then Zealot, as if getting the joke, laughed as well.

Christian expected Evangelism to cry again, but she looked more confused than insulted.

"Wait." Truth caught her breath and stifled her laughter. "If I were to say I wanted to confront the lost with their evil, what would you say?"

"I would say, we shouldn't confront," Evangelism said. "That would be destructive, like those in the Judgmental Evangelism camp. Our way is far more peaceful."

"No, it isn't," Zealot said.

"Yes, it is," Evangelism said.

Zealot and Truth went back to laughing.

"Stop it, you two," Love said. "I don't understand what's so funny but it's rude to laugh at philosophical personifications."

"Wait!" Zealot almost toppled over from the laughter. "Let me try one. All right, Evangelism Two . . ."

"It's just Evangelism."

"Of course it is. Of course. Let's say I am a boisterous and rude person who will call out evil whenever I see it, no matter what the context or ramifications. May I"—he held his side, stifling his laughter —"enter your base?"

Evangelism's confusion turned to revulsion. "No, we won't let such a destructive person be part of our camp. You're too confrontational. Also, you're being quite rude to me right now."

Zealot redoubled his laughter.

Even Christian felt uncomfortable.

Zealot and Truth continued laughing.

Interpreter put a hand on Zealot's shoulder. "Now, you two, that's enough. You're disrespecting Evangelism Two here."

"It's just Evangelism," Evangelism said. "Not Evangelism Two."

Truth wiped tears from her eyes and turned to Interpreter. "She is literally arguing against arguing. She's confronting us about our confrontation. You must say, objectively speaking, that is humorous. And thus, our laughter is justified."

Interpreter folded his arms in disapproval.

"It's all right. I can explain it," Truth relaxed her jovial tone. "In humor, there's this concept called irony—"

"We don't have time for this." Zealot walked past Evangelism and toward the City of Destruction.

Evangelism Two ran alongside Zealot. "But your way is so destructive." She struggled to keep up with his long strides. "Surely you don't expect us to go . . . talk to the lost. That's just ridiculous. Do you know how difficult it is to talk to strangers? Plus, its rude."

"Then find situations where it isn't rude," Zealot said. "Don't be lazy."

The rest of the party walked after Zealot and Evangelism.

"Besides, who cares if it is rude?" Zealot continued. "The people in that city are under threat of total atomic annihilation. The rudest thing to do would be a passive pursuit to inform them of their doom."

Evangelism started to get short of breath. "Do you think firing at them from guilt cannons will do any good? Surely you are not choosing to go back to the destructive ways of the judgmental camp?"

"No," Christian said, "but there has to be a choice other than doing bad and doing nothing."

"I'm afraid those are your two choices," Evangelism said. "Be confrontational and repulse non-believers. Or be passive like us."

Christian gave Evangelism a doubtful expression. "This is nonsense. All you care about is love. All those in the other camp care about is zealotry. There has to be a way of combining the two."

"Clearly," Truth said with a smile, "the solution is to find a camp that only cares about me."

"Those camps do exist," Interpreter said. "But you won't find them anywhere near the City of Destruction. With no motivation they end up just reading essays and listening to sermons."

"Ooh. Yeah, that sounds very nice. Let's go there," Truth said.

"Not while the lost need unlosting. And yes, I admit that is not a word. Here's a dollar."

Evangelism grabbed Zealot by the arm and tried to pull him away from the City of Destruction. If her efforts had any effect on Zealot's speed, it was impossible to tell.

"Zealot's right," Christian said. "Those people are in danger. We have to act, no matter how embarrassing or difficult."

"But if you"—Evangelism wheezed and pulled harder on Zealot— "if you are confrontational, it'll be counter-productive."

Zealot glanced at Evangelism. "Counter-productive, you say?" He stroked his chin. "That doesn't sound very . . . uh . . . productive."

After seeing her efforts make some difference, Evangelism pulled harder. "You can't go accusing people of things they don't feel conviction toward. They'll just resent you and be that much harder to convince to leave the City of Destruction."

Truth looked concerned. "That does make sense. Unproven accusations tend to breed contempt." She turned to Interpreter. "Are we doing the wrong thing?"

"You do lots of wrong things," Interpreter said with a chuckle. "Be specific."

"Is it wrong for us to return to the City of Destruction and endeavor to reach those trapped within it?"

"No," Interpreter said, weighing his words carefully.

"We already know that," Christian said. "The King's Highway has led us here."

Zealot walked back to the group, dragging Evangelism behind. "Then what other question is there? Let us confront these evil lost."

Love stepped forward. "But we'll make things worse. You can't just go attacking them. There has to be another way. Right, Interpreter?"

Interpreter thought for a bit. "You're sort of half right, half wrong. About both statements."

"What?" Everyone said together.

"You can't go attacking the lost—sort of. There is another way—sort of. As with most things, it's a bit complicated."

"Interpreter," Christian said, "if you don't stop following the cryptic mentor stereotype, I'm going to perform some very un-pilgrim-like actions upon your face."

Interpreter stepped back and raised his hands. "Please, I'm just following cryptic mentor law."

Zealot clapped and squealed in delight. "That's it!"

"What's it?" Truth said.

"Law!" Zealot said, as if he had just discovered all secrets to the universe. "Who finally caused us to flee to the Gateway? Who was the foe so powerful that we had to run to the Overseer for protection?"

Love laughed uncontrollably—bubbly and delightful, yet still washed with that twinge of sarcastic elitism that had wormed its way into Truth's and Zealot's elated bellowing. She paused, suddenly considering Zealot's meaning. "Wait. You're serious?"

Interpreter smiled.

Love looked worried. "You want us to get Law—that unstoppable, bloodthirsty, robot-bounty-hunting hivemind who tried to kill us and almost succeeded. You think he will help us? He'll just kill everyone in the City of Destruction."

"No, he'll *scare* everyone in the City of Destruction. He'll activate their Consciences, chase them to the Gateway."

"No, that won't work," Love said. "If the people of the City of Destruction are confronted by Law, they'll defend themselves just like the people in the City of Morality. They'll be slaughtered."

"I agree with Love," Christian said. "I know those people. They'll fight back."

"Then we shall die doing as we should." Zealot sounded calm, for once. Serious even. He always sounded like he was trying to be serious, but now he really did sound serious.

"It's not a question of courage," Love said. "It's a question of their hearts. If they're attacked, they'll defend themselves. And defensive hearts are not open ones."

"What if they aren't the ones being attacked?" Christian said. Realization suddenly reaching his voice.

He and Interpreter shared a look. The others looked confused.

Christian thought back to the simulations that Interpreter had shown him. "Could that really work?"

Interpreter considered the question. "Perhaps. But you'll have to do it just right. And I don't think you're going to like it. Odds are still good that you'll end up dead like so many others who face the City of Destruction."

"That's ok. If we wanted the easy route none of us would have started this quest."

"Then you have plan?" Zealot said.

"I think so. Interpreter, tell us what to do," Christian said

"But do it off-screen so the climax has more suspense," Truth said.

Interpreter sighed. "If you insist."

STAGE 24
THE LAST WRATH OF AKANE TSUNEMORI

T he alarm sounded. Obstinate rose from his bunk.

His compatriots rose from their bunks. There was a flurry of activity in the barracks. Men reached for rifles and slipped into combat gear.

"Another evangelist attack?" Obstinate grabbed a rifle from the rack and started for the door.

"This attack is different," someone alongside him shouted. "It's just a single man."

"Only one combatant? This should be the quickest defense in the City of Destruction history."

"Yes," another man said, "but if anime has taught me anything, it's to be afraid of one-person assaults on a large force."

"True enough." Obstinate burst through the door and ran outside the barracks. Before him lay the vast stretches of wilderness leading to the Dark Lands.

A beeping sounded by his wrist.

Obstinate swatted away the small metal figure on his wrist and consulted his data screen. Coordinates displayed an incursion. The location was a little distance from the city and near to where Christian had fought him long ago. Coincidence, surely.

Obstinate and his fellow marines trudged toward the coordinates, weapons ready. He looked around. The shadow of the City of Destruction still loomed behind them. Barren and forsaken earth stretched before them. Then he saw the attacker.

A single man walked toward the group, with no weapon in his hand. Christian. So, he had turned Evangelist after all. So many did. He would meet the same fate as all who encroached on their territory.

What attack would Christian use? Condemnation, probably. Or perhaps a temptation lure. Many had been tricked by false promises of easy lives. Most returned. Obstinate would not be intimidated by threats or coerced through false bribery. He knew that pilgrimage led through the Dark Lands.

Apollyon landed in front of the squad of marines, and they fell into formation. He marched up and down the line, inspecting the troops.

"All right, men. This man was once one of you. He will probably try some psychological trick to get you to follow him. Since he knows you so well, he'll probably accuse you of something specific. Don't let him push you around. Who is he to condemn you? He's part of those accursed pilgrims who keep shelling our city with their guilt cannons. Remember that and stay sharp."

"Didn't you say you had stopped this guy from being a threat to us?" Obstinate said. "How could he have made it here?"

Apollyon looked at Obstinate, annoyed. "Yes, I did say that. But I underestimated his three comrades. Thank you for bringing up such a painful reminder of my failures."

"That's what I'm here for, sir. I am Obstinate."

Apollyon turned toward the threat. "Yeah, that's fair." He jumped into the air. Two massive mechanical wings with rockets on the joints stretched out from his back. The rockets ignited, and he hovered in place. His wings spread across the entire line of space marines. "Obstinate, what's the status of our troops?"

Obstinate checked his wrist computer. "We've got anti-argument mechs in reserve. I see some flying gunboats on the way. Are those ours?"

"Yes, those are mine." Apollyon didn't turn his gaze from the approaching figure. "Spiritual interdiction gunboats."

"That should cover everything," Obstinate said. "I can't imagine what a single man can pull off."

"Forgive me for being less than optimistic," Apollyon said. "I've seen first-hand the damage a single man can do."

"He's almost in range," a marine said.

"Steady, men," Obstinate said.

Christian stopped and raised his hands.

"Here it comes," Obstinate said. "Anyone wanna make bets on if it's condemnation or bribery? Personally, I think bribery. Christian strikes me as a 'be a pilgrim, we have cookies and your best life now' kind of guy."

"Wait. I like cookies," a marine said.

Apollyon glared at the man "We have our own cookies. I am Apollyon after all, the baker of pies and the teller of lies."

"Wait, the teller of what now?"

"Never mind."

"All right then."

"Quiet," Obstinate said. "He's about to speak. Get ready."

"Ladies and gentlemen," Christian shouted for all to hear. He paused. "I . . . am evil."

An eerie silence crossed the entire formation of marines.

Obstinate took a step forward. "What?"

Apollyon sent Obstinate a worried glance.

Obstinate started to step back in line but stopped to listen.

Christian said, "I am a sinful, despicable wretch who delights in killing. Who delights in being lazy. Who stands idly by as others need my help. I am a hateful, murderous, lustful, tyrant." He continued to name vices and shortcomings, one after another. He didn't stop.

"Apollyon, what do we do?" Obstinate said. "He isn't attacking us. He's attacking himself. Should we open fire?"

"No," Apollyon shouted.

Obstinate looked up at Apollyon in disbelief. "What?"

Apollyon's face had grown white.

Obstinate couldn't remember a time he had seen fear on the Overlord's face. "But sir, he's preaching at us. We can't let him go on. What should we do?"

"I'm thinking!" Apollyon looked around, frantic, as if expecting a secret attack from any angle.

"Therefore," Christian said, "I am deserving of death. I thought death should only be reserved for those worse than me. But that was just a symptom of my inferior moral standings, thinking those more evil are the only ones deserving of judgment. Now I choose to point judgment toward myself. I know I deserve it."

"I can't hit him from this range," Obstinate said. "Changing to long range mode." Obstinate pressed a button, and his rifle made a complex and sudden mechanical transformation. Now it was a rocket launcher. "Sir, I've got a lock. Should I open fire?"

"That's exactly what he wants," Apollyon said.

"He can't possibly survive a rocket strike."

"That isn't the point."

"Don't we agree the evangelists are evil?"

"Yes."

"Then why shouldn't I shoot?"

"You don't understand," Apollyon said.

"I know the evangelists are evil. I am Obstinate. I will not stand idly by and let them continue their evil. I choose to pass judgment." He fired the rocket.

"No," Apollyon snatched for the rocket mid-flight, and with incredible speed of claw he almost grabbed it midair.

Almost.

The rocket sailed toward Christian and then . . . stopped, inches from his face.

Christian smiled.

"What?" Obstinate pressed a button and another rocket rotated into position. He fired again, which also stopped in front of Christian.

Christian walked forward. The rockets turned their trajectory and slowly spun around him.

"So, you wish to pass judgment?" Christian said. "How wise of you. I deserve judgment."

The rest of the marines switched their weapons to rocket launchers and fired. Each rocket turned aside from Christian and circled him, adding to the swarm of rockets.

"Stop firing," Apollyon shouted.

The marines didn't listen.

"Of course, if I deserve judgment that begs the question: Why?" Christian looked directly at Obstinate.

"Don't answer," Apollyon shouted.

Obstinate prepped another rocket. "Because you have done evil."

"According to what?" Christian said.

"According to . . ." Obstinate's voice trailed off.

Apollyon flew down next to him and grabbed his rocket launcher.

Obstinate wrenched it back. "According to all I know of right and wrong." He fired another rocket. "According to reason." He fired again. "According to my . . . my . . ." Now he saw that a small metal figure had fused to the rocket launcher, the same one he'd knocked aside earlier but paid little attention to.

"According to me," a hundred voices said from all directions. Obstinate glanced around and noticed tiny metal figures stood atop the rocket launchers of each of his comrades. Each robot had red eyes.

Obstinate spun back toward Christian.

Christian was no longer alone. He was now surrounded by flying missiles alongside thousands of large, metal figures with the red eyes. Each robot, of one accord, started chanting "blood, blood, blood," as they marched forward.

"Fire at the robots," Apollyon said. "Don't let them touch you."

The marines opened up on the red-eyed robots.

Apollyon swooped toward them.

All the missiles orbiting Christian stopped, turned toward Apollyon, and then flew at the flying baker. A cacophony of explosions. Apollyon sailed backward, each explosion tearing a chunk out of his flesh.

Obstinate ducked and Apollyon sailed over his head then back into the City of Destruction. Obstinate watched the winged demon baker smash into one of the skyscrapers. Obstinate turned back to the battle. He activated his com. "Guess I'm in charge now. Get those anti-argument mechs into position. We can't wait."

Obstinate looked up from his wrist computer. One of the robots stood inches from Obstinate's face. Eyes gleaming. Twisted metal jaws opened and closed, chanting the same words: "Blood, blood, blood."

Obstinate jumped back, raised his rocket launcher, and fired.

The robot caught the missile in one claw and kept walking forward. "What do you mean?" Obstinate shouted.

"Evil must shed its blood," the robot said. Oil oozed from its teeth, sending sprays of ick with every syllable. "All evil."

Obstinate raised his hand and spoke into his wrist computer. "Everyone, fall back till our mechs arrive." He turned and ran.

Five massive mechs, as big as skyscrapers, stepped from behind the buildings of the City of Destruction and trundled toward the battle. If Obstinate could just get to the mechs he'd be protected. Wouldn't he?

Obstinate reached the foot of one of the mechs, cowered behind it, and looked back. "Let's see them deal with this."

The red-eyed automatons formed a line in front of Christian, then grabbed onto one another. The one closest to Christian grabbed his arm and the rest of the robots twisted and broke apart. Then each grabbed ahold of the other. Each piece of each robot twisted apart and reconnected to the others till they were a single metal mass that moved and re-formed like living sinew. Then Obstinate saw what the robots were forming into.

A sword.

The sword was beyond long, beyond massive. Its shadow sliced across the City of Destruction and seemed to dwarf the monstrous skyscrapers. It continued to twist and writhe, changing length and shape with incomprehensible alacrity. Yet Christian carried it one-handed like the weight had no effect on him.

As the sword twisted and moved, it passed through one of the nearby boulders, slashing it to dust. And still Obstinate heard the mouths of the robots, now encrusted into the sword, chanting "blood, blood, blood," like a pack of hungry wolves. A hunger that seemed beyond reason. A hunger for him—Obstinate.

The anti-argument mechs stepped in front of the marines, and projected shields down to protect Obstinate and his compatriots.

One of the mechs pointed a fist toward Christian and fired the fist as a rocket. "Morality is relative," the mech said.

Christian's sword anchored him to the ground. "Relative, no. Complex, yes." The sword wrenched forward, launching Christian like a missile from a slingshot high into the air. Then the blade flashed through the air, cutting the rocket-fist from knuckle to knuckle. Both halves continued their rocketing trajectory, passed to each side of Christian and continued off into the distance. The blade of robots then shot down into the ground far below, stopping Christian's fall, and suspending him several dozen stories into the air.

Another mech's chest opened, revealing rows of rocket launchers. Each fired at Christian. Explosions shook the air, and Christian reeled backward, the force of the explosions shattered glass in the nearby skyscrapers and rattled Obstinate's bones.

"Reason is the only foundation for morality," The rocket-chested mech said with a thundering tone that sounded almost as loud as the rockets. "Religion is not necessary."

"Morality is but the application of true law," Christian said. How could Obstinate hear him when he was so far away. But the voice wasn't coming from Christian, high in the air. It came from the tiny robot on Obstinate's shoulder.

More missiles flew at Christian. Christian's sword retracted upward and latched onto one of the missiles. The propulsors on the missile swung the blade around like a metronome. Using the force from the missile Christian sped aside from the other attacks, then turned the missile around and smashed it back into the chest of his attacker.

"There is no truer or higher law then that of He who ordered the complexity of the universe." The blade caught another missile and slammed it back into the mech just like the first. Then another and another.

The mech started to topple backward. It reached out and caught the side of one of the skyscrapers to right itself. Its fingers tore through the glass and metal, ripping gashes in the sides of the structure.

Christian's blade flashed out again, striking the ground next to the mech's legs. How could a sword so long and heavy move so fast? And how could something so fluid be so strong?

"To disobey that perfect law . . ." Christian's blade sliced through the leg of the falling mech. "To lie, cheat, steal, fornicate. These violations of that infinite perfection of that infinitely perfect Lawgiver requires infinite punishment."

The mech fell back. Its fingers broke off in the side of the skyscraper and the mech toppled onto its back.

"Wait to attack," Obstinate said into his wrist computer. "You're trickling in. He clearly can take on a mech one at a time. Wait to attack all at once."

The other four mechs moved to group together. Christian looked toward the nearest one.

"Time to make some space." Obstinate entered a command into his wrist computer with all the speed he could muster.

An unnecessarily ominous beeping sounded from the chest of the mech Christian had felled. Obstinate swore underneath his breath. "I hate that OSHA requires self-destruct sequences to include that telltale beeping."

The beeping sped up. "Take cover!" Obstinate shouted at the marines.

The mech exploded. Christian went flying. He tumbled end over end, his sword flapping behind him like a snowboarder's scarf. He smashed into a skyscraper, leaving a large hole in the concrete.

"Ha! We got him!" shouted a nearby marine. "Now let's assume he's dead and go about our business without double-checking."

"No!" Obstinate struck his face with his palm. "We talked about this. Everyone! Fire the building!"

The marines looked at each other, shrugged, then raised their weapons, and fired. Missiles struck stone, steel, and glass. Missiles flew through the hole and sent explosions erupting from all sides of the building.

"Keep firing." Obstinate touched his wrist computer. "Anti-argument mechs, focus fire on the base of that building. We'll see how tough he is when he's buried under a mile of steel representing The Intellectual Cultural Resistance to Evangelical Efforts."

"The what?" a marine said.

Obstinate shrugged. "It's written on the side of the skyscraper. I don't know what it means."

The mechs reached the skyscraper together. The chests of each opened, revealing rows of missiles. They fired together. The missiles curved around and hit all four sides of the skyscraper. A rumbling sounded.

The skyscraper fell. Dust erupted from the sides and blasted past Obstinate and the other marines. The ground shook. The building continued to fall for minutes. Then the roof reached the ground and the collapse finally ceased.

The dust lingered in the air for several seconds. Then, in an instant the dust blew away as if fleeing some coming force.

There, standing atop a mountain of rubble, stood Christian. His armor shredded, blood dripping from his brow, arms, and legs. A shield crackled around him.

He glared down at Obstinate. "Ow."

"How?" Obstinate had to buy time for his mechs to ready for another missile barrage.

Christian motioned toward his hand that held the hilt of the sword. His hand seemed fused with the hilt. Strands of metal veined out from the hilt and into Christian's hand. Obstinate couldn't see where the sword began and Christian's hand ended.

"You can't destroy the Law. It exists regardless of your actions, opinions, hopes, beliefs or delusions."

The mechs readied to attack.

Christian raised his sword. "Your attacks mean nothing to me," Christian said. "I love you all, regardless of what you do to me."

One of the mechs grabbed Christian around the middle and squeezed. "Small crimes require small punishments."

The blade flashed, moving so fast that Obstinate didn't see it. The mech's arm fell to pieces.

"The Overseer, a perfect being, requires perfect justice." Christian landed and the sword whipped through the air like a flag. "And as I said before, a crime against an infinite being requires infinite punishment."

Obstinate ran toward Christian. Just as Christian looked his way, Obstinate tackled him. "Then you deserve infinite punishment," Obstinate said. "You aren't any better than us."

Christian smiled. "Exactly."

Apollyon flew out of the hole in the skyscraper then swooped down toward Christian and snatched him up. Apollyon flew, upward, away from the mechs. Up past the clouds.

Obstinate watched the winged demon rocket farther and farther into the sky. The sword of robots sailed up with them, its hilt still held by Christian.

Obstinate reached into his belt for a pair of omni-sensory binoculars. He homed in on Christian and Apollyon. The omni-sensory binoculars allowed him to see, hear, and for some reason smell everything he peered at.

The spiritual attack gunships moved into position. The giant vessels trained their guns on Christian and Apollyon. The gunships were large and flat. Suspended in the air by six parallel hover-engines. And on the edges of their surfaces bristled dozens of plasma cannons.

Apollyon held Christian in place before the spiritual assault gunships. Christian's sword whipped around to strike Apollyon but the demon swatted the blade aside. Its blade bouncing off his flesh.

"I'm no man," Apollyon said. "Your Law means nothing to me. Though I must confess it was pretty clever, pointing judgment toward yourself and letting empathy do the rest of the work. The Law is strong. Excellent against argument. But what do you have to say about spiritual attacks?"

Christian squirmed.

"You like the gunships?" Apollyon tightened his grip. Obstinate thought he heard the crunching of bones. "They're run by the newest model of Persecutrons. The real ones. Not those fakes you saw back in Palace Beautiful."

Christian muttered something.

"What was that?"

A voice came from Christian's wrist. "Status confirmed. Stand by for spirit fall."

"Stand by for what?" Apollyon sounded confused.

The gunships fired. But before their shots reached Christian, a massive object fell from the sky and crashed into Apollyon. Christian and Apollyon dropped and impacted into the ground with such force the earth split and a nearby skyscraper crumbled to dust just from the residual force.

Christian's sword zipped into the object and pulled Christian inside so fast a sonic boom echoed through the air and shook the spiritual interdiction gunships. Shots from the gunships hit the object just after Christian was pulled inside.

Dust erupted around the object from the gunships' assault.

Obstinate hit the dirt.

Shrapnel and bits of earth flew through the air.

Then the object stood up. It was a Mech. A Mech much larger than any that Apollyon had. The Mech crouched, then jumped into the air toward the nearest gunship. It sailed upward into the sky as if propelled by rockets.

Christian's Mech slammed up into the gunship, smashing through an engine, then landed onto the gunship. Christian's Mech leapt off the gunship and toward the other, the force of its jump sending the first gunship into the ground, followed by a trail of molten fire.

Then four figures shot from the chest of the Mech.

Christian, sword sailing out in front of him, was joined by a small white-haired girl, a large bulky man with a pistol, and a red-haired girl wearing an outfit adorned with shining shield projectors. The four landed in front of the marines, sending a shockwave of dust across the ground.

"Ha!" Obstinate said. "You think you can take on all of us? We have you outnumbered a hundred to—"

The man with the pistol drew his weapon faster than Obstinate could see. A stream of missiles hit each of the men's weapons, knocking their welders onto their backs. The man twirled his pistol and blew down the barrel. "You underestimate my resolve," the man said.

Obstinate rushed forward and slammed a first toward Christian's face. "I hate you!" His fist collided with an energy shield, and it flew aside.

"Is that supposed to be an argument?" Christian said.

"Are you trying to provoke my man here?" The magical girl slid up next to Christian and wrapped an arm around him. "Like that's going to work."

The remaining anti-argument mechs surrounded Christian in defensive stances.

"You have done evil," a mech said.

"Your judgement parameters are irrelevant," another mech said.

Christian smiled. "Those are some nice logical arguments you've got there. It'd be a shame if someone"—he snapped his fingers—"brought them to their logical conclusion."

The white-haired girl ran with unnatural speed toward the nearest mech, ran up its leg, kicked through the glass of the cockpit, and pulled the pilot out. All before Obstinate could even blink.

The hijacked Mech turned on the others, knocking them down and firing into their chassis. "Understanding that Christian has done evil shows you have an inherent sense of right and wrong." Its voice was now feminine. "How about we use that to our advantage?" The Mech fired its missiles into the other mech's chest, rending metal and glass.

Obstinate drew a sidearm and fired an explosive round into Christian, knocking him onto his back and his sword out of his hand. "You want to face me? Nothing can pierce my armor."

"Nothing but one thing." Christian grabbed the hilt of his sword. The blade snaked around and sliced the back of Obstinate's knee.

Obstinate fell.

"Your values are unchanging," Christian said. "Tell me, what can change the consequences of Law?" Christian swung the sword at Obstinate, slicing through his armor.

Obstinate screamed in shock, not in pain. For the first time in his life, he felt the cold, stinging air of the outside world rippling across his skin, which terrified him.

Apollyon swooped down and kicked Christian into the dirt.

Christian raised his blade.

Apollyon knocked the blade high into the air. "When will you learn? Those tricks don't work on me. I am beyond Law." His wing swooped down and struck Christian, its metallic weight knocking him down like a bowling pin.

"You're too late." Christian spat droplets of blood. "They have seen the Law and the evil of their actions. Even now, their Consciences are awakening."

Obstinate looked around. The tiny robots that had been stuck to the rocket launchers detached and clambered toward the marines. One climbed up to Obstinate's shoulder with spider-like agility. He struck at it, but the little robot was heavy, immovable, far stronger than before, when he could so easily knock it aside.

"No!" Apollyon growled and shot a gaze at Obstinate. "Very well, Plan B." He grabbed Obstinate and hoisted him into the air.

"What? Apollyon! Why?"

"Blame Christian for playing with such dangerous toys. Better to have you impaled than go evangelist."

Christian's sword turned and fell down toward them, blade first.

"Boss, stop! That sword is sharp enough to pierce my armor." Obstinate couldn't move, no matter how hard he struggled. The sword fell much faster than its upward movement had been. He saw the red eyes of the robots and heard their hungry chant for his blood. This was it. Only seconds to go until—

Christian took a great leap and sailed just between Obstinate and the falling sword.

The blade pierced Christian's side.

Christian fell.

The blade struck Apollyon's hands.

Obstinate fell to the ground.

Christian knocked Obstinate from Apollyon's grasp as he fell. The two fell onto the sand. Blood poured from Christian's side, the blade deep in his flesh.

Apollyon faced Christian.

Christian faced Apollyon.

"Well?" Apollyon said.

"Sic 'em"—Christian coughed up blood—"bears."

Then from literally out of nowhere a swarm of bears charged into Apollyon, ripping into him with righteous fury.

"Agh!" Apollyon tried to knock the swarm of bears aside with no success. "Where did all these she-bears come from? It's contrived I tell you. Contrived!"

Christian smiled and his vision faded. "Well what do you know? It did work."

Then Christian fell.

Dead.

Silence.

"Finally!" Apollyon flourished his wings and knocked the bears far from striking distance. "That was a tough one, boys. But we did it. Fornications all round. Now I've left a cake in the oven, and I'd like to get back to it before I—"

The Mech Christian had summoned ran into Apollyon and with a single kick, launched Apollyon up into the air. Apollyon continued upward till he vanished into the stratosphere, with a blink of light. Obstinate wondered when and where he'd fall back to earth.

Then Obstinate stared at Christian's dead body. A flood of thoughts, and feelings ran through his head. He had to do something.

Obstinate looked down at his hands, covered in blood. He had never noticed blood on his hands, but not because they had never been bloody. Firing hundreds of rounds of explosive ordinance into one's enemies was not a pastime conducive to cleanliness. But he had never *looked* at the blood before. Why was he looking at it now?

Where had the delight gone? Did it drip from the tubes and circuits of his burden? He checked himself. No, only blood dripped from his burden. As usual. His burden was a usual model, a suit of armor encased around him like a giant metal cage. Nothing seemed to be wrong with the machine. Had the work of battle drained him of his strength to delight himself? Why would this battle be any different? Why would—

"Aha!" a tiny grating voice screamed from Obstinate's shoulder. "I've gotten into the main programming. Don't worry I've almost got the conditioning down 29 percent."

Obstinate leapt aside, his powered burden acting before his mind had time to register his actions. He reached toward the sound on his shoulder. Searing pain sliced through his nerves. He fell to the ground, the power in his burden giving out, its weight pulling him onto the ground, immobilizing him. The weight of the burden didn't cause the pain. The memory did.

Obstinate looked down at Christian. Christian's blood seeped toward him. Now he understood. The blind delight he and his comrades had taken from the sport of raiding had drained from his soul like the blood from his face.

In Christian's hand was a small holographic display.

Obstinate picked up the holodisplay, slid it onto his wrist, and turned it on.

STAGE 25

GLADOS'S FIRST SERENADE

Christian gasped and opened his eyes. He was on a hoverpad, moving upward. The world was far below him. And above him was light.

"There you go, gasping again," Zealot said. "You really should quit that. Most unbecoming for a dead person."

Christian looked around. Zealot, Truth, and Love were standing around him, smiling. Well, for Truth, it was more of a bemused smirk.

"What happened?" Christian felt strange. "I'm dead?"

"Yes," Truth said in a matter-of-fact tone.

Christian expected to be shocked. He expected to be afraid. "Bummer."

"Not exactly," Love said. "You were beamed up. As promised."

"Then it's over. How unexpected." Christian walked past his friends to the edge of the hoverplatform and looked down. The world was so small, so far away.

A voice broke in from the far end of the hoverpad. "Yes, normally I prefer big musical numbers to end these sorts of things, but what can you do?"

Christian looked around. At the far end of the hoverplatform, a man sat at a set of controls. Christian's heartrate quickened and he ran over to the man. "Are you—"

"Jesus?" The man looked over his shoulder. "No. The author is too afraid to designate dialogue to Jesus as it's too much responsibility. My name is Steve. I work the hoverplatform."

"Steve? What kind of name is that?"

"They were out of allegorically obvious attributions. So I got Steve."

Christian folded his arms. "So, what happens now?"

"We take you to the Overseer."

"The Overseer?" Christian spoke with delight and anticipation.

"If you went through the Gateway, then yeah. Otherwise, Law gets you."

"I did! I went through the Gateway back in chapter 8." He caught himself. "Wait. Chapter 8? How do I know that?"

"Now that you're going to the Celestial Station, a lot of seemingly weird stuff will make sense to you." Steve's dismissiveness suggested he'd given this speech many times. "Well, not weird, just different from what you're used to. It's a good thing you went through that Gateway. I just had to yeet a couple of fakers named False Convert and Hypocrisy who tried sneaking their way in."

"I remember them from chapter 9." Christian stopped himself and felt confused. "Wait. Chapter 9?" Christian paused again. "Seriously, what's with my now seemingly universal understanding of chapter attributions?"

"You'd think more knowledge would make things less confusing," Steve said. "But that's human arrogance for you. Don't worry, it'll pass. Speaking of things passing away . . ." He gave a knowing look toward Christian's friends.

"Yes." Zealot stepped toward the edge of the platform. "I believe that is our cue to leave."

"Leave? Why?" Christian turned and faced his friends. "You've been with me through so much. You can't leave now."

Christian expected sadness. It didn't come.

"It was never us, Christian," Zealot said with a laugh. "We weren't the ones with you. At best we were simply gifts sent by the Overseer."

"Our job here is done," Truth said. "Your capacity for action and learning is now quite different now that you're dead. I'd specify further but the author actually is conflicted on what state human action and learning has after you die and doesn't want to risk teaching heresy so I'm not going to stipulate further."

"Plus, there are others who need us." Zealot took a half step over the side. Then he paused. "Christian, it may not have been glorious, it was a painful mess of an adventure. But . . ."

"Yeah," Christian said, "it was never about our glory, was it?"

Zealot winked, then turned back toward the edge. "Well, enough of this emotion. It seems that Steadfast has gone and gotten himself nabbed by the Sloth of Despond already. Impressive. That's a faster time even than you."

"Steadfast? Who's that?" Christian said.

"You knew him as Obstinate. That wasn't his true name of course. It's all too confusing to explain. I must away." Zealot saluted, then stepped off the platform and fell back toward the earth.

Christian looked over to Truth.

Truth shifted her weight in an awkward way. She coughed. "Well . . . you're still an uneducated idiot who got himself into more trouble than he should have. You wasted a lot of time. But I guess if we could do it ourselves, then we wouldn't need the Overseer."

"Your flattery never ceases to affirm me, Truth," Christian said.

"That's not flattery, Christian. I'm just saying accurate things."

"You always do."

Christian slipped off the projector for Book. Somehow, despite him seeming to remember Obstinate taking the projector, Christian still had it, or another that looked just like it.

Book flashed onto the floor in the form of some sort of multi-eyed, multi-headed beast.

"Uh, Book?" Christian said in shock and confusion.

Book changed back to her normal form. "Oh, hi, Christian. I see you died. That means I got nothing else to do. Dead folks can't read." Then she vanished.

Christian looked up at Truth. "Well, that was abrupt."

"Hey, Conscience," came Book's voice from the projector. "Let's make like a bad chiropractor and blow this joint."

Conscience reached up and took the projector then clambered over to Truth. He paused, then looked back up at Christian.

"Thanks, little friend," Christian said.

Conscience looked embarrassed.

Truth scooped Conscience up, and the three of them—Truth, Conscience, and Book—stepped off the platform and floated down toward the world.

"Well then," Christian said, looking at Love. "I suppose that means you're next."

Love looked different—older, more beautiful, and more vibrant.

"Nope," Love said with a smile. "I'm afraid you're stuck with me."

"Really?" Christian said, with an unhidden note of happiness in his voice. "That's good. But enough of this." He ran over to Steve. "I wanna see Celestial Station. I wanna see the Overseer! I have so much to say. To do."

"Yeah, don't get your hermeneutics in a twist. All I have to do is . . ." Steve paused, then stared past Christian, looking angry. "Hey, you. What do you think you're doing?" Steve pointed. But not at Christian. He was pointing behind Christian. But there was no one else here, was there?

Christian turned around.

A large, black-haired, fat man was sitting on the edge of the platform, typing on a computer.

He glanced up, looking confused. "Me?"

"Yeah you!" Steve walked toward him and away from Christian. "Get out of here."

"Who is that?" Love said. "Wait. Has he been following us this whole time? And writing down what we've been doing on that laptop?"

The fat man looked around as if Love's question was obvious. "Why? Is that not cool?"

"That's the author," Steve said. "Truth mentioned him several times in your journey. You never notice him?"

"No," Christian said in shock.

"Wait." Love paused, trying to comprehend what was going on. "Does this mean what he writes is controlling this entire reality or simply reflecting it? If the former, then how can he create himself?"

"That's an interesting question," the fat man said. "You see this specific allegorical format has a long proud history of self-inserted author characters which in this context I believe signifies—"

"Nobody cares, Fatso!" Steve charged toward the fat man. The fat man gave a girlish, cowardly yelp and backed away toward the edge of the platform. "Hey . . . what did I do?"

"Get out of here." Steve shoved the man toward the edge. "You aren't dead. Go back to the earth."

"But I want everyone to see what the Celestial Station is like." The fat man teetered on the brink of the platform.

"You wanna know what it's like?" Steve shoved the man again. "Go die. But don't actually die because killing yourself would be sin. Now beat it."

"But I need an epic, satisfying resolution to the story," the fat man said. "Everyone will want to see how everything wraps up in the Celestial Station. I can't just end my story here. It will be anti-climactic."

"Tough," Steve shouted. "The Celestial Station abides by a strict No-Spoiler Policy. Nobody really knows how great it is and they won't until they die so get lost." He grabbed the man by the collar and hoisted him over the edge of the platform.

"But . . . b-but . . ." the fat man sputtered.

Steve let go of the fat man and watched him fall back toward the world. Steve brushed his hands off. "Wow. That's the third time in two millennia that we've had someone sneak in here. We really need to get that cave covered up."

THE END

www.ingramcontent.com/pod-product-compliance
Lightning Source LLC
Chambersburg PA
CBHW060939030726
47503CB00003B/662